TIDES OF TORMENT

IMMORTAL REALMS

BOOK 2

ELLE BEAUMONT
CHRISTIS CHRISTIE

Midnight Tide
PUBLISHING

TIDES OF TORMENT

Copyright © 2023 by Elle Beaumont & Christis Christie

Published by Midnight Tide Publishing.
www.midnighttidepublishing.com

Cover designed by MoorBook Designs.
www.moorbooksdesign.com

Map designs by
Centaur Maps
centaurmaps.art.blog

Edited by
Meg Dailey
thedaileyeditor.wordpress.com/editing-services

N
W
E
S
Caithaird
Mointeach Bay
Fhregarde
Mointeach
Hillbride
Veil
Midniva

TORSKVALA
BEZOPASNYY
VEIL
SAHILLE
TRIBONIK
ISLE OF
PROPENTRI
*DEPENGAARD
SAVENTI
DARZGAARD
*CAITHAIRD
MOINTEACH
BAY
HIREGARDE
MOINTEACH
HILLBRIDE
VEIL

The Middle Realm
JOUJEW
CAIFU
* FINZU
MIDNIVA
N
NW
NE
W
E
SW
SE
S

For Papa, the sea will always be a part of me because of your love for it and passing it down onto all of us. ~ Elle

For Melana, who played with me by the water and helped to spark my imagination with our childhood adventures. Thank you for always believing I could do this. ~ Tiss

Prologue

Travion

It had happened. Travion had finally agreed to marry. After centuries of avoiding a union, and several more propositions, he'd decided it was time to wed. Not because the kingdom expected it of him, or because he needed an heir—his nephew Kian had been named heir long ago. Rather, his attention had been snagged by a certain Ferox daughter.

Sereia.

Amusingly enough, he knew her from a failed offer to Ruan, his eldest nephew. And the female was so daring, she'd sneak into Travion's courtyard to practice sword fighting. Never once approaching him. As if he didn't know.

So, when Lady Ferox approached him with hope gleaming in her eyes, he accepted the arrangement. Which was why he was currently standing before a tall mirror with his valet fussing with his overcoat.

Evun whistled a bawdy tune, one about taking a willing gent into a dark alley to have his way with them. Pointed ears peeked through a mop of sandy brown curls, and his clever green eyes stood out against his dusky complexion.

"Your Grace, I daresay your betrothed won't be able to contain herself," Evun purred, lowering his thick lashes.

Travion narrowed his eyes. Somehow he doubted that, for he'd seen defiance spark in Sereia's eyes when she didn't know he was watching her. "Something tells *me* she won't be able to contain herself either." He chuckled, but Evun didn't seem to catch on to his meaning, which was just as well.

Travion glanced over at his reflection again. He wore a pair of black breeches and a linen long-sleeved shirt. Over it, a deep navy overcoat with silver embroidery hugged his lean frame, and around his shoulders hung a navy cape, clasped by a silver knot.

In his reflection, he saw flashes of Ludari—his father—staring back at him. The turned-up nose, auburn hair, and chiseled jaw. He inwardly flinched and cast his eyes away. His father still haunted his dreams, and his waking hours, with what he'd forced Travion to do in the Lucem palace dungeons. He could still hear Draven's screams, as if they were occurring at that very moment.

No matter if he let his hair grow down to his chin or cropped it closer to his head, he still resembled his father too much for his liking. Thankfully, a smattering of freckles gave him a playful appearance, especially when he smirked. A gift from his mother.

"If I may, Your Grace," Evun interrupted his turbulent thoughts. "Perhaps let her see *you* this evening. Put aside the crown for an evening and be yourself."

Travion grimaced and shook his head. *Be himself.* A son of one of the originals, tormented by the past, who drank a little too much at times to escape the ghosts of his youth. "I don't think that is in anyone's best interest, Evun."

"Well, it was worth a try." He patted Travion's shoulder.

"Good luck this evening." Evun tilted his head, smiling, before he left the room.

Good luck, indeed.

Midniva's castle rested on a cliffside, overlooking the sea and the rest of the capital city—Caithaird. In the evenings, Travion enjoyed the sound of the waves crashing against the rocks below and the crooning of seals as they settled on the beach.

Beneath the castle, a long, winding road wove along the coast. Regrettably, travel was rough after a rather icy winter. But there was no other way to travel to Ferox manor, and so Travion would have to endure, and possibly swear a blue streak or two.

"By the sea!" Travion growled as one bump sent him sliding off his seat and into Finn. His guard steadied him by the shoulders, arching a pale brow in question, but remained silent as Travion settled back onto the cushioned bench. If he was going to be tossed about so violently, he would have preferred it be in the middle of the ocean. But alas, his coachman didn't give a damn.

Finn was an impressive fae who stood two heads higher than Travion. He made Travion appear short and deficient in muscle, and was just as lethal with a sword. Nearly two hundred years ago, Travion had witnessed Finn in one of the kingdom's tournaments, and the young lord had won the entire event undefeated. It was that as well as his family's good standing with Travion that had made him enlist Finn into the royal guard.

When push came to shove, he trusted Finn with his life.

As the carriage traveled farther into the city, the roar of the waves against the cliffside faded until there was nothing but salt in the air, mingling with fresh blooms. A far cry from the aroma of the changing tides.

Even in the carriage, Travion could see the orange-and-red-tinted sky. Soon, the crescent moon would replace its counterpart, shedding a soft glow on the middle realm.

Finally, they rolled up to an expansive marble manor with a quaint pond in the front yard. It reminded him more of the homes in Lucem than the houses of Midniva.

Other partygoers had exited their carriages and were entering the manor, eyeing the ensemble of guards outside. A safety precaution that was set in place by none other than Finn.

Travion leaned forward, his gaze shifting from the window to his guard. "Remind me why I thought this was a good idea?"

Finn snorted, then cleared his throat. "I don't believe you ever thought it was a *good idea.*" He shrugged, then ducked his head to peer out the window. "And in truth, if you wanted a way out, you could still escape."

Travion narrowed his eyes. "And say what, that I was overcome by vapors?" He dragged a hand down his face, groaning. "No. I agreed to this." He steeled himself, schooling his features into his typical small smirk and guarded eyes. "It's time," he grumbled before pushing open the door.

Guards bowed and inclined their heads as he passed but otherwise remained rigid and focused as Travion strolled by and into the manor. At once, he was met with the scent of sandalwood incense and the mouthwatering aroma of freshly cooked food.

As he strode forward, the guests scrambled to bow or curtsy, and even the herald had little time to announce his arrival. Travion had other matters to attend to this evening and couldn't linger and chat.

A panicked Lady Ferox rushed forward, bobbing a curtsy. "Your Majesty! Thank you for agreeing to this. Come, come, let's talk in private a little before the announcement." Her ebony hair was pinned back, showcasing her sandalwood skin and green eyes.

From the corner of his eye, Travion saw someone approaching swiftly. He glanced in the male's direction and realized it was Lord Ferox. Unlike his wife, his skin was pale and his eyes as dark as night. There was a certain ferocity in his gaze that reminded him of his betrothed.

"Shall we?" Travion motioned for them to lead the way.

The Feroxes cut through the throng of guests, passing the banquet table, which was laid out with a giant roasted goose, several other delectable goodies, and most notably, an oversized bowl of punch.

"Please bring some drinks to the sitting room," Lady Ferox ordered a servant as she brushed by and entered the room. Sconces lit the dark blue room, lending it a cozy appearance.

At the threshold, Travion laid his hand against Finn's chest. "Remain outside and see to it we aren't disturbed. Unless someone is bringing drinks."

"I might need one after tonight," Finn murmured.

Travion tilted his head back to glare up at him. "Aren't you opinionated this evening?" He pushed away and entered the room, but before he shut the door, the servant returned with a tray of silver goblets.

The female placed them on a table, then left, shutting the door and blocking out the slow whine of a violin.

Travion scooped a drink up, taking a generous sip of plum wine.

"I know we've discussed most of the matters, but is there anything you'd like to ask before the announcement?" Lord Ferox prompted.

There was one thing. All fae were born with an affinity, and it didn't matter what their parents' talents were, their abilities were unique to themselves. While knowing didn't make or break this union, it would help him navigate the waters with her.

"What is Sereia's affinity?" He ran his thumb along the engraved side of the goblet, watching them closely.

The Feroxes shared a look, then said in unison, "Water."

"Her most impressive ability is breathing underwater," Lady Ferox supplied. She pursed her lips and glanced down at the floor. "Your Majesty, may I just add . . . there is a slight chance that Sereia may push back on this agreement."

From what he'd seen of Sereia, he was counting on it. But he was curious about the maiden, who'd bested many of his swordsmen and who would consider denying the king her hand.

"I won't take a bride against her will, Lady Ferox. If she hasn't warmed up to me in three months' time, our agreement is void." He took a generous sip from his goblet, arching a brow in hopes the lady didn't argue with him.

She swallowed, nodding her head in understanding.

Lord Ferox, however, pressed on. "But surely—"

"But surely you aren't implying I should take your

daughter hostage?" His eyes narrowed, waiting for them to continue. To argue that he *should* capture their daughter because the union would bring wealth to their family. Politically and financially.

Thankfully, for their sake, the argument never came.

Lady Ferox placed a hand on her chest. "Before you seek her out, there is something my daughters have prepared for you."

"I look forward to it," he murmured, bowing his head before he spun on his heel and left the room.

Finn glanced down at him, his eyes widening a fraction as if to say, *Well, are you running yet?*

"I'm not going to run," he ground out, then strode down the dimly lit hall and into the open room, which was thoroughly alive with laughing guests.

Crystal lamps sparkled in the bright room, and the heady scent of alcohol swept around Travion, prompting him to drain his goblet. He eagerly made his way to the table, refilling his drink as the harps made a screeching noise.

Players beat against skin drums; fiddles whined along to the tempo as flutes tittered.

Travion strode to the edge of the dance floor, knowing that a dance had been prepared for him. Idly, he wondered if Sereia would be among them, or if she'd snuck out the back of the manor. The lights flickered as the Ferox daughters sprang through a darkened doorway, barefoot, with their hair tumbling down their backs. Three of the sisters Travion recognized at once: the same ones that had been thrust toward him several years ago. One he didn't know, and one stood out above all of them.

Sereia.

Her skin was the softer hue of her mother's sandalwood

complexion, but her eyes were a stark blue, and they were currently cutting through the crowd to glare at him. Perhaps it should have insulted him, but Travion laughed.

The sisters spun, grasping one another by the arm, only to leap toward another sister. At once, they all rushed forward, pushing everyone in the crowd back except for Travion, and they formed a circle around him.

His eyes never left Sereia and, much to his delight, her gaze remained on him.

The dance ended as they tumbled to the floor, breathless, and then the sisters went their separate ways. Except for Sereia.

Finn leaned down and whispered, "The nobles are chattering about a betrothal. That didn't take long."

"It never does." The only issue with everyone knowing was if this agreement didn't work out, the Feroxes would have a great deal to overcome in the eyes of Midnivian society.

"By the sea," Travion grumbled, shoving his half-empty goblet toward Finn. "Don't lose this, I'm going to need it." He crossed the room, and the guests parted for him. He felt rather than saw every eye on him because he was proving the rumors to be true. *Yes, Sereia is my betrothed.*

The fiddlers started playing a slow song, and the couples started edging their way toward the middle of the room once again.

Travion sauntered up beside Sereia, taking in the gauzy powder-blue fabric that clung to her curvy figure like a second skin. She looked like a daughter of Lucem, not Midniva. He cocked his head as she looked up at him. "You're a wonderful dancer." She looked at him through thick, dark lashes, and his heart galloped. He'd been with plenty of beautiful males and females, but Sereia's was the sort of beauty that could stop anyone in their tracks. There was also an undeniable intelligence swirling in her eyes that Travion wanted to tap into.

"Since we are to be married, will you give me the pleasure of a dance?" Travion didn't reach for her hand, but he offered a challenging look, lifting his brows and grinning.

Every one of her muscles seemed as taut as a bowstring, like she was readying to dart out the nearest door or window. Not in fear but defiance. She clearly didn't want to be here.

"If I must," she said through clenched teeth.

Travion chuckled, but if he gave her a way out, perhaps she'd back away. "If you're too tired . . ."

Her brow furrowed. "I can manage."

"Good enough." He offered his hand, and she took it. Travion led her to the middle of the room, and the couples who had stepped onto it quickly dashed to the side.

Sereia stared up at him, perhaps trying to read him, but she wouldn't have an easy time of that because this was not the time to decipher him. Now was the time to dance.

He pulled her in closer, until her body brushed against his. Selfishly, he wished she were like her sisters, flinging herself at him, willing to do whatever he wished. Because he'd capture her full lips between his that very moment.

The pace of the current song was too slow, aimed at the couples already on the floor, but Travion wanted something that would push him and Sereia to their limits.

"We are not here to slowly turn about!" Travion raised his voice, cutting through the party. "Play something livelier!"

At once, a bow dragged across the strings in a low, teasing tone, then quickened until it became a heart-pounding tune.

Travion stepped closer to Sereia, grinning from ear to ear. "I truly hope you can keep up."

Sereia's eyes widened, then she scoffed. "We will see who can keep up with who."

His arm slid around her waist, and he led her across the floor. It was no surprise when she initially fought against his lead, attempting to pull him in a different direction, but Travion remained steady in his stride.

Sereia's expression shifted into a scowl. "You're going to trip us."

"Me?" Travion laughed but nearly regretted the loss of breath. "I don't think it will be *me* tripping us." His heart beat as quickly as a hummingbird's wings, but it thrilled him, perhaps all the more when Sereia rose to the challenge.

Halfway through the dance, the tension in Sereia's face softened, but she still refused to end the dance. "You cannot hope to keep this pace," she rushed out mid-breath.

Travion was used to exerting himself beyond limits. In training, swimming, or fighting. How was dancing any different? "I can and I will."

Sereia narrowed her eyes, but she kept up the punishing pace with him until the very end, until they were both rendered breathless, speechless even. It was there, at that moment, Travion saw a familiar glint in her eye, one that he knew well from years as Midniva's sovereign: a silent truce.

A month after the fete, Sereia still hadn't eased into the idea of their union. Travion had gifted her jewels, sent for the finest dresses, but nothing seemed to gain him any favor. But on a particularly hot summer day, he called for her to join him at the castle.

When she arrived, he was in the courtyard waiting for her. He had foregone an overcoat and brushed off Evun's hands as he attempted to groom him. Travion knew he looked ruffled, with his windblown hair, rolled-up sleeves, and dust-covered trousers.

The carriage door swung open, and out stepped Sereia. Her hair was swept back into a braid, circling her head like a crown. The dress she wore was a sea foam green, with silver embroidery along the bodice. A slit ran up the length of her thigh, showing off her toned leg.

"Your Grace," she murmured as he strode forward, and even allowed him to help her down.

"Lady Sereia. It's particularly hot out today. What do you say we go for a swim?" He tucked her hand into the crook of his elbow, testing to see how much she would offer him. Travion hated having to push, but Sereia never let him know what she was willing to give him.

"In this gown?" Sereia motioned to it.

"If you'd like to keep it on, by all means. But clothing will only weigh us down." He chuckled and led them off the courtyard and down a beaten path.

"No clothing . . ." Sereia peered up at him, then down toward the beach and the small trail that was framed by overgrown white wild roses. The smell permeated the air, sweet and heady, reminding him of his younger years in Lucem.

At the end of the path, packed-down dirt turned into sand. Beach grasses spread off to the side, and in them, little brown and white sandpipers zigzagged through the tall blades.

Before them, waves splashed against the wet shoreline. The tide was low, bringing in screaming gulls and sending crabs scattering for cover.

Travion released his hold on Sereia and unbuttoned his shirt. When he glanced over at her, uncertainty flickered in her eyes, but he walked to the shoreline and discarded his top. "Would you like to race?"

"To where?"

"The red buoy." He paused for a moment. "I can help you with your dress . . ."

Sereia's cheeks reddened, but she nodded. "If I plan on winning, I'll need to be rid of it." She kicked off her slippers and turned her back to him.

Travion undid the clasps, careful not to let his fingers skim along the silken skin presented to him. He wanted to—by the sea, did he want to! But Sereia could scarcely stand to be in his company as far as he could tell.

He pulled away and finished undressing, leaving his clothes in a heap. It was difficult to not stare as she let the gown slide down her figure and pool around her feet. Even harder to convince his body not to find her deliciously attractive.

By the sea. How was he supposed to ignore the swell of her breasts and the curve of her bottom? This hadn't been his reasoning for the swim, but rather allowing her a moment to be carefree and surrounded by the freedom of *water.*

Sereia didn't let him think on it long. She ran for the water and dove beneath the waves, disappearing.

He ran after her, splashing into the water like a bumbling fool, then dove into the depths, propelling himself through the water. It was too murky to see much, but with the sun shining above, he could make out a distant shadow.

She didn't surface, not even once.

Travion popped up, sucking in air, and he glimpsed Sereia hanging onto the buoy with a grin. Amusement flickered to life, but rather than swim to meet her, he ducked under the water and swam for shore.

He surfaced as he entered the shallows, but just as his foot went to plant itself, something—or rather, *someone*—seized his ankle and pulled him back under, then relinquished him.

Travion shot out of the water, chuckling as he wiped the moisture from his face. "I'd forgotten that bit about you," he said as Sereia stood in the shallows. Her hair had come undone and now covered her breasts.

A sea maiden, indeed.

Sereia laughed, her eyes dancing with mischief. "I suspect my parents told you . . ." She canted her head and chewed her bottom lip. "You're different from what I expected."

Hope blazed within. This was the first time she'd genuinely seemed to enjoy his company, and he didn't want to muddle it. "Different how?"

"You're not . . . stuffy, for one. And for two, you broke a rule." She took a step closer and poked a finger into his chest.

He captured her wrist, letting his fingers lightly massage over her pulse. "Ah, but I never indicated there were any rules." Travion leaned in, and she didn't pull away. *Progress,* he thought.

Sereia moved close enough to him so that he felt the warmth of her body, but their skin didn't touch. He watched her, nearly holding his breath, wholly captivated by her. Then, she did something he didn't expect.

She leaned in and pressed her lips against his, tasting of honey and salty air.

And in that moment, he knew he was in trouble, or at the very least his heart was.

By the end of month two, there was nothing chaste about their interactions. Sereia was quick-witted, sharp-tongued, and longed to defy her parents in every way imaginable. And he was all too willing to help her do just that.

Travion let her set the pace every time, but just like their first dance with one another, she moved quickly, and every time, it left him breathless.

Days turned into weeks, weeks into months, and before long, Travion woke up with Sereia weighing on his heart as much as she did his mind. It was a foreign, terrifying feeling that blossomed inside of his chest, but all he knew was that he didn't want to lose it. For it was a beacon of light on his darkest, stormiest days.

Summer had wound down, and the first red leaves wavered in the autumn breeze.

Sereia stood by the cliffside, peering down at the crashing waves. The wind whipped her hair across his face, but Travion moved in front of her and brushed it out of the way as he lay a trail of heated kisses down her cheek, neck, and the top of her breasts.

She pulled him closer, and Travion had to reel himself in, remember why he'd asked her to meet him here.

"Sereia, I've quite enjoyed our time together."

She gazed up at him, searching his eyes. "You know I've enjoyed our time too."

A sudden burst of nerves erupted in him. "A betrothal by agreement is one thing, but I truly wish for you to become my queen . . ."

Sereia inhaled sharply and took a step back. A look of hurt passed in her eyes, one that would haunt him for years to come. "Travion . . ." She recoiled as if he'd slapped her.

What had he said? It was no secret they were to be married, and as he recounted their recent courtship, he thought she'd come to enjoy his company. "Please, let me finish." Travion rushed his words as he stepped forward.

Sereia stepped around him and glanced over her shoulder. A tangle of hair covered most of her face, but her eyes met his one last time before she made a mad dash toward the cliffside and leaped over the edge.

"No!" he bellowed and rushed forward, nearly losing his footing at the edge. "Sereia!" He saw the moment her body plunged into the depths of the turbulent sea.

With his emotions rising, black clouds filled the sky and blotted out the sun.

Anger filled him, as did hurt. A simple *no* would have sufficed. But she had leaped as if he was some sort of monster, bent on imprisoning her.

The guards standing by darted toward the edge and gaped down at the waves.

"Get my ship ready at once!"

"But sire, surely she's . . ."

Travion snarled. "Are you daft? She can breathe underwater."

For days the navy searched for her to no avail. Sereia

didn't want to be found. Her parents were dismayed to begin with, but when none could find their daughter, the Feroxes shot him accusatory glances, as if he had pushed her into the sea himself.

It wasn't until several weeks after, when Travion enlisted the aid of his hippocampus, Velox, that he found her aboard another ship.

"Sereia! Come back to Midniva!" he bellowed into the wind, sea spray coating his face. Travion was met not with words but with a shift of the waves. His ship tilted, and he grabbed ahold of the railing, but a massive wave rose before them. With a quick glance in Sereia's direction, he let her see the hurt, anger, and betrayal he felt within.

Then, in a thunderous crash, the ship capsized, pulling his crew and Travion beneath the tumultuous heaves of the water.

It was disorienting, no matter how many times he had been in the rough sea. It tossed him, pulled him under, and tossed him again. He flailed, trying to right himself in the darkness, but where was up? The cold water numbed him, dulling his ability to think.

Velox!

A shrill *whoop* filled his immediate space, then the familiar slick texture of his hippocampus's hide before his fingers grasped onto a frilled mane. In a quick movement, the sea creature pulled Travion above the water. He sucked in a greedy breath and fell forward against his hippocampus' neck. High-pitched clicking noises filled the air, and several of the sea beasts surfaced with the rest of his crew.

His ship, on the other hand, wasn't as fortunate.

Travion shifted his weight backward. "You could have said

no!" He coughed up some of the water he had swallowed and glared at her through his red bangs.

Sereia didn't say a word. She only turned her back to him and motioned for the ship to sail away. And with it, she took his heart.

1

Sereia

100 Years Later

The cannon boomed, smoke filling the air as the iron ball soared from the barrel toward the hull of the *Ackazanti*. Wood splinters exploded into the air as the ball crashed through it, leaving a large hole in the side of the merchant ship. A cheer rang out on the deck of *The Saorsa*, and Yannik prepped a second ball.

"Hold the fire," Sereia instructed. "Give them time to rethink their position."

Ackazanti was captained by a heartless tyrant, Domyk Mantivic, who took his merchandise from the hands of the impoverished and didn't care who he left destitute. Sereia would not tolerate him any longer. It was time to end the discord and strife he'd spread across the sea.

"They're preparing to fire back, Captain!" Adrik called from the bow.

Just as Sereia's lips opened to order Yannik to fire, the

water erupted around the *Ackazanti*, and two giant tentacles the length of the ship itself slithered around its hull. The sound of creaking wood echoed across the water as the tentacles tightened.

Sereia reached for her spyglass, extending it with a snap as she brought it to her eye. The deck of *Ackazanti* was pure chaos. Men and women ran frantically with whatever weapons could be found at hand, attacking the mast-sized tentacles with full force.

Beyond the merchant ship, her sister vessel *Prepik* fired a cannon, missing the creature and striking the hull of *Ackazanti* instead.

"By the sea," Sereia gasped as the bow of the *Ackazanti* began to dip beneath the weight of the sea monster. Two more tentacles rose from the water to crash down on the ship's deck, and the beast seemed to slither and coil around it. The creature had a large head and giant eyes, like two massive boulders, which blinked against the bright sunlight. It was unlike anything she had ever witnessed before, so large and violent. "It's going to go under," she muttered, mostly to herself.

"Captain?" Sereia lowered the spyglass to look down at Adrik, now just below the quarterdeck. "Should we help them, Captain?"

While she wanted their haul, Sereia did not want their deaths. "Yes, let's bring us closer and prepare to fire."

After a quick nod, Adrik hurried over the deck, barking out orders to the others, and Sereia reclaimed her hold on the helm and steered *The Saorsa* closer.

The crew's cries of distress and Mantivic's frantic commands drifted to them, a haunting song that was soon joined by screams of terror as a crewman was wrapped up in one giant tentacle and brought toward a gaping maw of razor-sharp teeth and dripping saliva.

"Fire!" Sereia shouted. The cannon exploded once more, but even the sharp impact of the iron ball against the side of the kraken's head was not enough to stop the beast from dropping the sailor into its mouth. His screams carried to her ears until the cavernous mouth closed upon him.

Several more cannons echoed from the other side: *Prepik's* captain doing her part to save the main merchant ship.

A deafening roar was the kraken's response, and then the loud crack of wood crushing in on itself as tentacles tightened until *Ackazanti* broke in two. The stern splashed down on the surface of the sea, sending out ripples. It bobbed momentarily on the sea, almost as if nothing had happened. Then it filled with water and slipped beneath the waves.

The bow sank even faster with the weight of the kraken pulling it into the depths below. Sereia released a shuddering breath as the last of the white sails disappeared.

She did not have long to absorb what she had just witnessed. *The Saorsa* gave a great lurch, and it forced Sereia to tighten her hold on the helm lest she tumble to the deck. Below, several of her crew found themselves facedown in wood or clinging to a railing.

Sereia knew that Adrik and her crew could handle the tentacles without her help should they rise from the water. She would be of more use in the sea, where she could see this beast for what it was.

She ran across the quarterdeck, pressed a hand to the railing, and leaped over the top of it, falling several stories down into the sea. As she sank beneath the waves, Sereia took her first deep breath of salt water, feeling her body adapt and change, the gills behind her ears filtering the water through them. While she had been born on land, there was a part of Sereia that did, and always would, belong to the sea.

The kraken was as large as the ship itself. A coiling demon of such mass, it was daunting to think of taking it head on. Why it had not been satisfied feasting on the crew of *Ackazanti*, Sereia wasn't sure, but she would be damned if she would allow her ship and her crew to join in on that devastation.

Treading water easily, Sereia stretched her fingers out through the silken sea and let her magic connect with each droplet. She could sense the very current below them that traveled along the coast of Tribonik and drove on farther toward Torksvala.

Sereia took a deep breath, filling her body with the sea water and letting it ground her as she pushed with her affinity to create heavy streams, mimicking the current below, to sweep between the kraken and her ship, forcing as much pressure onto the beast as she could. From above, the distant sound of cannons could be heard. She could only deduce that her crew were firing on the kraken, which was soon proven true as the iron balls propelled through the water and down onto the creature.

Its roar of complaint echoed through the sea, far angrier than the gentle whines and moans of the whales she'd swum with in the past.

The tip of a tentacle snapped into place on the bottom of *The Saorsa*'s hull, and the ship rocked on the surface.

Releasing her own roar into the water, Sereia pushed harder with her body, increasing the current that wove between the kraken and her ship, forcing every ounce of her willpower into it, until at last the kraken's hold on the hull was torn loose and the giant beast was shoved half a league away. Further from *The Saorsa* and directly into the path of *Prepik*.

Wasting no time, Sereia created a gush of water beneath her that helped her breach the surface and pushed her up onto the deck of her ship. Landing roughly on her side, she shook long strands of her hair out of her eyes and looked up to the quarterdeck. Boran had automatically claimed control of the helm in her absence.

"Get us out of here!" she yelled up at him.

"Captain." Adrik was at her side, a hand at her elbow hauling her up onto her feet. "Next time, give us warning before you launch yourself into the depths with a man-eating beast."

"No time," she ground out. "I've pushed the beast toward the other ship. I hope I haven't sentenced them to death, but we've only got a short window to make a run for it."

Adrik responded without hesitation, shouting orders that had the sails opening up to catch more wind. As *The Saorsa* turned in the water to head away from the creature, Sereia could only watch as the tentacles of the kraken shot from the sea and crashed around *Prepik*, taking down the foremast and all its sails in the process.

Sereia didn't take her eyes off the other ship, but instead forced herself to watch as it was crushed beneath the strength of the sea monster. She had chosen her ship over the others, and she would bear witness to their ending.

When it was deemed long enough for the kraken to have had its fill and return to the deep, Sereia directed her ship back to the scene of the attack. From the waters they fished up any who could be scavenged. Wrapped them in blankets against the chill, bandaged their wounds, and offered them some jerky to stave off hunger while they made their way toward the port of Bezopasnyy.

Night had fallen by the time they were docking in the harbor, but an apothecary was called for, and the survivors were relocated to a local infirmary.

As she watched the last of them carted off, Sereia sighed, weariness settling deep into her bones.

"What say you to us getting an inn for the night?" Adrik asked, sidling up beside her.

"I think perhaps after what was witnessed today, the crew is due some shore leave," Sereia bit out. Her throat was tight, emotion bubbling just below the surface. She wasn't proud of her actions today and knew they should have stayed to fight against the kraken rather than retreat. Had they stayed, they could have possibly saved the *Prepik* at the very least.

"Stop it, Rei," Adrik said firmly.

Sereia turned her head to look at him, a glare pinching at her eyes. "Excuse me?"

"Stop second guessing your actions today. You saved our crew with no casualties."

"At the expense of an entire ship. We could have—"

"What?" He swept his arms out wide. "Stayed and helped? Kept us in the fight?"

"Yes!" she snapped.

"And joined *Prepik* and *Ackazanti* at the bottom of the sea."

"You don't know that," she fired back.

"You know as well as I do that we weren't all getting out

of that. And if we had stayed, we would have all died. I wanted to help them as badly as you did, Captain. But there was no perfect out. You made the right call."

Sereia crossed her arms, teeth grinding as she breathed heavily through her nose. While she was a pirate, and her intention had been to plunder *Ackazanti* of all her wares, Sereia and her crew only stole from those who were tyrants on the sea. She took from those who had already taken from others, and when her treasures were sold, a large portion always went back to the people who had originally been wronged. There would have been those who were lost in the battle between the *Ackazanti*, *Prepik* and *The Saorsa*, but not to such an extent.

She didn't live without a conscience, and having to turn her back on others in grave danger cut deeply.

"Tell the crew they are free to take leave here at port. I'll claim us rooms at The Obstinate Goat." Sereia signaled to Yon and Chailai, who had seen the last of the injured off the ship. Her personal spy and second mate were quickly at her side. "Gather your things, we're going ashore for the foreseeable future." Both women nodded and then dispersed.

Sereia headed into her own quarters and packed up a leather satchel, taking only what would be needed. A spare change of clothes, a book should she decide to hole up in her room, and a spare knife that she slid into the bottom of her bag.

As their boots thudded across the wooden wharf, Sereia fought the internal rocking of her body that was in direct competition with the solidness of the structure beneath her. They had been out at sea for weeks, and it would take time to adjust to being on land once more.

Together, the three women made their way up the dirt

streets of Bezopasnyy, passing dark stone homes alight with single candle flames. Cracked wooden doors kept out most of the chill of the night, and occasionally the bay of a hound would drift into the air. At the top of the hill, The Obstinate Goat sat like a beacon of drunkenness and revelry, windows bright in the darkness.

Pushing open the door, Sereia was met with the din of chatter, broken by the occasional bout of raucous laughter or the thud of heavy tankards being set down on wooden tables. The tavern was alive with drinking and tall tales, completely at odds with her own internal thoughts and emotions.

It was good. For her crew, at least. They deserved this break on land after the battle at sea they'd just overcome.

Sereia stepped up to the bar and slapped her hands on top of it, allowing the solid wood to hold up her weight. The barkeep noticed her and stepped up.

"Well, well, well. Look what the seal dragged in. Captain Ferox." Kartok was a grizzled old man. Dark silver hair splayed out over his head every which way, and a thick leather patch rested over one eye. Rumors said he'd lost it in a fight, taking a broken bottle to the face over a beautiful girl in his youth. Sereia had it on better account he'd tripped while drunk and landed on something sharp. "Thought you were bound for Caifu, last I heard."

"The sea spirits had other plans for us." She didn't plan to elaborate. Her crew would have the tale of the kraken spread around port by sunup. They didn't need her aid in the matter. "I need four rooms. You've got them to spare?"

Kartok grumbled like she was tasking him with something unpleasant rather than putting coppers directly into his pocket. "We're full up." He brought a fist to his face to cough a haggard sounding wheeze into it.

Sereia slanted a glare at him and fished a silver coin from her satchel, which she held up between them. "The tavern's not that full, Kartok. Why don't you check your keys again?"

He eyed the silver piece, and she could see him fighting the urge to lick his lips. "Three," he coughed out. "I can do three."

She sighed but used her thumb to fling the coin into his waiting hand. "I'll take them." Once the keys were in hand, Sereia turned to Chailai and Yon, who waited behind her. "I'm afraid the two of you will have to bunk together, unless either of you wishes to share with Adrik."

Yon, who was always stoic and typically silent, only squinted. It was Chailai, her second in command, who plucked one key from Sereia's hand. "Yon and I do not mind sharing. We live on a ship, two to a room is a dream."

She watched them disappear up the creaky wooden steps while leaning against the bar. The edge of it pressed into her spine, and she relished the bite. While Adrik may have spoken true, she wasn't ready to accept her failure as needful.

Eventually, Sereia made it up to her room to bathe in the first hot water she'd seen in weeks and change into fresh clothing. Her salt-stained garments were given to the maid to be cleaned. Feeling somewhat put together, Sereia returned to the tavern below to fill herself up on beet stew and bread.

When her belly was full and the ache of her muscles had settled into heavy weariness, Sereia settled herself beside the large stone fireplace, propping her feet up on a log stool and clasping her ale in her hands.

Bringing a tankard to her lips, she gulped down some of the foamy ale, blue eyes staring into the fire. Outdoors, the wind rattled the shutters and rain beat against the window panes as a fresh storm unleashed its woes upon the coastline.

For once, she wasn't being rocked to and fro by violent waves but found herself on solid ground—steady and dry.

It felt like more than was deserved.

Across the tavern, she could hear the excited shouts of Boran, her third mate, and Batteo, a deckhand, as they won at a round of dice. Perhaps it was with the aid of ale, but they were putting the horrors of today behind them. Relishing in the chance to either win or lose a handful of coin.

"They say all of Lucem was pitched into darkness." A voice drifted over the din of chatter and cheers.

"For how lon—"

"Can I interest you in a top up, m'lady?" the barmaid asked, appearing suddenly at Sereia's side with a pitcher in her hand.

Sereia held up her tankard, glancing at her cooly. "There's no lady here." Sereia trained her ear on the voices coming from the table off to her side, and her dark brow furrowed slightly at what she was hearing.

"Jousin hasn't told ye all of it," a new voice chimed in. "They say the king was sliced clear in two."

King Zryan is dead? Surprise flared inside her at the news. Had his queen finally tired of his philandering ways and taken a sword to him?

"Not that one, y'fool. The Midnivian king. I heard some creature crawled out of the depths of the dark realm and bit the top half of him clean off."

"The nightmare king! I bet it was all his doing."

Sereia heard nothing else. Her peripherals darkened as the room closed in on her. Suddenly, she found the leather corset encasing her ribcage too tight to breathe in, and the ale in her stomach turned to acid, burning at her throat.

Sereia tossed her tankard into the fireplace, causing the

flames to sputter and then flare, and her boots hit the roughened floorboards with a thud. She stood quickly and was at the table in a breath's time, hands slamming down on their table as she leaned in. It wasn't possible that Travion was dead. While his elder brother was known to be a monster of nightmarish proportions, they were on good terms . . . as far as she had been aware.

Her heart beat rapidly in her chest with dread that threatened to pull her down into a pit of darkness she did not wish to fathom.

"What is this bloody nonsense you're spouting?" She growled so that her words wouldn't come out trembling. Her pulse thrummed loudly in her ears, and there was a storm of panic brewing within her.

The men at the table looked surprised at her sudden appearance before them but took it in stride. Sereia was a frequent enough visitor in these ports for her and her behaviors to be known by the locals. She was not spooked by forceful men and did not back down when there was something she wanted or needed. Most recognized that it was better to give in than to go to battle with her. Her mother had always said she was stubborn to a fault, and that had not changed in the one hundred years she'd been away from Midniva.

"The news coming in from the west is that there was a battle in the three realms of the immortal brothers. No one's sure who started it, but they say many were lost."

"King Travion." Her voice shook lightly on his name. "He was killed?"

"Killed? I'd say so!" said the youngest at the table, a man with half an ear missing and a gold ring in one nostril.

The man who'd been speaking shot him an annoyed look.

"I never said he died. Just that he was attacked by one of them dark creatures from the pits of the afterlife. They say his dark brother betrayed him, and the light king as well."

What could have happened for King Draven to betray his brothers? Had the darkness of Andhera twisted him into something so menacing that even once-beloved brothers were no longer safe? While there was no love lost between him and Sereia, there had never been a rift between King Zryan of the light realm, King Draven of the dark realm, and King Traven of the middle realm. Could something have taken place between the brothers to result in not only an attack but death?

The thought of Travion, bloodied and torn, drawing in his last breaths while she lay thousands of leagues away, made it hard to breathe. The men at the table were eyeing Sereia oddly, waiting for her to respond, and perhaps wondering what was going through her mind.

Sereia said nothing, only straightened up and strode quickly across the room to where her first mate sat face deep in a pair of voluptuous breasts. The wench was producing such moans there was no doubt they were the kind bought and paid for. Sereia kicked his chair leg hard enough to make it lurch a little and rouse him from his foreplay. Adrik lifted his head with a snarl, a heavy glare on his face until he realized who was disturbing him.

"Aye, Captain?" he muttered, arms still tight around the wench's waist.

"Plans have changed. We set sail at dawn."

"The storm . . . they say it's meant to last."

Sereia continued to stare down at him without blinking. Storm be damned, there was no time to wait. If she ever wished to breathe properly again, she needed answers now.

"But you promised the crew a week of shore leave—" His words died off as he caught the hardening look in her eyes. "Aye, Captain. I'll make sure it's known. What heading will we be taking?"

"West. We head to Midniva."

Sereia

The waters of Mointeach Bay glistened in the bright sunshine overhead, and the white cliffs of Caithaird farther down the coast glinted more proudly for it. There was a familiar scent in the air that caused a flash of nostalgia to surface in Sereia. It was fierce and tasted suspiciously of homesickness. It was not a weakness she cared to acknowledge, and it did not mix well with the depth of unease and grief that had grown inside of her during their trip from Tribonik.

When she had fled Midniva a century ago, Sereia would never have imagined that she could miss the place that had stifled her. Living as a lady of nobility had not been enough to sustain the thirst for adventure and life itself that rushed through her veins. The need to go out and simply live had been a current too strong for her to ignore.

Sereia had snuck her way onto the first ship, only to be discovered and eventually thrown off at the next port. But that had brought her to the shores of Tribonik, where it was possible to forge an entirely new life. After proving her mettle in a sword fight against one sea captain's best fighter, she'd earned her place onboard a vessel.

She worked her way from the bottom rung upward. Swabbing decks, prepping food, swashbuckling with the best of them. Sereia learned her way around the ship, hauling ropes until her hands bled and spending so much time on deck, her lips grew chapped and her skin burnt from the sun.

None of the pain mattered, because she was at sea, and the salt water was all she had ever hoped for. Ever needed. It was her home.

But a part of her, even if she did not like to pay it any mind, missed her homeland. Missed the white cliffs and the sun-bleached castle set atop them. Missed the call of the gulls over the harbor in Mointeach, and the scent of beef stew and ale filtering down the cobblestone streets.

"I did not expect to see these shores again." Adrik stepped up beside her at the railing, the wind whipping at his shoulder-length, medium-brown hair. He wore most of it pulled back from his face with a leather string at the back of his head while the rest hung loose.

He was a tall man, broad shouldered and firmly muscled from his days on the ship. His blue eyes tended to glint with mischief and mayhem, and his tongue bore more sass than was appropriate for a first mate. He was lucky she viewed him as family and let him get away with it.

"Well, take pleasure in the unexpected. The crew can have their shore leave here." She fought to keep her tone casual, hiding the swell of emotions inside her.

Her sea adventures had not kept her from Midniva. Over the years, she would return when her captain saw fit to dock at port here, and later, after she had commandeered ownership of

The Saorsa through a well-placed bet and duel. Each time she'd stepped on shore, she had found herself heading back to the capital. Sometimes to see her family, but always to see Travion.

Their first interaction after the failed betrothal had been tense and full of many unasked questions. Yet, from there, they'd developed an understanding. When she was here, she was welcome in Travion's bed, no questions asked and no presumptions made. It was a liaison without expectations and without shackles.

But even romances without romance can take their toll. Each time Sereia found herself in Travion's arms, she was drawn more strongly to him. It became harder and harder to resist the desire to lose herself in his presence. To forget her life at sea and promise to stay there with him on land despite what she needed for herself.

It had been five years since Sereia had last stepped foot in Midniva, and when she'd left, she hadn't been sure she would return. Adrik kept his face turned out to the approaching land, but his eyes flicked momentarily to her before returning to Midniva. "And you, Captain? What will you be doing back in your homeland?"

Sereia's eyes narrowed a little, and she turned her head to look at him. Adrik's beard was scruffy along his rugged jaw and made the high cheekbones in his face all the more prominent. Currently, his hair was straggly and in a mighty need of washing. His fitted blue shirt was stained and starting to look a little threadbare. As was the red scarf tied about his lean waist. He needed off this damn boat and a thorough bathing.

They all did.

"What I'll be doing is no worry of yours. See to it that the ship is restocked and that any repairs needed are made. And for the love of sea and shore, find yourself a tub to wash the filth off."

Adrik's smirk was quick and broad as he scanned her over from head to toe. "You could use one yourself, Captain. Especially if you plan on visiting your ki—"

"Yes, I'm not much better than a barnacle myself. I'm aware." There would be no discussing Travion. She couldn't bear to, not until she knew whether the rumors were true. She also didn't have the patience for Adrik's taunting. Not now. Not with the cliffs of Caithaird in the distance. Did Prince Kian now reign there?

Sereia returned her gaze to the shores of Mointeach, the quaint seaport town, a familiar, welcoming sign. Small colorful homes nestled along the banks of the coast and worked their way toward larger structures that were used to house nets and process fish as they came in off the water. The seaside fishing shops and warehouses then gave way to proper shops, a market, taverns, and a small temple to the fae of creation.

Men and women bustled right alongside fae, selling wares and preparing fishing vessels. It was a healthy town. A welcoming port. A safe refuge from the unsteady nature of the sea.

She wondered momentarily how her mother and father were, as well as her sisters. How had they fared in the battle? Had any of them come under attack? Were any of them injured? Had any of her nephews joined the Midnivian army or the royal guard? It had been so long since Sereia had seen any of them. While she loved her family, Sereia had always felt so separate from them. Her sisters had been happy to follow along with their mother's plans for their lives. Had loved the notion of beautiful homes, fancy gowns, and endless balls. All the things that felt like a noose about Sereia's neck.

This life of piracy was not something that her mother or father understood, nor did they accept it. The idea that one of their daughters should choose to sail the seas with a group of swarthy ruffians instead of accepting the coveted role of queen had been incomprehensible. She'd had everything her mother ever dreamed of within a fingertip's reach, and still, Sereia had fled from it all. It sent her mother into a fit of nerves, which was why she had not crossed the threshold of the Ferox family estate in over five decades. She wasn't exactly certain she was welcome there anymore.

Lord and Lady Ferox had been born and raised in Lucem. They came to the middle realm centuries after King Travion staked his claim and settled himself and his court on her white cliffs. While they made their life here, they had never truly left behind their Lucem ways. But Sereia, who had been born to this seafaring land, had the water in her blood.

The salty breeze always called to her, and the ships disappearing on the horizon had beckoned her along with them. While her mother focused on seeing all five of her daughters married into well-off families—ones of power and acclaim—Sereia had sought any opportunity she had to escape to a world of freedom. Ballgowns and soirees were not the life she had ever seen for herself. Instead, Sereia had wanted the open sea before her and the wood hull of a ship beneath her feet.

"You'd tell me if there was something greater at work here than just a sudden desire to see home, right?" Adrik pressed, concern in his eyes as he studied her. "You seemed hell-bent on getting here, whatever the sea chose to throw at us."

More than one storm had hit *The Saorsa* and her crew since they'd set sail from the port in Bezopasnyy.

Sereia turned from the small portside town of Mointeach and looked up at the bright scarlet sails of her beloved ship. They had withstood the winds well, but the foretopsail was in tatters.

"There is always something greater at work, Adrik. When you have need to know it, I will tell you. Until then, see to it that my ship is fixed." Aboard *The Saorsa*, the only one Sereia trusted more than Adrik was Yon. In the nearly thirty years he'd been aboard her ship, he'd morphed from a mouthy teen to a mouthy friend who felt more like a pesky sibling. Despite him often being her sounding board, she did not have to share everything with him.

Now was not a time when she felt like sharing.

Adrik merely nodded. "Aye, Captain." Knowing not to press her further, the first mate walked away to oversee their docking at port.

Shouts rang out around her as *The Saorsa* drew nigh to the docks, waves crashing on shore as the large ship drifted up to the wharf. Her crew hurried over the deck to reel in sails and toss ropes to those working atop the wooden structure. As the ship came to a final halt, lurching slightly as the anchor took root, Sereia turned from the railing and made her way from the forecastle deck down the stairs to the main, searching for Yon.

She found her climbing down the shrouds from the crow's nest. As Yon dropped the last few feet onto the deck, Sereia waved her over.

"I have a task for you," she said in a hushed tone.

Yon nodded and stepped closer.

"I need to know what happened with the supposed

insurrection and if a new king sits on the throne in Caithaird. It is imperative you find out everything that is happening in the castle and a means for getting in unnoticed. I don't want anyone in the palace to know that we're here." If Travion was well, Sereia could head straight back out to sea, and he would have no need to know she had rushed across the waters to check on him.

Yon's large brown eyes peered up at her. While the other woman was petite and slender, looking as delicate as a water lily, she was an expert tracker. If there was ever a moment when Sereia needed information, it was to Yon she went. Yon never asked why, and Sereia never asked Yon how she acquired it. Her information had come in handy on more than one pillage of a merchant ship or when offloading goods once they were acquired.

"Should I leave immediately? Is this why we have come to Mointeach?" She studied Sereia carefully, questions brewing in her dark brown eyes. It made Sereia wish to shuffle in place, as if Yon were seeing down into the heart of her. The crew closest to her had all recognized the desperation within Sereia. Had known it was something greater than a need to return home. She wasn't so good at hiding herself from those who saw her day in and day out in tight quarters.

"This is top priority. Leave now." That was all she was going to give her. Just like Adrik, there were things Yon didn't need to know.

Without another word, Yon disappeared down the ramp and into the crowds on the dock. And with her Sereia's concerns went. Whatever word Yon returned with would decide how this shore leave was going to go for Sereia, and for any who got in her way.

3

Travion

Travion drummed his fingers against the wooden table in the war room. All the eyes of his council were on him, waiting for direction. The recent reports of monstrous sea creatures terrorizing Tribonik, capsizing ships and slaughtering crew, weighed heavily on him. Beasts that size weren't normal, and he had a sneaking suspicion it had everything to do with The Creaturae. The damn book was capable of creating *anything* and destroying in equal parts.

General Quillan's tense features suggested he was ready to send their troops into the unknown, but Travion knew better than that, and it was foolish.

Which was why it was so essential to retrieve the book.

Again, he bemoaned the fact that his brothers had been so preoccupied with his grievous injury from the manticore, and that somehow, someone snatched the book when they were trying to piece Travion back together.

They should've let him bleed out on the floor.

"We don't know the cause of any of this, but what we can do is send out half of our armada to scout. We need to inform the surrounding countries of what is happening and warn them."

"But what about us?" Lord Tywil stared down his long nose at Travion, his calculating beady eyes narrowing on him. "What should your citizens do?"

His tone rankled Travion, and he sat forward, glowering. "Tell me, do you expect your daughter to dive into the water, readying for battle?"

Lord Tywil sputtered. "Absolutely not, Your Grace."

"Then, nothing. Midniva's *army* will increase their security around the Veil and across the kingdom. Anything that seems amiss is to be reported back to me at once. Because I will not have my *citizens* fighting."

Travion stood and placed his palms on the table. He turned to look to his left, and Admiral Callahan shifted his jaw. Tension oozed from his broad figure, but it wasn't directed toward his king but rather at Tywil. "Admiral, be certain those you send out have an affinity for wind and water. Make certain they keep their distance from where the attacks occurred. I don't want to lose anyone if I can help it."

"Of course, Your Grace." Admiral Callahan bowed his head.

"Until we need to assemble again, we're done here," Travion said roughly and left the room. If he was quick enough, he could avoid speaking with anyone else and have a moment to breathe.

He descended the marble stairs and took a sharp left, heading toward the doors to the garden. Travion stepped outside, and the smell of fresh blooms struck his nose. The warm, sugary fragrance of honeysuckle wafted toward him, coupled with the sweet, velvety scent of gardenias.

The castle's gardens—his gardens—were one of the few

places he felt at peace. He wound his way through the flora, following the stone pathway all the way to the rail. From here, he could watch the ships sailing in the bay, not that it would soothe him any. All he could think about was the lives that were lost.

Although it had been two months since he'd nearly died, there were days his body screamed at him to rest, to cease pushing himself to the extreme. But Travion had already rested for weeks while he healed, and lying on his back while his kingdom suffered wasn't something he could do. These past few weeks, the skin itched around his scar, and his muscles ached.

His gaze settled on a small craft and, not for the first time in the last five years, he wondered where Sereia was. In the past century, she'd returned to him long enough to mess up his bed, heart, and mind alike, but never to stay. It was a torturous cycle but one Travion longed for, because while in Midniva, she was at least in his arms, however briefly.

But as the years drew on, her time away from him grew longer, and he knew the last time was likely just that.

There had been a look within her eyes, and the drawn-out kisses that tasted of sorrow and goodbyes. Travion had clung to them, but they had long since faded.

He hoped, for her safety, she remained as far from Midniva as could be.

Travion sighed, closing his eyes as he absorbed the warmth of the sun. Spring had ended in Midniva, and most of the flowering trees had dropped their petals, which coated the ground in yellow, pink, and white hues. Flowering vines crawled along the trellises not far from where he stood, reaching for the brightest rays. Said garden had been designed to mimic Lucem's lush landscape, and outside of the harsh winters in Midniva, there was rarely a season without a bloom.

He leaned on the rail, letting his shoulders sag, but he should have known better. Peace didn't last long.

"Your Grace." Taimon's voice carried to him; then came the footsteps.

Travion regarded his steward with a lazy lift of an eyebrow. "Please tell me you have good news, Taimon." He spun around but remained leaning against the rail.

Unlike his king, Taimon was always well-dressed. His dark red hair was combed back and held in a neat bun at the nape of his neck. He had a youthful but narrow face that made it appear as though his lips were always twisted in disapproval, and maybe they were. He had to manage Travion, after all.

Taimon's thin lips tilted into a smile. "Actually, I had a thought. Seeing as your health has returned, don't you think it's wise to throw a small soiree for your courtiers? Show them you are well, give them a distraction from all this madness."

A fete, at a time like this? "Surely not. There are beasts lurking in the sea, and who knows where they'll surface next. They are growing closer to Midniva, Taimon." Travion shook his head and pushed away from the rail.

Taimon followed close on his heels. "It may not be the right time in the broad scheme of things, but it is a *good* time for your citizens. If not a large fete, then at least the well-known families."

Travion frowned but considered what others may have needed. A reprieve from reality in the form of a party may not be a terrible idea. It may not have worked for him, but perhaps the gossip, the normalcy of interacting with the realm's peers, would be enough for his courtiers.

"Very well," he said at last. "You may begin the preparations. Ensure it's in the evening so that Draven and Eden can attend if they're available to do so."

Taimon quickened his stride to keep up. "As you wish, Your Grace." He paused, then, "Is there anything else?"

"That'll be all for now, Taimon." He nodded and watched as his steward bowed and walked away.

The half-fae had only been in his service for twenty years. He was young, sometimes a little too serious, but he was efficient and respectable. His mother was a human and nearly at the end of her life. Eighty years was long indeed to a mortal, but to a fae? It was the blink of an eye.

Nevertheless, he truly hoped Taimon was right.

Invitations had been sent out the day Taimon mentioned the soiree, and just a few days later, the castle was bustling with activity as they prepared for guests.

Travion reclined on the marble bench in his garden and watched the glittering sea. Silver threads of moonlight touched upon the surface, but the sea was darker than the sky.

As much as he'd prefer to remain outdoors, his guests would soon arrive. He pushed himself up with a soft groan and strode across the path. Inside, chandeliers lit the open spaces, the crystals twinkling like stars.

The scent of food tickled his nose, reminding him he

hadn't eaten a thing during the day. He could nearly taste the breaded fish filets, crispy potatoes, and dark, velvety ale.

Taimon swept into view, and at once, Travion tensed. Right away, his mind went to several possibilities—including more casualties along the distant shores.

"Your Grace, I know that guests are set to arrive at any moment, but these missives wound up on my desk. I thought you may want to take a look at them." His lips pursed, and his bottomless brown eyes mirrored the mounting disquiet inside of Travion.

He plucked the letters from Taimon's hands and scanned the parchment. At once, the muscles in his face tightened. Survivors from the latest wreck were in Midniva, spreading their tale of woe far and wide, which meant there wasn't any more time to prepare. But how had the armada fared? He hadn't received a seahawk from them with an update. Still, danger was imminent, and the kingdom needed to be addressed as soon as possible.

"Why wasn't this brought to me instead?" Travion folded the papers and thrust them back at Taimon.

"Your Grace, I don't believe it was done on purpose. When you were bedridden, I'd taken on more tasks to alleviate your stress. Nevertheless, I'll make certain it doesn't happen again." Taimon bowed his head and clutched onto the papers tightly.

Travion scoffed. "There were few things I could do in bed, but reading was one of them." He flicked his hand to the side in annoyance and grumbled. "Any news should be brought to me at once. I appreciate all your help, but this is not for you to address."

Taimon's pale cheeks reddened, and he cast his eyes

downward, but not before Travion caught a curious expression in his gaze. Frustration? Possibly annoyance.

Perhaps he was only placing his own emotions on his steward and not reading him properly.

"You must excuse me, Your Grace. There are some more missives waiting for me in my study."

"Not more for me, I hope," Travion muttered as his steward bowed and walked away without another word.

He knew throwing this fete was a terrible idea, yet the possibility of alleviating unease among his people had convinced him otherwise. Travion didn't want Midniva taking another hit, not after Naya Damaris unleashed discord on his kingdom, nearly killing him in the process.

Travion turned on his heel, readying to help himself to a goblet of ale in the ballroom, when a breathless servant rushed up to him. "Your Majesty, Queen Eden has—"

His brow rose as he glanced around, hoping to catch a glimpse of Eden. The last time she'd been in his castle for a ball, Zryan had convinced Travion it was a *good idea* to betroth her to Draven. Had Travion been sober, he never would have agreed to it, but the drinks flowed heavily that evening. Still, it worked out for the best.

She was exactly what Draven needed—sweet but with an underlying tenacity.

"Travion!" Eden rounded the corner and ran toward him, arms outstretched.

She collided into him, and his arms coiled around her slender frame in a gentle embrace. "Eden. I didn't expect you to be without—"

"Yes, well, she sprinted from the chariot the moment it came to a halt," Draven drawled as he strolled into view.

Flanking him was a blond were-wolf and an impressive harpy guard.

Travion pulled back and grinned at Eden. "Is that so?"

Eden's full lips twisted. "You'll be occupied tonight with your guests." She flicked the red cape hanging from her shoulders out of the way, then glanced between Travion and Draven. She reached out and lightly squeezed his bicep. "I wanted to make certain you'd save a dance for me."

Travion barked out a laugh, then slid his thumb beneath her chin and tilted her head back. "Ah, for you, Eden, I'll save the very first one." He winked at her. For the one who had saved his life, he'd willingly dance until his feet fell off.

Eden lowered her hand, grabbing his to squeeze it. Her eyes remained on his, and he wasn't keen on how she seemed to look beyond the surface of his expression. "Are you all right?" she asked softly.

"Well enough, my dear." He nodded his head toward his brother. "Now go, your husband is giving me dirty looks." Travion peered over at Draven and shared a look, relaying the need to talk.

Eden sighed. "I'll be with Dhriti in the garden." She glanced over her shoulder at Draven, then exited the room.

"So, you've heard more?" Draven closed the distance between them, frowning.

Travion nodded. "Survivors have made their way to Midniva, and whatever fresh hell is brewing out at sea isn't far off from here. If we manage a week without one of those beasts hitting my waters, I'll be surprised." He bit his bottom lip before he sucked it into his mouth. "You should have let me bleed out on the floor. It would have been better than whatever awaits us." If they'd only snatched the book up instead of piling his innards back in, they wouldn't be in this predicament.

Draven narrowed his gaze. "You know that was never an option."

"It should have been. I'm only one, and who can say how many will pay for it now. Hundreds? Thousands?"

Draven's shoulders stiffened. "Only one—"

Travion lifted a hand to silence any further argument. "I'm not squabbling with you. It's neither here nor there at this point." Now the book was seas-only-knew-where and wreaking havoc on not only ships but ports too. If Eden hadn't chosen an apt punishment for her mother—to remain imprisoned in the dungeons, reliving her worst nightmares indefinitely—Travion would have hauled that damnable banshee from the depths of the castle and exacted a gory punishment on her.

Travion sighed. "Before you join your wife in the gardens, I've had a room in the depths of the castle furnished for the both of you. Should you wish to extend your stay beyond the evening, now or in the future when she stays with me, it's there." It was the least he could do for them. Travion knew all too well what it was like to be separated from the one he loved. But to be parted for six months and just out of reach was a different kind of torture.

Draven remained quiet for a beat, then a small tick of a smile formed. "Thank you, brother." He started to walk away, then paused to clap a hand on Travion's back. "Since this evening's gathering is smaller, I'll do my best not to frighten your courtiers off."

"Where is the fun in that?"

The courtiers filed into the castle, filling the ballroom with chatter, laughter, and no doubt juicy rumors that Travion couldn't care less about.

Some days were better than others for Travion, and on the good ones, he enjoyed being in the company of his courtiers. But on the bad ones, he drank deeply and yearned for the quiet of his room.

While he adored his subjects, he didn't care for trivial babble or their endless need to stir trouble when there were far too many genuine problems to sort through.

Lord Seaver, one of Midniva's notoriously pompous nobles, faced Travion. His bulbous nose seemed to glow brighter with every additional sip of wine he took. "Your Majesty." He bowed. "We are so glad you've recovered from your injuries. My brother's niece is staying with us, and I thought—"

Before the lord could finish, Eden looped her arm through Travion's. Her freckled cheeks glowed beneath the chandelier's warm light. "What of that dance, my dear brother? Surely everyone has had enough food and drink?" She lifted her light red brows in question, an impish gleam in her green eyes.

Bless Eden for coming to his rescue.

"Ah, thank you kindly, Lord Seaver, but I cannot allow my brother's wife to wait a moment longer. You must understand . . . "

Travion escorted Eden to the center of the ballroom. "Ever the savior, Eden." It would seem pulling him from the brink of death wasn't the only way she could rescue him.

He chuckled, placing his hand on top of hers as he stepped back. Bowing, he curled his fingers around hers. Travion's free hand slid to the small of her back, and he lifted a brow. "What sort of dance would you prefer?"

"Preferably the moving kind."

His brow furrowed at Eden's quip. "You've spent far too much time with Draven. His humor has rubbed off on you." He shook his head in mock disappointment.

Eden's hand lighted on his shoulder, and she squeezed in a not-so-subtle reprimand.

The drummers quickly pounded on their skin drums, and the sound of a bow across its violin filled the room, and they hastened their music until it was a lively tune that had even the most stoic of individuals tapping their toes.

Eden smiled, and it lit her face in a way that was infectious. She bounded across the floor in his arms, laughing.

Travion led her into a spin and caught her in his arms, only to pull her along into a series of quick turns.

For the moment, he forgot the worries of the kingdom and simply enjoyed himself. After all, it had been a long time since he'd allowed himself that luxury.

4

Sereia

S ereia wore her dark brown hair pulled back into a low, twisted bun at the back of her head. Large emeralds dangled from her earlobes, an age-of-maturity gift from her father that she'd hung on to. Tonight's soiree was not a masquerade, but she had no desire to be recognized and so wore a black lace mask that covered the upper half of her face. From beneath it, her blue eyes popped.

It was very likely one or more of her sisters and their husbands would be present tonight. The four of them had all married members of the nobility, fae males her mother could be proud to call sons. A part of Sereia longed to mingle with her sisters. To remember fond memories of their youth and learn of their lives now. Were they happy? Were they angry with her? Did they miss her? But there were more pressing matters than building a bridge to her family.

As her carriage brought her through the large gates of the castle and into the first courtyard where the guards' barracks were stationed, memories flooded her, so strong she had to open the window to let fresh air in.

In those first months of Travion courting her, she'd taken

this path many times. But even before that, Sereia had been familiar with the inner walls of the castle, beyond the high stone walls that surrounded it.

She'd made friends with the soldiers inside. Dared them to test her sword-fighting skills, gained from lessons that had been hard earned and only found acceptable because she relented to taking every other feminine lesson her mother could foist upon her.

In this inner courtyard, she had been knocked to her bottom in the dirt and learned to get back up and keep on fighting.

From there, the stone street wound up the hill, past the stables and the castle gardens, until passing through the final gates that lead to a bridge and ended in the main courtyard before the large stone steps. The castle was many stories high, with proud dormer windows and a turret on either end.

It was old, but beautiful. A little wild in appearance from the salt breeze but dignified and sturdy. A lot like its king.

A footman helped Sereia down out of her carriage, one of her hands in his while the other clutched the silken skirts of her emerald dress. As she stepped down, the wind caught it, and one tanned leg was exposed nearly up to her hip from the high slit. The footman was polite enough to look away, but it only made Sereia smirk.

There was nothing subtle about her gown. Cinched tight around her waist, it had a full skirt that flowed down to the floor. Thin straps held it up over her shoulders, and the neckline plunged low. There were some aspects of Lucemite culture she could appreciate. Raw sexual decadence without the need to pretend one was a modest, innocent mouse. Not like the mortals of the middle realm who seemed to value virginity over their own pleasures.

Climbing the broad stone steps up to the solid wood doors, Sereia took quick note of those strolling around her, but focused on the strains of music coming from the direction of the ballroom. It had been a party similar to this one where she had first met Travion, King of Midniva. He had represented all the chains and restrictions her mother had wished to tie about her, the lifetime of rules and obligations that would have broken her. Until the fateful day of that damned proposal, Sereia had thought he recognized that.

Stepping into the ballroom, Sereia wove her way through the crowd of courtiers. Some noticed her, their eyes following the elegant trail of her gown, while others whispered about the black mask that hid her features. She didn't care.

A sharp breath left her lips at the first sight of Travion, who was very much alive and healthy. Yon had managed to find out that much, and that he had been gravely injured during a surprise attack on the three realms. But no one had been sure of his current state. Had he bounced back quickly from the injury? Or was he ailing still?

From the ease with which he spun his partner around on the dance floor, Sereia could only assume he had overcome the attack. For the first time since that tavern in Bezopasnyy, Sereia felt herself relax.

He was alive and well. Perhaps she should take this happy glimpse as all she deserved and slip back out unseen. But there was a pang deep within her. A need to draw closer. To smell the scent of him, fresh breeze and spice. Her fingers twitched at her sides, the desire to press them to his solid chest and reassure herself that he was whole running through her. He was not meant to affect her so. In all the years that they had known each other, through all of their interactions, Travion had never given Sereia cause to believe that he cared about her as anything more than a companion at his side. Someone he desired and enjoyed, but not an equal. Not a soulmate.

He was alive. She had seen it for herself. Proven it with her very own eyes. And now she should leave. Turn and go before he had a chance to spot her in the crowd and know that she had come back.

But Travion was smiling down at the female in his arms with such happiness that any relief she had felt disappeared, and instead, an ugly monster brewed in her chest. The red-haired nymph smiled back up at him with a familiarity that bespoke intimacy.

Reaching out to grasp the sleeve of the man nearest her, Sereia looked up at him, blue eyes alight with fury. "Who is the harlot dancing with King Travion?"

The man looked startled at her words, and stepped back as if he were deeply affronted. "That, you disrespectful maiden, is Queen Eden. I would mind your tongue." He wrenched his sleeve free.

Sereia's mind reeled for the second time in as many weeks. *Queen Eden.*

"Me? That little wench should have minded *herself.*" She was saying words without really thinking them through, her eyes following Travion and the queen around the dance floor. Could he have truly settled down? "Impossible," she spat out. "The brat looks barely out of her cradle. Damn her."

The man turned away, muttering something she did not hear to the woman beside him, who then looked over to give Sereia a fierce look. Another couple who had overheard also shot her a series of glares, shaking their heads at her. But she paid none of them any heed as they moved away to other groups of people, spreading the atrocious words of the masked woman.

Travion had married . . . After a century of insisting he could never be bothered to propose to another, he had found someone. Ensorcelled by an innocent looking creature with big green eyes and a sweet smile. Sereia could feel her jaw tightening as her teeth ground together.

As the dance came to an end, she watched Travion lift his queen's hand and press a kiss to the back of it. They smiled at each other, and then he leaned in to say something to her, which both of them laughed over.

The nasty emotion churned in Sereia's stomach, making her hands clench and her back straighten.

Travion walked the redhead over to the buffet station, where they parted ways. Rather than following him, Sereia pushed through the guests in the room, eyes never leaving the queen.

The queen looked startled when Sereia appeared suddenly at her side but quickly offered a small, uncertain smile as she took in her masked face.

Sereia curtsied before her, biting the inside of her cheek to keep from making a snide comment. "Good evening, Your Majesty. I hear that congratulations are in order on your nuptials. I have been out of the country and had not realized His Highness had wed."

A brighter smile covered the younger female's face, and Sereia wanted to snatch her happiness away. Travion deserved it, she realized that, but it didn't mean she had to like it. And she didn't. "Thank you, and you haven't missed out on the news for long. It was only last month."

"Oh," Sereia breathed. "So recently? How ever did you manage to get such a set-in-his-ways bachelor to long for marriage?" Was it her sweetness that had won Travion over? That didn't seem to suit him.

"To be frank, I'm not so certain myself." The queen laughed, a happy, musical sound. "May I ask your name?"

Sereia held out her hand, about to introduce herself, when she heard the hushed voices sounding out around them. The courtier she had accosted earlier was standing nearby, whispering none too quietly as he watched them together.

Suddenly, a dark presence was upon them both, and a black sleeve slipped around Queen Eden's thin waist, pulling her into a black-clad chest. Looking up, Sereia found the almost feral face of King Draven glaring down at her.

"Darling! I was just making the acquaintance of this—" Eden began, only to be cut off by the king's soft, furious words.

"Did you or did you not refer to my wife as a harlot and childish brat?"

"What? Draven, no, she was . . ." Queen Eden looked between the two of them, confusion turning into a pained look as her eyes settled back on Sereia.

There were even more eyes upon them now, as King Draven's fury radiated off him strong enough to be a physical presence in the room.

Sereia blinked and looked between the two of them. Draven's words echoed in her mind. My *wife. My wife.* She laughed suddenly, her hand lifting to cover her lips as her mistake became all too apparent.

Draven's face darkened more.

"I apologize. I do believe a grave misunderstanding has taken place," Sereia stifled her laughter enough to say. A second bout of relief washed through her.

Travion had been dancing with his sister-in-law, not his wife.

"Would you care to explain exactly *why* such a misunderstanding happened in the first place?"

Sereia wasn't certain exactly what words she could offer him but knew she had to say something before he exploded and the courtiers were awarded with the scene they were all hoping for. Reaching up, Sereia grasped the mask and pulled it off her face, letting Draven get a full view of her features.

He growled at the sight of her, and all she could do was flash him a broad, confident smile.

"Sereia?"

Her smile froze before disappearing. Slowly, she turned in the direction of the familiar voice already sending a flush of warmth through her body.

Travion stood there, stopped in his tracks and looking as if he had seen a ghost.

"Travion." Seeing him from across the room had not prepared her to come face to face with him once again. Suddenly, she felt uncertain what to do with her hands. Their rendezvous had ceased being a public affair long ago, and while she did not care who saw her with him, as their opinions did not matter, meeting Travion for the first time in five years with King Draven glaring down at her added a whole new weight to the situation.

Travion's throat worked as he swallowed roughly. "What are you doing here?" he asked, eyes meeting hers steadily. Travion wasn't one to shy away, but there was some warmth missing.

She longed to move to him, check his body for injury, and truly prove to herself that he was in one piece, but the distance between them felt much broader than a few feet.

Instead, she cocked a hip and rested a hand on it. "Is that any way to greet me?"

"I believe the only greeting he owes you is an escort out of the castle and into a departing carriage," Draven stated coldly.

His words had Travion moving once again, and he stepped into their small cluster, offering his brother a perturbed look. One that was matched and surpassed by the one Queen Eden was offering him.

"Draven . . ." she scolded.

The king of the night realm did not appear to be repentant at all, and Sereia did not expect to see that emotion change. He had never taken that kindly to her or her intermittent presence in Travion's life. Who knew what he'd thought as the time between her appearances grew even more distant.

"I would like to apologize for whatever gossip you may hear concerning me and yourself, my lady. I can admit wholeheartedly that I was mistaken." Sereia bowed slightly to Eden, who still appeared perplexed by all of this but nodded.

"What . . . gossip?" Travion asked. "What did you do?" His blue eyes focused on Sereia, a slight frown marring his features, and she offered him a small shrug in return.

To discuss it would mean disclosing the *why,* and Sereia had no desire to let Travion know she had seen him with another woman she thought was his wife and had become incensed with jealousy. What right did she have to be jealous over a role she had turned down?

Travion wasn't hers.

"The two of you clearly have some catching up to do.

Draven and I will leave you to it. It was lovely meeting you, Sereia."

Draven snorted at Eden's words but allowed himself to be drawn away, though not before pinning Sereia with one final glare of death.

"What did you do?" Travion repeated, stepping closer to her, his hands coming out to grasp her upper arms. He held her firmly, as if she were likely to flee at any second.

His nearness made her breath catch. The terror that had filled her for the two-week mad dash from Bezopasnyy had not been relinquished, even by Yon's assurance that he was okay. It hadn't mattered that it wasn't Draven who had attacked him, just some noblewoman. It hadn't even mattered that he was alive. Because she had learned he'd been tragically injured. That he *had* almost died, and that fact alone was enough to send her spinning into thoughts she didn't want to dissect.

"I may have confused the new queen's role in your life and spoken a few unchoice things."

Travion sighed roughly. "Why am I not surprised?" Glancing around, it was obvious he'd become aware of the stares leveled on them, his courtiers no longer attempting subtlety. He dropped his hand to her wrist, and with a quick motion, pulled her out of the room, into an alcove that ran along it, taking them well out of the way of curious eyes.

The need to prove fully to herself that he was okay became too fierce to ignore, and Sereia could no longer hold herself back. She caught Travion by surprise, pushing him up against the nearest wall and capturing his lips in a firm, demanding kiss. She felt the hesitation in him, as if he weren't certain if he should return the kiss, and then his lips became more pliant, responding to her onslaught. Her hands clutched onto the silver embroidered lapels of his navy velvet jacket, and Travion's hands captured her cheeks, holding her lips well and truly against his own.

Her body flared with a fiery hunger, all of her pent-up emotion from the past few weeks rearing its ugly head, and suddenly, she needed him more than she needed her next breath. Her lips parted, and she met his tongue, the taste of him both familiar and exhilarating. But also different.

It was still Travion, someone she had kissed more times than she could count, but kissing him felt almost like kissing someone new. Like the closeness that had been there in whatever form they'd had it was missing. Had she been gone too long? Had Travion known she wasn't intending to come back?

Was this thing between them wearing itself out?

Needing more contact, desperate to find that connection again, to experience a Travion who was full of life and strength, she slid her hands beneath the lapels of his jacket and up to his shoulders, pushing it down over them. Travion assisted by dropping his hands from her cheeks and shrugging the garment the rest of the way off. As Sereia focused on the buttons of his vest, he moved to her waist and, with a soft grunt, picked her up to rest on his hips. The high slit in her gown allowed the skirt to part, and her legs wrapped around him easily.

Travion spun and pressed her against the wall behind them. Her heated flesh, bared by the open back of the gown, hit cold stone. It was a sensation that made her purr, and she captured his lips again as she discarded his vest.

Their hungry lips parted as she moved to the top of his shirt, and Travion began kissing down the expanse of her throat. Sereia tipped her head back against the stone, moaning happily at the shivers of pleasure that coursed through her body. He still knew her body. The places that made her quiver and sigh.

"I miss your beard," she rasped suddenly. Last time she had been here, he had not been clean shaven. It was a minor change, but only added to everything else that had taken place while she was gone.

"There was a run-in with a chimera, and then I had an incident with a manticore," he murmured, nipping along her collarbone. "Seemed a proper time to shave it off."

His words were a douse of cold water to her passion-clouded mind, and she stiffened. "So the rumors were true."

Travion lifted his head, a questioning light in his eyes as he looked into hers. "The rumors?"

"That you were attacked and severely injured." Her fingers played with the buttons at the top of his shirt, her thumb brushing over one small pearl piece.

"Is that why you've returned?" Travion asked, his gaze searching hers.

"How bad was it, Trav?" she whispered, a stern look in her eyes. He had better not lie to her. They were . . . friends . . . after all, and she needed to know the truth if she was ever going to rest easy again.

"Draven had to hold my innards in while Eden put me back together." His response came softly but honestly.

Sereia shut her eyes for a moment, fighting the scream of fury that wanted to burst out of her. Who had dared to hurt him? Who had dared try to take him out of this world? The thought of him gone from it made her want to burn everything down around them. It was a response that shook her, made it impossible for her to deny emotions she tried her best to keep buried deep within.

"They're mostly back where they belong," he stated in a jesting tone, trying to lighten the mood.

Sereia opened her eyes so that she could shoot him a cold glare. Without saying anything else, her fingers began working at his shirt once more, until she was able to spread it wide over his chest.

Her breath caught at the sight of the angry red scar that traveled from his shoulder to his hip.

"By the sea . . . Travion." Sereia was at a loss for words, fingers lightly brushing along the angry flesh.

Travion's eyes shut at her touch. "A beauty, isn't she?"

"I'm sorry I wasn't here to help."

"I'm glad you weren't."

Their eyes met in the silence that fell between them, and without needing to say anything else, the distance between them was gone. Their lips met with a new fervor, one that spoke of near death and deep relief. Amplified by the length of time since they had last been together like this.

5

Travion

A hunger that Travion had tamped down for far too long erupted within, consuming every fiber of his being. Sereia was there, truly there in his arms. He had longed for her return, but now—amid the discord in the sea? His heart thundered in his ears as their kiss deepened, chasing away his tumultuous thoughts and replacing them with his need for her.

Travion dropped a hand to one of Sereia's thighs, pushing the silken fabric aside. The skirt glided away with ease, and as his thumb met the bare skin beneath, he discovered she was slick to the touch. It drove him mad, even more so as the scent of her arousal rose between them. He swore into her mouth. There would be time for more drawn-out pleasure, but Travion needed her now, as much as she seemed to need and want him.

Sereia rolled her hips against him in a steady rhythm as he withdrew his hand to unbutton his breeches.

Travion's length sprung free from the confinement, and Sereia wriggled lower in his grasp until her scorching heat met him.

He nudged her warm center, allowing her warmth to coat him.

"Trav," Sereia whined against his lips as she bore down— or at least attempted to.

Travion chuckled as his lips moved away from her mouth, then down her neck. His hands shifted to Sereia's bottom, angling her for better access. This would be no sweet reunion but a heated, frenzied one.

With a thrust of his hips, Travion entered the welcoming warmth of Sereia's folds, which enveloped him as he filled her to the hilt. He left a trail of heated kisses down her collarbone and to the valley between her breasts. *By the sea,* she tasted like a mixture of salt and honey, which only intoxicated him, muddying his thoughts but spurring on his actions.

"Don't stop now," she grumbled, shifting against him.

"So impatient," Travion tutted. Moving forward to support her better against the wall, his hands aided her as she rose. So began the punishing pace he set for them. Each quick stroke, each rise and fall of Sereia, filled him with pleasure that rose like a tide.

Her fingers trailed along his neck and into his hair, clutching tightly as she collided with every thrust. Tossing her head back, she arched herself into him. Travion's mouth pulled the dress aside to reveal one of her hardened nipples. His lips circled the tender skin as his tongue ran around the outer flesh.

Scissoring his teeth along the nub, he delighted in the gasps that were none too quiet. Midniva wasn't as open when it came to their debauchery, and their king didn't have a history of flaunting his indiscretions. However, if anyone stumbled upon them, neither Travion nor Sereia would have burned in shame. They were both children of Lucem, whether by blood or birth, and Sereia simply didn't give a damn.

A groan slipped from Travion as her inner walls clamped tighter around him. "By the sea . . ." His lips stilled on Sereia's nipple as she collided with him quicker than before, and he met every downward motion with a thrust.

Travion knew every curve, every inch of her body. So, as her completion drew near, he pulled his head back and watched the moment unfold. Her eyes slammed shut as she rasped his name over and over. Which proved to be his undoing, for he gave into his pleasure, spilling himself into her.

Travion sucked in a greedy breath. His arms wrapped around her, holding her sagging form tightly. It took all he had not to sink to the floor. Chuckling, he trailed soft kisses from her breast to her neck, all the way to her full lips. There would be another time to raise a wall between them again, but this wasn't it.

When Sereia shifted; they both groaned. "Oh," she breathed. "I missed this too." She dragged her fingertips along his neck, then cupped his cheeks and leaned in to press a firm kiss to his lips.

The words, though simple, softened his heart, which he'd done well to harden over the years. Since she left, he hadn't entertained anyone, because no one was Sereia and no one could rile his temper or his passion as she did. But he'd be lying if he said he hadn't begun withdrawing himself from the ghost of her.

Even he knew it wasn't healthy to hold on to an *idea* of someone.

"A quick rutting in a corner?" Travion scoffed. "I could do better than that."

"I know you can. Just like I *know* that is only the beginning of the evening." Sereia pulled a hand free of his cheek to tug her dress back into place and slid down his frame to stand. Her blue gaze swept along his mussed clothing, which brought a smirk to her lips. "What a state you're in, Your Majesty."

By the sea! She was so quick to think it would continue? His gaze dropped to her kiss-bruised lips, and he knew then that was exactly where they'd wind up—in his bed. "No thanks to you." Tucking himself back into his breeches, he secured them again and set to tidying his appearance. Evun would be distraught at his ragamuffin looks but would no doubt revel in the fact that Travion had finally broken his bout of celibacy.

"I'll do better next time. I'll ensure there is no way you could possibly stroll casually into the soiree without requesting the aid of your valet." When she leaned forward, her lips left a heated path in their wake along his jawline.

Travion shut his eyes. "Mm, if that were the case, you'd have no dress left to wear." He would have reduced it to tattered scraps if he'd had his way with her in their usual manner. Aggressive, drawn-out, and frenzied.

Travion tucked in his shirt and leaned against the wall as he buttoned it. He sighed heavily and threaded his fingers through his hair. How long would this last? How long before Sereia left again, and this time for good?

She leaned against his shoulder. Her arms looped around his torso and back. "Say it."

"I have nothing to say." He paused, having more than

enough to say, but then glanced down at her. "I do have something to ask . . ."

She quirked a brow.

"Did you see anything out there? I've read the reports of giant creatures, and survivors have been tended to, but did you come across anything?" A frown creased his brow, but despite the worry that crept in in place of his fading pleasure, he lifted a hand to brush back her hair.

"Yes," Sereia murmured. "A kraken bigger than my ship . . . Trav, we were in the thick of it." She lifted her head from his shoulder and placed a hand to his cheek. "What do you know?"

Travion shook his head. "Those creatures have been turned by The Creaturae."

"The Creaturae?"

"An ancient tome of old magic with the power of ultimate creation and destruction. And it was within our reach . . ." His eyes flicked toward the ceiling.

Sereia tapped his cheek—not enough to sting, but it wasn't light either. "Don't do that. Talk to me, tell me what has happened."

This time, Travion's entire face scrunched up. "Did you just slap me?"

"No." She lifted her hand, but this time he was ready, and he caught her wrist. "If I were to smack you, everyone would know I did." A wicked smile spread across her face. One that Travion adored.

Sereia squared her shoulders as if she were readying to leap into battle already. "Don't blame yourself for this. It isn't your fault." When the last words left her lips, she looked away and put distance between them. "Tell me, what are we actually dealing with here?"

What *were* they actually dealing with? With Naya in the pits of a mental hell, they'd assumed it was all finished, but that wasn't so. Not with the book gone, not with giant sea monsters destroying ships and killing citizens of Midniva and Tribonik. The question was, who was orchestrating the discord?

He licked his lips. "I'll summarize it for you."

Travion relayed the events of the past four months, including Zryan's foolishness. Some details were spared, but the more important ones he didn't skimp on. Like Lucem being tossed into darkness, or the first bout with a manticore, and how Travion's efforts with Draven had been nothing but a wild goose chase.

It had taken two months for Travion to feel *normal* again. With the aid of his nephew, Kian, he was able to heal physically and, for the most part, mentally.

"'Tis a shame, honestly. Kian would have made a wonderful king." Travion's lips tilted into a small smirk.

Sereia hissed at his words, shoving his shoulder, which happened to be the one that was still quite sore. "That isn't funny."

He grunted, wincing as he ran his fingers along the tender muscle. "It's the truth. Nevertheless, I'd not wish your fury on him had you returned only to discover I was dead." He watched as she began to pace, her hands on her hips as she spun on her heel to march in the other direction.

"I wish I'd been here to fight with you."

Folding one of his arms across his body, Travion dragged his free hand down his face, working out the lines of frustration. He was glad she hadn't been, for if Sereia had been fighting by his side, he knew she would have taken the brunt of the manticore attack, or possibly endured something worse—if that was possible. "You are here now, and it appears a new battle is on the horizon. If you'd like to join me in arms, then you'll have to stay on land for a little while."

She flashed him a seductive smile in reply.

"And your room is ready for you, as always." He tapped his fingers against his hip. "Minus one outfit, Eden lifted one after . . ."

Sereia nodded as a flurry of emotions passed over her gaze. Relief, regret, and something else. "She could take all of it for all I care. It's only clothing." She lowered her eyes to his vest, but Travion imagined she was seeing the scar instead of his clothing.

"Sereia," he murmured, closing the distance between them and wrapping his arms around her in a tight embrace. Travion inhaled the scent of her, the smell of sunshine and the sea. "I am here, and aside from a ghastly scar, I am well." His arms squeezed her. "Don't conjure a fight in that head of yours that isn't here. I'll need your head in the present for what's about to come. If what everyone says is true . . . it'll make the sun disappearing in Lucem seem like child's play."

In return, she squeezed him, her face pressed against his chest, where his heart thrummed steadily. "And what is coming?"

"I fear something terrible. Nothing you've faced before, and if I could spare anyone, especially you, I would."

Sereia frowned, pulling back. She lifted her hand and ran her fingertips along his kiss-bruised lips. "We will face it together."

Travion brushed kisses along her fingers. He wanted her there with him, selfishly, and more than that, he needed her. The ache deep in his chest had nothing to do with the unsightly scar and everything to do with how he missed Sereia.

A trill of laughter down the hall pulled him away from their intimacy. Unfortunately, it was still the early hours, and he had guests to entertain, at least for a while longer. He glanced down at Sereia, her light sandalwood skin flushed with their shared pleasure.

"If you want to clean—"

She smirked at him as she withdrew. "Let them see me rumpled. What do I care?"

Travion closed the distance between them, his arm looping around her waist. "It will at least give them something to talk about."

Sereia's eyes flashed in challenge. "I will give them plenty to whisper of."

"I have no doubt." Travion laughed as he escorted her into the ballroom. Few glanced in his direction, but it meant little to him. Their eyes didn't need to be on him for their tongues to wag. Whatever they whispered couldn't touch him tonight, not while Sereia graced him with her presence and cast him glances that threatened to bring him to his knees.

6

Sereia

Wrapped in nothing but a sheet, Sereia moved across Travion's room to the silver tray that sat on the table. Beneath the intricately decorated dome sat a plate of eggs, potatoes, blood pudding, and sausage. Another plate held a stack of toast and slices of tomato. Her belly grumbled at the smell, and she picked up a piece of sausage and bit into it greedily.

Sereia wasn't sure when someone had entered the room to leave the tray, but she wasn't surprised that she hadn't woken. Once she and Travion had left the ball last night, their lovemaking had carried on into the early morning. From the position of the sun, it would seem she had only been asleep for a few hours.

"Travion?" she called out, but there was no response. Likely, kingly duties had pulled him away.

After securing the sheet around her like a dress, Sereia dropped several slices of tomato and a piece of toast onto the plate. She then poured piping-hot tea into the waiting teacup. With a cube of sugar and a dollop of cream, it was ready. After carrying both the cup and the plate out onto the balcony off Travion's quarters, Sereia settled herself down onto the chaise lounge there.

She took a welcomed sip of the tea, sighing as she looked out over the water. Today, the sea was calm, its surface nothing but glistening sunshine that beckoned. She wondered how her crew was doing, and if the repairs to the ship had been completed yet. She'd only left Mointeach yesterday morning, but a lot could be achieved in a day when they were at port in a proper town.

A lot could also distract them.

Adrik would be on top of his duties, however, so long as he hadn't gotten too deep into his cups last night, or too caught up in a pair of breasts. The man had never been enraptured with anyone that Sereia had noticed, but he *did* seem to enjoy his tavern wenches.

She set aside her teacup and dug into her breakfast, her stomach rumbling happily as the savory food was consumed. This was much better than the swill she typically feasted on aboard the ship or in the portside inns where they took up lodging.

Being royalty did have its advantages.

When she was finished and pleasantly full, Sereia set her plate aside and settled back, her feet drawn up on the lounge and her teacup resting on her knees. There was a peace inside her for the moment that had only come from setting her eyes upon Travion herself. Even when Yon had returned with reports that he was safe and alive, she'd needed to know for sure.

If the ache between her thighs and the tiredness of her muscles said anything, it was that Travion was well and truly alive. He may have borne a large scar across his chest to prove how in peril he had been, but he was okay.

Sensing a shift behind her, Sereia glanced over her shoulder, expecting to see Travion. Instead, it was Yon. She was dressed in her standard attire: cotton trousers, leather boots, a leather vest that also acted as armor, and leather vambraces protecting her forearms. On her back she carried two swords, pieces she was never without.

"What are you doing here?" she asked, startled.

Yon bowed lightly in greeting, her jet-black hair bound tightly with leather in a topknot. "Sir wished to know that you were well and that everything had gone smoothly for you last night."

Sereia's brow shot up. Adrik had sent Yon because he wanted in on the *gossip*? He was well aware of the fact that she had a tendency to slip in and out of the castle. Sereia hated that he knew this time was different because of her inner turmoil.

It felt like a weakness had been exposed.

"Well, as you can see, I am quite all right," she said dryly. "And so very happy to see that Adrik is concentrating on the truly important tasks I've left him to oversee."

"The ship repairs are coming along, Captain. The sails have been sewn or replaced, and the minor holes in the hull have been patched. Sir was working on restocking our stores when I left."

"Mhm." She sipped her tea, which had grown cold. Standing, Sereia tossed the remainder over the balcony and slipped past Yon. "Did anyone see you enter the castle?"

"No, Captain."

"The king isn't going to like that." Along with her talent for acquiring information, Yon also possessed the ability to sneak through places undetected. It was nothing against the alertness of Travion's soldiers, but Sereia had never known

Yon to be caught yet. Her training in Caifu had been centered specifically around the ability to get in and out of heavily guarded places unseen.

Her skills were truly wasted on *The Saorsa*, but Sereia was happy to have her.

"Have you eaten?" she asked, pouring herself more tea.

"Is that tea?" Yon asked, a hopeful light in her eyes.

Sereia chuckled. "It is. Come, make yourself some." She waved at the teapot and corresponding amenities.

Yon stepped over to it quickly and poured herself a cup.

Sereia took her own and moved to sit on the end of the bed, sipping from the steaming porcelain. "You can report back to Adrik that I am alive, and the rest is none of his bloody business."

Yon, always so stoic, offered the slightest of grins—really just the twitch of her lips—as she carried her teacup across the room, where she chose to lean against the wall beside a chair rather than sit down.

"I will relay your message verbatim, Captain."

Together, they took a sip of tea, mutual delight shining in their eyes. Yon, ever the professional, tended to keep herself distant from the other crewmen. Sereia had a feeling it was to do with her past and an inability to truly let herself get close to anyone. However, Yon had grown fond of Adrik, Sereia could see it. His brash behavior amused the serious fighter, which Sereia always assumed was due to his ability to walk a fine line between loyalty and insubordination.

The moment of quiet reflection was interrupted as Travion waltzed through the doors. He wore a dark green jerkin over a white linen shirt and even darker green trousers.

"You're up! I thought perhaps I was going to have to

come in here and stir you awake." The smirk on his face told her exactly how he'd planned to awaken her. Travion strode across the room and came to press a kiss to her forehead. "Good morning."

"Morning," she replied.

"How did you sleep?" His voice was soft, gentle. And it warmed her belly.

"I don't remember getting much sleep last night." She eyed him, pursing her lips.

Travion chuckled and leaned down to steal a quick kiss. "And I don't remember hearing any complaints."

Yon cleared her throat from across the room, her eyes on the floor as she sipped casually from her teacup.

Travion glanced over at her, a look of surprise on his face. "One of yours, I presume?" he asked, peering down at Sereia.

"She was sent to check on me." Travion's brow lifted in question. No one had been sent to check on her during any of her other visits. But that had been before she'd thought he was dead. Before she had raced through every storm the ocean had thrown at her to make sure he was still alive.

He seemed to read that, and perhaps more, in her face, for he did not press her on the matter. "And how *exactly* did she get past all my guards?"

Yon remained nonplussed, sipping her tea.

"I don't ask Yon how she achieves any of the miraculous feats that she performs. It is simply accepted."

"Truly?" Travion glanced between the two of them, then shrugged a shoulder.

Sereia only smirked and looked over at Yon. "Can you give us the room?" Yon bowed and left, stopping only to first refill her teacup. "Yon is a highly trained warrior, and it is best for both me and her that I do not know the ways in which she acquires her information."

"Highly trained by who?" Curiosity lifted his brows, but he didn't appear angered.

"A vicious nobleman in Caifu who stole young children from their homes or bought them from their impoverished parents to fuel his personal army."

"What were you doing in Caifu?" he asked, frowning.

Sereia eyed him. "I have been in all the nations that surround the vast ocean. The kingdom of Caifu is widely known for its many great tinctures and herbal remedies that can be kept on ship for long periods of time without spoiling." Infections were the worst to deal with out at sea. Injuries could be stitched back together, but if infection set in, there wasn't always time to make it to port before blood poisoning followed. The Caifuese possessed an herbal remedy that would not only store well for long durations of time but was a blessed relief.

"How did you pluck a soldier from the ranks of this man's army?"

"Yon wasn't actually a mere soldier. She was one of his trusted assassins. When I met her, it was in a dark tavern on the outskirts of Joujew." Perhaps one of the more dangerous ports along the coast of Caifu. "I was meeting a man who wished to purchase something I'd acquired at sea, and she was there to end the life of that same man." They'd come to an agreement in the end, that she would finish her deal first, receive her coins, and then Yon could follow through with her duties.

"That doesn't explain how she came to be aboard your ship."

"In the end, all slaves are for sale. No matter how

valuable." The deal struck between them had proven to be more beneficial than either of them would have thought, for it provided the funds to free Yon. "She has been on my ship for over ten years now, and her dedication has never faltered. She would never do anything to harm me. Which means you have nothing to fear from her either."

Travion sighed but nodded. "You certainly have an interesting group of people on that ship."

"You have no idea." When he gave her a questioning look, she waved it off. "Just a motley crew of humans, truly. Odds and ends I've collected from across the sea." Sereia stood and pressed a kiss to his lips. "Do you need to stay in the castle today?"

His jaw shifted, and he hesitated before asking, "What were you thinking?"

"Heading into the city proper. It's been ages since I've gone to the markets of Caithaird."

Travion brushed the hair back from her face. "We can do that."

Sereia nodded. "Let me just go and get dressed." She slipped past him and out into the hall, where Yon leaned against the wall, appearing calm and at peace. "I'm going to dress, and then we're heading into the capital. You may head back to the ship."

"Is that an order, Captain?"

"No."

"Then I'll stay here with you."

Sereia eyed her closely before nodding. While Yon had learned to sail as well as the best of them, she preferred to remain where Sereia was, acting as a protector for her captain.

"There is, perhaps, something else I should have

mentioned, Captain."

Sereia halted on her way down the hall to the room where Travion allowed her to store some Midniva-appropriate clothing. "Yes?" She looked back at Yon.

"There was word in the pub last night before I left of an attack off the coast of Tribonik. A fisherman had gotten word from a family member who lives there. It sounded as if the entire seaside town had been destroyed."

Sereia cursed. "Did they say what it was?"

"The kraken, Captain."

Sereia's teeth clenched. That damnable beast. If only she had been able to kill it. "What town?"

"Novgor."

Clothes forgotten for the time being, Sereia turned back to Travion's room, finding him at the table munching on a slice of tomato.

"There was another attack."

"What?" He looked up, a frown creasing his features. "Where?"

"Novgor, on the coast of Tribonik. It's a small fishing village, likely five hundred citizens in its entirety. Yon overheard a fisherman in the pub—the attack happened in the last day or so. It was the kraken."

Travion growled to himself and plucked a knife from the table. Piercing the tip of his finger, he dropped blood into a goblet of water. After the quick muttering of a spell, he spoke Admiral Callahan's name.

It took a moment, and then a deep voice arose from the goblet. "Your Majesty."

"Callahan, new reports have come in. There was an attack on the Tribonik town of Novgor. Where are you presently located?"

"We are a few days from Tribonik still."

"Have you come across any signs of the attacks?"

"One downed ship. All that remained were bodies and a mast," Callahan responded.

While she listened, Sereia paced back and forth, feeling her own agitation rising. The beast attacked with no rhyme or reason.

"I want you to head to Novgor, see what news you can gather from whomever may remain."

"Aye, aye, Your Majesty."

They signed off, and Travion's shoulders sagged as he leaned forward to rest his hands on the table. His head hung forward, and there was a tightness to his jaw that spoke of anger. "Useless," he muttered.

"You have your ship out there, you're searching. What more can you do?"

He slammed his fist on the table top and straightened. "There has to be more than this."

"Let Callahan do what he is trained to do. Once you have more information, you can plan your next move."

His jaw was still working, and she could tell he hated this inactivity.

"Come, let us go to the market."

"There is no bloody time for the market."

"Perhaps not, but I think you could do with the distraction."

They took a carriage from the castle, down into the outskirts of the city, then asked to be let out there. It was better to walk in on foot and have a slight chance of being unnoticed than to announce their presence at the center.

They walked together, side by side, with Finn and Yon following at a good distance behind. She had insisted on accompanying her captain into the city and now looked rather comical strolling alongside the gigantic captain's guard. Yon was slight and came just about to mid-bicep on the tall fae. Yet, Sereia didn't doubt that if pitted against each other, Yon would find a way to climb Finn like a tree and take him out at the neck.

The sun was bright in the sky, and the day was turning out to be a warm one. Though clothing options in her quarters were limited, Sereia had decided on a simple white blouse that came off her shoulders, flowed down her arms, and widened into long trailing cuffs. It was paired with a layered hunter-green skirt that gathered up on one side to show off an impressive view of leg. Around her waist was a matching corset that laced up the front and ended just below her breasts. Evun, Travion's valet, had tried to talk her into letting him do her hair, but she'd sent him away and simply braided her hair, then wound it just below one ear in a bun.

The homes nestled on either side of the cobblestone streets at the city's center were small but well maintained. Stones from the shoreline as well as the ground around them had been used to build their walls, and natural grasses were woven for thatched roofs. It was easy to see that the kingdom was prosperous, the homes cared for, and the citizens coming and going from them cleanly dressed and nourished.

"You would never guess that you had been at battle not too long ago," Sereia commented offhandedly.

"The attack was more centered on the castle and myself, fortunately. Lucem took the hardest hit for devastation."

Sereia studied him for a moment, the ease with which he spoke of his own near demise. Like he'd rather it be him than any of his people.

As they passed a larger structure, Sereia took a deep breath and grinned. The sign over the shop read "O'Quinnlan Whiskey." While other nations produced their potables in small shacks in the woods, Midniva was the only place she had ever seen where their whiskey was proudly brewed along the city streets. The scent of it mixing with sea air was something she had missed.

Their walk didn't last long, and soon the street opened up into a large market area. Stalls with wooden structures over them and carts overflowing with vegetables and other wares filled the inner square, while the outside was lined with shops. People bustled, and it caused a soft hum.

"Is it everything you remembered?" Travion asked, peering down at her.

"That and more." She nodded. That wave of emotion she'd felt at seeing Mointeach for the first time in many years washed over her again. Her chest tightened, and she was struck with a sense of nostalgia. This was the city where she had spent her younger years. Where, as a young fae, she had raced through the streets with a small hoodlum gang and learned to play hide and seek quite efficiently, how to best even the boys at marbles, and how to swipe an apple from the fruit seller without getting caught.

Naturally, she gravitated toward a table run by a young woman with light blonde hair twisted into many plaits. Her table was covered in small hand-carved stone items.

"Good morning, madam." The young woman smiled.

Sereia bristled at the term but only nodded in a friendly manner. "Morning. Do you craft all these items?"

"I do." She looked from Sereia to Travion, who stepped up beside her. The girl's eyes widened a touch, but instead of saying anything, she merely curtsied.

Travion waved her off. "That isn't necessary."

He was at ease here with his people, Sereia noted. Almost as if he weren't a king but simply another citizen wandering the marketplace with nothing more serious to concern him than looking at trinkets. A true warden of both their security and their peace of mind.

Sereia smiled a little as she picked up a small hand knife. The handle was made of beautiful gray stone that had been carved to mimic a wave. It fit nicely into her hand, the waves naturally flowing with her grip.

"Thinking of acquiring a new weapon?" Travion asked.

"For Adrik, actually. He recently lost the one he keeps in his boot." Sereia looked over at the young woman. "How much for this?"

"Ten coppers, madam."

Sereia pulled her coin purse out of the pocket at her waist and handed the coins over. She then bent to slip the knife into her own boot.

As she stood, a pendant hanging from a stand at the side of the table caught her eye. It was carved from a white stone with veins of green. Her fingers reached for it, brushing over the smoothness of the outer curve. The shape of the pendant was a selkie curled around itself. Its nose was at the heart of the piece, with its tail wrapping around the outer edge and creating the only point, where a small hole was drilled for the chain.

She considered buying it for herself for a moment but thought better of it. What purpose did pirates have for pretty baubles? No matter how lovely.

Dropping her hand, Sereia smiled at the young woman, thanked her for her help, and turned back to the rest of the market. *So many people coming and going.* It was a thriving city, and it was easy to tell how well Travion cared for his people.

Unlike many villages in Tribonik, which were taxed beyond their means by high-ranking lords, they did not starve, they did not fear being oppressed or locked away for speaking out of turn. They were not selling their children just to survive like those in Caifu or going off to war for a senseless need for more land.

Sereia stilled as the pendant fell within her view and a chain was clasped around her neck to nestle against her breasts. Wrapping her fingers around the stone selkie, Sereia turned to Travion, who stood behind her.

"You did not have to do that."

"No, but I wished to."

There had been a time when receiving gifts from Travion had felt like him attempting to buy her favor. When he'd been seeking to make her his wife, and fancy dresses and jewelry were deemed the course to a female's heart. This, however, felt like nothing more than a gift. She stepped closer. He, in turn, trailed his knuckles along her jaw. It seemed fitting and only right to tip her head up for his descending kiss.

"Thank you for my gift," she murmured against his lips.

"You are most welcome."

"*Fish!* Get your fish!" A man close by shouted, carrying a large trout, breaking the spell that had woven around them and causing both to laugh.

"Shall we grab lunch?" Travion suggested.

"Absolutely. I haven't had beef and ale stew in far too long."

7

Travion

Sereia could have easily plucked the pendant and paid for it herself. But she didn't, and he wondered if it was because she warred with the two sides of herself: the lady and the pirate. He'd lived long enough to know that one could live with a dual nature and, in fact, if they allowed themselves to live in such a way, would be happier for it.

After his first month with Sereia all those years ago, he'd wished that he wasn't a king. That he could leave his responsibilities behind and watch her experience life. But the fates were cruel, and he couldn't relinquish his control of Midniva. And he learned rather quickly that co-existing with Sereia wasn't meant to be. At least not in a permanent way.

"In all your travels, no beef stew or ale since your last time in Midniva?" Travion groaned and placed a hand on his chest. "That is a shame and should be a crime."

"Well, that would be absurd, wouldn't it?" Sereia countered with a sly smile. "But no. None tasted like Midniva's stew. Maybe it's the sweet grass, or the magic that has touched the soil. Either way, it paled in comparison. So why bother to eat it?"

Well, wasn't that true enough? The honey cakes in Midniva were delicious, but they weren't the same as Lucem's, especially those of the Blossom Festival. Still, Midniva was known for many other things that were far superior that simply couldn't survive in the tropical climate.

"Fair enough," he said at last and led the way down the cobblestone streets of Caithaird. In the distance, the cathedral's bells rang out a new hour. Even from where Travion stood, he could see the spire on the building rising above the other brick structures.

Children wove in and out of the busy streets, and some hopped up onto wooden boxes, hoping someone would take a chance and play a game with them—for coin, of course.

A little girl ran out in front of him, and he nearly tripped over his feet to keep from stepping on her. She had eyes the color of spring grass and hair the shade of night. When she looked up at him, tears stained her rosy cheeks.

"Sorry," she murmured, ducking her head, and her free hair tumbled forward, revealing short, pointed ears. She tightened her fingers around a wreath of shells and tried to move around him, but Finn was blocking her, and she would have to shove past Travion.

"Oh, it's nothing. But what is that in your hands?" He pointed to the wreath.

Sereia drew closer and peered down at the girl too. Yon sidled up beside her, silent but curious.

The girl shook her head enthusiastically. "I made it for my Da." Her voice cracked as she spoke.

Travion's heart twisted at the sight and he knelt so he was eye level with her. "Is he here?"

"No." Her bottom lip wobbled, and she brushed away

fresh tears. "A monster attacked his fishing vessel, and he died."

Travion glanced over at Sereia, who frowned, and as he peered back down at the girl, sobs wracked her small body. He scooped her into his arms and ran his hand down her back. "I'm so sorry." He pulled away and dipped his head to meet her tearful gaze. "What is your name, darling?"

"Annabelle! By the sea, there you are, child." A breathless woman rushed up to them. It was clear by her gnarled fingers that she was a fisher and had spent years in the sun, weaving nets for daily catches. The old woman glanced up at Travion, and her weathered face paled. "Your Majesty, I'm so sorry," she hurried to say, bowing her head. "She ran away on our way to the beach."

Travion stood and shook his head. "My condolences to your family," he offered. Now the wreath of shells made sense. It was a common gesture for the seaside folk to fashion wreaths of shells and send them out with the tide as a gift to their loved one who was lost at sea.

"And may I offer my sincerest condolences as well," Sereia said softly.

This was what he'd wanted to avoid. His kingdom suffering once again in such a short amount of time. "I don't wish to impose, but may we join you and pay our respects to your kin . . . I'm sorry, I didn't catch your name?"

"Oh, we would be honored to have you present." She touched her chest lightly, swallowing roughly. "Sophie. I'm her grandmother."

It was clear that the woman was mortal. Age lined her face prominently, as did the days in the sun, and if Travion looked hard enough, he could discern that her hair had once been a dark shade, for it twined with silver strands. Like her granddaughter, she possessed sparkling green eyes, and even time couldn't hinder their vibrancy.

"I wish we could have met under different circumstances, Sophie." Travion set Annabelle back down on her feet. "Please lead the way, and we will follow."

Annabelle stepped beside her grandmother and led the way down the cobblestone street. The pathway steepened as they drew closer to the water, and Travion could smell the rich, salty air once again.

The road continued on, but they strayed and instead stepped onto wooden planks that stretched all the way to the sand at the bottom of the wooden structure. Hip roses bloomed off to the side, permeating the air with their sweet fragrance, and in a few months, their fruit would grow.

When at last they stood before the receding tide, Annabelle turned to look at Sereia, who was murmuring something to Yon. "Is she a pirate?" Annabelle blurted. "She looks like a pirate."

Sophie gasped in horror.

Pirates, no matter what coast they skirted along, were not kindly looked upon. They were thieves, lacked honor, and were filthy.

While it was true in some cases, Travion knew not *all* pirates were filth of the sea. And he knew Sereia enough to know that she had honor and a code she abided by.

Even so, she could have ignored the child's outburst, let it float on the wind, but she spun on her heel and flourished a courtly bow. "That I am. But no ordinary scallywag, I assure you. I am a *captain*."

Annabelle looked more impressed with the fact she was in the presence of a lady captain than the king himself, which utterly amused Travion.

He was glad for the moment of levity, and with one glance at everyone, he saw they were also thankful for it too.

"My boy was a fisherman just like me, and his father too. This was the life he always wanted, but to die how he did . . . " Sophie cut herself off, as if remembering her granddaughter was there.

As much as Travion wanted her to continue, he didn't press, only waited.

"One of the crewmen survived and said there was a whale the size of the ship. Its fluke so large, one slap was enough to capsize their small fishing boat."

Dread unfurled within him. Of course he knew this news already, but to hear it from the families affected by it was a whole other ordeal.

Finn swore beneath his breath and put distance between himself and the rest. Sereia, however, kept her eyes focused on the grandmother and the girl.

Annabelle took a deep breath and walked toward the shoreline. Travion didn't blame her for exiting the conversation and decided to join her as well.

"May the wind always fill your sails," she started saying as she placed the wreath in the water. "May your net never —" Annabelle's voice broke and she couldn't continue.

"Never be empty, but let it be so bountiful, you share it with kin." Travion knelt in the sand beside her. Despite the turmoil in the sea, it was beautiful, and there was little wind to disturb the waters. If the wreath had any hope of journeying out to sea, they'd need a little help.

Velox, come to me.

His hippocampus surfaced just beyond the shallows. Travion stood and realized the others had joined them.

"Come with me," Travion said softly, reaching for the

girl's hand. She held onto his, and together, they ventured into the water.

The cool water grew deeper, up to his waist, and Annabelle was starting to tread in place. She used her hand and pushed the wreath toward Velox. His blue scales glimmered in the sun, and although he couldn't understand the girl, his soft hum came across as mournful.

"I'll always miss you, Da," Annabelle cried and leaned into Travion.

Velox scooped up the shells in his mouth and sped away through the water, disappearing into the deep.

Travion wrapped his arms around the girl, planting her onto his hip before he waded toward the beach. He deposited her beside her grandmother.

Sophie's gaze remained fixated on the distance. "Thank you," she murmured.

"Be well, Sophie and Annabelle." Travion strode away, his feet squelching in his boots. His clothes chafed against him, but that was the last thing on his mind.

Sereia quickened her stride and followed him. "Trav," she called out quietly.

He turned to glance at her, noticing Yon and Finn making their way toward the boardwalk. "I need to get back to the castle. I'm wasting time out here." His words came out harsher than he'd wished.

Sereia flinched but shook it off. "You cannot just sit in your study beating yourself up for this."

He clenched his teeth, anger rising. Not with her but with this entire situation. "Can't I?" Already he began to withdraw from her, despite the fragile moment they'd just shared with Sophie and Annabelle. Travion didn't want Sereia to see how much it truly bothered him.

She knew, of course, a fraction of it.

By the sea . . . Guilt weighed heavily on his chest, and it threatened to suffocate him. Travion didn't want to come off as coarse with her, but what was the point? She was only going to leave once the battle was through.

Even he had realized they were better irregular bedmates than constant lovers.

Once they arrived back in the castle, Sereia didn't linger long. Travion assumed she'd gone to find a sparring partner to take her frustrations out on. He wished he could do the same, but there was something that he needed to see to. But first, he needed a fresh outfit, for sand clung to him, and his skin had pinkened from the abrasive texture of his clothes.

He ventured to his room, changing quickly before he set off down the hall in search of Taimon, but the sound of metal clashing against metal gave him pause. Travion approached the window in the hall and pushed the gauzy drape out of the way.

There, in the training yard, Sereia lunged forward, sword outstretched as her opponent—Yon—leaped backward, narrowly missing the strike.

Seeing Sereia like this brought a wave of memories back. Of him, standing just like this, watching a fiery female learn her way with a blade. As he watched, there was no doubt she'd grown in so many ways—as a female and with a sword —all without him. It was a bitter thought, but without him, she'd flourished.

Travion's attention flicked away as a door shut nearby. *I*

need to find Taimon, not watch Sereia. He took a sharp right and nearly slammed into his steward. Travion took one step back so Taimon didn't stumble.

"Just the one I was looking for," Travion offered. "There is something I need to do for Midniva."

"Your Grace," he murmured and inclined his head. "How can I be of service?" Taimon's brow furrowed.

"The families who suffered from the assault on Midniva have been compensated, but those who have lost recently have nothing. We're focusing our resources into the army, increasing security, sending out fleets . . . We can't spare anything at the moment, but after all of this, I want a monument erected in honor of those who have fallen. Let no one forget the sacrifices made."

Taimon nodded. "As you wish, Your Grace." He was quiet for a beat, then, "I was on my way to find you. A seahawk brought a letter from General Quillan. Our forces are in place and ready for what may come."

"Very good. Let's hope we can thwart the threat long before it comes to our shores. But mark my words, whoever is behind this better hope they die before I get my hands on them."

Taimon's lips twitched into a small, nervous smile. "Let us hope it doesn't come to that."

Sea help the bastard who orchestrated this discord, because it wouldn't just be Travion in line to execute them, but the whole royal family too.

8

Sereia

Giant tentacles shot from the water and wrapped around the center of The Saorsa. *The pressure against the mainmast sent it careening down. Batteo was unable to escape the fall and lay pinned beneath the weight of it.*

"Kill it!" Sereia screamed.

With a jerk, Sereia sat up in bed, panting as her heart raced. Lifting a hand to press against her chest, she forced a slow inhale and then an even slower exhale.

A dream.

It had been nothing but a dream.

After an afternoon of sparring with Yon to make up for their missed morning sessions on the ship, Sereia had spent the night with Travion. Neither of them had felt much like talking. She had collapsed into bed and expected to sleep soundly.

But the kraken would not leave her be.

"Sereia?" Travion murmured. "Are you okay?"

She dropped her hand back down to her lap and released one final steadying breath. "I'm fine, it was simply a dream."

"I've never known you to have nightmares before."

She snorted and shook her head. She didn't typically have them, not that he truly knew. A few nights shared here and there over the last century did not leave much time for either of them to know what was or was not normal.

"I've seen a few more things since the last time we shared a bed."

Travion sat up and leaned back against the headboard. While she didn't glance back at him, she could feel his eyes on her in the early morning sunlight. Glancing out the window, she could tell that it was just past dawn. Fishermen would be heading out on the water, gulls beginning their circling movements on the lookout for any scraps available. The world was waking up, but so too was the darkness of death that was creeping over the waters.

"What exactly happened with the kraken?" he pressed.

She wanted to curse him. Both because he had read her correctly and because he seemed intent on forcing it out of her. Why did he need to know? This wasn't what they did.

Sereia looked down at her hands, clenching and then unclenching her fingers, remembering them wrapped around her spyglass, watching the horrors unfold. She pressed her lips tightly together against the flood of words that fought to come out. It was the press of his hand against her lower back that released them at last.

"We were in the midst of a battle against two merchant ships when the largest tentacles I had ever seen just appeared out of nowhere and wrapped around the bow of *Ackazanti*. The chaos . . . The screams . . ." She shook her head as it washed over her once more. "There was nothing any of them could do. Nothing we could do. All of us shot cannons at the beast, trying to take it down, but it simply crawled onto the ship until it cracked it in half." A shudder went through her as she recalled watching the monster feast on one of the men aboard.

Travion didn't say anything. Instead, his arm slipped around her waist, and he pulled her in against his side.

There had always been a comfort in his arms, tucked away securely in his bed. The moments when she allowed herself this pleasure had been few and far between over the past century. Not because she didn't want to be here but because she wanted it too much. When she lay here, his hands on her body and his lips trailing kisses over her skin, it was easy to forget the sea and its very particular hold on her. He made her contemplate coming back and finally giving in.

But how long would it last? How long before the salty breeze tangling in her hair or the splash of a wave on her feet called to her so fiercely, she couldn't stand to ignore it? What would happen then, if she were settled into a life here with Travion? How could she abandon him if she had promised to stay, and how long would it take for her soul to wither away once she ignored that call?

This comfort, however, was something new altogether. This went beyond physical pleasure and a sense of peace in his arms. This felt like solace for her soul, and it struck her deeply.

"It came for us next, rocking the ship from below, and I knew that there was only so much time before we were wrapped up in its tentacles as well." Sereia brushed a hand over her face, fighting against the anguish of that moment as it all rushed back.

"How did you get away?"

"It didn't fully latch on, and we were able to separate its tentacles from us and flee. But the other ship—" She cut herself off, hating how cowardly she'd been. No one else should have died that day.

"It took them down as well." It wasn't a question, simply an understanding.

"Yes. We went back for survivors, but there was barely anyone left."

"You did what you needed to do to protect your ship and your crew. Any captain would have made the same decision."

Perhaps, but it didn't help with the guilt that gnawed inside her chest. She didn't want to focus on it any longer, nor speak on the matter further. Instead, she turned to press her lips to Travion's, silencing him before anything else could be said. He did not hesitate, recognizing her need to wash away the thoughts clogging her mind, and their hands found each other beneath the covers. With a growl, Sereia rolled herself into Travion's lap, straddling him.

Their kisses grew more heated, and Sereia scraped her hands down over his chest, paying reverence to muscle and scarring alike. He was alive and whole, and she would delight in every aspect of that. Purposefully, her hips rocked over the hardening length beneath her, and she moaned happily as it parted her to brush against her nub, causing a shiver of pleasure to course through her.

Travion's hands were on her bottom, clutching the cheeks tightly as he dipped his head to brush his lips along one full breast.

A heavy knock sounded at the door, and both of them groaned as Finn's voice sounded from the other side of it.

"Come in," Travion grumbled.

As the door opened, Sereia looked over her shoulder to see Travion's mountain of a captain standing in the doorframe, attempting to look somewhere over her head rather than directly at her. Smirking, she dropped back down to the bed, drawing the sheet up over her chest.

"Finn, someone had best be dead," Travion growled, moving his arm to rest between his head and the headboard. He looked glorious in the early morning sunlight. Bare chested with bedding slung low over his hips, with his auburn hair mussed from her fingers. Sereia felt a rising desire to have her hands on him once more and slanted a less-than-favorable look in Finn's direction.

"Actually, Your Grace . . ."

Travion instantly sobered and sat up. "Who?"

"Word just came in by seahawk. The entire scouting fleet has gone down, and Admiral Callahan and his crew are believed lost," the captain announced solemnly.

Beside her, Travion cursed harshly. "Call my council to the strategy room, we'll be there shortly," he demanded of Captain Finn, who nodded and left.

Travion glanced over at her, a pained look on his face.

"We?" Sereia asked.

"You have firsthand experience with these beasts, and we could use your insight."

Sereia nodded and, leaning in, she pressed a firm kiss to his lips. "I'm sorry about your fleet."

"As am I."

Without another word, they both climbed from the bed, and while Travion dressed in fresh clothes, Sereia plucked her dress from the day before up off the floor. Now was not the time to be concerned about wearing a dress two days in a row.

Dressed, she gathered her hair at the top of her head and wound it up in a warrior's knot, something Yon had taught her for emergencies.

Together, they left Travion's quarters, leaving the wing entirely to head to the opposite side of the castle, where his study and strategy room were located.

Three men already sat waiting for them, with Finn standing at attention in the corner. On the long oval table at the center of the room lay a map of the entire middle realm, with Midniva fully sketched out, as well as Tribonik to the northwest, and Caifu to the northeast. At the top of the map, bold letters declared the portal into Torksvala.

"Sereia, this is General Quillan, Lord Tywil, and my steward Taimon." He motioned to each as he spoke. "Gentleman, this is Captain Ferox."

Sereia nodded as she came to stand at the table, looking down at the map.

"*Lady* Sereia Ferox?" Lord Tywil asked, eyeing her closely. Sereia could only assume he was aware of her parents and her absolute abandonment of all her daughterly duties.

"*Captain* Sereia Ferox," she corrected him, staring him down until he was forced to look away.

"For those of you who have not heard, word was sent of an attack, and it is believed that Admiral Callahan and his fleet have been lost."

There were curses around the table.

"Do we know where?" General Quillan asked.

"When I spoke to Admiral Callahan yesterday morning, they were three days off the coast of Novgor." Travion picked up a small ship from the map and moved it to just off the coast of Tribonik, along the tip closest to Midniva. "Where did you encounter the kraken, Sereia?"

Plucking up another ship, Sereia scanned the upper east coast of Tribonik and then placed it down on the correct location. "Approximately here. We were on our way back from Caifu when we ran across a small mercantile fleet in distress." Better to talk of them being in distress than to admit her pirating acts to a group of high-tier nobles.

Travion shot a quick glance toward her but did not correct the lie.

"The one possessing The Creaturae has traveled a great distance," Lord Tywill muttered.

"And how long ago was your battle with the kraken?" Travion asked, studying the map.

"Almost two and a half weeks. We harbored in Bezopasnyy overnight following the attack, then headed here the next morning."

"So, the kraken isn't traveling exceptionally quickly, but it is heading in our direction," General Quillan stated.

"Which means we have time before it reaches our shores, but not much." Travion ran a hand through his hair.

"I know you've mentioned that this Creaturae possesses creation and destruction magic, but how ultimate of a power are we talking about?" Sereia asked, needing a true picture of just what was out there.

Travion sighed as his eyes met hers. "Once my father came into possession of the book, he used its spells to create the veils between the middle realms, linking all three together. And from what Zryan has told us, he created an entirely new realm for Torksvala to exist in because he found the Torks too powerful an adversary."

Sereia swore softly under her breath, a chill coursing down her spine. The kraken was nothing compared to what this book could do.

"It is a power we must control once again," Quillan said. "At any cost."

Travion glared down at the map, and Sereia studied his face. "What are you thinking, Travion?"

He didn't answer right away. His blue eyes remained on the map spread out before them in a contemplative way.

"We've lost too many men to this already. I cannot ask more to go out alone." Finally, his eyes left the map, and he surveyed his council before looking at her. "It's time I set out myself to see what this is about."

A muscle in Sereia's jaw flexed. It was standard Travion to settle on running into the oncoming danger himself. But who would keep the fool from winding up dead this time?

"If that is the case, then you'll sail on *The Saorsa*."

"What?" Lord Tywill sputtered, and in the corner, Finn shifted uneasily on his feet.

Sereia chose to ignore him and kept her eyes on Travion.

Travion's brow shot up. "No."

"Excuse me?"

"I said, no. I will take my own ships."

"With half the fleet lost, we may only be able to spare one. The rest will need to remain here and protect our coastline," Quillan interjected.

Sereia motioned to him. "One ship is not enough. One ship manned by a crew that has not faced such atrocities. Your admiral could not even escape these things. I am the only one standing here who has actual experience facing off with this kraken. If anyone has a chance of doing it again and coming out the other side, it is my crew and me," Sereia shot back.

"She has a point," Finn quipped, and Sereia shot him a quick look and nod of gratitude.

"Ignoring my captain, Sereia, this is not your fight."

"Your Majesty," Quillan began, but Travion raised a hand to silence him.

Her teeth clenched against the swell of curse words that wanted to spew from her mouth. "This is as much my fight as it is yours."

"A pirate does not have the same fight as a king. Nor does that make you fit to wage battle."

The world was awash in red, and Sereia clenched her hand into a fist so that she would not strike him. "A pirate I may be, but a pirate who has spent a century out on that water, living through every storm and leaving every battle brought to me a victor. Don't tell me I am not fit to fight this battle. It was mine before it was yours, and Midniva is my home too."

He snorted. "Your home? Is that so?"

This felt like a fight that was becoming about more than just the battle at hand. "Yes, my home, and I have every right to wish to defend and protect her."

Her parents were still here. And her four sisters, their husbands and children. While they weren't a part of her life, this was where they lived, and Sereia would fight to protect them if she could.

She also couldn't bear to let Travion walk into the battle alone and not come out of it alive. "This is what I *do* Travion. This is my *life*. You need me and my crew."

"We are down ships . . ." Quillan reminded the room once more.

Sereia's gaze locked onto Travion's in a firm stare that neither was willing to break from. Silence filled the room as everyone waited. It took Finn clearing his throat for the two of them to break eye contact.

"Very well," Travion grunted reluctantly. "We will take *The Saorsa*, but also one of our fully armed battleships."

She waved him off but didn't argue the point. Let him have his backup if he felt the need of it. Sereia knew what *The Saorsa* and her crew were capable of, and he would come to see for himself.

"Let the captain of HMS *Speedwell* know to prepare to set sail. The ship should be ready to leave port first thing tomorrow morning."

The men in the room nodded and began to stand.

"Your Majesty," Taimon finally spoke up. "Will Prince Kian be here in your stead?"

"Yes, I will notify my nephew personally."

When the room was cleared, Travion's arm moved around Sereia's waist to pull her in against him. "While I appreciate your aid, this truly isn't your battle. You don't have to join in on the hunt."

Sereia pressed her hands to his chest, leaning her hips into his as she quirked a brow. Had they not already discussed this? "Are you jesting? You are about to head out on the open water . . . into *my* world, and you think I would choose not to be there at your side for it?" She shook her head. "There is no place I would rather be right now than facing off against some monstrous beast on the open sea with you."

And it was the truth. While she had not lied when she said she wished to fight for Midniva, there was another part of her that also wanted Travion there on the water with her. To be able at long last to share this part of herself with him. Everyone questioned why she had left; let him see it for himself.

Their lips met once more, and her arms slid up and

around his neck. It was a firm kiss, filled with the frustrations of their argument, the unrelenting wills inside both of them that did not wish to give in. It would be easy to lose herself in this moment with him. To chase the residue of anger and work it out with their bodies. To let the feel of his warm hands brushing over her curves and the eager way he met each brush of her tongue with his own soothe the snarling creature inside her. Sereia wished there were more time to hide away in his chambers here at the castle and forget the outside world.

But that was never their lot in life, and there was a battle brewing.

Pulling away from him, Sereia allowed her lips to stay within a whisper of his own. "If we are to leave at dawn, I should return to Mointeach. I have to round up my crew and break the news to them that their shore leave is being cut short once again."

Travion nodded.

"Try not to miss me too much until tomorrow?" Winking at him, Sereia left the strategy room to fetch Yon.

The Saorsa sat bobbing lightly on the water, her scarlet sails a bright contrast against the blue sky above. Sereia walked down the wharf with Yon at her side and could hear a bawdy tune being sung somewhere on her ship's deck.

As her footsteps sounded on the gangway, the song faltered, and Batteo's head popped up over the railing to see who was approaching.

"Captain!" he sputtered in surprise.

"Quite the lurid tune you were singing, I don't think I've heard that one before."

He didn't look shamefaced but grinned proudly. "Learned it last night."

Sereia stepped onto the main deck and cast an eye around her ship. Everything looked pristine and taken care of. There was a mop in Batteo's hand, and it appeared he was working his way across the ship. "Glad to hear you're making use of your time in Mointeach."

"Aye, Captain." He chuckled.

"Where is Adrik?"

"On shore. Think there's an issue with our jerky stores."

Sereia nodded and turned to Yon. "Locate Adrik, and between the two of you, track down the rest of the crew. I need to speak to them all."

In the end, it took nearly an hour for the crew to be rounded up and returned to the ship. While she waited, Sereia had changed into clean clothes and prepared a map of the seas to begin plotting her own path back to Tribonik.

When at last they were all gathered on the main deck, Sereia surveyed their faces. Several seemed rather hungover, or perhaps close to being done for already. They were a rowdy group and desperately loved a bottomless tankard of ale when it could be found.

Their current state would have to do.

"I've gathered you all together to inform you that we set sail once more at dawn." A loud protest rose up, and she had to lift her hand to silence them. "I know we haven't had much rest between Bezopaznyy and here, but it cannot be helped. The kingdom of Midniva is in peril, and we have been asked to join in on the hunt for sea monsters."

"What?" Surprised, Adrik, now at her side, turned to look at her.

"You can't be serious, Captain. We've just escaped it!" another shouted from the back. One of her boatswains.

Sereia frowned. "I am absolutely serious. We'd never run from a fight before that, and what happened on the coast of Bezopasnyy will never happen again. Tomorrow at dawn, one of the king's most trusted men will be joining us, along with the battleship HMS *Speedwell*, and we will launch forth on a mission to track down the sea creature and destroy it."

"Captain, are you certain that this is the best thing for us to do?" Chailai's face was creased with a frown of uncertainty. "We barely escaped from the kraken."

Sereia's hands lifted to rest on her hips. "When did we become a group of lily-livered cowards?" she growled. "People are dying out at sea, and it's always been our prerogative to help them. I, for one, am not okay sitting back while this monster terrorizes helpless villages." Sereia shook her head, her shoulders stiff with anger. "If any of you have a problem with this, consider this your moment to get the bloody hell off my ship." With that final snarl, she turned on her heel and marched into her quarters, slamming the door behind her.

They were afraid, she knew that, but they weren't going to run from this. She could not run from this. Not again.

Dropping down into the chair behind her desk, she sighed roughly. Somehow, she would find a way to defeat this beast and keep her crew out of its hungry maw.

The door to her quarters opened, and Adrik appeared, coming to rest against the doorframe. "One of the king's most trusted men?"

Sereia signaled for him to come into her quarters. "Shut the door."

He stepped in and did as commanded, eyeing her.

"It will be King Travion himself."

"You just couldn't help but bring your toy back here with you, could you?"

Sereia shot a glare at him. He was backlit by the fading sun, but that didn't mask the bottle of rum tucked beneath his arm. He knew how to calm her temper once it was riled.

"If you give me that bottle of rum right now, I will refrain from informing the King of Midniva you referred to him as my toy." Sereia stretched back in her chair, lifting her legs to drop her boots down on the corner of her desk with a *thunk*.

Around the two small windows on the right side of her quarters were built-in shelves which bore books, navigation equipment, and bits of memorabilia she'd collected from each port she'd ever been in. Sometimes a shell, other times a bottle of alcohol or a scrap of fabric. To her left, beneath two more small windows, was her bed, neatly made and calling for her. She wished she were laying in it right now, staring up at the stars in the night sky, being gently rocked to sleep by the waves, rather than glaring angrily at her first mate.

"He's not my king, I don't care what he knows I've said." Adrik grinned but strolled across the cabin to place the bottle of rum on the desk before her.

Sereia reached down and quickly opened the bottom drawer to pull out two tumblers. They were gorgeous pieces that she had picked up in Tribonik. Hand carved from crystal so fragile she kept them nestled in wreaths of fabric in her drawer to protect them from the turmoil of the open water.

The glasses clunked on the desk's surface, the rum bottle

was unstopped, and soon the tumblers were filled with amber liquid. With the ease of familiarity, Sereia and Adrik silently cheered each other and took a sip.

She watched Adrik drop down into the seat across from her as she gratefully swallowed her alcohol. "We have to keep it hush-hush, you do realize?"

"That we've got one of the immortal brothers on our ship? Yeah, I gathered."

Sereia shot him a look. "I'm being serious. We'll have a battleship following us, so the crew will be curious as is, but they can't know. If word got out, we'd have more trouble on our hands than a giant kraken. He has enemies abroad, far greater than that beast. The kraken isn't just a coincidence. It was created by someone with a desire to hurt, and should they find out that Travion is on this ship, it will put us all at great risk."

"I understand." Adrik nodded, seriousness replacing the teasing from before. "Don't worry. I'll tell the crew to mind their own business when it comes to our visitor and that you have a purpose in all you do. Mind you, it would be an easier thing for them to accept if you stopped interrupting their shore leave." It was his turn to shoot her a look.

Sereia sighed and took a larger gulp of rum. "I know. And once this is all done, they can have an extended leave, but I can't control the circumstances as they now stand."

"And how did these become our circumstances to deal with?"

"You know how."

"Because you love him."

Sereia's eyes narrowed on Adrik, who seemed fully confident in his statement and entirely unconcerned with having voiced it out loud. "Be careful what you say," she growled.

"What? Are you going to try and tell me he isn't the one you continue to come home to?"

"Midniva is not my home. *The Saorsa* is."

Adrik snorted and lifted a brow. "Saying something doesn't make it true, Rei."

Sereia downed the entirety of her cup, inhaling sharply between her teeth at the burn. "Did you come in here for a purpose or only to antagonize me?"

Adrik grinned. "I came to tell you that your ship and crew will be all ready to set sail at dawn, and your royal toy is welcome any time he'd like to appear."

"Gods, you are annoying at times."

"At times?"

"*Most* times." Sereia dropped her boots to the floor and sat up. Opening the small satchel on her desktop, she pulled out the stone-handled knife she'd bought in the market. "Here." She lobbed it through the air at him. "I bought you a gift. Though I'm second-guessing that decision now," she tacked on.

Adrik caught it easily and examined the piece. His eyes lit up with delight, fingers brushing over the detailed work. Shifting it into his hand, he waved the knife, then tested out its balance by holding it up on two fingers. He then flipped it in the air to grab it up again, so it now pointed down in his hand. "It's great." He looked at her across the desk. "Thank you. Did it come from the same place as that necklace?"

Sereia looked down, having entirely forgotten about the pendant that Travion had given her. Wrapping her fingers around it, she gazed at the selkie engraved in stone. If only she could know the kind of peace the selkie bore on its face.

"Am I crazy, Adrik?" she asked suddenly. He opened his mouth, then closed it, a pinched look coming to his eyes like he didn't know how to answer her. "Am I going to get us all killed hunting for this beast?"

Adrik downed the rest of his rum and then sat forward, leaning both elbows on his knees. "Let's be honest, Rei. We always knew you were going to go back for the kraken—it was a matter of when, not if. You don't sit back when others are in need, and *The Saorsa* doesn't run from trouble. I think you're asking us to do what we all signed up for."

"And what is that, exactly?"

"Fight."

She stared across the desk at him. *Fight.* They could certainly do that. She just hoped she wasn't steering them into a battle that was already lost.

9

Travion

Sereia had left promptly for the port, leaving Travion to handle the other side of Midniva's matters. Kian had to be summoned—again—and he was fairly certain that his nephew would soon go into hiding. As his named heir, when Travion was indisposed, Kian sat on the throne.

Despite his nephew's help over the past two months, it was clear this wasn't where his heart was. Yet, there was no other option presented to Travion. With no child of his own, the crown had to be passed on to another family member, and with Ruan the heir to Lucem, it was left to Kian to shoulder Midniva.

Travion was bound to the castle walls for yet another day while more suffered. He loathed this waiting game, but soon his nephew would arrive, and Travion could finally set out and hunt down the person responsible.

The loss of the fleet infuriated him. Midniva couldn't afford to lose those numbers, not when the assaults seemed to increase by the day.

He wound his way down the upstairs hall and strode to

Taimon's office. The door was ajar, allowing Travion to peer inside. Red walls were bare of any paintings or portraits. A golden high-backed chair sat in front of a dark cherry desk. Bookshelves were lined with several volumes that Travion had a sneaking suspicion were more likely to be accounting figures than novels of adventure or romance.

"Your Grace." Taimon's voice startled Travion. "Are you in need of something?"

He shoved off of the door frame and glanced down at his steward. His hair hung loose rather than in its typical bun or topknot, and his nostrils flared as if he'd hurriedly made his way through the hall. In the short few years his steward had been in his service, Taimon never seemed to relax. His shoulders were always bunched by his ears. Travion knew he wasn't the easiest to deal with, but to cause such anxiety all the time?

"Prince Kian shall be arriving this evening, although he doesn't know that yet. I'll be calling on him soon."

Taimon had been in the strategy room, he knew what they'd planned. Still, he didn't seem to approve.

"Are you certain? I know we discussed this, and I don't want to second guess you, Your Grace, but with so many unknowns and you sailing into dangerous waters?"

Stiff muscles wouldn't keep Travion from leaping into battle. Not when innocents were dying while he sat and twiddled his fingers. "We are running out of options, Taimon. With every day that passes, I grow more impatient. We cannot simply wait around any longer."

Taimon nodded and fidgeted with the gold buttons on his overcoat. "I see. Will you need me in the castle? It's unfortunate timing, you see. My mother is ill, and I fear her last days draw closer. I'm not sure how long I'll be in Hillbride for."

As much as Travion couldn't afford to lose an important member of the castle, he wasn't so cruel as to deny the male what could be his mother's last days. "Of course. Take all the time you need, Taimon. You may leave whenever you wish."

Taimon bowed his head. "Thank you. I'll take my leave at once."

"Send my regards to your mother," Travion said before he turned away and continued down the hall until he arrived at his study. Once inside, he walked up to the basin on a white marble pedestal. The water rippled from his approach, then stilled. With a sigh, Travion picked up a knife and pricked his fingertip. Blood dripped into the water as he murmured over it. The red spun around in a circle until an image slowly formed.

Dark, mussed hair fell over the male's brow, nearly brushing against green eyes. "Brother!" Zryan cried. "I'm so glad you called on me."

Zryan was not at all who Travion wished to speak to. "I didn't. I was actually calling for Kian."

Zryan rolled his eyes, smiling broadly. "Come now, my son left Midniva not long ago. You can spare a moment with me."

"No, actually, I can't. I leave for Tribonik at dawn."

Zryan's smile faded. "What? So soon?"

Travion shifted his weight to one leg and used the basin to hold himself up. He sighed, shaking his head. "It appears so. The attacks have increased, decimating one of my fleets, and I cannot have this on my conscience. It's because of The Creaturae, and it is our responsibility. We're more than the royal family, we're the caretakers. It's time we took *care*, Zryan."

His brother glanced away from his basin. "Nothing good can come of this." His voice was barely above a whisper.

Travion didn't make a habit of soothing Zryan when most of his woes stemmed from the discord he created. Still, he was his younger brother, and it was only a matter of time until the relative peace came to an end, wasn't it?

"Likely not. But together, we can put things back to rights. We've done it before, and we can do it again." Like after Ludari had been slain and the kingdom was in utter chaos. It had been up to the brothers, and later on, Alessia, to mend the damage that had been done.

"Travion, don't do anything foolish."

He barked a laugh. "That is rich, coming from you, Zryan." But his brother's face scrunched into an expression of frustration. "I will be with Sereia's crew, and you know she wouldn't let me do anything—"

"Sereia?" Zryan's tone lightened. He drew closer to the water and grinned. "Well, well, look what the tide brought in for you, brother. A lady of the sea." He nodded. "I feel better knowing she's accompanying you, considering she'd flay someone like a fish for looking at you sideways. And did she honestly call Eden a *harlot*?"

Travion rapped his fingers against the basin and ground his teeth together. "I'm so pleased to know your nerves are soothed, but I have a lot more to do than simply gossip." He paused, glancing up at the ceiling, wondering if she actually *had* said that. But judging by the murderous look on Draven's face, it was true. "Just send Kian at once. If he leaves within the hour, he'll be here at sunset."

"Very well. Give my regards to Sereia." Zryan lifted his brows and winked.

Not wishing to endure his antics any longer, Travion dashed his hand through the water, severing the connection of the basin.

Travion was already outside, pacing the courtyard, when Kian's gold-maned griffin landed on the grassy hillside. Long black talons scraped against the earth, digging it up. And as the wind blew, it ruffled the beast's feathers. It must have been annoyed, for its lion's tail lashed out behind it.

The gold of his nephew's arm gleamed in the fading sunlight as he dismounted, and he smirked as he sauntered forward. "Uncle, it's been far too long."

Travion chuckled and gripped his hand, shaking it firmly. "Far too long, indeed." At this rate, his nephew may as well have just remained in Midniva. "I hope you're not too tired to rule in my stead."

Kian pulled him into a half-embrace and pounded his back "Surely you jest," he said as he withdrew. The breeze ruffled his dark brown hair. "We won our last battle, and you know how my parents get. Their sounds of *celebration* echo in the halls. It's impossible not to hear." He motioned to the castle, toward where the kingdom lay. "This is my reprieve."

Oh, did Travion ever. Zryan and Alessia were riotous with their sexual endeavors, indifferent to any that may hear or catch them in the act. It was the only time Alessia cared to entertain her husband, not that Travion could blame her. Zryan's eyes wandered too much, and he had strayed from his wife countless times—it was a wonder Alessia even let him touch her any longer. But who was Travion to judge, when the female he loved couldn't endure his presence for too long? And the idea of remaining with him drove her away.

He grimaced. "My apologies, then." Turning away from Kian, he motioned for him to follow. "Supper is ready for us, and while you know the gist of what is happening, there are some new developments."

Over the course of the evening, Travion enjoyed the company of his nephew while he relayed the new information. In truth, he hadn't a clue when he'd return to Midniva, which was likely not the answer Kian wanted, but it was the only one he had.

Eventually, sleep called to Travion, and he knew he needed the rest. It wasn't likely he'd get any while he was out at sea.

Gulls flew above the masts, chattering to one another in annoyance as the wind worked against them. They circled the deep red sails as if they yearned to perch, in hopes of finding scraps to eat. *The Saorsa* wouldn't be the wisest place for them to land. Neither would HMS *Speedwell*, which rode in the wake of the red-sailed ship.

Travion leaned against the railing on the quarterdeck, peering down as a vibrant hippocampus surfaced and shook its frilled head. Velox, his beast of the sea, looked no different than a horse as far as his face went. Full, rounded cheeks puffed as he drew in air, and the gills behind his cheeks puffed wildly. Then his face tapered as his muzzle drew down toward a pair of nostrils. From his chin, two long whiskers resembling a catfish's dangled into the choppy water. Instead of a thick mane of hair, he possessed frills that looked more like seaweed than not. Velox was an impressive creature of muscle. His tail looked like a whale's, and his front legs were that of a horse until they morphed into streamlined fins, made to better cut through the rough sea.

Words were not needed to communicate with Velox. They spoke through images and feelings, which Travion did to warn him, then to pass it on to those who also lurked beneath the sea. The last thing he wanted was for his companion to fall because he yearned to follow him.

At last, when the very last image filtered into Travion's head—dark, tumultuous water—Velox shot a mouthful of liquid at him. He didn't have time to duck out of the way and wound up with a face drenched by seawater. Grumbling, Travion pulled a cloth from his back pocket and wiped it away.

"Maybe I shouldn't have warned you," he muttered and wiped his face off. "Before you leave, can you and your pod be on the lookout for monsters?" Travion relayed the urgency by projecting imagery of a kraken and a whale.

Velox whistled his agreement, then shook his head in what Travion assumed was his version of a shudder. A moment later, Velox dove beneath the water, but Travion was wise to his tricks and shoved away from the rail before a wave crashed onto the deck.

"Ingrate," Travion spat before he hopped down the stairs toward the captain's quarters. Down below, lamps were lit to offer extra light. His interest wasn't in the table with the map rolled out onto it but the woman bent over with her brow furrowed in concentration. Sun-kissed brunette locks tumbled down her shoulders, spilling onto the table before her. A small, slightly turned-up nose scrunched in annoyance as she shoved a scrap of parchment away, but it was the woman's eyes as she flicked them up to gaze at him that always undid him. A blue so deep it rivaled the sea's glittering hue.

"Why are you wet?" Sereia narrowed her eyes as she inspected the front of his shirt.

"A foul creature sprayed me."

Understanding softened her expression. Her fingers toyed with the golden compass on the table.

Travion sat across from her, bent on having something akin to a normal conversation. There, of course, was nothing wrong with heated kisses or gasps of pleasure, but they had done little conversing since the night of the party.

As a pen rolled toward him, he stopped it with a slender finger. "You know, I never did ask . . ."

"What?" Sereia folded her arms and leaned on the table.

"What exactly did you say about Eden the other night? It's been ages since I've seen Draven so furious." He chuckled.

Sereia, to her credit, had the grace to look apologetic. Travion surmised it wasn't at all because she'd offended Draven but because of how her words might have hurt Eden.

"I happened to call her a harlot, a wench, and a brat barely out of the cradle."

Travion let the pen tumble from his fingers in response. "Well, thank the sea he didn't haul you off to the afterlife on the spot. Draven isn't fond of you on a good day, let alone when you're insulting his wife."

She shrugged. "I care little for what he thinks of me. Still, I cannot believe someone *chose* to be with him."

Travion arched a brow. "No?" He glanced up at the lantern as it swayed with the gentle rocking of the sea. Although he knew Sereia wasn't likely to change her mind, just as it was unlikely Draven would change his, Sereia didn't know his brother—not for who he was or his truth. Perhaps if she knew how his companionship in the dark cell had kept Travion sane, or how the rough squeezing of his hand reminded him that he wasn't alone, she would see past the scowls.

The taste of the cell threatened to choke him. Damp, foul, and stale. He could almost hear the barking of orders from down the way, signaling that the worst was yet to come with a visit from their father.

Ludari always came with the intent to inspect them, as if to see if he'd made the right decision, his visits full of taunts and mistreatment. Draven, of course, tried to spare Travion the worst of it, but as both grew, it didn't matter.

"Trav?" Sereia grabbed ahold of his hand and held it between both of hers. "Are you all right?"

Her voice brought him back to the present, chasing away the stale air and the bite of iron in his flesh. "I'm fine." He lifted her hands to his lips and placed a kiss on her knuckles. "One day, I hope you'll see how and why someone *would* choose my brother." Travion couldn't bring himself to look into her eyes, knowing full well that the demons were clawing their way through his memories, his mind, and if she took one look at him, she would see them.

If Sereia couldn't fathom why anyone would choose Draven, it was no wonder she couldn't remain with him in Midniva. No, he wasn't as severe as his brother, but he was more like him than not. The idea that her distaste ran so deeply left a bitter taste in his mouth.

With a sigh, he released his hold on her hands. He didn't want to dwell on his tormented past, but Sereia, in all their years of on-again, off-again, he'd never asked what she had been up to while out at sea.

Part of him didn't want to know, because he still clung on to hope that the same Sereia Ferox he'd first met was in there too. Travion wasn't daft, though; he knew she'd made a name for herself, just not the extent.

"Tell me, what fresh hell have you been wreaking on the sea as of late?" A small twitch of a smile touched the corner of his lips.

Sereia's shoulders fell ever so slightly, as if perhaps she'd been waiting for a different slew of words to tumble from his mouth. "First of all, you assume it's hell, but in fact, I've been aiding those in need."

Travion's hands opened with his palms facing upward as he rocked back in surprise. "Is that so? I'm listening." He chuckled, tucking loose strands of his hair behind his ear. The image of Sereia aiding someone wasn't so far-fetched, but it was the *how* Travion wanted to hear. He didn't picture her cradling someone on their deathbed or immersing herself in a sick house to take care of orphans, so her explanation of aid would no doubt be a good one.

"I've spent the last few years balancing the scales on the water. You have no idea how many greedy merchants pollute the sea, or what ill they inflict on the less fortunate." She paused only when Travion lifted an eyebrow as if to say *Is that so?* Sereia continued on, her face lighting with a familiar passion he knew all too well. She grew animated with her hands and even the shift of her body as she submerged herself in her element. At peace and truly happy. It was selfish of him to even think it, but he wished he could bring the same light to her eyes as the sea did.

"Thanks to *The Saorsa,* there are less than there were. We've taken back what should belong to the poor merchants and fishermen."

Travion's good sense disagreed with the notion. There was a way to go about exacting fairness, and stealing or destroying another's property wasn't it. Nevertheless, he didn't exactly disagree with the sentiment, and he'd be lying if he said the impassioned look on Sereia's face didn't make him want to join her efforts. Alas, he was King of Midniva, and he was to lead by example.

"And here I thought you'd lived a dull life until now. What was I thinking?" Travion slid his palms along the smooth surface of the table. The light flickered in the quarters as the ship rocked more. He felt the crackle in his veins, the unfurling of an impending storm.

A knock came at the door, snapping them from the moment. It was something Travion was used to, but Sereia looked annoyed. Her full lips pressed together as she tilted her head toward the door. "What is it?"

Adrik's tan face peeked in first, then the rest of his body followed. "There is a storm ahead, and it looks bad."

Travion didn't turn to face Adrik, he only stared down at his hands. The electric current of the storm swirled around him, and he could nearly pluck the strands from the air. They didn't have time to be slowed by an inconvenience.

"Lightning every few seconds and black clouds. It's going to get even choppier the farther we head into it."

"We can't afford to anchor and just ride it out." Sereia glanced toward the window across the cabin.

Travion curled his lip in annoyance. "No, we can't." His weight shifted on the chair, then he stood up and quickly shoved past Adrik, ignoring the grumble that followed him.

Sure enough, the sky on the horizon was nearly black. The clouds above them had turned an unwelcoming gray, but it was the erratic streaks of purple darting across the sky and dancing along the water that grated on Travion's nerves. If only it were Zryan playing games—but this was no trick, and his brother was far from the sea.

Sereia burst from the cabin, holding her hands out to the side as she approached him. He twisted at the waist to glance at her. "Would you mind telling me what that was about?"

Time wasn't on their side. Each passing moment was precious, and it was possible more lives would be lost. "Everyone is in agreement that we can't waste time by anchoring, so someone has to do something about it."

She gawked at him. "Like what? Talk the clouds into obedience? Shame the sky for storming?"

Travion rolled up the sleeves of his shirt. His face crumpled in discontent, furrowing his brow and pinching his lips. "Well, when you put it like that, it sounds rather silly. You don't discipline a force of nature, but you can persuade it." He licked his lips, then smirked as she folded her arms.

It would take a great deal of his energy to command the weather, but he could do it. In his lifetime, there hadn't been much need outside of ensuring a day of sailing went as planned, or to bless someone's wedding with sunshine instead of rain. There had been the need to try to pull the clouds from the sun during the attack on Lucem, but with a spell repelling his attempts, it'd been futile.

"What are you doing?" Sereia's voice sounded so far away already. "Travion!"

Travion closed his eyes, homing in on the tug of the air and the electricity pulsing within, then reached out for it with his magic. Once, he'd been told it looked as though the sea churned within his blue depths when he called to the sky, to the earth, and that it was unsettling.

The ship rocked in the uneasy waves, but Travion tuned out the sounds of the crew and of Sereia hissing at him until she swatted at his shoulder. His hand darted out, caught her wrist, and he tugged her closer. When he opened his eyes, she sucked in a breath but said nothing more.

The wind whispered through his hair, humming with a life of its own, and he pushed it back. But it wailed in fury, longing to rage over the sea. Travion glared at the sky, the horizon, the water, and with every ounce of determination he possessed, he pushed the storm away. It wasn't instant, but it slowly rolled back in the direction it came from. Little by little, the sky brightened, the sea calmed, and the wind steadied.

When it was done, his shoulders sagged, and he drew in a deep breath. In comparison, it felt as though he'd swum laps for an hour. His limbs felt fatigued, his mind hazy.

"What in the great depths was *that*?" Sereia slammed a hand against his shoulder once, then again. "After . . . after all these years! Your ship in that storm . . . You could have stopped it."

Travion relinquished his hold on her and narrowed his eyes. "You knew I could control the weather." He tore his gaze from her and surveyed the crew, who were studiously looking anywhere except for them.

"Yes, Travion, I did. Clearing a drizzly day, blowing a cloud or two from the sky, but this?" She motioned toward the sky. "You stilled the sky, the wind . . ."

He sighed tiredly. "That ship was a nice one, but by the sea! Forget it."

Sereia's eyes remained wide. A hint of betrayal melded with the surprise written across her face. "We're not done here," she muttered.

He arched a lone brow and shook his head. "I'm too exhausted to have this conversation right now."

Sereia swore before advancing on him. "We are *not* done. Can we stop and talk about how you glared a storm into submission?"

"It's a familial trait—glaring something into submitting. But it doesn't always work." He raised his brows pointedly as he stared at her.

"That's not funny."

But it *was* true.

10

Sereia

A week had already passed at sea. One week of storms and grumpy pirates upset about their lost shore leave, of watching Travion stare frustratedly out at the horizon waiting for word to come back from any of his many sea creatures, with faithful Finn standing guard and silencing her crew's questions about Travion and his abilities. While her crew were plucked from Tribonik and Caifu mainly, there were a few who had come from the depths of Midniva seeking something more than a farm life.

There had been suspicion in their eyes since his performance with the storm a few days ago, and she wasn't certain if it had given him away or not. If those from Midniva weren't certain of their king's abilities, it had certainly shown him to be a man of true strength.

Sereia had seen the waves rolling in Travion's eyes as he had connected with the storm. It had been both terrifying and exhilarating, the power brimming from within their bright blue depths. He was as mercurial as the weather, so it was no surprise his affinity was connected to it. But such a level of power was awe-inspiring. To be able to call a storm into being or stop one before it even began . . . Travion could rule all the lands of the middle realm if he truly wished to.

Though it was a shock to learn the depths of his abilities, Sereia couldn't really hold it against him that he had kept them from her. What truths about himself did he truly owe her? None. She had never stayed around long enough to earn them.

Sereia woke a little later than usual to find Travion already dressed and gone from her bed. As she exited her quarters—in a leather vest paired with dark red breeches that clung to her legs, showing off the length of them, calf-high boots laced up the front, and leather vambraces in case battle broke out on the water—it was to find her crew busy at work.

Overhead, the morning sunshine was bright, casting a heat to the early summer day. Currently not a cloud in the sky to speak of, and if the wind remained just right for their sails, they would have a good day of sailing ahead of them. Sereia guessed that they were a day, maybe two, from the coast of Tribonik. Tonight, when the stars reappeared, she would be better able to gauge it.

Closing her cabin door behind her, Sereia took in her crew slowly. Batteo was busy mopping, singing another of his lurid tunes, while Yannik and Xiu sat nearby humming along with him and repairing nets. While their stores were plenty, it made the days easier to have a fresh catch of fish each night with their meal. Toward the bow, Boran was busy showing young Svenik how to work the harpoon guns. They had taken on two new crewmembers just shortly before heading for Caifu two months ago. They were fitting in well but still had plenty to learn.

Sereia straightened her leather vest. Already the heat of the day was beginning to make the contact of it against her skin feel hot. Fortunately, the ocean breeze was cool on her skin, something she'd learned to relish. The water was in her blood, and with her affinity for it, she was built for its chill.

Casting another glance around, Sereia spotted Travion at last. He leaned over the railing, speaking with who she could only assume was his hippocampus, Velox. She and Travion had had all this time together, far longer than their typical stints, and yet there still seemed to be an undeniable space between them. They had shared stories of their times apart, and the only moments when their conversations grew serious was when it turned to their current mission.

Sereia had never minded it before, but she was beginning to realize that she needed more depth from their encounters. That flitting in and out of his bed was no longer enough for her. It may have been smarter for her to have simply stayed away as she had previously intended.

She crossed the deck toward Travion and reached him just as he straightened up. She nodded in greeting to Finn, who stood just a few feet away, and then looked to Travion. "Morning, have we any word?" she asked.

Travion turned, his eyes falling to take her in before he met her gaze and nodded. "Velox came to inform me that there is debris several leagues from here, just to the northeast."

"Could he tell if it was the armada or not?"

Travion shook his head. "He's only able to give me pictures, and none of it was telling. I just know that whatever went down out there was entirely destroyed."

Sereia sighed. "At least we've got a proper heading."

Together, they turned and made their way to the stairs leading up onto the quarterdeck. Adrik stood at the helm with his arm draped over the top of it between two spokes.

On his face he wore a cocky grin that only grew when he saw her being followed by Travion.

"Morning. Captain, I see you've finally decided to join us. It seems His Majesty is wearing you out. Earning his keep in more ways than one." The grin only deepened, eyes bright as he gave them both a suggestive look.

Glaring at Adrik, Sereia shouldered him out of the way. "How about you go earn yours elsewhere?"

Chuckling, he stepped away from the wheel, winking as he swept past them and headed toward the steps.

"Adrik, we have word from one of the hippocampi that there is debris just leagues from here, so tell the crew to prepare for anything."

"Aye, aye, Captain." He saluted before heading down to the main deck.

Shaking her head, Sereia watched him swagger along. He stopped to clap Finn on the back before moving on to check on the crew and informing them to be prepared to both scavenge and recover. Unclasping the compass at her hip, she held it up and adjusted their direction.

"Charming," Travion muttered.

"He has a tendency to be an arrogant ass, but he's a loyal first mate." Adrik had proven himself time and time again over the almost three decades he'd been on her ship.

"He's the one you fished out of a Tribonik prison, is he not?" Travion watched her crew with a careful eye, noting the interactions between them.

Sereia nodded. "It was a bar brawl over some tavern wench. He was but a hot-blooded boy on the cusp of adulthood back then. With no parents to speak of and a home on the streets, he had a tendency to come out swinging." Sereia chuckled. "His first weeks here, I had to break up more than one senseless squabble and toss him in the brig a time or two. Finally, I threatened to abandon him at sea with nothing but the clothes on his back and a barrel to cling to unless he could choose to be a part of this crew and earn his place." Sereia had let him know that if he chose to hold his own, he would have a place here for as long as he lived. That he would find himself with a family that would die for him. "He needed to be given a purpose."

"And you gave it to him."

Sereia glanced at him from the corner of her eye. "*The Saorsa* did."

They fell silent, the great stretch of the sea surrounding them and the shrill cries of the gulls overhead. It was strange, having Travion here in her world. While it delighted her, it also left Sereia feeling vulnerable and exposed. Out here on the sea, she was Captain Ferox—that was the only form in which any of them knew her. Her past life, the one with luxury and feminine expectations, was long gone, usually easy to pretend that it had never existed.

Travion's presence was making that impossible. She saw the way her crew eyed him when he'd boarded her ship; she'd seen the way their minds were recalculating Sereia herself. She didn't know if it was a good or a bad thing. They didn't realize exactly who they carried on their ship, but they knew he was important, and suddenly her connection to one of the immortal brothers was becoming apparent. Pirates didn't simply get asked to join in on a royal mission. While they knew their fae captain came from Midniva, none of them outside of her most trusted three, Adrik, Chailai, and Yon, were aware of her noble status.

No matter how much she hid from it, her past could never be entirely outrun.

"Debris!" came a sudden shout from the bow of the ship. Yon pointed out toward the horizon.

Pulling the spyglass off her hip, Sereia stretched it out and lifted it to her eye. Scanning the area around them, she caught sight of ship remnants and supplies floating on the surface of the water. "Drop the main sails!" she shouted and snapped her fingers at Boran, who scrambled up to the quarterdeck to take the helm from her.

All over the main deck, men and women hurried to obey her orders, reeling ropes with the speed of experience. Without the force of the wind propelling her sails, *The Saorsa* began to slow. While they wanted to reach the debris, they did not want to ram through it and unknowingly put a hole in their hull.

Sereia shared a look with Travion, but words weren't needed. Together, they headed to the bow to assess what had been found. Leaning over the rail of the forecastle, Sereia watched chunks of wood and discarded crates sweep past them as they entered the debris field. "Was it one of yours?" she asked him.

He shook his head. "I'm unable to tell, I see nothing of identification."

Neither did Sereia. But they had certainly found one of the latest attacks.

Their attention was captured by Velox, who leaped from the water, chattering in a way that denoted upset. Frowning, Sereia looked to Travion. "Can you tell what he's saying?"

"Man . . ." he whispered. Awareness suddenly filled his eyes. "Survivor! There's a survivor in the water!" He pointed to a spot on the sea's surface where a body lay draped over a barrel, bobbing on the waves.

"Lower the dory!" Sereia shouted, turning to look over

the main deck. Spotting Adrik, she pointed out toward the space on the water. "We've got a survivor."

Making quick on her orders, Adrik and her second mate Chailai were soon over the side of *The Saorsa*, Xiu and Svenik lowering them down to the water on their dory. Returning to the railing, Sereia looked through her spyglass once more, and this time she caught sight of the dark navy coat and white trousers. He didn't look like a common sailor.

"He looks to be a naval officer." Handing the spyglass to Travion, she let him take a look.

"It's one of mine," he confirmed her suspicions.

In due course, Adrik and Chailai had hauled the body out of the water and returned to the ship. Steadily, Xiu and Svenik hauled the dory back up, where Finn and a deckhand carefully lifted the officer out and laid him onto the deck itself.

Chailai's fingers pressed to his throat, checking for a pulse, and she leaned down over him, listening for breath. Chailai had been found on another trip to Caifu. A young woman who had trained tirelessly alongside her father as a medicine woman but who was not allowed to practice on her own due to her sex. Sereia had offered her a position on *The Saorsa* as its second mate, where she would not only be allowed but encouraged to practice her medicine.

"It's faint, but he's alive." She looked up at Sereia. "I'd say severely dehydrated and near frozen." Uncapping her flask, Chailai poured a little water into the man's mouth. At first there was nothing. And then he coughed, a ragged sound, and weakly opened his eyes.

"Ser . . . pent . . ." he managed to rasp out before his eyes closed once more.

"Get him below deck and see what you can do for him, Chailai." Her eyes met Travion's. "A serpent is new . . ."

"You ever seen a sea serpent large enough to destroy a naval scout ship?" he asked. "And take down an entire armada?"

The chill of foreboding washed through Sereia, and she shook her head. "No, but I have a feeling I'm about to." Her eyes returned to the water. If the serpent was in proportion with the kraken, the sheer size of it would be impossible to contend with.

Adrik moved to her, tugging at the water-soaked shirt on his form as Chailai oversaw two deckhands lifting the survivor and carrying him down below. "What are your orders, Captain?"

"Keep searching for any more bodies. Send two of the deckhands out in the dory to survey the area, but tell them to be cautious. We don't know if the beast is still here or how far all of this debris has drifted."

It was as if her words had called for the beast itself. *The Saorsa* rocked violently on the water, tipping so far and so suddenly that none of them had a chance to prepare and steady themselves.

Sereia hit the deck hard and rolled over herself until she slammed into the railing. Her elbow screamed in protest as she connected with the wood. There was barely enough time to take a breath before the ship tipped back in the other direction, and she rolled with it. This time she landed on Adrik, who groaned in pain as they smashed into the opposite railing.

"Hold on and grab me!" Sereia ordered Adrik, who fortunately moved quickly, looping one arm and leg through the rail and the other arm around her waist before the ship tipped back drastically to the other side. The tall mast and her bright red sails swung dangerously in the air.

Fearing they were going to capsize, Sereia reached out to the water, feeling her body hum as the sense of the sea depth filled her. Her fingers curled as, in her mind's eye, she grasped the water itself and pulled it up to form a wall. Gritting her teeth, she used that wall to stop *The Saorsa*'s sway, pushing it back up. As they began to level out, then tip back to the other side, she brought up a second wall of water.

When at last their violent tipping had ceased, Sereia's forehead was dotted in sweat, and she sat panting on the deck floor, leaning back against Adrik.

Travion raised his brows, surprise filtering into his gaze as he and Finn approached. "Water manipulation?"

"Not the time," she growled, and with his offered hand, got to her feet.

Seeming to need to make itself known, the serpent's giant head, which could easily swallow a man whole, lifted from the water. It seemed as if it stared the two of them down before opening its large mouth and releasing a deafening screech.

When its blue head descended back into the water, Sereia leaned over the rail to see it sweep its way toward HMS *Speedwell*. She readied herself to support that ship as well. Behind her, Travion and Adrik barked orders to prepare the harpoon guns.

The *Speedwell* tipped dangerously on the water as the serpent attacked it from beneath, just as it had done with them. Shouts from the crew could be heard as they went tumbling. Sereia called up another wall of water to prevent it tipping to the other side, grunting as her muscles shook from the strain. Manipulating water was one thing; keeping it solid enough to protect a ship was another.

"You're not going to be able to do that forever," Travion said, coming to her side.

"I'll do it for as long as it takes."

"It's on its return!" Yon shouted from the crow's nest. Sereia wasn't sure when she'd climbed the rigging to get up there, but her eyes were the keenest on board.

Adrik turned the harpoon gun mounted on the bow of the ship. Beside him, Xiu stood prepared with another. As the serpent cut through the water toward them, the harpoon launched, merely a weapon, free of any rope.

It entered the water aimed directly for the serpent's head, but the beast coiled out of the way at just the right moment, and the harpoon disappeared into the deep instead. Travion cursed at the sight of it.

The ship shuddered from a severe impact, the bow lifting off the water and then crashing back down. Sereia dropped to her knees from the force of it, while Travion barely managed to stay upright.

"It's coming at us from below," Adrik said, climbing back to his feet but keeping a hand on the rail. "We're not going to be able to get a shot off."

Sereia drew herself back up as well. "We need to draw it to the surface."

"Something to act as a snack and lure it into our trap so we can get a clear shot."

Across the water, HMS *Speedwell*'s bow rose into the air and came crashing back down, waves of water cascading through the air around it. The ship then teetered, swaying drastically to one side and then the other as the serpent assaulted it from below.

Travion began disrobing, kicking his boots off and unbuttoning his vest.

"What are you doing?" Sereia snapped.

"We need bait."

"Your Grace . . ." Finn was frowning with uncertainty.

"Travion, you are not getting into the water! What can you hope to do against something that size?"

"I can swim and I can act as something tasty is what I can do," he growled. Tossing aside his vest, he tugged his shirt out of his trousers.

"This is ridiculous. You of all people shouldn't be used as bait."

"Why don't I go?" Adrik offered.

"Or me," echoed Finn.

"No!" Sereia and Travion shouted at the same time.

"I'm doing this, and that's final."

Sereia narrowed her eyes at Travion and began unlacing her own boots.

"What are you doing?" he asked.

"Last time I checked, I am the only one who can breathe underwater and control the sea. My experience with the kraken was similar, and I had to get down there to use the current and push it away from the ship. I will be of more use out there than you. I am going."

Travion reached out and grabbed her arm, pulling her up from her boots. "No. You are not." His face was pinched, and she wasn't sure if it was in concern or anger. Perhaps both. "This is my decision."

"This is my ship," she snapped back. Kicking her feet violently, she threw off first one and then the other boot.

"And I am ki—

"Don't," Sereia growled. She wasn't going to hear it. Him

being king was even more reason not to let him get in the water. He also didn't need to slip and reveal his true position to her crew by announcing his title. "This creature is unlike any sea serpent that's been seen before. You have no idea what to expect once you get down there. Look around us! Nothing has drifted from where the attack happened! There is more magic at play here than simply a large animal. My abilities make more sense down there right now." The beast must have some sort of power to keep all the debris here; better to pick off survivors if none of them floated away.

"And yet, I am not allowing you to go down there by yourself. Someone needs to be down there with you, and no one else on this ship, nor on *Speedwell*, is capable of aiding you like I can."

She could agree that this was a foolish task for anyone to take upon themselves, but it felt like anyone else would be a hindrance if she had to make certain they didn't drown.

"Here." Adrik had returned, a harpoon in each hand, and cut off her snarling response. "Since you're both being foolish, at least take these down with you."

Both Travion and Sereia snatched one from him, eyeing the other with frustration.

"Thank you, Adrik," Sereia said. "And Travion, make no mistake about it. You have no right going down there and risking your life. But if you insist, at the very least, I can provide you with some secondhand breaths if we're forced into the depths." Gracefully, she swung one leg over the railing.

"You are impossible," he grumbled.

"Mmm, I am," she agreed. With ease, she swung her other leg over so that she was resting with her bottom on the railing and her heels braced between the rungs. "Keep an eye on the water, Adrik, and do what you can to keep the ship afloat. Once the beast's head is above water, take aim. And if we are pulled down into the depths, don't wait long. Consider us lost and get *The Saorsa* as far from here as possible."

Looking over her shoulder at him, she winked, trying to reassure when there was no assurance to give. He looked uneasy, but he nodded. "Understood, Captain."

She took a moment to eye Travion, who had moved to the railing as well and was still looking less than pleased that she was coming along. "See you down there, darling."

With ease of practice, Sereia dove into the sea. It took only a fraction of a second for her body to accept that she was now in the water, and with a happy breath, she felt the gills behind her ears open, and the first rush of salt water went through her.

A splash sounded beside her, and turning her head, she saw Travion had joined her, his auburn hair caught in the tendrils of water, and his lips sealed against the sea. Quickly, he kicked his feet and returned to the surface.

Sereia stayed below, letting her eyes adjust to the difference in light. At first, she could see nothing, but then she saw the large dark form of the serpent heading their way. Their splash into the water had done what they hoped and attracted its attention.

Sereia kicked up quickly to the surface, throwing her head back to knock her wet bangs out of her eyes. "It worked," she gasped to Travion as she readjusted to air. "It's headed this way at full speed."

He nodded. "We should expect it to attack from below."

"I agree. I'll stay under to watch for it and do my best to

push it away from you at the last minute, if you're ready with the harpoon?"

"Works for me."

Sereia glanced up to the ship quickly to see that Adrik and Yannik were ready with the harpoon gun. Nodding to them, she ducked below the water.

She was just in time, because the beast was rising up from the deep, its mouth wide and ready to engulf them. Sereia smacked Travion's foot to warn him, then reached out with her hand in preparation.

Had she been above water, she would have started sweating from the nerves. Heart pounding in her ears, Sereia held off until the last minute, and then she pushed a current of water directly into the serpent's mouth, propelling herself backwards and away from it and pushing the creature's head to the side so that as it breached, it narrowly missed Travion.

Kicking to the surface, Sereia saw the harpoon protruding from one of the large fins running along the side of its head. Aboard the ship, Yannik was quickly reloading the harpoon gun.

The serpent's large body circled them quickly, preparing to squeeze them into submission. Its large head, easily three times the size of Travion, turned to snap at him once more. Sereia forced it back with another wave of water, which angered it. At the same time, Travion took advantage of its distraction and drove his harpoon deep into its body, just a few meters from its head.

The beast roared, a sound which only increased in volume as a third harpoon sunk into the flesh at the base of its head. Furious, the serpent's form rolled and writhed in the water, and Travion, who had not released his harpoon, went with it.

It must have decided that the surface was not the place to be at the moment, for it dove, the long coils of its body surfacing before receding into the water. Knowing she couldn't leave Travion on his own, Sereia thrust her harpoon into the tail just before it disappeared and held on tight as the beast wove its way through the waters, heading directly for the bottom.

Many meters down, Travion had finally let go of his harpoon. The need in his face as she came upon him told Sereia all she needed to know. Releasing her harpoon, she grabbed his shoulder and pulled him in, pressing her lips to his and blowing oxygen into his mouth.

After a couple of helpful breaths, they pulled back from each other, and Travion pointed to himself, then his throat, and lastly motioned to the water at large. Sereia nodded, letting him know that she understood he had reached out to the creatures of the sea to aid them. She pointed downward, and together, they dove lower.

The deeper they went, the darker it became. But from around them, glowing jellyfish suddenly appeared, helping to light their way. An answer to Travion's call, she was sure.

At the bottom, they found the discarded remains of the naval ships. Two were cracked entirely in half, sections lying leagues apart from each other. The third had lost its bow, but the rest of the ship was intact. Mostly. The mast had cracked in half with part of it jutting out of the seabed. The hull around the mast was now a gaping hole. It was too dark to see more, but Sereia was sure the rest lay out there. Lost and forever gone.

Pausing to exchange more breath, they began to swim around the ship, a little jellyfish bobbing its way along beside Sereia's head. She felt a hand at her shoulder, and looking to Travion, he pointed to a large cavern in the seabed. Their eyes met, and they did not need words to understand what the other was thinking. It was likely the serpent had descended into that hole to lick its wounds.

A wave of apprehension slid up Sereia's spine, causing the skin along her scalp to tingle. They were not currently in a great position. However, neither of them were good at choosing the safe route, so they swam over to the opening of the large hole to peer down into it.

As she grasped onto the edge and kicked lightly with her feet to keep herself in place, Sereia could smell it in the water: blood. There was nothing good down in that hole. Looking to Travion, she pointed to her nose before indicating the hole, and then drew a line across her throat to mimic death. He nodded in understanding, and then he froze.

Sereia tensed, knowing exactly what he was seeing behind her. The serpent had not gone into the cave.

She didn't spare a look back but pushed away from the cavern to swim quickly toward the sunken ship. Travion was right beside her, and all she could hope was that he could hold out for more air until they could get inside.

They were, of course, not fast enough, and the serpent's giant body cut them off, swirling around them in such a way that it created a whirlpool, sending them colliding into each other and then away. Sereia grasped for her powers, trying to somehow orient herself in the chaos.

Just when she had lost all hope for Travion and his ability to hold his breath without passing out, an orca struck the side of the serpent, stopping it in its attack. A second orca, and then a third appeared, joined by the rest of their pod.

The serpent reacted, biting out at the nearest orca, its sharp teeth sinking into its back. Secured there, the beast shook its head, and a trail of blood filled the water around them. The pod cried out in distress and began attacking the serpent more fiercely.

Using this distraction to her advantage, Sereia swam quickly to Travion, finding him in the darkness thanks to a jellyfish. She pulled him in to offer much-needed breath. They didn't have much time to spare and quickly broke apart to swim for the nearest sunken ship.

Grasping onto the edge of the hole in the deck, Sereia pushed herself inside. Grabbing onto Travion's hand, she pulled him in to herself once more, giving him another quick breath just before the ship began to tumble around them.

Losing her hold on Travion, Sereia was slammed into the side of the hull and then felt herself spinning as the ship itself was rolled along the seafloor. Grasping for something to stop herself from spinning out of control, Sereia found nothing within reach and instead slammed into the end of a cannon. The breath was knocked out of her as several of her ribs cracked in protest.

Worried that the weight of the cannon was going to end up resting on top of her, she pushed off of it, trying to swim toward the middle of the ship where the spinning wouldn't affect her as much. A large crate struck her back, dragging her down to the present floor of the ship, only for a third roll to send her and the crate tumbling once more.

Grasping onto the piece of the mast that was still attached to the bottom of the keel, Sereia finally managed to stop her own spinning.

Frantic, she looked around for Travion.

11

Travion

Precious air escaped Travion as the boat thrashed. He tried to relax, but given the situation, that wasn't an option. His lungs burned for more air, and it didn't matter how many years he'd spent diving deep in the sea or how many times his father had held his head beneath the water hoping to urge a new ability to the surface.

Travion didn't *have* gills. And he was currently every bit the hindrance Sereia hadn't wanted. But how many crew members could endure this—or call upon the aid of nearby sea creatures?

The floating jellyfish illuminated the hull of the ship, and Travion saw Sereia get tossed aside, but to his horror, a rusted cannon hurled toward her. Unable to shout, he pushed himself through the water, but she shifted at the last moment, narrowly escaping the crushing weight.

A cluster of jellyfish swarmed next to the hole in the ship, then, in a rush, the light extinguished. That meant one thing: the blasted serpent was making its rounds again.

Wasting no time, Travion attempted to reach out to the

serpent, hoping to coax it into peace with his mind. Typically, he felt the emotions of the beasts of the sea, saw through their eyes, and with that, he could control them. But this creature possessed a wall of resistance.

Unable to tap into its mind, Travion gave up and propelled himself toward Sereia. He grabbed her by the arms, and relief washed over her face. Travion leaned in and cemented his lips against hers, allowing her breath to pass into him. Once his lungs were filled with air once again, his hand cupped her face. He slanted her a look, which she read as it was intended. *Are you okay?*

She nodded.

In the distance, he could hear the orcas' low, pulsing call. He didn't need to direct them, for they were the wolves of the sea, and hunting—as well as attacking—was a game for them. The serpent had angered the pod by injuring one of their own.

Thud, thud, whoosh, thud.

The whooshing this deep was dull, but there was no missing the pod's aggressive attacks. Travion glanced out of the hole just in time to see an orca bite into the tail end of the sea beast. Except the serpent was too close.

The beast snapped its tail against the wreck, shifting it again, and the serpent's cry pierced the water.

Travion grimaced, twisting to see the snapped mast shifting as the ship tilted again. He shoved his hands against the wooden hull, but his eyes darted from Sereia to the splintered piece of wood heading straight toward her.

By the sea!

Panic rose within him, and the need to shove the mast-turned-missile out of the way urged him to dart forward. He cut through the water, struggling against the burning in his lungs as his body ran dangerously low on oxygen. He knew his limits, and he was pushing them.

Bubbles escaped his mouth as he rammed into the wood, redirecting its path.

Every moment that ticked by only seemed to make the growing aches in his body more pronounced, but as he stared at the mast, a thought occurred to him.

They could use the mast. If they could lure the sea serpent into the ship and time it just right . . .

With the orcas already in the area, and the addition of Velox's pod, it would be enough of a distraction. One they desperately needed.

He swallowed down the burning need for his lungs to suck in air and forced his mind to calm. *Just a moment more.*

Travion mentally reached into the sea, and it was like dipping his hand into a bowl of strings. Each one was a life form that he could call to, and they whispered to him, letting him know what they were.

Moments later, the whooping trill of Velox with his pod cut through the scraping sound of the ship sliding across the seafloor.

The serpent screeched again.

Travion chanced a glance out a small window and regretted it. The ship now teetered precariously close to a crevice. If it plunged over the side, he was as good as dead, and Sereia would be at the mercy of whatever wretched fates watched on.

Closing his eyes, he shook his head, then, opening them,

he turned to catch Sereia's gaze. Travion lifted his hands and mimed their current predicament.

The stream of curses flowing from her lips weren't muted by the sea. Sereia motioned to her chest, and he caught her meaning. She knew he desperately needed air again.

She swam toward him, secured her lips to his, and passed a mouthful of air to him, then another, but when she attempted to pull back, he halted her.

Travion motioned to Velox, then mimed him darting in and them shoving the mast toward the serpent.

Sereia nodded, grim determination hardening her expression.

If the fates were kind, they'd both make it out of this alive.

The serpent cried as the orcas continued their assault. Travion called to Velox, and the hippocampus swam close to the hole in the ship, his clever eyes watching his rider. As best he could, Travion relayed the plan to his mount.

Velox trilled lowly. A sound that Travion knew to be one of displeasure. But they didn't have a choice. One more whip of the serpent's tail, and the wreck would tumble over the crevice, and he and Sereia would be gone.

He gritted his teeth, and a knot formed in his stomach. Velox was quick and had survived many a foolish battle, but Travion would be lying if he said he wasn't worried.

The hippocampus swam away, calling to his pod, weaving through the furious orcas.

Grunting, Travion manipulated the mast, using the floor of the wreck to steady it. He focused on the beasts under his command, relaying orders to herd the serpent toward them.

The grating moan of the serpent's anger filled the area,

and Travion motioned for Sereia to join him. Together, they shifted the mast into place, steadying it. The moments passed by excruciatingly slowly, but then Velox darted into the hull, zipping to the farthest side.

There was a blur of movement, then the serpent bolted inside, nearly slamming into Travion and Sereia. The rush of water was enough to send the mast tumbling down, even with the two of them steadying it.

Damn it to the depths!

Velox, feeling cornered and frightened, darted from the wreck and into open water, but the serpent's attention was on him instead of inside the wreck.

Dread unfurled in Travion. They couldn't allow it to escape the hull.

He peered over his shoulder and motioned for Sereia to swim into view of the creature, then out the hole behind him if she could.

She nodded her understanding, and in a rush, she cut through the water, in front of Travion, then back toward him, darting through the hole.

The furious serpent opened its mouth as it rounded on him, bolting forward. It took every ounce of strength he possessed to steady the mast, and his lungs felt as though they'd burst. Seconds ticked by, and his vision narrowed, but he was bent on ending this abomination.

Whether the creature believed it could avoid the large spear-like object or simply didn't care, Travion didn't know, but as it sped toward him, it didn't change its course and impaled itself on the broken mast.

The force of the blow sent Travion against the side of the ship, and his body crashed through it. Splinters pierced his back, and the mast shoved into his shoulder with such force, he heard something snap.

Stunned by the force, he sucked in a breath—or rather, a lungful of water. *Calm yourself, Travion, calm yourself.* But sea below, it was hard. He blinked, trying to focus on the serpent. The blasted thing was dead, but the weight of the corpse and mast were much like an anchor, dragging him down into the crevice.

Every part of his body screamed, and as much as he wanted to call out to Velox—to anything—he couldn't string together a coherent thought.

The last thing he recalled was water bubbling beneath him furiously, like a volcano was readying to erupt. Then his vision faded, and he knew no more.

The sound of the crew crying out orders sounded so distant, but then there was Sereia's voice, and Travion couldn't quite make out what she was saying.

His lungs felt full and heavy, he was unable to breathe. Travion coughed and rolled over as he vomited seawater. Then the pain bloomed in his arm and back, he groaned hoarsely. Finally, his eyes opened, and blurred faces stared down at him.

Sereia cupped his face gently. "By the sea, don't ever do that again!" Her voice broke as she leaned her forehead against his, pausing for a moment before sitting back up.

"W-what . . ." Travion's voice was hoarse from the salt water.

"Your shoulder is dislocated, and you have half a ship's

worth of wood in you," Finn offered, and his voice shook with concern. "Sereia gave you breath, but Your Grace." He lowered his voice so none of the crew could hear him. "You nearly died."

Travion lifted his good arm and draped it over his face, blocking out the sun's too-bright rays. "But I didn't."

"Have a care with yourself," Finn bit out. "There are countless people who care for you, including myself."

"Truly," Sereia breathed out.

Slowly, he sat up, then wished he hadn't. But as his last moments in the sea tumbled around in his head, something didn't make sense. "How did I make it to the surface again?" He supposed Velox could have fetched him . . .

"Oh, you shot out of the sea like a fae-missile." Finn mimed it, adding the sound of an explosion, then the splatter of Travion hitting the deck. "Sereia. It was the captain." He popped his lips when he only received a glare from Sereia.

"What?" He glanced at her, wondering how she'd propelled him from the sea with such force. "How?"

"I can control the sea." She said it quietly, as though she didn't want to have this conversation now.

And neither did he. "The walls of water earlier," he murmured, even more memories returning. Travion lacked energy in every way, and his body screamed. He nearly wished he could fade into the darkness again. "So, we both have secrets," he managed to say through clenched teeth as a fresh wave of pain shot through him. "Finn, I need you to set my shoulder. I can't function like this." His voice shook.

His guard nodded and moved closer, grabbing ahold of Travion's left arm. "On three," he warned. "One, two—" Except Finn didn't pop his arm back into place on three, he did it on two.

Travion howled in pain and fought to grab his guard by the scruff of his shirt. "You said *three*! You bastard."

Finn's pale brows pinched at the insult. "My mother would very much disagree with that," Finn said, as if scolding Travion, then he shrugged. There wasn't an ounce of remorse on his face. "Besides, you would have been tense at three."

Sereia laughed, but then inhaled sharply. Pain marred her face.

"What's wrong?" His bruises and aches were still there, but at the moment, all Travion cared about was that *she* was okay. When he leaned back, he caught sight of a deep red and purple bruise already blooming on her side and back.

Unfortunately, the crew consisted of humans, minus Finn, and his affinity wasn't in healing but rather in working with the earth, which did them no good in the middle of a damn sea.

"It's my ribs. When we were being tossed around, I think they were too." She drew in a shaky breath.

"You've got a nasty bruise." He closed his eyes and mustered the strength to stand. Sereia stepped forward, steadying him with a hand.

Finn looked ready to catch Travion at a moment's notice. "The captain said you were able to kill the serpent?"

"It was almost the other way around." He groaned as he leaned to grab his clothing, but Finn snatched them up and held them out. His underclothes were wet, but it wasn't something he'd fuss over. The mood was far too heavy for Travion's liking, as if the crew had already lost him. With a sigh, he cast a glance over the rail. "It's a bloody shame such a trophy went to waste."

Finn cocked his head as if Travion had sprouted an extra

limb. "You're upset about leaving the corpse on the seafloor?"

Sereia tried to hold back a laugh, which just came out as small hisses. "Yes. Skin like that would've made an exceptional pair of boots." She huffed a pained breath.

With his pain only increasing as his wits returned, and with Sereia in clear discomfort, now wasn't the time for jesting. "We need Chailai's assistance."

Sereia shifted her jaw. "She tends to you first." Her tone brooked no room for an argument.

"I'm going," he muttered as he gingerly crossed the deck and took the stairs down into the depths of the ship. He entered Chailai's room, Sereia following behind.

Oil lamps swayed with the rocking sea, and Chailai sat beside the sleeping naval officer's form.

"How is he?" Travion frowned as he walked up to the table, where the man lay cushioned by blankets and pillows to keep him from rolling.

Chailai's eyes were a bottomless brown verging on black, lined by thick dark lashes. A beautiful woman by anyone's standards. She caught him assessing her, and her brow furrowed. "It's hard to say. He took in a lot of water, and he was stranded for days. It may yet still take a toll on him. Fortunately, he didn't sustain any other injuries."

Sereia stepped up to the table, a frown wrinkling her brow. "What does he need? What can we do?"

"Time, mostly. Or a fae healer."

"Of course," Travion muttered. The *Speedwell* had those with wind and water affinities, but the *healer* on *The Saorsa* was human and had no true healing abilities. "May the fates have mercy on him, because we are far from land."

"I'm doing what I can." Chailai's words held a bite to

them. Apparently, he'd ruffled her feathers, which he hadn't meant to do.

"I realize—" Travion started.

"Enough." Sereia glanced at him, one eyebrow raised. "Chailai, before Travion decides to jump ship again, can you see to his injuries? He has half a wreck's lumber in him."

The pain had blossomed into a stinging burn, and it spread from his shoulder to his back. He wasn't going to argue about being cared for, because he needed to be in prime condition for the journey. Hopefully, this was as exciting as today would get. "Don't let your captain avoid being tended to. She needs her ribs checked."

Sereia crossed the floor and reached to open a wooden cabinet along the wall. Inside, there were several small shelves, with some holding sliding drawers. She rummaged through them, glass bottles clinking together as she searched. When she found what she was looking for, she twisted the stopper and pulled out the dropper; a dark amber liquid bubbled at the end of it. Lifting her tongue, she deposited two drops. "See? I've been seen to. Now it's your turn. Don't make me pin you down."

Her words garnered a smile from him, then a chuckle. Travion wouldn't complain overly much if she did.

"Since the table is occupied, you'll have to sit here." Chailai pointed to a cushioned chair, and the tight expression she wore brooked no argument from Travion. However, he was still of a mind to be obstinate.

He plopped down in the chair. The sound of Sereia's feet on the floor had him following her movements until she sat down next to him. "Should I hold your hand?" Without waiting, she reached forward, scooped up his hand, then ran her fingers along his palm.

The soft, featherlight touches on his palm soothed him. Travion wished they could've remained locked inside his bedchamber for several more days to do as they pleased. Whether it was reacquainting themselves with one another or relaying stories of the past five years. He didn't care. He only wanted to absorb as much of Sereia as he could.

"I may need you to—" A sharp burning pain blossomed in his shoulder. "Why doesn't anyone warn me?" He twisted his head, shooting Chailai an accusatory glance. "You are no gentler than Finn." Travion clenched his teeth as tweezers dug into the wound on his back. The scrape of the metal against his flesh didn't feel delightful.

Once the splinters were removed, Chailai opened a jar containing a red poultice. It didn't smell like much of anything, but the consistency was similar to tar. "This will speed up your recovery and also disinfect." She gingerly smeared it over his wound and around it. In a few moments, Travion's skin tingled. "Try not to rush into battle any time soon."

"You clearly don't know me," Travion remarked with a weak grin.

"Don't tempt him." Sereia shook her head. The salt-crusted pieces of her hair dangled in her face. He reached out, brushing them back and tucking them into place. "He is even more reckless than I am."

"Great," Chailai grumbled. "I should have packed more supplies."

All Travion could do was laugh. It was true that he was reckless. He often hurled himself into precarious situations. It didn't always serve him well, but sometimes it paid off. But if he had time to dissect the reasoning, it'd likely stem from the fact he trusted few, and those he did, he wanted to spare.

There was one thing he was learning on this journey rather swiftly, and that was that Sereia was a force to be reckoned with. He needed to trust in her abilities if he wanted the same in return.

12

Sereia

The soft splash of water against the hull and the gentle creaking of the rigging lulled Sereia into a mild sense of peace. Overhead, the sky was clear, allowing the constellations to twinkle and shine across the vast darkness. Gazing up at them, she could tell they were steady on course for Novgor. Boran, though likely half asleep where he stood at the wheel, was keeping them heading in the right direction.

Lifting her bottle to her lips, she took a deep swig of the amber liquid inside, enjoying the slosh of it as it swirled around. Seated on the deck, Sereia leaned back against the foremast, her legs stretched out before her and crossed at the ankles. She wore one of Travion's linen shirts, the stays left open at the top, and a pair of her own breeches. She hadn't even bothered with boots as she'd slipped from bed and made her way out of the cabin.

Idly, her fingers twined around the pendant hanging from her neck.

"Shouldn't you be curled up in the arms of your king?" came a deep voice from behind.

Rolling her eyes to the heavens, but not bothering to look in his direction, she took another sip of rum. "Can't sleep." It was turning out to be impossible to find a position that didn't cause her ribs pain. Chailai had informed her she'd managed to break two and badly bruise another.

At least she hadn't returned with a series of wood chunks embedded in her flesh and lungs full of sea water.

"Are you sure that's all it is?"

No, she was well aware it was not. Sleep was hard to come by when the notion that Travion had been right about her needing him chafed so badly. Him being down in the depths of the sea, unable to breathe, had been one of his most idiotic moves yet, but she *had* needed his help. What they had accomplished neither could have done on their own.

"What else would it be?" She would deny anything else until she was blue in the face.

"Perhaps this latest incident with your king nearly drowning at the bottom of the sea?" Adrik asked pointedly.

"What he does with himself is his business," she argued pitifully, causing him to snort. She took another swig of rum from the bottle.

Aggravatingly, Adrik had pinpointed the issue directly. Despite everything else, the thing weighing most heavily on Sereia's mind was the realization that Travion truly did not seem to care about his own wellbeing at all. Not but two months ago, he had nearly died, gored terribly by a manticore, and now, without thought for himself, he had gone into another near-death experience.

If left to his own devices, Sereia was sure this trip would kill him.

Adrik reached down to swipe the bottle of rum from her hand, bringing her thoughts back to her company, and dropped a small vial into her lap instead. "Why don't we try Chailai's healing tinctures first, rather than the spirits."

Hissing in irritation, Sereia watched him carry her bottle to the railing, where he took up a leaning position and drank from it just to torment her. "I don't like the way they make me feel afterward. Clouds my thoughts."

"More so than this?" He shook the bottle in her direction, earning another glare.

"Yes."

"Still wearing that, huh?" He nodded at the pendant.

Sereia dropped her hand, having forgotten she was even playing with it. "Mhm."

"I'm not used to you wearing jewelry."

"And your point?"

Adrik simply chuckled, shaking his head. For a moment, he looked up at the sails, taking another swig from the bottle. Then his eyes fell back to her, and he studied her silently. His shoulder-length hair tumbled into his eyes as the wind grasped gently at it. For a moment, the only sound was the soft flap of the sails in the wind and the gentle crush of the water beneath their hull. "Come now, Rei. Be honest with me. Why are you really out here rather than in there with him?"

"Where I choose to sleep or drink is none of your concern," she growled.

With Travion in her personal quarters, there was no escaping her feelings for him, and what had once been her sanctuary was quickly becoming a place of torment. To always have him within arm's reach—it was the embodiment of the secret desires she never dared give voice to. And now, on top of that was fear that at any moment she might lose him forever. It was more than she could take.

Adrik shrugged and took another swig of the rum, letting out a guttural sigh as he finished swallowing. She wished that it was her throat the alcohol was burning.

"We both know that someone has to—"

She didn't listen to the rest of what he had to say because a flickering in the distance caught her attention. She stood up, pressing a hand to her side as her ribs burned in agony, and moved to the railing.

"You can't just ignore me," Adrik complained.

Lifting her hand, she pressed it over his mouth, which seemed to *always* run, and nodded to the fire. "I see flames."

Her first mate turned, squinting out over the water. "Shit."

Sereia turned and cupped her hands over her mouth. "Boran!" she shouted. "We've got fire ahead! Approach with caution." It was hard to know what they were coming upon, and it would be best to go carefully.

Adrik was already moving to loosen the main boom and push it into a better position for capturing the headwinds. *The Saorsa* responded, picking up speed as it sliced through the mildly choppy waters and brought them closer to the fire. Boran angled the bow of the ship away from the potential wreck so that they would come up alongside it.

Sereia cursed herself for not having her spyglass on her hip but stared out over the water as they drew nearer. Squinting, she was finally able to make out what they were looking at.

"Rocks! Drop the sails!" She spun on her heels, racing down the steps to the main deck, ignoring the way her ribs screamed in protest. "We're coming up on an island!" she shouted up to Boran.

The flames lighting the sky were from a fishing boat,

caught up on a series of rocks below the water's surface. They were always a danger as one neared islets in the middle of the sea.

Leaving his post, Boran joined Adrik and Sereia in reeling in the sails. Sereia's hands slid over the ropes, feeling the burn against her palms and fingers as she wrenched on the leads. Every jerk made her ribs throb, and sweat formed along her hairline. Gritting her teeth, she worked through the pain.

Seeing that they were still coming up on the island faster than she would like, Sereia rushed over to the anchor. Releasing it with a groan, she watched it sink into the water, then waited.

The Saorsa gave a bit of a lurch as the anchor caught at last, beginning to drag on the bottom of the sea. Barely keeping her own footing, Sereia heard the curse come from the direction of her cabin and couldn't help but smirk.

"Wake the crew, Adrik. I want boats out on the water searching for survivors."

"Aye, Captain." He moved quickly to the bell hung from the mainmast. It rang out, shrill and clear, a signal to all to be up and ready. There were duties to be seen to.

Sereia pressed a hand to her screaming side and panted short breaths to see her through the pain. "Signal HMS *Speedwell*, Boran. They'll need to know there is an island and survivors to collect."

"On it." Boran moved to the mainmast and dug around for the appropriate flags. Then, with ease and haste, he climbed the rigging to the top to string them up and light the lamp so they would be visible in the night sky.

Sereia steadied herself and headed back up to the bow, peering out over the water. Until the fire was out on the other boat, they wouldn't be able to look for survivors onboard. And if left to its own devices, the fire wasn't going to be done until the ship sank beneath the waves. They couldn't leave innocent people to potentially burn to death. Not when she could do something about it.

She took a deep breath, her body shaking from the pain, and climbed over the railing. Sereia looked back over her shoulder in time to see Travion coming out of the cabin, hair a mess and face scrunched in a surly expression. She smiled at the sight of him and knew then she was making the right decision. He could not be put at risk again, not so soon. Not when he was still injured.

Preparing herself for agony, Sereia looked out at the burning ship and jumped into the water. The fact that she could breathe underwater saved her. The minute the impact of hitting the sea rocked through her body, she inhaled involuntarily, sucking in a large mouthful of water.

As she surfaced, she could hear Adrik shouting at her. "Dammit, Captain!" he roared. "What in the bloody hell are you doing *now*?"

Waving up at him, Sereia buoyed herself. "Someone's got to put the fire out!" she shouted back up at him.

"You're not well enough for this, get back up on the ship."

"The wrong person is giving orders right now, Adrik." She growled in frustration. "I'm the only one who can do this. Just focus on getting those on *Speedwell* caught up and searching for survivors."

She turned from him and focused on the fishing boat. There wasn't any more time to waste. Not if they hoped to find anyone alive.

Knowing that her side wouldn't handle the stress of

swimming, she reached out to the water around her and created a small whirlpool to propel her smoothly across the distance between the ships.

Once she was bobbing on the surface alongside the fishing boat, Sereia lifted her hands and sent a wave of water up and over the deck. The flames hissed and sputtered, continuing to burn strong until she increased the amount of water falling down. She continued doing so until the flames had flickered entirely out, and only dark smoke drifted lazily up from its surface.

Behind her, she could hear the dories being lowered to the sea as her crew began their late-night search. Shouts mingled with the splashes as the *Speedwell* arrived and added to their numbers. Now she needed to get up onto the ship to see if there was anyone to be found.

Sereia used her whirlpool once more to lift herself out of the water. As she hit the wet surface of the deck, she lost her footing and dropped to one knee, cursing as her side flared in agony.

"Damn the high seas," she growled under her breath, inhaling slowly through her nose in short bursts.

Sereia climbed carefully to her feet and crossed the blackened deck, being cautious of weak looking spots. Such loss and destruction was heartbreaking to see. This had been someone's livelihood. And now it was all gone. The thought of losing her own ship in a similar manner made her stomach knot.

Seeing no one on the deck, Sereia moved to the hatch, which lay wide open. A quick look down into the bowels of the ship told her the most severe damage had happened below. Carefully, she ventured down into it as best she could, careful not to slip and fall once more, knowing the chances of piercing a lung only increased the more pressure she put on the broken bones.

Below, the insides of the ship were dark, lit only by the full moon shining in through the open hatch. However, it was enough to see the large hole in the hull where jagged rocks had broken through as the ship fetched up on the outcropping. That wasn't the only thing. Inside the hull lay a severed tentacle the length of the ship itself. It was seared longways, and from the charred remains of the hull around it, she would say the crew had set fire to the ship in hopes of killing the beast.

"Hello?" she called out, peering around.

Eerie silence was her only companion. Other than herself, there did not appear to be a living soul aboard. There was a heavy stench of burnt wood and charred flesh that made her upper lip curl in distaste. The bottom of the hull was filled with water that had poured in from the open hole.

Slowly, Sereia waded through the water. Crates and apples floated on its surface, along with a wooden goblet. She moved to examine the tentacle more closely. It appeared to be the same shade as the creature that had taken down the *Ackazanti* and *Prepik,* which made her think it was from the very same kraken.

Which meant the monster was traveling down the coast and had likely come here after decimating Novgor.

Sereia halted as something brushed against her thigh. Looking down, she jerked back, gasping in horror as the charred remains of a fisherman floated by in the dark water. Lifting a hand to her lips, Sereia shuddered at the sight and could only pray to the sea spirits that he had already been dead before the flames found him.

With the greatest of care, Sereia used the water in the

bowels of the ship to lift the body up onto the main deck. He couldn't be left down here, not to rot away in the hull of this tragic ship. He deserved either a proper burial at sea or to return home.

What had the captain of this ship done when the kraken appeared? Had it all been lost before they struck rock, or had that been their one saving grace?

Had she been foolish in bringing her crew into this whole sordid affair? Every ship that came across these monsters was lost, and in some cases, entire crews killed. Her need to help Travion had sent her barreling into this without a thought, just as recklessly as he threw himself in the way of harm. But it wasn't only herself she had placed in danger; it was everyone who called *The Saorsa* home. Her family. And they were her responsibility to protect.

With a newfound heaviness weighing upon her, Sereia looked to make certain there were no other bodies, then climbed back up through the hatch. As she crossed back over to the railing, she saw one of her dories floating below.

"Anyone aboard, Cap?" Yannik called up.

"No one alive. I do have a body, however, that I need you to come and fetch. We'll be taking him back with us for a proper burial."

"Aye, Captain."

"And Yannik? Please show him the utmost respect."

"Of course." He nodded, and Svenik, who sat in the back, echoed this sentiment.

"Where are the others?" she asked as he pulled his dory up alongside the ship and tossed up a rope to tie on.

"The other dory is headed for the island in case survivors made it to shore."

Sereia nodded. "I'll see you back on ship, gentlemen, and hopefully some survivors."

There had to be someone left. They had gone somewhere. Hopefully they had managed to escape to the island just beyond the ship.

Once Sereia was back in the water, she used her abilities to once more to carry her across the water and back to *The Saorsa*. Travion's linen shirt clung uncomfortably to her form in a less than concealing manner, and her side threatened to buckle her knees. But satisfied that there was nothing else for her to do, Sereia let herself lean against the railing, breathing heavily.

Boots shuffled across the deck, drawing closer. Someone leaned next to her and sighed heavily. "What was that about not rushing into a battle any time soon?"

Sereia peered up through the strands of her wet hair to gaze over at Travion. "That was a recommendation for *you*, and there's no battle. Just putting out some fires. Captain's duty and all that." She tried to make light of it, but truth be told, her heart ached as badly as her side did.

How long would it take for Tribonik to heal from the pain The Creaturae had brought to its shores?

He simply shook his head at her, and an indiscernible expression flickered in his eyes. "Might I say, captain, your affinity is rather impressive to watch."

His words surprised her. He didn't lecture her, only teased, and if she weren't mistaken, pride glimmered in his eyes.

"Take care of yourself, we've got this for now." He nodded and stepped away from her to join the rest of her crew.

Nodding, Sereia waited until she passed him before her hand went back to her side. She rather wished she was still in the cool water, letting it ease the sting of her aching body. Once in her cabin, she stripped out of the wet clothes, moving cautiously to avoid aggravating her ribs further, and grabbed a towel to begin drying herself off. She pulled on a dry pair of breeches and a shirt of her own, then braided her hair quickly to keep it out of the way.

Nothing was worth the hassle of tugging boots on at this moment. She longed to drop down in bed, but there were survivors to oversee, and hopefully a captain to locate.

Back out on deck, the first dory had returned, and injured men were being hoisted up onto *The Saorsa*. Sereia stepped up beside Travion, and his one good arm, not bound up in a sling, naturally wrapped around her lower back, his hand coming to rest on her hip. Accepting the touch, she leaned into his side, feeling the weariness of her body even more.

"They managed to sever one of the kraken's tentacles," she murmured to Travion as they watched the haggard men drop down to the deck in exhaustion.

Their clothes were torn, sandy, and singed. Some were relatively whole, while others looked to be bloodied and beaten. Sereia was happy to see Chailai was already making her way through them, a small notepad and charcoal in hand as she triaged the injuries and noted the supplies she would need from below. Finn and Yon were working together to stop the bleeding on some of the worst ones, while Yannik and Xiu helped each new survivor brought aboard find a place to sit.

"So, it's both injured and pissed," Travion finally muttered back.

"True. But the key word there is 'injured.'" She looked up at him, and Travion peered down at her in agreement.

"Captain." It was Adrik. "The second dory is arriving. We

have the last of the men that survived the wreck. Those on *Speedwell* are prolonging their search farther down the coast of the island, they'll send a seahawk if they discover anyone else."

"Where is the body Yannik brought back from the ship?" she asked softly, not wanting to disturb any of the crew around them.

"It's currently in Chailai's quarters."

"Can you see to it that it is wrapped appropriately, and the sooner the better. I don't want any of his crew members to have to see him in the state he's in. Once their injuries have been dealt with, we can ask how they would like to handle his burial."

Adrik nodded in understanding.

"Please assign any deckhands not out on a dory to aid Chailai with whatever she needs. We'll make our way to the nearest port. While I figure out our new heading, hunt down the captain of the fishing boat, if he is still living, and send him to my cabin."

Her first mate nodded, then headed off to do just that. Sereia looked at Travion and nodded at her cabin. "Come . . . There's not much either of us can do out here."

Travion cast a look around them, and she knew that a part of him wanted to stay out here and oversee it all. He preferred to have all the information there was to be had rather than wait. But with his own healing shoulder and an arm that was bound, he wasn't any more use to these injured people than she would be.

Together, they headed back into the cabin. After retrieving her octant and spending some time measuring the stars, Sereia lowered herself carefully into her chair and sighed roughly. Before her, she spread out one of her maps, and after some quick calculation of their location from the stars, she tapped her finger over a small unnamed island. Picking up a paperweight shaped like a boat, she set it down near the island.

Travion came to stand behind her, studying their current position.

"I know you wished to see Novgor for yourself, but with the injured men on board I'm afraid we will need to make our way to the nearest port instead." Sereia looked up at him, but his eyes were on the map.

"The living come before the dead. It's more important to get these men back to land." He reached over her, tapping a finger on the map.

Her eyes drifted to the port he was indicating—Darsgaard —where once she had stabbed a wealthy man's son for forcing himself upon one of her crew. No one had cared about the harm done to a pirate, not when a rich benefactor's beloved child lay dying. Sereia had barely escaped with her own life, and had it not been for the backup and support of both Yon and Adrik, she may not have.

"Seems to be the closest," he muttered. "We could be there in a few hours."

"It is," she replied. "But *The Saorsa* can't sail into Darsgaard." Travion's brow lifted as he looked down at her. "I'm not highly appreciated in those ports," was all she was going to say on the matter.

"I'm sure there is a tale worth hearing behind that reason, and perhaps one day you'll tell me. Over a tankard and horrendous sea ballads."

Her eyes skimmed the coast of Tribonik, then she rested her finger next to another port situated on the island of Propentri. "Saventi will be our safest bet." It was a small coastal village, rather impoverished and desperately in need of new leadership, but it would at least get the survivors from the fishing craft on land. And if they were truly lucky, there would be a fae healer resting at port.

Before he could respond, there was a knock at her cabin door.

"Come in," she called.

The door opened, and a man she did not recognize stood in her doorway. Gray hair was shorn at the sides of his head and grew only a little longer on top. Along his jaw was a thick white beard. His left eye had been wounded, a deep gouge running along the length of that side of his face. The blood had dried enough that it was no longer flowing, but the wound was red and angry and would certainly need some of Chailai's poultice.

"I am Captain Zaitsev, and I must thank you for rescuing my crew." He was gruff and burly, with the look of a man who spent most of his days out in the sun upon the waters.

"Welcome aboard, Zaitsev." From the drawer of her desk, she pulled out three of her crystal tumblers and a spare bottle of rum that Adrik hadn't confiscated from her yet. "I'm Captain Ferox." She motioned a hand to the chair across from her desk. Then she looked up to Travion, who had straightened up, crossing his good arm beneath his wounded one. "And this is my compatriot . . . Lord Trask." He squinted at her but made no move to correct her.

There was no telling who all Zaitsev would talk to once he was in Saventi, and until they knew who they were up against, it was best not to risk the knowledge of Travion's presence spreading along the coast.

Zaitsev took the offered seat and accepted the tumbler of

rum gratefully. He drank down a good half of it before he settled back into his chair.

Sereia slid Travion's glass over to him, then relaxed in her seat, hiding the way her side twinged and throbbed with the movement. By the sea—forget a couple drops of Chailai's tincture, she was going to bathe in a tub of it. The gulp of rum burning down her throat helped.

"What happened out there?" she asked.

"It came out of nowhere." Zaitsev's eyes grew distant as he returned to that moment on the water. "The sea was calm, and then it was bubbling. The ship started to rock, and we knew something was coming. We're a fishing vessel . . . not a battleship, but—" He shook his head and gulped more rum.

Seeing his glass was empty, Sereia leaned forward, offering him more. Extending his glass, he allowed her to top it up. "But what?" she encouraged.

"We brought harpoons just in case." His harrowed eyes met hers across the expanse of the desk. "We've all heard stories."

Sereia nodded. It didn't take long for the tragedies of the sea to carry from one port to the next. "And that didn't stop you from setting out?"

"A man has got to make money to live. Fish are what feeds my family and my crew."

Sereia could only nod once again. When all a man knew was the water, what else was there to do but keep heading out on it despite the dangers that lay ahead. They all took risks. Storms. Assailants. Starvation. Fear kept none of them home. "It was bigger than we could have imagined." He shook his head, continuing. "It wrapped itself around the bow and was trying to drag us down. We shot harpoons . . . thought that would kill it." His voice drifted off a little as his eyes grew distant, and he appeared to be lost in studying the contents of his glass. At long last, he gulped more rum, then continued. "It didn't die. The harpoons just made it roaring mad, and it thrashed about in the sea like a drowning man. The harpoons were attached to the ship . . . a catch like that—"

"Would have made you rich," Sereia finished for him.

"It wasn't what we were out here for, but tithes have increased at home, and the boys are all near starving. I just wanted—" His voice cracked, and he brought a hand up to cover his face, fighting tears.

Sereia felt a twinge of pain for the broken man. He and his crew were in need; he'd wanted only to line all of their pockets to help keep the strain off. "All any of us can do is try," she said, trying to soothe him.

The captain nodded, brushing the back of his hand across his nose. "It started swimming, pulling the ship along with it until we were dragged into that cropping of rocks. After that, it forced its way through the holes in the hull. My first mate managed to harpoon a tentacle to the bottom of the boat. Blasted thing just . . . *ripped it off* and kept coming for us. There didn't seem to be any way off the boat but to set it ablaze and pray we made it to shore."

Sereia watched him finish his second glass of rum, then finished her own. She remembered what it had been like to watch the kraken go for one ship and then come directly for her own. There had been great fear inside her when she'd thought her crew was going to follow the path of the *Ackazanti* and sink beneath the waves.

"I found a body in the hull of your ship," she said carefully.

He cleared his throat against tears. "Alixandre, my first

mate. After he harpooned the beast, it caught him with another tentacle." His voice broke, and he could not continue.

"He's below. Do you wish for him to be buried at sea, or would you prefer he go home?"

"He has a wife and kids," Zaitsev said, voice hoarse. "She'll want to bury him."

Sereia nodded. "Then we'll take him home." She glanced at Travion, his face stern and contemplative. "Should we assume it will react the same way as an octopus would at losing a limb?"

"My best guess would be yes. I don't think this will slow it down any."

Sighing, Sereia leaned forward on her desk, looking at the fisherman once more. "I'm sorry about your ship, and your first mate. I know as a captain, the last thing you want is to lose one of your sea family." Her eyes fell to her desk for a moment, and once again she thought about her own crew and the risk they were all taking because of her. "I appreciate you sharing your tale with us, I know it wasn't easy." She looked back up at him. "Go, join your crew below and get some food in you. By mid-afternoon, we'll be in Saventi."

"Saventi? That's not where—" Sereia cut him off with a look. "Appreciated." Captain Zaitsev stood up, giving them both a nod.

When he was gone, Sereia slumped back with a deep moan, pressing a hand to her side. "That thing is relentless. And it just keeps leaving so much devastation in its wake."

Travion's hand was suddenly brushing strands of hair back from her face, a gentle, soothing touch. As she looked up at him, his fingers slipped beneath her jaw. "You're not blaming yourself for this, are you?"

Her heart clenched, and for a moment, Sereia let herself accept the comfort he was offering. Let the weight of her responsibility leave her and simply focused on the understanding in his eyes. He bore the weight of an entire kingdom. He knew.

"If I had just stayed to kill it then . . ."

"You may have succeeded, and you may have died."

"I won't flee next time." She kept her eyes locked with his. "I meant it when I said I would face this with you." When they had first met, she was nothing but a young maiden full of rebellion and dreams. Now, Sereia possessed experience. Hard earned and respected.

Travion nodded, his fingers curling around her jaw and up into the hair at the back of her head. "And I value your help. But we still don't know how to kill this bloody beast."

"There's got to be something that can be done." Sereia slammed her fist down on the desk, which sent a ricochet of pain from her ribs all the way through her chest, like a tight fist wrapping around her middle. She gasped, unable to keep it in.

Travion grumbled and straightened up. He moved across the cabin to grab up the vial of pain medicine Chailai had given him and brought it to her.

"Take it," he demanded.

Not having the desire to argue with him, Sereia accepted the vial and released several drops beneath her tongue.

Travion was eyeing her, a frown on his face. "Why did you go?" he growled, clearly still upset she'd headed off into the waters alone.

Sereia smirked up at him, feeling the faint line of cold sweat along her hairline. "So you wouldn't." She released a dark laugh, wincing. "Would you mind fetching Boran for me please? I'd like to tell him where we're headed, and I don't think I can move just yet." The admission cost her a lot. Vulnerability was a despised trait on the sea, and Sereia hated showing it. But if she was going to trust anyone with it, shouldn't it be Travion?

Shutting her eyes, Sereia wondered if she could perhaps sleep in her chair.

13

Travion

Sweat glimmered along Sereia's forehead, and lines of exhaustion as well as pain pinched her features. Travion wished to shield her from *everything* stemming from this blasted book, but he was quickly realizing that Sereia didn't need sheltering. The years apart and on the sea had molded her into a fierce sailor, there was no doubt about it.

"Fine, I'll fetch Boran for you, but next time—" Next time *what?* Next time let his foolish self leap into the waters with an arm he couldn't use?

Sereia's eyes flicked open, and she stared at him through dark lashes. "Did I wound your pride?"

Travion scoffed and turned away from the table. He pinched the bridge of his nose, willing his annoyance away, but it was futile, especially with Sereia. "Maybe a little. I'm not keen on being useless."

"Of course." Her features softened, and she sighed. "Being alive isn't useless, Travion."

He shifted his jaw. "Sometimes it can feel that way." Travion said no more as he left the quarters.

In another setting, he would have laughed because they were the same, he and Sereia. Thick-headed and driven by the need to protect the ones in their care—the ones they loved. But out here, on the dangerous waters, he honestly didn't know if they'd survive these ordeals.

But she was no wilting flower, shriveling from the harsh sea spray. No, she was the wind howling with rage across the waves and the tide rolling in to claim the shore.

The notion that she didn't *need* him both soothed him and caused an ache to form within his chest. If she didn't need him, there was no possibility of staying.

Travion made his way onto the deck, and he homed in on Boran, his face lit by the torches in the dark of the night. He was in the middle of making his way to another crew member when Travion interrupted him. "Boran, your captain wishes to see you."

The other male nodded, then ducked his head and walked away.

"Why do you look as though you're ready to take on the sea itself?" Finn, who had been lurking seas-knew-where, stepped into view. He folded his arms across his chest and sighed. "Please tell me that isn't your next course of action."

Travion chuckled darkly. "Maybe it is, who can say at this point."

"Not in your condition, Your Grace," Finn said firmly, then inclined his head. "I've watched you do this to yourself for years now. I cannot begin to understand what has happened in your lifetime."

"Don't, Finn." Travion held up his good hand. "This is my responsibility, and to see others endure loss and pain they shouldn't have to—"

"It's not your fault. None of this is. And you cannot take

this all on yourself. You cannot hope to face this alone. You *need* help, and it's okay to accept that." Finn's gaze remained on Travion, and intensity swirled within their depths.

Damn it to the depths! Travion didn't want him to be right, and certainly didn't want his words to be sound reasoning, yet they were.

Cries rang out near the bow of the ship, then the distinct sound of a fist colliding with skin.

"Oi! Knock it off!" Adrik's voice cut through the thunderous waves around them.

Travion spun to regard the crew member, but the words weren't directed at them. One of Adrik's hands was plastered against another male's chest. With Sereia temporarily occupied, Travion rushed over and stepped between Adrik and the other human. "Enough." The shorter male leaned forward as if tempted to strike Travion. As far as etiquette went out at sea, striking down a first mate wasn't exactly *polite*. To strike a king, on any surface, was pure foolishness. "I really wouldn't," Travion warned.

Adrik hissed behind him. "They're exhausted. We were on our shore leave when it was cut short because of you."

Travion turned to face him, catching the quick shake of his head at the crew member. "Because of me?" Sereia had disrupted the entire crew's rest only to ensure he was . . . alive? He frowned. It was a wonder the crew didn't lash out at him directly. "I see."

Movement from the corner of his eye snagged his attention. Sereia and Boran emerged from the cabin, and she studiously avoided his gaze. "We will make port in Saventi. There is no use in pushing ourselves in our current state." The breeze caught small strands of her hair and plastered them against her profile. "Get a move on."

With the captain's final word, Travion set to helping the crew, ignoring the screaming muscle in his shoulder. He could rest at port when everyone else was at ease.

Finn ran his fingers along his short-cropped hair as he stared at the Squid's Ink Tavern. The clever wooden sign with tentacles wrapped around the words hung by one hinge and shifted in the wind rolling off the harbor. The thunderous voices from within held a promise of flowing drinks and lively entertainment.

"Are you sure you wish to lodge here, Your Grace?" Finn murmured, curling his lip in distaste. Prior to joining the royal guard, he'd been a spoiled earl's son. And while he had no qualms about bloodying his hands, Finn preferred high-quality establishments.

"I'm not trekking across an island to find more adequate lodgings. This will do for the night. Unless a certain highbrow lordling disagrees?" The question earned a chuckle from his guard.

"Fair enough." Finn shook his head, eyeing the inn as if it would collapse at any moment. Travion had to admit, he wondered if a swift wind would send it crumbling to the docks. "This will do."

Sereia walked up beside him, still nursing her side, although she tried to hide the discomfort. "I've seen worse." She narrowed her eyes, truly assessing the building. "Been in much worse than this."

A shingle fell off the side, as if to prove how dilapidated it was. "Worse?" He considered the tavern again. The wooden siding had rotted in some places, there was a shattered window none had bothered to patch, and a well-fed rat nosed around a barrel of discarded food. "I am not comforted by that in the least." Somehow, the image of Sereia squatting on a floor-level chair surrounded by pots holding rainwater didn't soothe his doubts about this establishment.

Travion stepped forward and pushed the door open. He cleared his throat, peering over his shoulder. "After you, Captain."

She lifted a brow in response but went inside.

When he moved in behind her, a wall of heat rushed against his face. It was several degrees warmer and verged on stifling. But the fragrance of freshly baked bread and ale permeated the air, enticing him.

His stomach growled, needing sustenance, and his mind longed for the numbing influence of ale. So did his aching body. But this wasn't the time to fall into a tankard; his senses needed to remain sharp because there was no telling what danger lurked around the corner.

"There is bound to be talk about the recent attack. I'll have Finn and the *Speedwell*'s crew spread out to see what they can gather." He glanced around, taking in the cramped space of the tavern. Instead of smaller tables, there were half a dozen long, wooden tables lined with bench seats that were mostly occupied. There was a bar against the back with a row of empty stools in front.

"It's a sad day when we have to rely on the recountings of drunken sailors," Sereia offered with a sigh, then strode toward the bar.

Travion took up one of the empty stools, and from the corner of his eye, he saw Sereia shift and grimace as pain no doubt radiated up her ribs.

He frowned. "I'll see if I can find someone—"

"I just need a drink."

Travion rolled his eyes. "As much as I need one as well, I think you need a little more than alcohol."

"*Trask*, darling, I didn't take you for a nanny." She huffed, motioning for the barkeeper.

The barkeeper shuffled forward, lifting his bushy gray brows. He shrugged a shoulder after giving them a once over. "We only have two things here as far as drinks go. Hard or piss-like. We have fresh bread and chowder."

"Hard," Travion said at the same time as Sereia.

Her lips twitched into a hint of a smile. "Just bring the bottle."

Although it'd been a few moments, the notion Sereia thought him to be a nanny didn't settle well with Travion. He wasn't annoyed, but by the sea . . . a nanny?

Travion held up a finger. "Just to be clear. I'm not a nanny, but I know broken ribs well, and they can shift enough to pierce your lungs, which is a whole other world of hurt." He shook his head and glanced to the side, shifting to try to find a comfortable position. The sling chafed at his neck, and he growled, readying to rip it off.

Sereia poured herself a shot and downed it, wincing. "I don't think fighting with it is going to help," she said dryly.

"Thank you for pointing that out." He shot her a glare, then glanced up as a lanky male passed by. He had dark eyes, which contrasted with his porcelain skin, and pointed ears poked through raven hair. He was fae—all the way out here.

A fae this far out wasn't unheard of, but it was a rarity. The neighboring kingdoms weren't fond of any beings that weren't *human*. Magic was something mortals feared, always assuming fae would incite a war they couldn't help fight in.

Not that they were wrong, especially considering the current predicament.

Nevertheless, he grabbed a bottle of whiskey for himself and turned to the fae, who'd sat next to him.

"The seas have been unkind as of late, have they not?" Travion asked by way of greeting and took a moment to assess him more closely. He wore a loose linen shirt and a tight pair of breeches. Every angle on him was sharp, but there was a beautiful quality to him, and his full lips only enhanced it.

The other fae squinted at him, and suspicion crept into his gaze. "So I hear." He turned away from Travion and took up his drink, savoring it.

Sereia laughed, more than likely at the less-than-chatty fellow beside him. He shot her a rueful glance, but it softened as she drew in a sharp breath.

Casually dancing around a topic had never been one of Travion's strong suits. "Have you heard any word of healers in the area? Those who have an affinity for it, not mortal medicine. I'm in dire need of aid, as is my companion."

It took a moment for the male to glance at Travion again. "Do you have something against mortal medicine? It has benefited several travelers these past few days." He twisted around on his stool, readying to hop down and get away from Travion.

Unwilling to let the fae go, Travion grabbed him by the bicep, wincing as the skin pulled taut on his back. "But you are *not* mortal, and I asked a question."

He lowered his eyes to Travion's hand. "I do, but I don't believe it's wise to accost the only healer on this island."

Sereia slid off the stool and cut between them, pushing

Travion's arm down so he was forced to loosen his grip. "Don't mind Trask, he can be moody."

"Trask, is it?" The male's brow furrowed as he smoothed out his linen shirt. "Lefyr, at your service." He tipped forward as much as he could considering he was on a stool, bending in half as he swept into an awkward bow. Lefyr's eyes drifted to Sereia and lingered longer than Travion cared for. "Let me eat and I'll address your ribs."

Sereia cocked her head. "What?" Her tone sharpened. "How did you know?"

"Your breath keeps hitching." Lefyr leaned against the bar, his eyes flicking to the barkeeper. "A bowl of chowder, if you don't mind. And then"—he cast Travion a brief look of annoyance—"I'll heal you as well. Your shoulder is oozing."

Travion rubbed at his shoulder, and sure enough, his fingers came away damp with a hint of blood. He grumbled and motioned for the barkeeper. "May as well grab some of that bread and chowder for us as well."

"I'm assuming the sea wasn't kind to your lot," Lefyr murmured. "Was it?"

"No, it wasn't." Sereia poured herself another shot, then drank it down. "We took down a serpent the size of three ships."

"An entire scouting fleet from Midniva was taken out. And we fished someone from a wreck," Travion added. "If you're inclined to help, I'd prefer you to see the others first."

Lefyr's lips pressed into a grim line, and he nodded, focusing on his chowder. Steam billowed from the bowl, wafting toward Travion, teasing his stomach.

When the barkeeper placed his food down, Travion hastily plucked up a spoon. Lefyr chose that moment to find his voice. "Midniva," he drawled. "I was born there."

That answered the question as to where he was from.

Travion's mouth thinned. If he was born there, surely he knew he was the king? Depending on how old the male was, his guise could've easily been blown. "Truly? Small world. Whereabouts?" He shoved a spoonful of chowder into his mouth and felt Sereia's gaze on him.

"Caithaird." The capital city of Midniva. There was a slim chance that Lefyr didn't know who Travion was. Still, the male didn't grin knowingly at him.

"So then you know more about the troubles on the sea than most," Sereia cut in. "Have the locals seen anything else?"

"According to them, some have seen crabs the size of a cow. I've heard mention that either a woman or a man wearing a cloak, and they were seen carrying something bulky in their arms that seemed to hum with power just before the crabs appeared."

"That isn't...quite a description," Travion muttered.

"No. But some said they saw a man's pale face in the moonlight, and others, they saw a woman so beautiful it stunned them. But all of them did mention each one was holding something—either that bulky item or a piece of paper." Lefyr shrugged. "I wish I could offer more, but that is only what I have heard. You may have better luck asking around."

Travion tore a piece of bread in half and dipped it into the chowder. *Something bulky that hummed with power.* Did that translate into the book? "That clears everything up." He scoffed. What this meant was that there would be no retreating to a room, cleaning up, or sinking into the mattress. There was more to learn from this Lefyr.

"Did they say where they saw these mysterious figures

heading?" Sereia chimed in.

"Just that they remained close to the water." Lefyr dunked a piece of bread into his own chowder. "It's strange, though. The locals have a nightwatch, and when they went to inspect the beach, they didn't find a thing."

Travion sighed. Nothing could be so simple.

After eating, Lefyr rolled his sleeves up and moved to stand behind Sereia's stool. His hands hovered over her ribs, and his fingers flexed as if he were plucking on invisible strings. Sereia gasped, leaning forward, and dug her nails into the counter.

"I thought we agreed I'd be after the passengers," she rasped, glaring at him from beneath her long lashes.

"Yes, well, I have to walk by you first," Lefyr said all too cheerfully.

Sereia pulled coins from her pocket and left them on the counter. She slid from her perch with her typical grace and jerked her thumb in his direction. "Since you're feeling chipper, he took a small forest to his shoulder."

"So, that's why you're bleeding." Lefyr cocked his head. "I didn't take you for a lumberman."

Travion started to stand, but Lefyr carefully planted both hands on his shoulders, securing him in his seat.

"What did you do?" Lefyr locked eyes with him, and a surge of warm relief passed into Travion as the throbbing, dull pain eased little by little. When Lefyr was done, small circles formed beneath his eyes.

"Just tending to those in need," Travion added before fetching the remainder of the bottle of whiskey and polishing it off.

Lefyr smirked. "Lead the way to the ship, and I'll do my best."

Travion stood and crossed the room, noticing the *Speedwell*'s captain sitting by the door. The male glanced up at him as he walked by. "Drink up, Darragh," Travion murmured, unfastening a coin pouch at his hip and handing to him.

Sereia brushed past them, but before Travion left the tavern, he stopped Lefyr by barring his path. "I don't suppose I can bribe you into joining us on our travels," Travion drawled, but when the other male made no move to reply, he continued outside. The cool air rolled off the sea, whispering across his face and teasing strands of his hair.

"Depends on what the bribe entails," Lefyr eventually said, smiling like a cat about to pounce on a canary.

Travion shot Sereia a look. Annoyance rippled through him, but what were they to do when they were in need of a healer?

"More coin than you could ever dream of," Travion supplied.

Lefyr lifted his brows in interest. "I'll think on it."

Back on *The Saorsa*, Lefyr made his way to the unconscious naval officer. Chailai had done as much as she could, but she didn't have magic, and this man desperately needed that. Lefyr placed his hands over the man's chest, shaking his head. "He has so much water in him still," he said, more to himself than to Travion, Sereia, or even Chailai.

Soft blue lights danced along the man's chest, and a moment later, he coughed up water, spewing it onto the floor. He didn't rouse any more than that and laid back down.

"He will recover, but he does need to rest." His dark gaze swept from Sereia to Travion. "As should you. I'll continue tending to those who need it."

Travion nodded, then left the confines of Chailai's quarters. Sereia followed close on his heels. "You should get some rest." He crossed the ship's deck and climbed onto the dock. The moon's glow illuminated the port, and he spotted a small beach in the distance.

Sereia's hair whipped across her face, and she brushed the sea-tangled tresses away from her eyes. "You managed to find us a healer, well done."

His lips twitched into a small smile as he bent low and grabbed another stone. "Between the both of us, I figured it was necessary."

Sereia only nodded, then she, too, bent to pick up a stone. "Will you answer me a question?"

Travion paused mid-throw and twisted to look at her. She was watching him closely—too closely for his liking. "That depends on what the question is." He lobbed the stone into the water but didn't bother to watch it skate across the waves. His eyes were trained on Sereia's features. The smile tightened, and tension crept in.

"Why have you not married yet?"

A laugh unwillingly bubbled out of him. Perhaps from surprise or the notion that Sereia was the one inquiring about marriage. Still, the question was much like a punch to the gut. He hadn't married at all in three millennia. His reasons were fair enough: too damaged, too busy, too unwilling to compromise. There were a thousand things he could have said, but in the end, he stuck with the truth.

"It was never expected of me, and with a named heir to Midniva already, I didn't see a point in it." He shrugged and chanced a look in her direction. A pensive expression knit her brow. Of course she'd wonder why the hell he proposed to her then. "There are other ways to achieve political balance than marrying someone you cannot stomach. I never wanted to force you into marriage."

And he meant it. By the sea, didn't she know that by now?

"Then why did you agree?" she asked softly, her gaze never wavering from his.

"I had my terms," he said as he walked down the dock and smiled at the memory. "If in three months, you still refused me, the arrangement was off. I was so certain of myself by the end of month three, but ah . . ."

They wound their way down to the beach, and when Travion's boots touched the sand, he crouched to pick up a rock and lobbed it.

"Have you bothered to look for anyone, or have you become complacent in your bachelorhood?"

Perhaps if the question had come from anyone else, he would have been annoyed at the probing. But given that it was coming from Sereia, who fully possessed his heart, it amused him. In one hundred years, he'd learned the steps to the seductive but heartbreaking dance between them. He'd learned how to guard himself, prepare for the inevitable departure, but he knew what to expect—that one day she'd leave and never return with his heart.

"Complacent," he echoed with a chuckle. "Hardly. I stopped looking one hundred years ago." There was little point concealing the truth of how he felt about her. At this point, Travion had nothing to lose.

14

Sereia

Inwardly, Sereia's heart stopped, then began racing faster than a bob of seals hurtling toward land to avoid a shark. Her parents had never once mentioned the agreement between them. As far as they—and Sereia herself—were concerned, the betrothal had been made with the king, and so long as she lived in Midniva, the marriage would be taking place.

When Travion had proposed, Sereia really felt that she had no choice but to flee the kingdom. Had she realized she had a say in the matter, they could have ended on better terms.

Outwardly, she remained calm, leaning in against him, his arm snaking around her waist to hold her.

He'd stopped looking. Was this Travion's way of saying he loved her, or that he had simply given up on the idea of marriage after his one shot with her?

He'd never actually said the words to her. Not after their heated sessions of tumbling with one another, and not even when he proposed. Each time she returned to port, Travion had been there to receive her without question and without hesitation. But while they shared his bed and their bodies, they did not share words or feelings.

At one point, about fifty years ago, Sereia had been ready to voice her thoughts on the matter. To tell Travion why she had leaped from that cliff, why she hadn't been ready for marriage—that she loved him. But when she'd begun to speak, he'd cut her off, pressing kisses to her lips.

She'd never broached the topic with him again.

Sereia hated to show weakness. Vulnerability was the worst kind of weakness, when anyone would take it as a sign of her being unfit for her command. A mere lady of the court who set sail thinking she belonged to the high seas. It should have been different to reveal her vulnerabilities to Travion, but after everything that had taken place between them, it felt like leaping over a ravine without knowing what was on the other side.

"I've never been tempted into it by anyone else, either." She could have added "except for you," but that was as much of an admission as she was willing to give right now.

Sereia rolled the flat stone over in her hand, smoothing a thumb over one silken side, then pulled her arm back and let loose the stone, watching it sail through the air and skip over the surface.

"We haven't slept much in the past few days. We should head back to the inn," Travion suggested, breaking the silence that had fallen between them.

Sereia only murmured in agreement, pulling away for the walk back. Being with Travion consistently and for so long was making her wish that she could take the leap. Even while they had courted, they hadn't really been able to see what life together could be like. Not like this. They had argued over the last week, but they had also begun to learn about each other. It made Sereia long to spill her secrets. Unleash all of her fears and hopes upon him. But there were monsters to kill and shields to keep up.

From the beach, they climbed rocks that led up to narrow streets. Small, weathered homes made of clay nestled on either side, their seagrass thatched roofs requiring repair. There was no glass in their windows, only wooden shutters, which revealed their large cracks by the amount of light filtering out through them. In the doorway of one home, a small, grubby child stood, stick in hand. His clothes were tattered and ill-fitting. Most likely stolen, or old hand-me-downs already worn by many siblings and cousins. There wasn't a lot of extra or new around these parts. Parents were more invested in trying to feed their children than clothing them in fresh garments.

Much like the inn they were staying in, Saventi itself was worn and ready to fall down around itself. The feudal lord who governed the entire island of Propentri took all that he could from the people and left them with barely enough to see themselves through. Though a nation that owed its allegiance to Tribonik, it was offered no help or resources, only forced to pay tithes.

While coming to port in Saventi wouldn't get Sereia lynched, it took everything within her not to force her way into Lord Alekhin's home and slit his throat.

Sereia watched as Travion stopped and pulled a coin from his pocket, flicking it into the hands of the small boy, who caught it with a glowing smile on his face.

As they continued walking, Sereia slid her arm through

Travion's and leaned upon him a little. "Something's been niggling at my mind . . ."

"Yes?" He looked down at her.

"Lefyr mentioned rumors of a man or a woman along the waters during the attacks . . . What are the chances we find anything helpful here? I am assuming we'll be tracking the witnesses down and questioning them ourselves?"

Travion sighed. "We will. People are confused, which either means no one here has witnessed it firsthand or we are dealing with more than one person controlling The Creaturae. With any luck, tomorrow, the locals can be persuaded to speak the truth."

"Be prepared to loosen tongues with a little help from coin. Nothing speaks to the desperate more than something that will help alleviate their need."

Travion nodded.

"Should we rent horses tomorrow?" They'd reached the inn, and she grabbed the door, stepping back to hold it for him. He quirked a brow at her, and she quirked one back at him.

"Yes. I'm not keen on walking the length of the entire island."

Inside, Adrik sat in a back booth, a couple of hired girls on either side of him. He appeared to be blissful and content. The only other crew members who had not yet retired for the night were Finn and Yon, who sat together at a table before the large fireplace. Each clasped a tankard of ale. Neither said a word, but both stared contemplatively down at the flickering flames. Although they didn't acknowledge it, Sereia got the sense that both were more than aware she and Travion had returned.

Neither she nor Travion waited around to chat. Having already booked rooms earlier, they instead mounted the stairs to the chambers above. Sereia stopped at her room and pulled her key from the pocket of her vest to unlock the door. Stepping into the room, she kicked the door shut with her heel, slamming it in Travion's face.

She heard him grunt on the other side and smirked to herself. It was hard not to torment him, even just a little.

"Suppose that's a goodnight then," he muttered to himself, which made her smirk broaden.

Sereia waited only a heartbeat before she turned back around and opened the door. Travion had already turned away, ready to head back downstairs and request another room for himself.

"Where are you going? Get your ass in the room." He paused at her words, turning back to look at her. "My apologies, *please* come into my room, Your Majesty."

Travion wasted no time, taking her about the waist and hoisting her up onto his hips. This time, it was he who kicked the door shut. "Why must you be so trying?" he growled.

"It makes the ravishing all the better."

Travion chuckled and then carted her across the room, where he unceremoniously dumped her onto the bed. "Shall I swat your bottom for such behavior?"

Sereia's eyes narrowed. "You can certainly try."

He was upon her quickly, his kisses wringing moans from her lips. She unbuttoned his vest, divesting him of it. In turn, Travion's fingers moved to the buckles of her leather corset, making quick work of unfastening them, and Sereia lifted her hips from the bed so he could pull it out from under her.

With the corset gone, Travion hurriedly pulled her linen shirt up over her head and tossing it over his shoulder. His darkened blue eyes traveled over her bare flesh, and her toes curled at the lust she saw there. Travion's firm hands pressed her thighs apart so he could kneel between them, and then his lips captured one hardened peak.

Sereia's hands moved into his hair, holding him against her as her hips lifted involuntarily from the mattress.

He did not disappoint her, pressing his thumb to her, finding the needy bundle of nerves through her trousers, and rubbing with just enough friction to make her whine for more.

"By the sea, Travion," she panted. "Don't tease."

He chuckled darkly against her skin, tugging at her nipple with his teeth. He then lifted his head to look at her with such pride and devilment she felt herself grow even slicker with want. "I thought tormenting made the ravishing all the better?"

Sereia growled as her words were thrown back at her, and grabbed his face, pulling him up to her lips. The kiss was a clash of wills, tongues warring for dominance and pulling moans from both of them. In a frenzy, the rest of their clothes were discarded, and Travion had flipped Sereia onto her stomach before she had a chance to react. Grabbing her by the thighs, he pulled her up onto her knees, and then, in fact, did lay a stinging slap to her ass.

Sereia gasped, her cheek pressed into the bedding, muffling the sound a little.

"You are going to pay for that." Two fingers were thrust into her suddenly, cutting off anything else she could have said as a groan of pleasure left her instead, and she ground back against his hand.

"Is that so?" he taunted, voice thick with desire. Slowly, he stroked her, crooking his fingers in just the right way to hit her internal spot.

Sereia shut her eyes. The slick sounds of his actions and her own heavy panting were the only sounds in the room. Travion leaned over her and pressed kisses down her spine, nipping roughly between her shoulder blades.

Hissing once more, Sereia opened her eyes to peer up at him. "Enough teasing."

"What do you say?" He stroked her faster and deeper, making her body quiver. And yet, she needed more.

"Now," she growled.

Travion's eyes darkened, and instead of giving her what she demanded, he pressed a third finger into her, stretching her further. The burn made her whine, her lips parting to haul in more air.

"By sea and shore, *please!*" Travion growled triumphantly at her plea and withdrew his fingers. The loss left her empty and aching. He did not enter her right away, however, just brushed the tip of himself through her slick heat, gliding against the bud that throbbed greedily there. "Travion," Sereia grumbled, her frustration mounting.

He didn't make her wait any longer. He entered her in one long stride, driving her up the bed a little and making her cry out in pleasure. No one had ever filled her so perfectly as he did, stretching her just enough to make her aware of it.

Travion's first retreat was slow, a gradual glide almost fully out of her, and then a sharp return that pushed her forward once more and made her body quake from the force. Sereia raised herself up onto one hand and pressed the other to the wall before them, using it to brace herself so that she could experience the full force of each thrust.

Behind her, Travion panted, and when his hands moved to clutch her hips tightly, fingers pressing into the flesh, Sereia could feel how they trembled with his own need.

She looked back over her shoulder, their eyes meeting in the short distance between. His skin was flushed, his auburn hair falling down into his eyes. He was both fierce and beautiful, and Sereia had never wanted anything more. "Don't hold back, Your Majesty."

Travion's eyes flickered with the challenge. "As you wish."

The pace he set for them struck forcefully and quickly inside her, leaving Sereia unable to do more than cry in pleasure and brace herself. Each snap of his hips against her bottom a sharp sting that only added to the pleasure building within.

When she thought she could take no more, he reached around to press his fingers against her clit, pinching it between thumb and forefinger. That action sent Sereia spiraling. She cried out, not caring who else heard, and let the wave of her pleasure wash through her. Travion's thrusts quickened, his own breathing labored, and he, too, was moaning harshly as he spent himself inside her.

Together, they collapsed onto the bed, sweaty and panting.

Turning her head, Sereia kissed him slowly, letting their breath mingle and his scent fill her nose. "That was not an incentive to behave," she whispered as their lips parted.

"It wasn't meant to be." He smirked and kissed her brow.

Even after a busy day and late night, Sereia still woke up early, as did Travion. After dressing in a white linen shirt that fell off her shoulders, with the pendant nestled against the swell of her breasts, and a pair of dark blue trousers, Sereia headed for her door. Yon stood on the other side, her swords crossed at her back, black hair tied in a topknot.

"We're coming with you."

"We?" Sereia asked. Somehow, despite not mentioning their plans to Yon, she was evidently not only aware of what was going on but had properly gauged the time at which Sereia would rise.

She should be concerned with how well Yon knew her.

"Finn," Yon responded. "We're not leaving you and His Grace to go out scouting on your own."

Sereia felt Travion step up behind her before he spoke. "Are we not to be trusted on our own?"

"No, you're not." It was Finn, coming down the hall from his room.

Clearly, some talking *had* taken place between the two of them at the fireplace last night, as they'd managed to plan this bombardment.

"Well, let us at least eat before we head out." Sereia slipped past Yon and headed down the stairs to the tavern below.

While they waited for their breakfast to be served, Sereia caught the arm of the innkeeper's wife. "Do you happen to know who in town we could speak to about the giant crab sightings?" The elderly woman eyed her suspiciously, and Sereia pulled a coin from her pocket and held it out to her. "We would greatly appreciate your help."

The woman took the coin, and though she didn't look any

less suspicious, she answered. "You're going to want to speak with Yergin Ologov."

"Where can we find him?"

"Go down the lane to the right when you head out the door, and at the next lane, turn left. His home is the one with the black dog tied out front."

"Thank you."

Once they finished their hearty breakfast, the foursome stepped out into the bright morning sunlight. The sunshine should have made the village of Saventi more appealing. Unfortunately, all it did was highlight the truly impoverished state of the homes and buildings around them.

"Do their leaders not care about the state they are in?" Travion asked as they turned right.

"The mortal on the throne in Tribonik cares only about the tithes his lords send him from their districts. As long as he has what he feels he is owed, he doesn't care what becomes of his people."

Travion shook his head, a muscle in his jaw ticking. "A king is meant to be a caretaker, not a tyrant."

And that was why the people of Midniva were so fortunate and lived good lives. Travion hadn't come to the middle realm with the desire to rule with an iron fist and steal everything from his people to fill his belly and his coffers. He'd come to help and protect them. Sereia had traveled the seas and had never found a ruler who cared for their people nearly as much as Travion did.

The home of Yergin Ologov was just as decrepit as all the ones that had come before it and was made only sadder looking by the mangy old black dog out front. It was tied with weathered rope about the neck and tethered to a hook on the side of the house. The animal whined as they approached, and Sereia wondered how long it had been since it had eaten.

As she and Travion stepped up to the door, Sereia could hear the bustle of someone moving around inside and voices. When Travion knocked, a hush fell over the house, and it took long enough for someone to answer that she started to wonder if they were going to at all.

When the door opened, it was to reveal a woman in her middle years, with graying hair and a faded floral dress. Her dark brown eyes scanned them both over, then narrowed. "Yes?"

"We're looking to speak with Yergin Ologov, please," Travion informed her.

"Who're you?" She looked from him to Sereia once more, and then her eyes flicked up to their ears. Sereia saw the wariness build in her eyes.

"We're trying to track down the being responsible for the atrocious attacks happening at sea and now along the coast. We just want to know what he may know about the giant crabs that were spotted."

The door was suddenly wrenched open even wider, and an angry looking man stood behind the woman. "What business is it of yours what I've seen or not seen?" he growled, glaring at them.

From the corner of her eye, Sereia saw Yon shift closer to her.

Travion held up his hand. "We would greatly appreciate—"

"We'll pay you," Sereia cut him off, elbowing Travion in the side.

Yergin eyed her. "How much?" Travion held out his hand with an offering of coins. Yergin looked and then reached out to accept the coin. However, he didn't step back so they could enter the dwelling. "What do you want to know?"

"Did you see the crabs coming from the sea?" Travion asked.

He nodded. "Huge as a bull. Came out of the water and attacked a herd of sea lions. Pinchers cut them right in two."

"Bloody hell," Sereia cursed softly.

"Was there anyone around? We've been told that some have seen a man while others have spotted a woman near the beach at the time of the crab sighting."

Yergin shook his head. "I just saw the crab. You want to talk to Borsik. He saw someone strange when they came at night."

"Where can we find this Borsik?" Travion asked.

Yergin lifted a hand and pointed down the lane. "Keep going that way until you come to the end, then turn right. Up the hill to the house at the top."

"How will we know we're at the right one?"

Yergin scoffed. "It's at the top."

Helpful. "One last thing," Sereia cut in. "Where were you when you saw the crab?"

"Two miles north of here, on a beach filled with rocks."

"You've been most helpful," Travion murmured, and together, they stepped away from the door.

"Borsik?" she asked him.

Travion nodded. "If we can find him."

With Yon and Finn at their backs, ever watchful, they headed down the long lane, passing more homes in shambles. At the end of the lane, they turned right and began to walk up the steep hill. The homes had ended, and instead, there was a browning hill dotted with tombstones, and one scraggly looking crab apple tree that did not appear to bear any blossoms.

Yergin's words about them knowing what home it was made sense as they crested the hill. It was the only building around. Though, to call it a home was an exaggeration. "Shack" would be more appropriate. The holes between the wood boards would allow not only the wind to enter the residence but several small animals as well.

The roof, which was also made of wood slabs, had several holes that were covered with seaweed and grass patches.

"This village saddens and depresses me," Finn muttered behind them.

"Welcome to Tribonik, where only the truly wealthy can survive." Sereia shook her head. Perhaps Travion should sweep the middle realm over and stake his claim to all of it. The only ones who would lose would be the worthless rotters sitting in places of power.

This time when Travion knocked on the door, they were met with the sound of cursing from inside, several thumps, and a shuffling noise before the door opened wide. An old man with a wrinkled face and sparse white hair over his head peered out at them, squinting at the bright morning sunlight.

"I've got nothin' worth stealin'!" he shouted and moved to shut the door.

Travion was faster and shoved his hand against the door to keep it from closing. "And we have no desire to take." This time he was prepared and simply held out the coin. "We just want some information."

Borsik took the coin and then used all of his weight to shove the door closed. Travion growled, and Sereia huffed. They looked at each other, and with silent understanding, both of them drove a shoulder into the door at the same time, sending it falling off the hinges.

As the door crashed to the floor, dust filled the inside of the house, almost like smoke. A shocked Borsik stood staring at them, wide-eyed and coughing.

Travion and Sereia stepped farther into the shack as a united front. Finn dipped his head low to walk in behind them, and finally, Yon followed, stopping just behind Sereia, to the side.

"I believe I paid you, and I'd appreciate getting my coin's worth."

Still coughing, Borsik waved the dust away from his face and moved to sit down at the one small table and rickety chair in the room. "Fine," he rasped. "What is it you want?"

"I need a description of the being you saw just before the giant crabs came out of the water." Travion stood not too far from Borsik, looking down at him intently.

Sereia took the knife out of her boot and stood tapping it on her palm—just a little added incentive for him to be honest and to be quick about it.

Borsik looked between the two of them apprehensively before his eyes landed on Finn, who had to tip his head down a little to properly fit inside his shack. "All I saw was a figure, didn't see no face. Don't know if it was a man, woman, or fae." He pointed at Travion, indicating his ears. "But . . ." He drifted off, becoming distracted as he stared at Yon. "My, she's a tiny one, isn't she? Rather opposites with this walking tree over here." He nodded at Finn.

"But?" Sereia pushed, voice heavy with irritation and impatience.

Borsik shook his head. "Didn't see a face but felt a strange hum in the air. Like a spell was goin' to be cast, or one of you strange fae was manipulatin' somethin'." His eyes narrowed on them, as if at any moment, Sereia or Travion would begin doing "strange fae" magic.

"Was this figure holding a book?" Travion pressed.

Brosik's brow furrowed, and he fell silent, looking to be in thought. His fingertips drummed on the table. "May have been a book . . ." he mused more to himself than to them.

"Where did you see this person?" Sereia asked, fighting back another growl. She hated the fact he seemed to be dawdling so much.

"If you take the road out of town headin' north, the crabs come up along the coast. Not a rhyme nor reason when they show. Some have gone an' see nothin' at all, others have passed and barely made it out alive. It's like somethin's lyin' in wait, watchin' for somethin' in particular to set them off."

Sereia and Travion shared another look. "Thank you for your time," Travion said briskly. "We'll leave you to the rest of your morning. Best of luck with the door."

Both Yon and Finn waited until Sereia and Travion had passed outside before they left the house. On his way out, Finn was kind enough to pick the door up and rest it against the wall for Borsik, then he ducked his way back out into the sunshine.

"Well, I say our best course of action is to get back into town, hire some horses, and head north." Sereia slid her knife back into the top of her boot.

Travion nodded. "I agree. We've got a heading, there's no sense wasting more time here in the village."

As the four set back down the hill, heading into the main part of the village once more, Sereia decided information gathering was not her favorite task and she was very glad she had Yon to typically do this for her.

She looked over her shoulder. "How do you do this for me all the time?"

Yon's head tipped slightly to the side. "What, Captain?"

"This." Sereia motioned back to Borsik's shack and then in the rough direction of Yergin's home. "Seeking out tidbits of information and dealing with the likes of them."

Yon's hand disappeared and then reappeared with a small jade-handled knife, which she spun around her hand before grasping it carefully to rest with blade edge against her throat. "There are more entertaining ways to get information than paying with coin."

Finn coughed at this announcement, and at her side, Travion chuckled darkly. "Now that is a sentiment I can support."

"We can*not* get banned from another port," Sereia warned them both. Though a smirk bent her lips at the edge. She had to agree with them, even if silently.

Beside their inn sat a stable, and with a more than fair portion of coin, they were able to hire four relatively healthy looking steeds to take them on the road out of Saventi. Sereia fell in beside Travion as they rode down the dirt-packed street, leaving Yon and Finn to take up a protective and watchful position at their back. Both Adrik and Captain Darragh had been given instructions to see to any ship needs for both *The Saorsa* and HMS *Speedwell*. They would need to be ready to return to the sea at a moment's notice.

As they left the village behind them, the morning grew hotter. Bright sunshine beat down upon their shoulders and there was not a cloud in the sky to offer any relief. The cry of gulls came in off the water, and the scent of salt wafted in on the gentle breeze. Despite the heat, it was a good day to be traveling, by either land or sea. Sereia was not displeased to be atop a horse rather than on her ship.

The northern road they followed was well worn from travelers, and it curved along the coastline. Salt damaged trees lined the roadway. Their tall, skinny trunks were barren until the very top, where lush green leaves blew in the gentle summer breeze. The coastline was rugged, the side of the road giving way to rocks and small cliffs falling down into the deep blue sea that surrounded the island.

"So, is it our hope that something simply crawls from the sea into our laps or that we stumble upon someone looking suspiciously devious?" Sereia lifted her voice and glanced over at Travion.

He shook his head but shot her a slightly mischievous look. "I suppose I was counting on your habit of finding misadventure wherever you go."

She eyed him. "What makes you think I have a habit of misadventure?"

"Krakens, sea serpents, burning ships?" He glanced up at the sky as if trying to recall more happenings.

"Now, I would not label those as a mis-anything. Those were a delight, plain and simple, m'lord." She grinned at him, and he returned it.

"We'll look for the beach Yergin mentioned," he added more seriously. "And perhaps, if you don't mind getting wet, you can dive in to check in the water to see if there are any signs of disturbances."

Sereia nodded. "I can do that." There was an odd sense of pleasure trickling through her that she didn't necessarily want to admit to, but which absolutely came from the fact he had said *she* could and not *we*.

By the time the noonday sun was in the sky, they had

made their way quite far along the coast with nary a sight to be had. They passed through a small collection of shanties, some nestled on the rocks and some built on stilts leading out to small wharfs. Not enough to be considered a town, just a group of people who supported and protected each other. They did not take kindly to the sight of four strangers —and three fae, at that—very fondly, but at least they responded to questions when asked. The beach they were looking for was only another half-hour journey ahead of them.

As they came out on the other side of the shanties, they spotted an older gentleman who had just pulled his small boat ashore and flipped it over on the beach so it wouldn't wash away. He spat on the ground near his feet as their party pulled up before him on the road. Dressed in a worn looking button-up cotton shirt and slacks rolled up to his knees, Sereia could tell he was not wealthy. His skin was tanned almost to the point of leather, which not even the cotton hat with a small brim on his head could help to protect at this point.

"We've not got any extra fish for you," he called out in a gruff tone, speaking the native Tribonik language with a little bit of island flare. Fortunately, it was a language Sereia had well mastered.

"We're not looking to claim any of your fish. Alekhin steals enough from your pockets and nets as it is." Together, she and the old man spat on the ground at mention of the lord. "We're searching for a foreigner, possibly a fae, who may have been seen carrying an old tome. They would have been spotted just before or after the emergence of the giant crabs that have been attacking as of late."

The man stared at Sereia as if she possessed six heads.

"You're the only foreigners I see about these parts." He then tossed his small catch of fish over his shoulder and headed down the road, back toward the shanties.

Travion grumbled. "I think I caught enough to understand he was of no help."

Sereia sighed, feeling hot and underwhelmed by their findings. "No help at all." The noonday sun only seemed to be intensifying. A dive into the ocean to search for crabs could not come soon enough.

"Well, there's nothing to do but continue on," Travion muttered, sighing his own frustration. "The beach isn't far now."

Using her knees to keep her seat on the horse as they began moving once more, Sereia gathered her long hair up on top of her head and knotted it with a spare piece of string she had tied around her wrist just for this purpose. With some relief from the sea breeze now blowing against the back of her neck, she relaxed a little.

Her muscles strained, and her bottom ached from riding in a saddle for the first time in months, but it was a pleasant ache. It reminded her of the burn in her arms after a proper sword fight, when she battled for not only her own life but the safety of her ship and crew. While the purpose of this journey was strained and tragic, Sereia was glad she was taking it with Travion. To properly see him as a king, the way he pushed himself to protect what was his responsibility . . . They were the same, in more ways than she had ever realized.

The calm did not last. They had not ridden very far when Travion stiffened beside her, and it instantly put Sereia on edge. She followed his gaze out to the water and saw what had caught his attention.

Across the rocks exposed by the receding tide, giant green crabs made their way toward them. Seven in total. Just as the villagers had warned, they were each as big as a dairy cow with claws the size of a large sow. Black beady eyes peered maliciously over the beach, and the click of their scuttling legs over the stones sounded like a blacksmith's hammer falling on an anvil.

"Bloody hell!" Travion growled at the same time Sereia exclaimed, "By the Sea!"

She looked over at Travion. "Please tell me you can communicate with these things and order them back into the water?"

In response, Travion squinted, and a look of concentration came over him before he finally shook his head. "All I'm getting is a sense of hunger. There is no turning them back."

Sereia cursed.

"Your Grace, they don't appear to be slowing down," Finn called out.

"What do you say about battling crabs large enough to pinch you nearly in two?" he asked her rather than responding to Finn. His blue eyes sparked with both frustration and excitement.

"I say, what are we waiting for?" Throwing her leg over the horse, she withdrew the sword from her hip as she slid quickly to the ground.

Behind her, Yon was already on the ground, both of her swords pulled free from the scabbards on her back.

Sereia raced over the pebbly beach toward the first crab. The creature's black eyes focused on the fresh meal approaching, and it reached for her with its pincer. Sereia raised her sword in a two-handed grip, blocking the attack. Her blade scraped along the outer curve, setting off sparks and a ring of metal. Narrowly ducking the clutch of the second claw, Sereia stepped just out of reach, striking once more with her sword. The sharp blade made the barest of chips in the hard shell.

"How are we to kill the damn things?" she shouted quickly, muscles straining as she pushed away another attack. Sereia took a moment to search for Travion in the throng and nearly lost her head to another crab behind her.

"Captain, *duck!*" came a shout from Yon, and having learned to trust her entirely, Sereia dropped to her knees and rolled beneath the crab in front of her.

The move confused both crabs, the one above her scuttling to the side in search of its prey. Sereia rolled to her left, her elbow painfully digging into rocks and shells that slit her open, and narrowly missed being speared by a sharp crab foot in the process.

Shooting to her feet once more, Sereia brandished her sword and ignored the torn sleeve of her shirt, now dripping with blood.

"They've got to have a weak spot somewhere," Travion shouted out to them all, ducking beneath a claw coming his way. He managed to lodge the tip of his blade in the joint of one front leg only to have another crab approach him from behind.

"Behind you!" Sereia shouted, but she didn't have time to see how he made out. The crab closest to her turned at her voice and snapped forward with its claw. Sereia leaped back quickly, but the tips of the claw caught her side, tearing shirt and flesh alike, and she tripped over a large rock, tumbling onto her back.

Wincing from the screaming protest of her spine against stone and the searing throb of her fresh wound, Sereia swung out with her sword as the crab moved to loom over her, hissing threateningly. She blocked the first strike of its claw and rolled just out of the way of the second, feeling the brush of it against her neck.

Panting with adrenaline and desperation, Sereia thrust her sword upward, aiming for its mouth—and stabbing clear through and up into its head.

The crab released another softer hissing noise, and a large white bubble popped from its mouth before its legs folded beneath it, and it dropped.

"Curse the seas!" Sereia shouted as the crab's weight landed on her, pinning her legs and part of her torso to the beach.

It was a crushing weight that impacted her diaphragm and reduced her breathing to short, shallow pants. Yanking her sword free of the crab's mouth, she dropped it beside her. Placing her hands on the underside edge of the shell, Sereia pushed, groaning through her teeth as the weight barely shifted. Sharp clips sounded against the rocks around her, and the shadow of a second crab blocked the hot sun above.

Sereia had just enough wiggle room to roll her head and shoulders out of the way of its strike but felt the graze of claw against her neck. Frantically grabbing her sword, Sereia raised it to protect her head, blocking another attack. But without the ability to free herself from the dead crab, she was as good as lost.

The beast grabbed onto her sword with one claw, pulling it from her hand, and struck with the second. Sereia could only lift her arms up and wait for the deathblow to land.

However, it never came.

A hard grunt sounded, causing Sereia to open her eyes to find Finn above, pushing the crab claw away with his hand.

Angrily, the crab lashed out and grasped Finn's thigh with its free pincer. He gasped in pain but punched forward into the crab's dark black eye. The creature released an ear-splitting sound of pain and released him.

Panting, Finn brushed the back of his hand across his forehead and plucked his sword back up from the beach, then advanced on the crab. For such a large fae, he was swift and moved inside the crab's reach before it had a chance to react. With a roar of anger and a flex of savage strength, Finn flipped the crab over onto its back, and amidst its frantic waving legs, drove his sword down through the weak abdominal shell.

The crab jerked violently, and then stopped moving.

"Well that's one way to do it," Sereia said, peering up at the tall fae now panting over her.

Without missing a beat, Finn was at her side, gripping the edge of her dead crab and lifting so that she was able to slide out from under it.

"Are you alright, Captain?"

"Much better now," Sereia grunted as she rose to her feet. "Thanks for the assistance, Finn."

Travion's guard nodded, then swung around to fend off the advance of a third crab.

Beyond him, Yon was being pulled out from beneath the legs of a crab she had just killed by yet another crab that had caught her ankle. The creature lifted her into the air, and Yon dangled, both swords crossed before her. As the crab lashed out at her with its free claw, she blocked it with the cross of her swords, shoving it back, but cried out as the beast clenched her ankle more severely.

Sereia raced to her aid, darting around a small boulder. Lifting her sword above her head, she brought the blade down on the weakest point of the crab's arm, the first joint before the claw. The crab hissed as the shell cracked, but her sword didn't go through.

When it swung Yon violently through the air and turned on her, Sereia leaped to the side, trying to keep away from its face and second claw so she was able to make another harsh chop at the joint. This time, her blade went clean through, and the claw as well as Yon fell to the ground.

The creature forgot Sereia's crumpled assassin and instead advanced on her. Had she not thought the thing was just hungry, Sereia would have sworn there was vengeance glowing in the depths of its dark eyes.

Prepared, Sereia blocked the swinging claw, distracting it, while Yon climbed to her feet and, ignoring her injured ankle, launched herself at the crab's legs, then swung herself up onto its back. Sereia parried another strike from the claw and kicked out with her foot, connecting with one of the crab's eyes.

Kneeling on its back, Yon clung on as the crab reared up, trying to shake her off. To help her, Sereia swung at the other arm. When the beast settled its front feet back on the ground, Yon struck, driving one of her swords deep into a weak spot just above its mouth. The crab shuddered and crashed to the rocks.

Yon fell forward from the force, and Sereia opened her arms to catch her, the two of them tumbling to the ground.

"And that's another way to do it." Sereia groaned through the burning pain in her side.

With no time to waste, Yon rolled off of her, and the two of them climbed to their feet. Sereia pressed a hand to the wound in her side, and Yon leaned most of her weight on her right foot, favoring the injured left.

There were three crabs left. Travion, blood coating his back and coursing down the side of his face from a wound in his hairline, faced off with one of them. He blocked its attacks with his own sword as it rose up on its back four legs, ready to fight but exposing its underbelly. He did not hesitate but fought his way past two legs and claws to spin inside its guard, then impaled it on his sword.

Trusting Finn to finish the one fast approaching him, Sereia headed for the third, Yon joining her. There was no need to talk. While Sereia stepped in front of it, her sword ringing against the hard shell of claws, Yon dove between its legs, positioning herself just beneath it.

With Sereia once again acting as distraction, the beady black eyes leering down at her, Yon was able to thrust one sword up into the crab's belly and swiftly thrust the other into the beach. This acted as a prop, so when the monster crashed down, its shell struck the handle of her sword and tipped sideways, leaving Yon free to roll out from under it.

When at last the cast of crabs had been slaughtered, their large hulking forms already attracting scads of hungry gulls, the four of them stood looking sweaty, spent, and stinking of shellfish.

"I've never wanted to bathe so badly in my life," Sereia muttered, sniffing at her thoroughly stained shirt.

"We could always slather you in some butter and garlic and call you a feast," Travion taunted, breathless.

Eyeing him, Sereia shook her head. "You've spent too much time with your youngest brother of late, haven't you?" Though she could admit, standing there with his auburn hair plastered to his forehead, stains of battle across his cheek, and a slightly torn shirt, she was tempted to lead him off to a bush and see them both satisfied.

Perhaps it was the after-affects of battle or the adrenaline still racing through her veins, but Sereia could never find her fill of him.

Tearing the tattered bottom of her shirt off, Sereia wrapped it around her waist, binding her wound to stem the flow of blood.

15

Travion

Travion sucked in a breath of precious air and flicked a hunk of shell from his torn shirt. He frowned as he glanced down at Sereia's waist. "Are you okay to continue on, or should we bother Lefyr?"

"I'm okay to press on," Sereia offered with ease, and Travion didn't miss the way her eyes tightened, as if she expected him to call off the rest of the day and haul her back to Lefyr over his shoulder.

And maybe a part of him wanted to, but she was holding her own, and he respected that.

"How about you two?" He jerked his head toward Finn and Yon, who were just as breathless and caked in blood as him.

"I'm fine," the two said in unison, then grinned at one another.

"A moment to catch our breaths then." Travion grimaced and placed his hands on his hips. He chuckled as he tilted his head back. "I think this journey has aged me another millennia."

Sereia teasingly reached out and flicked a strand of his bloodied hair out of his face. "Is that a gray I spy?"

He narrowed his eyes, catching her wrist. "Never."

A strong wind blew off the water, sending grains of sand tumbling over the crabs. In a day's time, the creatures would start to rot and attract more than just the gulls. The seabirds were already crowding the shore, and who knew what else would pick up the scent? Wild cats, wolves, and if hungry enough, possibly a feral griffin.

The crabs confirmed what Travion had suspected all along —the book had a part in the discord. In his youth, his father had summoned small dragons from their caves. They had been lizards, no larger than an alley cat, but with the book, he spelled them to grow, and grow they did. Until the dragons were the size of the palace.

But his father was *dead*. He and his brothers had killed him themselves. They'd scattered his body across the realms, ensuring no one could retrieve and attempt to resurrect him.

After they'd all recovered their breath, Travion gestured toward the fallen crustaceans. "We should bring the carcasses back to the tavern." They were still standing beside the slain overgrown crabs, and knowing how destitute the locals were, he figured they could use the meat.

Finn lifted his pale blond brows.

Sereia shrugged. "It's better for them to use it than have it go to waste." The wind tousled her hair, whipping it across her face, and Travion knew he had never seen a more beautiful fae. Despite the flecks of meat clinging to her blood-soaked blouse and the sweat from battle dripping down her cheek, the sight of her still stole his breath away.

"This would feed plenty of patrons, and the owner

doesn't have to spend a coin." Travion flicked a hunk of shell off his torn linen shirt.

"I know." Sereia groaned, her shoulders sagging. "The townsfolk in general could desperately use a feed like this. Perhaps put a little meat on those starving bones. But by the sea, how will we get them back?"

Travion hadn't thought that far. His eyes flicked to the water and the choppy waves. Buoys bobbed back and forth. "There are traps just off the shore. We can cut the lines from them." He didn't want to disturb someone else's livelihood, but they hadn't trekked out with ropes and lacked enough clothing to fashion into tethers.

Finn had already started toward the water, and Sereia joined him. Soon, Yon and Travion followed.

He dipped below the surface, spotted the trap, and yanked it up. Rather than leave it behind, he hauled it onto the shore and cut the line free.

They repeated the process until they had enough line to secure the crustaceans to each horse. Luckily, they didn't have too far to travel.

Sereia leaned in close to him and wrinkled her nose. "Your Grace, you're in dire need of a bath. You smell like a lukewarm tide pool."

Travion leaned in closer, smoothed loose strands of hair from her face, and brushed his lips against hers. "And you, my heart, smell like you crawled out of a whale's arse." And yet, he'd still haul her off into the beach grass and show her how little he cared *what* she crawled out of. He winked, kissing her quickly, and pulled away. "Before we head back, let's ensure there are no other beasties lingering, be it crustacean or other."

"Let's hope we can find something other than enormous

crabs." Sereia walked up beside him, focusing on the distance beyond the beach grass, where a line of tall trees formed a wall.

"Well, now you've done it. You dared to hope."

"Oh, ye of little faith."

Yon and Finn followed behind them but offered enough privacy that they could talk. Although, if Travion was honest with himself, he didn't know what to say to Sereia. Their moments together were typically rushed, and he never wanted to taint it with anything heavier than light-hearted bickering and heated kisses, knowing all the while that she'd leave.

Sadly, he didn't have Zryan's gift for weaving eloquent words together. He couldn't fashion a declaration that would make a poet weep.

And rather than sound like a complete fool, he kept his mouth shut.

Sereia moved forward, squinting as she surveyed the woodline. "We could spend hours, days even, searching for this phantom."

"She's right, Your Grace," Finn chimed in as he jogged up the path. "Yon and I haven't even detected disturbances in the land. No footprints, and we would have seen them since the tide is just coming in."

Travion frowned. Were they being run around on purpose? Naya Damaris had duped Draven, had set plans in motion with her minions, distracting himself and Travion from what she was truly doing in Midniva—trying to kill him.

He sighed and jammed his fingers through his hair. In his experience, uncertainty was dangerous. Doubt crept in, clouded one's judgment, and accidents happened.

"Why not look a little longer and then head back?" Sereia interrupted his thoughts.

Every time he felt as though they were making strides, it seemed as though they stalled. "Whoever they are knows we are here. I find it strange that the moment we arrive, cow-sized crabs appear."

Finn and Yon had spread out ahead again. Yon hugged the trees, peering down to inspect the lesser-traveled area. Finn stuck to the higher-traffic pathway, ducking down to check on mud prints. Sereia waded into the water and dove beneath its surface, searching for other signs as he'd requested earlier.

"No horses have been this way. All the prints in the mud are geese or gulls," Finn grumbled, looking as forlorn as everyone else.

"I see no broken stems in the brush to suggest someone has been traveling through the woods," Yon announced as she returned.

"Anchor marks!" Sereia shouted from the water as she popped back up to the surface. Soon she was back on the beach with the rest of them. "I can see where the rocks have been recently disturbed by an anchor. I think whoever was here came by boat to this beach."

"By the sea!" Travion ground out. "And yet there is no boat." Neither dolphin nor hippocampus had signaled the *Speedwell* indicating they'd found anything.

Sereia sighed. "Let's head back and get some food in our bellies."

When they arrived back at the horses, gulls were squabbling over the slain crustaceans. Travion grunted and mounted his horse, urging it forward. Initially, the palfrey didn't get far as it met the tug of the rope. The crab's heavy body was enough weight to give it pause, but when Travion drove his heels into its sides, it bolted forward, yanking the cargo behind it.

The small party set off, back to the inn, but along the way, they stopped at nearby homes. The state of them twisted Travion's heart. If they'd been citizens of Midniva, there was no way he would have allowed these *shacks* to remain in such condition.

At least some good came of the fight with the crabs, and these people would eat better for it.

By the time they reached the inn, they were down to one crab. Finn hopped down from his horse and ventured inside to grab one of the inn's workers, while Travion and Sereia returned the horses to the stable.

She poured fresh water into its trough, and Travion did the same. All the while, he couldn't stop fussing over the thought that the book wielder was one step ahead of them.

"We will figure it out," Sereia said, attempting to soothe his aggravation.

"Before or after the surrounding islands are destroyed?"

Sereia placed a hand on his cheek and turned his face toward her. She lifted a brow as her eyes drank in his features. What she saw, he didn't know, and he wasn't certain that he even wanted to.

Travion gently pulled her hand down. Navigating his way around Sereia was much like exploring the darkest abyss. While she may have been the brightest spot in thousands of years, there were so many unknown and unexplored territories in their relationship.

Everything they had seemed to skim the surface, driven by physical need. Yet, he wanted more from her. Yearned for emotional depth that ventured beyond the physical. But Travion knew it was *he* who was at fault. Unwilling to offer that same depth to her.

If she knew about the darkest parts of him, would she still seek his gaze out? Would she still press her lips to his scarred flesh so tenderly?

Sereia turned away from him, impeding whatever tender moment had been about to unfold. It was his own damn fault, but it stung nonetheless.

He sighed as she disappeared around the bend. "You idiot," Travion murmured before following after her, which seemed to be a theme of his.

Once inside the tavern, he unlaced the top of his linen shirt and headed toward the stairs leading to the rooms above. But before he could get there, Lefyr barred his path.

"Tra-ask," he stuttered, which gave Travion pause. The first half of his farce name sounded closer to *Travion* than the moniker Sereia had given him.

"Were you just keen on saying my name, or was there a pressing matter?" His words caused Lefyr to swallow roughly —not in fear but rather *interest*, and in turn, Travion's lips twitched into a small grin. Had they met over a hundred years ago, he would've explored what the other male could offer and showed him what three thousand years of experience could give him. But gone was Travion's desire to take the first smiling face he saw to bed. "Well?"

"There is a man from Sahille upstairs. He came in quite injured. I've done my best to heal him, and he's resting now."

Lefyr paused, and there was a grand *but* in his tone. "I thought you'd be interested to know that his home port was destroyed by giant sea creatures. And he was muttering something about a book."

It did, in fact, interest Travion. He ran a hand down his face and shook his head. Three days' worth of sailing along the coast, farther away from Saventi, away from Midniva. None of it added up. "Is he awake?"

Lefyr shook his head. "No. If I hadn't tended to him, he would've succumbed to his injuries within the hour. He's in room four."

"I wish we could let him rest, but waking him is our best potential lead right now." Travion brushed past Lefyr and jogged up the stairs. Lanterns lit the hallway, illuminating his way. Shadows leaped and stretched, no different from the monsters he'd seen at sea.

When he arrived at Sereia's room, he rapped his knuckles against it. When no reply came, he opened the door. She'd lit the lamps already, but there was no sign of her save for the pile of clothing on the floor. His eyes flicked to the privacy screen as a shadow moved across it.

Beautiful.

"Sereia, as much as I'd prefer to watch your little show, there is a man down the hall that possibly has information regarding the book wielder."

Sereia poked around the privacy screen. "What?"

"Lefyr said he was nearly dead. I don't know how much we'll get out of him, but it's all we have right now."

Her eyes widened, and she rushed across the room to grab her clothes and yank them on. "So much for ridding myself of dead crab," Sereia huffed as she pulled her boots on.

Travion stepped into the hall, waiting for Sereia to follow him. As she fell behind him, he headed down the creaking hallway. Each door was black with a golden number painted on it.

When he reached the fourth room, he knocked. There was no answer. He shifted the door knob—it wasn't locked, so he pushed in. "Hello?" Travion called out. "Are you awake?"

Sereia crept up behind him, then brushed past and into the darkened room. There was only one lamp on the side table next to the bed, and the flame burned dangerously low to the wick mount.

The man lay still, and it took a moment for Travion to notice the rising of his chest. The movement was so minimal, that he feared they were too late. That this man had also succumbed to the terrors he suffered.

Sereia must have read his expression, because after she glanced back at him, she advanced on the bed. She placed her fingers to the man's pulse. "He's alive still."

Relief washed through him as he took another step forward. "Wake him, it'll be less terrifying seeing a beautiful face looming over him than my mug."

She nodded. "Sir, can you hear me?" She gently rocked his shoulder, then stepped back as he came alert and nearly leaped out of the bed.

The sheet hung from his body as one foot planted on the floor and the other sat tucked beneath him. His eyes were wide as he scanned the room, confusion scrunching his features. "Where . . ." The man touched his head, and Travion could almost see the pieces clicking together in his mind. "Who are you?" the question came roughly.

Lefyr had performed wonders on this man. If he'd been at death's doorstep when he started healing him, this was a stark contrast to that. Although the wounded man's face was drawn in discomfort, a touch too pale still, his eyes were alert—bright, even. His salt and pepper hair hung loosely around his shoulders, and a fresh scar puckered the skin near his shoulder.

"I'm Lord Trask." Travion stepped around the bed, and confusion rumpled the man's brow. "This is Captain Ferox." He motioned to Sereia but didn't move any closer to the bed, in case the man felt surrounded. "We're here to help and to hunt down these creatures. But we need information about what you saw in Sahille."

Suspicion swirled in the man's eyes. "No." Every muscle visibly tensed, making him look more like a cornered rabbit.

"We can help you," Sereia offered, shifting forward, but she quickly halted as the man recoiled.

"Tell us your name and what you saw." Travion's tone was gentle, but it still held a king's command in it.

"Jonathan," he rasped, then darted from the bed, grabbing something he'd hidden beneath the mattress. "You're fae." His voice dripped with contempt. "So was he. You cannot have the page back."

Another fae?

Travion held out his hands as Jonathan put space between them. He squinted, catching the words on the paper. His pulse roared in his ears. "Where did you get that?" A page from The Creaturae. The yellowed, thick parchment teased him, laughing in defiance because it should have been locked up or buried so deeply, none would ever find it.

"From him," the man rasped, his knees buckling, but he caught himself and lowered into an awkward sitting position.

Travion lurched forward, readying to catch him, but as Jonathan sank down, he stopped. His skin prickled. He gritted his teeth, but rather than prod, both he and Sereia waited until the stranger continued.

"A man with hair the shade of blood and eyes so black . . . " He stammered, then paused to collect himself before he continued. "He was holding a book, reading from it, and I knew I had to stop him. Every time he murmured something, the beasts grew." Jonathan shook his head, and his eyes grew unfocused, like he was reliving the moment. "So, I lunged for him with my sword in hand. I struck him once in the shoulder and ran him through another. I managed to tear this from him before he fled." Jonathan lifted the page and crumpled it against his chest. "I wounded him, but he still got away." His shoulders heaved as a silent sob racked his body. "Sahille is in ruins because of him. I won't let you take it from me." Jonathan's eyes darted to a small table, where a plate of rolls and a butter knife lay.

"Jonathan, listen. We are here to stop that male. While we've been in port, we've already slain crabs before they had time to reach town. We've stopped them."

The man's gaze flicked to Sereia, as if weighing out his options and whether he could manage taking on two fae. Fear trickled into his expression, but exhaustion seemed to win out. He lifted his hand, offering the paper to Travion.

"You have?" Jonathan whimpered. "I've never seen a crab so . . . enormous." He trembled and shook his head, as if trying to rid himself of the image.

"What else can you tell us about the male?" Travion pressed.

Jonathan closed his eyes. "Narrow face, thin lips . . . He looked young. Around your ages."

Travion highly doubted that, but to a human, he looked as though he were barely in his mid-thirties. He nodded, easing forward to slowly take the paper away. He unfolded it, the lines smoothing out at once as it restored itself. A power hummed through it, one he hadn't felt in centuries.

"Is it . . . ?" Sereia's brows rose in question.

Unfortunately, it was every bit a part of that damnable book. Travion folded the page and sighed. "It is." But there was one good thing to come from Sahille's destruction, and it was this man wounding the treacherous person who wielded the book. "You did well because now we can hunt the bastard down. If he's wounded as you say, we may be able to catch him before he sets sail again."

"With how much he was bleeding, I don't think he's capable of sailing," Jonathan muttered.

With the book wielder injured, there was hope they'd find him, but would he be alive? By the sea, Travion prayed to the blasted depths that he *would* be. "You did well, Jonathan. Let me help you back into bed."

The man waved off his offer and hobbled back to the bed. "If you truly are here to help" —Jonathan sucked in a breath, winded from his earlier efforts—"avenge Sahille for me —for us."

Sereia glanced at Travion, and she was the first to speak. "We vow it, Jonathan."

"For now, rest well, and thank you for everything."

Travion quietly crossed the room and didn't utter a word until both he and Sereia were on the other side of the door. "We need a sketch."

She focused on the page, as if in a trance. "And where do you propose that we find an artist at this hour?"

"I have it on good authority that the first mate on *Speedwell* is an adequate artist."

Sereia cocked her head. "How do you know?"

"Because he was showing off his naked portraits when I checked on them last."

Outside the inn, the wind howled through the streets, sounding like a siren wailing a warning of impending doom. By the sea, it felt like it. Not knowing what invisible foe they chased, just that they needed to obtain the book, was exhausting. Sailing for days on end was one matter, but fighting one gigantic beast off after another was purely exhausting.

Between the moon and the lit lamps, the street was bright enough to see where the dirt road ended and the dock began.

"This better be it, Sereia. I don't know how much more senseless chasing I can do."

"I know." She looped her arm around his waist, squeezing gently. "Believe me, I want this to end. We all do."

He remained silent for the rest of the walk down the dock until they reached *Speedwell*. The ship bobbed as much as it could given that it was moored, but she still strained against the ropes as the waves rose and fell quickly.

Sereia crossed onto the ship's deck first, and Travion followed closely behind.

Captain Darragh sat perched on a barrel, smoking a pipe. When he realized who approached, he stood abruptly and bowed at the waist. "Your Grace, what can we do for you?"

Travion ran a hand down his face. "I need your first mate's drawing abilities."

It was clear that whatever Captain Darragh thought Travion had been about to ask for, it wasn't *that*. His brow furrowed, and his lips twisted to the side. "Beg your pardon?"

"We need a sketch done. Is your first mate aboard the ship?" Sereia's tone was crisp but straight to the point.

Darragh used his pipe to indicate the bow of the ship. "Callum! We need your drawing skills, but I don't think they have naked females in mind."

Travion chuckled darkly. "No," he bit out and turned his gaze to the approaching male. "We're in need of a sketch of the one who is behind all of this."

"By the sea," Callum murmured as he approached. "Follow me, Your Grace." The male crossed the deck to the steps leading to the belly of the ship. Lamps swayed as they walked through the small hallway and into the crew's quarters. "Let me grab my things."

Sereia sighed, and he knew what she was thinking: every moment that ticked by was a moment they lost.

Callum lifted his gaze from his sketch pad and looked up at them. "Now, tell me what the person looked like, as best as you can."

Travion reiterated the missing fae's appearance and as he did, Callum's adept fingers brought the figure to life, line by line, angle by angle. Soon, a narrow face appeared, boasting thin lips and pointed ears. Then came the hair and eyes. Familiarity nagged at Travion, but he couldn't place the face.

"I was hoping I knew who it was," he said with a frown. "But this is good, it gives us something to go off of." Travion turned at the sound of boots scuffing, and Darragh's bright eyes connected with his. "We set sail for Sahille tomorrow. Gather any extra supplies if you have need, and collect whatever missing crew there is."

"Of course, Your Grace," Darragh said with a nod, then disappeared down the hall once more.

Sereia grabbed Travion's elbow, pulling hard enough that he spun to face her. "We're not taking this useless ship."

Travion sighed. He hadn't the energy to argue at this point. "Your crew is beyond exhausted. They have gone out straight, Sereia."

She rocked back on her heels, arms folded and head tilted back. "Fine. We'll take *Speedwell*."

On the deck once more, Travion heard a familiar trill. He made his way to the rail of the ship, and Sereia joined him. Below, Velox bobbed in the turbulent water. "Have you seen anything, you rascal?"

Velox clicked and whirled around in a circle, sounding dismayed as he let out a rush of air.

Neither he nor his pod had seen anything.

"What did he say?" Sereia asked softly. "He seems rather upset."

"He is, because he hasn't found anything yet." Travion frowned. "It's all right. Keep looking, and spread the word to the dolphins too. But when you do, look for a man who looks like this . . ." Travion pushed the image of the sketch to Velox's mind, and he nodded vigorously, then flicked his tail in renewed excitement.

Velox enjoyed being helpful, but more than that, enjoyed being *right*. But who didn't?

"Well, to Sahille it is." And he hoped this lead wasn't a bloody dead end.

16

Sereia

HMS *Speedwell* was a beautiful ship, a true gem in Travion's navy. She cut through the water seamlessly, her white sails capturing the wind without a tear or rip in sight, and the hull a gleaming dark teal against the clear blue waters of the sea.

But she was no *Saorsa*. Sereia would have been envious if she didn't love her ship so dearly. It wasn't the *Speedwell* that brought her and the crew freedom they sought so often.

Only one full day at sea, and it had already grated sorely upon Sereia's nerves. Being but a passenger on the deck of this naval vessel chafed at her spirits and rankled her fury into an almost living thing. She tried her best to be content with the journey but found even the crew of the ship so efficient, any attempts at lending a hand were automatically shot down.

The *Lady Sereia* was a guest of His Majesty, not a humble crewman.

Seated on top of a barrel, leaning against the wooden wall at her back, Sereia watched Adrik catch a hard chunk of loaf tossed at his head by a *Speedwell* crew member with a laugh. Adrik had insisted on coming along this time, not wanting to be left out of the adventure. So Chailai had been left in command of their crew. Behind him, Yon tucked into her bowl of chowder, looking casual but keeping a watchful eye on the crew at large. She didn't take to new people easily. The bowels of the ship hummed with chatter and the clank of spoons against wooden bowls.

"Not hungry?" Travion came to lean against the wall, nodding down at the full bowl of chowder in her hand.

Sereia had helped with the catch because diving into the water to scare fish into the ship's net was the one thing she could do to assist with their current journey. But her lack of being able to do anything else still chafed. "I've eaten enough chowder in my life to fill an entire ship."

Travion reached over to take the bowl from her hands and replaced it with a bottle of rum instead. Gazing up at him, Sereia lifted a brow in question.

"It's time for a little fun," he murmured with a grin, then turned to the crew. "Whoever can beat me in a game of liar's dice wins a bottle of scotch from my personal stores!" Travion shouted to the room at large, which erupted in cheers and whistles at this battle cry.

Laughing, Sereia shook her head and uncapped the rum to take a deep swig. "Very well, Your Majesty, I'll hedge that bet."

After that, it didn't take very long for the evening meal to be finished and cleaned up. The crew converged on the deck with bottles, cups, and dice aplenty. One of the deckhands brought out her fiddle and began to play. The uplifting melody swirled through the air along with the clatter of dice rolling over the deck and the cackles of delighted sailors as they drank and gambled their concerns away.

After losing nearly her full pocket of coin to Travion, Sereia finally accepted defeat and left the circle of liar's dice to wander the deck, coming to stand at the bow. Listening to the slosh of the waves below, she sighed and let some of the tension slip from her shoulders. While it was hard to relinquish control, Sereia could admit that it was good for her crew to have the break. And while he was still present, Adrik was looking more relaxed and rested, not having to fulfill his first mate duties.

A wild cheer rose up behind her, and Sereia turned to look over her shoulder. A number of men were clapping the boatswain on the back, while Travion's hands were lifted in the air, his head bowed in reverent loss.

Sereia turned back to the water, inhaling deeply the salt on the breeze and letting it lift her hair off her shoulders to dance behind her. She had always known that Travion was beloved. The people of Midniva were happy and content, enjoying their cups and their dances, with fair taxes and enough crops to go around. But she had never truly seen Travion with his men. Not in this capacity.

Her heart felt pained, as if she were missing out on something she'd never even known she had. Could a life with him be happy? Could it be enough?

She felt him before she heard him. "You let him win, didn't you?"

Travion slid up beside her, leaning forward with his arms on the rail. "There was something more enticing over here."

Turning, Sereia leaned toward him. "Is that so?" she murmured.

"It is." Travion moved in a little closer.

Sereia's breath caught slightly at the nearness, and she wished the crew and the ship were many miles away so that she could give in to the draw of Travion. He made the pain in her heart both increase and lessen. Her body and her spirit yearning for a physical connection between them. To feel connected to Travion, even if for only a moment. "Should I tell him it was a hollow win?"

Travion growled, his hand slipping around her waist to pull her closer to him. "Why you—"

"Oy! Captain!"

Their eyes, which had been trained on each other, narrowed at the interruption before they turned to glare down at Adrik, who didn't even bother having the decency to look contrite.

"Yes, Adrik?" Sereia snarled.

"I've been telling the boys how great a dancer you are, and they seem to be having a hard time believing me." His eyes gleamed with delight, and his lips twitched with amusement.

Sereia's eyes narrowed further, and she could feel a tick in her jaw. She was fully aware of what her first mate was up to. "And?"

"And it had me thinking, Captain, that you should prove them all wrong." His smirk was broad and proud, a defiant light within their depths. The defiant light became a dare, and he held out his hand to her.

She wanted to kick that smirk clean off his face and watch it sail over the horizon. However, she cast Travion a look for their lost moment, then jumped down off the foredeck to land before Adrik and claim his outstretched hand. A shout rang out for a lively tune, and as the music claimed the night, Sereia leaped into the song, dark hair swirling around her shoulders as her knees skipped and her feet tapped quickly over the deck. Those not entirely caught up in their gambling soon joined in, and the deck came alive with dancing forms.

It was hard to remain frustrated when she was letting herself be swept up in the moment—something her first mate was more than aware of. While it wouldn't chase away all her irritation at being rendered useless aboard someone else's ship, it would help ease the tide of her storm before she unleashed it on some undeserving deckhand.

Adrik's eyes gleamed back at her in victory. "There's a happy Captain." He did nothing but bow out in satisfaction when Travion cut in to claim her for the next dance.

Paying him little heed after that, Sereia pressed her palms down into Travion's upturned hands and let him swing her around as a new melody filled the air. Those along the railing of the boat had forgotten their dice for the time being and began to clap or stomp their feet to the tune.

Someone in the crow's nest sang along to the jive with a lovely deep baritone that was soon joined by a willing tenor.

Through the crowd, Sereia noticed Yon approach Finn. While she could not hear what was said, she saw a shift on Finn's face from serious to surprised. The two then moved out into the midst of the dancers to join in.

Grinning to herself, she returned her attention to Travion, letting herself simply enjoy this moment.

Travion's eyes were a deep blue, sparkling back at her with a levity that she hadn't seen within them for many a day. It was only during this most recent trip back to Midniva that Sereia had taken note of the sorrow in them. Had she never spent enough time truly studying them to realize they were typically so sad behind the glint of merriment he presented to the world?

Now, however, they shone with glee as his quick footwork carried them over the deck of the *Speedwell*. At some point, Sereia could only tip her head back and let her laughter spill into the night sky.

When their song had concluded, Captain Darragh cut in, and from there, Sereia was passed from one member of the ship to another until her feet hurt and her legs felt like jelly. At long last she called for a ceasefire and collapsed onto the deck, propped up against a barrel.

Soon someone was pressing a bottle into her hand, and she poured liquid fire down her throat, heating her belly and causing her continued panting to exit on a wheeze.

"I'd say you did a fair job proving them wrong, Captain," Adrik chuckled from above her.

Kicking out with one foot, Sereia caught him on the ankle.

Yelping, Adrik jumped back, lifting the injured foot up a little. He laughed deeply.

"I can't feel my feet."

"They seem to be kicking just fine," he shot back.

Travion had come to lean on the railing near them, an elbow resting back against it as his other arm lifted a sloshing bottle of rum to his lips. "Reminds me of the time Zryan tried to dance his way into a maiden's bed, only to wind up with her mother."

"What?" Sereia laughed. "How does this circumstance remind you of that?"

"He nearly danced his feet clean off as well."

"Well, you can't leave off there, sire," Adrik interjected.

A smile slid over Sereia's lips as she watched Travion fall into the role of storyteller. He took another sip of rum and then swiped the back of his hand across his lips before he began.

"It was the early days, after Ludari was tossed into his watery grave, and Draven, Zryan, and I were attempting to bring peace and joy to the kingdom once more. There were many a party and soiree in that day. Zryan's thought was, if everyone was enjoying themselves, they would forget to hate each other."

Sereia snorted. She'd continued to hate plenty of the snub-nosed pincushions who'd looked down on her for her disinterest in the marriage market, despite the fun she was having at their balls. Though, perhaps the issue had been her displeasure in attending the balls in the first place. Her mother's attempts to foist her onto an available noble hadn't helped matters any.

She'd aimed for the Lucemite royals at one point, thrusting her before Prince Ruan, who, in his stormy, indelicate manner had wasted no time in telling both of them he had no desire to be wed. It amused her now to think that she'd gone from one displeased prince to his uncle, and there had found her proposal.

"A sentiment I can stand behind," Adrik said. He hopped up on top of a barrel, his hands resting on the edge of it between his spread thighs.

He reminded Sereia of a young lad, caught on every word of an older, more experienced boy. In many ways, he would always be that lost boy to her, seeking out a place to belong and finding it with a group of swarthy pirates who took him in and made him their own.

"This one particular night, Zry had set his sight on a young maiden who was the center of many a male's fancy. Once he managed to get her to accept a dance with him, he thought the best way to keep her away from any other male in the room was to keep her dancing. So that is what he did."

Sereia shook her head, sipping at her bottle.

"But with much dancing comes great thirst. So, with each spin around the room, either myself or Draven would exchange his empty glass of wine for a full one, until he was so knackered, he could barely stand. It was at this point I swept the mother of the maiden onto the dance floor and then swapped her out for the girl instead of the wine. I don't think he even noticed until the next morning, after staggering off the dance floor with the mum and waking with her in his bed." Travion was smirking as he finished his tale, and Adrik was chuckling in appreciation.

"I am going to go out on a limb and assume His Highness never did end up with the maiden?" Sereia grinned.

"Oh no, he pulled some Zryan nonsense and still bedded her as well."

Adrik hooted in pleasure and slapped his thigh. "And you make the peerage sound boring and stuffy!" he crowed at Sereia. "Sounds like a grand time."

Sereia rolled her eyes at her first mate. "Yes, and the last time you had a truly great time with some of the peerage, you wound up hanging by your boots from a tree. I've already vowed never to save you from one again, remember that." She tipped her bottle at him.

Grinning broadly, Adrik winked at her, slid from the barrel, and bowed to Travion, then walked away to lose some of his coin in a game of dice.

A contemplative look crossed Travion's face, though not an unpleasant one. "You seem quite close," Travion murmured, sliding down to sit beside her on the deck. "Have the two of you ever . . ."

"Adrik and I?" Sereia's brow shot up, and she laughed darkly, wrinkling her nose. "For sea's sake, no." She shook her head, watching Adrik for a moment as he laughed and slapped one of the sailors on the back. "In many ways, he's the little brother I never had."

Travion's arm snaked around her waist, and he pulled her into his side. Content to be tucked in against his sturdy frame, Sereia leaned her head back against his shoulder. His nearness brought a sense of peace that was often missing in her life these days. It was unsettling, being made to feel so calm by someone else.

Cries of surprise broke out from the middle of the ship, capturing her attention, as Lefyr began to dance a jig well known in the inns and taverns of Midniva. Clapping along to the fiddle, the crew cheered him on until he had finished the lively dance.

"That was splendid! Where did you learn that?" one of the sailors asked him.

"My mother taught me. She always grieved for the daughter she never had and forced me to endure hours of dancing."

"Oh, is that so?" Travion called out to him, earning a sheepish look from the healer. "A pity your mother wound up with you instead," he teased. "What is your family name?"

"Sebdula," he responded.

Travion arched a brow. "As in Adavu Sebdula?"

Lefyr nodded, dragging his hand along his sweat-slicked brow. "He is a healer in the castle." His expression turned to one of smugness. "How is His Highness these days?"

There was silence over the deck, and then the sailors laughed. One gave Lefyr's shoulder a squeeze, and they returned to their dancing and drinking.

"Does this mean Trask is dead?" Sereia asked quietly, laughing a little. She turned her head to peer at Travion, who shook his head, a gleam in his eye.

"You'll find he's as impossible to kill as I am." He then captured her lips, effectively silencing any further comments.

17

Travion

Death was not impossible. Although it seemed that way, as many times as Travion had evaded its icy clutches. Perhaps it was the fact his brother would only scold him if he turned up in Andhera's halls, nothing more than a wisp of chilled air. Or maybe it was that, after enduring Ludari's punishing hands, he only wished to defy death at every turn.

Regardless, his attention was on Lefyr, and Travion wondered if the fae knew who he was. The obvious thought was *yes*, which brought a grumble forth.

Sereia snaked her arms around his neck, dragging him away from thoughts of Midniva, of being the king, and centered him there, in that moment. Alcohol buzzed in his veins, sea spray clung to his skin, and a beautiful female's devilish blue eyes attempted to pierce his soul. But Travion had years of practice assembling impenetrable barriers.

Did he want to keep them up though? He supposed it was a wise thing to do, since she was bound to leave and bound to wound him grievously if he didn't.

"My heart," he murmured softly. The notion that Sereia

would return to the farthest corners of the sea after this ordeal plagued him. Travion would return to the throne in Midniva, and he'd force himself to finally move on, to live with the knowledge that half of his soul lived elsewhere.

This would be their last time together. And he knew that.

His lips twitched, and he tucked a strand of hair behind her pointed ear.

"Yes, Your Majesty?" She brushed her knuckles along the stubble on his chin.

Travion raised his other hand, swishing the rum around. "We are running low on our alcohol stores. I'm afraid it's a sad day." His brow rumpled as he squinted. "I may even throw myself overboard."

Sereia gripped the collar of his shirt. "Only if you take me with you." She leaned in, pressing her lips to his in a slow, demanding kiss. Her tongue grazed his, and he tasted promises of things to come.

"We are done out here," he murmured against her lips and hauled her into his arms. She laughed, sprawling in his hold as he hauled her to the captain's quarters. His boots clumsily slapped against the dark wooden flooring. It was a spacious room, with a dining table in the center, a desk off to the side, and on the farthest wall, a full-sized bed with a privacy curtain.

Travion set her down on the bed, her breasts heaving from laughter. By the sea, what net would capture her? But that was just it, wasn't it? She was of the sea, and sadly, not a creature he could control. Not that he wished to.

He set the rum down on the table and knelt on the mattress, crawling toward her.

"What if Lefyr knows?" she interrupted his thoughts with the name of someone else on her lips.

Travion dashed a hand through his hair and closed his eyes, shaking his head. "What?" he asked incredulously, not because he didn't know what she'd said but because her mind had drifted to thoughts of Lefyr instead.

"Oh good, we are on the same page. You'll not venture off in your head, and I won't utter someone else's name." She laid back on the bed, wriggling her hips.

"You better not utter someone else's name," he growled, crawling over her. His hands were at her waist, undoing her trousers. "But just in case, I'll be sure to render you breathless."

Sereia propped herself onto her elbows and glanced up at him through her eyelashes. "I'm afraid you can't do that while talking, Your Majesty." A devilish gleam entered her eyes, daring him to continue.

"Did we learn nothing from last time?" He arched a brow and rolled his sleeves up, then unlaced her boots, taking his time. When it came to her trousers, he dragged his knuckles down her thighs roughly until she sucked in a breath.

"I need a thorough reminder of what I should have learned from last time."

He chuckled darkly and hooked his hands beneath her knees, dragging her to the edge of the bed. "Don't you worry, I'll make certain you won't forget this time." Travion slid his hands beneath her backside, gripping her undergarment and slowly removing it.

"You're going to draw this out, aren't you?" She almost whined the words, and her hips raised in want—need—of attention.

Travion kneeled before the bed, pressing his chest against the wooden frame. "How else will you learn?" But he was done with talking for now, because she was right. He couldn't teach her if his lips were moving.

"Easily, I jus—"

He scraped his nails along the outside of her thigh, then tugged her closer so that her legs draped over his shoulders. Travion trailed heated, wet kisses along her thigh, letting his teeth scrape the tender flesh.

She sighed the moment his lips coasted to her center, and when his tongue dipped into her seam, Sereia arched into him. His hands stilled her, pressing her back down, but she wasn't the only one reeling. The taste of her arousal hardened him, but he used it to fuel his ministrations.

"By the sea! Don't tease me again," she whined.

Travion chuckled and thrust his tongue into her entrance, pulsing his tongue inward only to withdraw and do it again.

Sereia moaned, fisting the blankets to keep from lifting her hips again. However, when he pulled his mouth away, she tilted her hips in search of him.

His lips circled her bundle of nerves, but then his tongue replaced them, and he brought a finger to her, teasing the sensitive flesh.

"Travion, I swear . . ." She sucked in a breath the moment he dipped one finger inside of her, then another.

With his tongue, he set a demanding pace, using quick thrusts within her to strike in a way that made her legs tremble. He grinned but continued and groaned as she clutched onto his head, driving his face forward into her.

As much as he yearned to withdraw and replace his fingers with his length, burying himself deep within her, this wasn't about him.

Travion wanted Sereia to unravel, to lose herself in the pleasure he brought her. And the moment her fingers tugged at his hair, then loosened, he felt her muscles spasm around him.

"Trav!" Sereia rasped and rocked her hips into him as she rode herself through the waves of pleasure.

He didn't cease his ministrations until the last waves of her climax washed over her, and only then did he withdraw. "By the sea and shore, Sereia . . ." he half chuckled and half groaned as he crawled up the length of her and hovered over her heaving form. "I hope you learned something."

She sucked in a breath and shook her head. "You'll no doubt have to show me again."

And he would. Over and over again.

Travion opened his eyes, the taste of blood and mildew on his tongue. It was dark, save for a few dregs of light filtering in from a grate in the stone wall of the dungeon. His heart leaped wildly, his breathing rasping due to what was likely a broken rib.

"Don't move," a stern voice commanded, but in it was a hint of kindness. "He is sleeping, but not for long." It was Draven. He reached his hand out and brushed his fingers through Travion's matted hair. "You're not alone, Travion. Don't be afraid."

But he was. So afraid. Mostly of hurting Draven, as their father ordered it, forcing them to fight, to find a weakness and exploit it.

Sandals slapped against the stone floor, alerting them to Ludari's arrival. Their father stopped in front of their cells, a torch in his hand. Flames danced, casting harsh shadows on his chiseled face. Travion knew his cold, storm-blue eyes and his dark auburn hair that was so much like his own—like Draven's too.

"Wake him up," he spat at Draven. "Or I'll do it myself."

"*Get up,*" *came Draven's clipped words. Showing affection only meant it would be used against them.*

Ludari unlocked their cells. Freedom teased Travion, but he knew better than to run, and his ribs wouldn't allow it.

"*Out.*"

They obeyed, and while Travion stole a glance at Draven, his brother didn't so much as blink in his direction.

"*For a child, you're resilient.*" *Ludari's remark would've stroked the ego of anyone else, but compliments from him were vile things. "And I know we haven't seen what you're capable of. For whatever reason, you're hiding it.*"

He wasn't. At least, not on purpose. He had already shown he could speak to the creatures of the sea. What more did his father want?

Ludari led the way, and they passed several cells, which held forlorn fae who were more like corpses than anything. Their clothes hung in tatters from their malnourished bodies, and their eyes, which should've been bright and full of life, were dull, sunken in. He stopped at a wall with chains hanging down and motioned for Draven to step forward. There was no reluctance on his part. Travion only assumed it was because of Draven's obedience—and not that he had no will left.

While Ludari secured Draven to the wall, Travion glanced down at the water rushing into the dungeon's trench. Light reflected off it, bouncing onto Draven's stricken face.

"*Child. Call on your magic, or your brother will pay.*" *Ludari moved to the wall, and to Travion's horror, he realized there was a crank.*

"*No,*" *he whispered, eyes saucering.*

"*What did you just say?*"

"*Fuck,*" *Draven ground out and hung his head, twisting his hands in the restraints.*

The crank shifted, tightening the chains suspending Draven to the point that pain creased his brow.

"I won't ask again. Every moment that passes, the chains will tighten, and when you fail to call on your magic, your brother will suffer. He will die because of you."

Panic rose like a tidal wave. Travion couldn't think, let alone call on magic he didn't possess! He lifted his hands and dragged them down his face.

"Stop! I can't!" His voice cracked.

Draven bellowed in pain as his limbs were stretched beyond their limits. His teeth gnashed together, and Travion didn't know how he hadn't bitten through his tongue.

Ludari chuckled, cranking the handle again. "So much for brotherly love."

Draven shook violently, his face contorting as he yelled.

Travion sunk to his knees, anger melding with hopelessness, and balled it up. Energy sizzled in his veins, rushing through him, and he drew on it as hard as he could.

"Enough!" Travion screamed.

Lightning crackled outside of the castle, and the wind howled in fury. Waves rushed through the tunnel, bursting over the lip of the trench and flooding the floor of the dungeon. Chairs slammed against the walls and iron bars of the cells from the strength of the current.

More anger coursed through Travion, spinning through him viciously. The wind grew louder, roaring until the castle quaked. No— not the castle, the very ground.

The stone floor started cracking, spider webbing until it reached Ludari's feet.

Their father would stop now, surely, since Travion had done it. He had shown Ludari that he could do it.

Ludari only smiled coldly, like he always did. "You're too late." As the crank spun around again, blood sprayed Travion's face.

He jolted awake, tumbled out of bed, and tripped over his feet, landing on his backside. "I'm not. I'm not too late. He's alive," Travion panted, blinking several times, attempting to fight off the dream clashing with memory.

He was in the captain's quarters, he reminded himself, half dazed. The distant cry of the crew shouting orders as the sea rocked violently was another grounding factor. Someone was shouting close by, but his ears were ringing too loudly to decipher who it was.

Travion swallowed roughly and squeezed his eyes shut, trying to drown out the sound of his pounding heart. Then he realized someone was near, shaking him.

"Travion! By the sea!" Sereia cursed, slapping his cheek, then cupped his face. "Trav? What is wrong? Talk to me."

In their time together, he had done well to dance around his past because Travion didn't want Sereia's pity. But with the rawness of what had transpired in the depths all those centuries ago, he pulled her into him and buried his nose in her hair.

"I have not told you . . ." His voice broke, and he closed his eyes, inhaling her scent—fresh air and salt water—to will the stench of his cell away.

Of course, in part, she knew Ludari's transgressions, as any fae did. But the extent of the scars Ludari left on each of his sons was unknown.

Sereia remained in his arms for a time, then pulled back and gently stroked his back. "Come back to bed and tell me," she said quietly.

And for once, he did. He followed her into bed and

wrapped his arms around her, needing to know she was real and not a trace of another nightmare rising. "Ludari sired us, but he was no father." Travion sucked in a ragged breath. It didn't matter how many times he blinked or rubbed at his eyes, the images still flickered in his head as if they'd just happened. "Draven was taken to the dungeons long before I was born, but when I was eight, the old bastard found me playing with the fish in our pond. He realized my powers were taking shape and studied me for months before whisking me away to the depths of the palace." Travion shook with a mixture of rage and fear. "He pitted us against one another, testing our weaknesses and our strengths in the worst ways. So many times, I wished I'd die, not only to end my suffering but Draven's as well." Travion laughed bitterly. "But when my little brother was born, I knew I couldn't let him endure this, and Draven would never allow it. He did his best to shield me, and I him." Travion sucked in a ragged breath, recounting the numerous nightmares that had been his reality.

Sereia was quiet at first, then she cupped his face and leaned her forehead against his. "If Ludari was not dead already, I'd gut him myself."

The sun peeked through the small windows in the captain's quarters, and from looks of the port coming into view, they were just sailing into Sahille's harbor.

Travion had hardly slept after the dreadful night terror, and although Sereia's body eventually stilled beside him, she hadn't fallen asleep either. He'd felt her muscles tense and refuse to relax.

He rolled out of bed, padding over to the wash basin, and splashed water on his face, not daring to glance at his reflection in the mirror. Someone pounded on the door, and it opened moments later.

Sereia grumbled from the corner of the cabin and pulled her shirt down.

Finn poked his head in through the door, carefully scanning the area to ensure he wasn't intruding on a *moment*. Although it hadn't stopped him before.

"Your Grace." Finn's voice shook ever so slightly, and the stricken expression on his face said it all.

"What is wrong?" Travion was already picking a fresh shirt up to yank over his head.

"There is a spider crab rampaging through what is left of Sahille." Finn swallowed roughly.

"By the sea!" Sereia yanked her boots on and headed toward the door. "Still?"

They knew from reports that Sahille had been ravaged, but never did he think that the beast would *still* be at it. Travion finished dressing and shared a look with Sereia. In the depths of her gaze, he saw his thoughts reflected there. *How much worse could it be?*

A dangerous thought, for certain.

He grabbed his sword and secured it to his trousers as he hopped up the stairs. At the top, he was immediately faced with the crew staring at the dock. His heart plummeted to his stomach.

The crabs on Saventi's beach were nothing in comparison to the beast before them. Legs as tall as a cedar tree, body as wide as the ship.

More than that, the entire port had been destroyed. Beachside huts had been reduced to rubble, and smoke billowed from the sand. Barrels, no doubt filled with whale oil, had been rolled out.

The villagers had half-fought a battle, but it was far from over.

"By the sea!" Travion cried in unison with Sereia.

"Push the ship dockside! Use your bloody affinity. We need to get to land!" Travion growled above the sound of the whipping wind.

Darragh complied, but amid barking orders, he paused. "Your Grace, surely you're not thinking of—"

"And let this port suffer more? Get us to that dock, *now*."

Wind filled the sails, and the sea lurched as those with water affinity aided too. Although it took mere minutes, it felt longer.

Travion grabbed a mooring line, securing the ship in place, and Sereia and Finn made quick work of the lines too. When it was tight enough, Travion moved the gangway into place and quickly strode across.

The crab was missing a leg on the left side, and a pincer claw on the right.

Travion glanced over his shoulder as Finn, Yon, and Adrik hopped onto the dock. "Attack the joints on the legs, and if you have an open shot to the mouth, take it. At that size, the underbelly is going to be hard too." He looked to Darragh and jerked his head toward a barrel with extra rope on it. "Hand over that rope. If we can cut enough limbs off, we can flip it over and impale it. When the threat is gone, send Lefyr ashore. I think he's still sleeping."

Finn took the rope, shouldering the thinner cord. "Isn't he the lucky one?"

"Not for much longer," Sereia offered.

"He's going to need all that rest and then some if this is anything to go by." Without another word, Travion turned on his heel and ran toward the merchant storefronts, where the beast was still shuffling around, focused on something—or someone—in the ruins.

They needed to lure it away, toward the water. The crab was too close to the establishments. "Finn," Travion shouted. "It's your turn to act as bait."

Finn swore but unraveled the rope from his shoulder. "Whatever you're thinking, be quick about it, Your Grace."

"Get its attention, we need to get it as close to the beach as we can." Travion unsheathed his sword as he jogged toward the beach. Adrik and Sereia were on his heels, but Yon remained closer to Finn.

"What exactly is your plan, Trav?" Sereia finally asked.

"Finn can hold his own for a while. But he needs to lead the crab back here so I can create a sinkhole. By dropping the beast, we can cut off its legs. This one isn't the same as Saventi's horde." Sweat trickled down his brow from adrenaline coursing through him. He shook his sword arm and watched as Finn created a loop with the rope. When it caught on a needle-like leg, he pulled.

Immediately, the crab spun around, facing Finn and ultimately them too. Rocks vibrated around the area, leaping across the sandy soil before hurling directly at the crustacean.

Travion had only seen Finn use his affinity a handful of times, but it always made sense that he could manipulate something as large and powerful as him.

One of the bigger stones collided into a lower leg, snapping it off. The crab stumbled but regained its balance. A hiss, sounding more like a growl, emitted from the beast as it focused on Finn and quickened toward him. He dropped the rope by the dock and ran, zig-zagging in hopes of dodging the pounding, sharp limbs as they crashed to the ground with every stride.

"Do whatever you're going to do now!" Finn bellowed as he raced past them.

"Oh, sh—" Adrik never got to finish because one of the legs towered over them, intent on impaling one if not all of them.

Travion reached for the earth with his mind, clung to the strands that whispered by him. One mental tug was all it took to pull the earth out from under the crab. It toppled in awkwardly, long, spindly limbs jutting out of the hole and flailing, hoping to find purchase.

"Now!" More sweat trickled down his brow from the exertion of his affinity. He darted forward, striking down on one of the weak spots. His sword bit into the meaty sinew, and in turn, the hissing from the crab only grew louder.

With only a few legs left, the crab pulled itself up. The pincers near its mouth opened, revealing tusk-like teeth. Unable to balance on the loss of legs, it teetered forward.

"Get out of the way!" Sereia screamed.

Travion bolted to the side, but as the crab collapsed to the ground, one of the spikes from its shell pinned him down by the very edge of his shirt. He wheezed, facedown in the sand, and grimaced.

Sereia rushed to his side and yanked his shirt free. "Travion! Are you okay?"

"Just had the wind knocked out of me," he said in between sucking in a breath. He peered over his shoulder and caught sight of Adrik approaching the crustacean.

Adrik rammed his sword into the crab's mouth, twisting until a loud *pop* sounded. Whatever tension remained in the beast's body fled.

"Is everyone okay?" With a quick glance over at Yon and Finn, he didn't see any visible injuries.

"All's well," Finn said, but his face, which had been cherry-red moments ago, was steadily paling. He stared at the shoreline, his brow furrowing. "Your Grace."

A seahawk flew above, diving down to chase off seagulls and ravens that were picking apart its meal. To Travion's horror, the birds were feasting on the dead of Sahille.

"Get off!" Travion bellowed, rushing to his feet and running closer. He stopped only a few yards away, but even from here, he could see the flies buzzing around. The man's eyes had long since been plucked from their sockets, and his throat's flesh had been ripped away. There was a massive hole in his chest from where a leg had no doubt impaled him.

His knees threatened to buckle. All these people were dead because of the blasted book. The town now so drenched in the reek of death. All because the book had been stolen.

"Finn, grab Lefyr and the remainder of the crew. We need to see if there are *any* survivors in the area," he bellowed.

"And everyone else, spread out, see what everyone needs!" When they didn't move fast enough, Sereia hissed. "Now!" She raced down the beach, but Travion's attention was on the tree line not far from them. Perhaps the treacherous individual was hiding in the woods, orchestrating the madness.

Travion traipsed through the overgrowth, surveying the area. He spotted a trail a blood that hadn't coagulated yet.

Someone whimpered nearby.

He narrowed his eyes as he stepped further into the

woods, following the trail until he reached a gathering of bushes.

Heart pounding in his ears, Travion moved the branches aside. A fallen man lay sprawled out, bleeding from his chest and side. Behind him crouched a sobbing boy. His tawny hair was slicked back with blood, but it didn't seem to be his. Travion didn't see any wounds on him, but the older man— his leg had been shredded, and one arm was missing.

"Boy," Travion said gently. "It's all right." He held out his hand as if speaking to a cornered animal. "I'm sorry," he whispered, hating how many times he had said those same words as of late.

"He tried to stop him!" the boy said, sucking in a breath. "There was someone with a book, speaking strange words. Every time he did, something grew. My father and some other man attacked . . ." He rocked back and forth, holding his arms. "The other man got away, not my father . . . Not my father."

Frowning, Travion rested a hand on his shoulder. "I'm sorry," he offered again. "Did you see where the person went?"

"East, I think."

Travion nodded solemnly. "What's your name, boy?"

"Radomir."

"Tell me something, Radomir, what color hair did this person have?"

Radomir's hazel eyes flicked to his father and then back up to Travion. "Red as my father's blood."

Travion sucked in his bottom lip. At least that detail had been holding up through the various witnesses. Now they just needed to find the fae and bring them to justice. "Thank you. Let me help you carry him out. There is no need to worry about the crab any longer. It's time to honor the fallen." He slid his arms beneath the man's legs and dipped his head down. "When you're ready . . ."

Together, they carried the boy's father out, and by the time they'd reached the beach once again, the entire crew of *Speedwell* was present.

Travion enlisted the aid of everyone aboard the *Speedwell* to pitch in, clean up the streets, extinguish fires, and move the bodies indoors. But when everything was said and done, the monstrous crab's corpse still served as a hideous reminder of what was lost.

Sereia slid her arm around Travion's waist, leaning into him. "Are we to leave it for the birds and other scavengers?"

He shook his head. "No. It'll only haunt the locals."

"So, what then—tie it to the ship and pull it out to sea?"

"Close, but I have a better idea." He jerked his head toward the water. "Call on the sea and haul the beast out. It'll cleanse the land in the process." And deposit some fresh seaweed and other critters for the gulls to snack on instead of the monumental crab.

Sereia nodded in understanding, then closed her eyes as she reached for the sea. Little by little, the waves grew larger, until a tidal wave formed at the shore, rising and rising until it darted forward. It didn't crash and disperse as a natural occurrence would but kept its shape. The water swirled around the carcass until it was entirely covered, then as it receded, it yanked the crustacean with it.

She was a force to be reckoned with. Unfettered, fierce, and courageous.

And by the sea, did he love her for all of that and more.

His lips twitched into a small smile. "Now, that was a lot easier, don't you agree?"

"Says the one not breaking a sweat." She sucked in a deep breath and used her sleeve to wipe away the trickle of sweat running down her temple.

"Somehow, I don't think the villagers would appreciate an earthquake or cyclone. I have a feeling both of our affinities will be put to the test sooner rather than later." He sighed, rubbing the bridge of his nose as he turned away from the shore. "Let's head back to the ship. I need to call on Draven and Zryan. They need to know about this destruction."

18

Sereia

Back in the captain's quarters, Travion made quick work of pulling out the summoning bowl and calling for his brothers. Fortunately, both answered the summons, and the sound of their voices filled the space of the cabin. Sereia perched on the opposite side of the desk; close enough that she could comment if needed, but not so close that Draven could bore a look of death into her flesh.

"Travion! I see you're very much still alive and in one piece. Splendid." Zryan's voice was cheery.

"I'm honestly surprised to see you uninjured," Draven drawled.

"Not for a lack of trying, trust me," Travion muttered.

Sereia snorted. They didn't know the half of it.

"What have you found?" Draven asked, cutting to the heart of the matter.

"Destruction, everywhere we go. The rumors are true. We very nearly lost both our ships to a sea serpent larger than you can imagine. Shortly after that, we rescued a group of fishermen who had been run aground by the kraken. We've battled crabs the size of cows, and we are currently in Sahille where an entire village was decimated by one the size of a ship." His tone was grave and his expression dark.

Both brothers cursed in response.

Someone was leading them on a merry little jaunt along the coast. And Sereia was quite certain they were aware Travion was out here. But were they trying to cover their tracks, or was this all to keep Travion preoccupied and away from Midniva?

"Any luck finding the culprit?" It was Zryan this time, with hope in his voice.

"Not yet. But two men here in Sahille tried to stop him. One was terribly injured and the other killed in the process, but they did manage to wound him with a sword and rip a page from The Creaturae."

"What have you done to find him?" Draven asked.

Sereia ruffled a little at the question. She realized Draven didn't mean it the way it came off, but she wanted to growl that they had followed every lead that had come their way.

"It's why we've come to Sahille. We're hoping to track him from his injuries. I wanted to catch you up quickly on what has happened thus far, and then Sereia and I will go out in search."

"What can be done on our end?" Draven asked.

"Send aid to Kian. If what Sereia and I have met out here at sea is any indication of what Midniva can expect upon her shores, my forces alone will not be enough. We must be ready, and assume that I will not be back in time for the initial attack."

"I can send Ruan with my forces at once," Zryan offered. "Draven can be of aid if the beasts come at dusk," he quipped, taunting his eldest brother.

Sereia watched Travion roll his eyes and wondered if his

elder brother's expression matched. The two were similar in many ways, and now that made far more sense to her than it ever had before. Draven had been Travion's only solace for many years while simultaneously being the greatest weapon used against him.

A part of Sereia softened toward the nightmare king, knowing that he had done what he could to be there for Travion.

"Yes, I am useless in the daylight," Draven muttered irritably. "But if my harpies or wolves are needed, I will send them to Kian."

"Thank you. I will reach out once we have found the man in question. Once we have him and the book, we can return to Midniva. But keep watch over your own realms and Midniva's shores. An attack is coming, of that I am certain." Travion straightened and dragged his fingers through the water, severing the connection. He stood from the desk, running a hand down his face with a heavy sigh.

"They are capable. They will watch the shoreline until you return," Sereia assured him.

"Well, mostly capable—one of them is Zryan after all." Travion cracked a small grin.

In return, Sereia reached out and grabbed the front of his shirt, pulling him in to nestle between her spread thighs. She rested both her hands on his chest, looking up at him. "We will find this man. With a wound, he's bound to slow down and not cover his tracks as well. Now, would you like to begin our hunting party?" Her hands slid up around the back of his neck.

His face was lined with exhaustion, and Sereia echoed the feeling within herself. But it had already been three days between the battle of Sahille and their arrival. If there was any chance of finding his trail, they had to set out now.

Travion settled his hands on her hips and pressed a kiss to her forehead. "Yes, let's go and find our culprit."

Tracking by lantern with only the shine of the moon overhead adding additional lighting was not ideal. Dusk had just settled over the land when they had headed out, and now there was nothing but night sky above. Too many times, Sereia found herself releasing a string of curse words as she tripped over a stone she hadn't noticed.

Their one saving grace was that Yon was in no way deterred by the darkness. In fact, it was as if she had come alive, so fully in her element that she moved with stealth and ease over every obstacle. Sereia, not for the first time, was very glad to have brought the former assassin with them.

After young Radomir had been coaxed into showing them where his father battled the man with the book, Yon was like a hound following the scent and located a trail of blood that left the scene and headed south along the coast. From there, it had made sense to let Yon lead the search party.

"We are fortunate that it has not rained since the attack of the crab and that the wielder of the book stuck to the upper portion of the beach," Yon stated as they made their way through tall sea grass. She paused to show them a heavy patch of red on the tips. "He is not familiar with tracking, that I can tell. He was still bleeding heavily and has left a very easy trail to follow. Had this been me, I would have walked along the waterline so that the tide would wash away any traces of my path."

Yon was in motion once more, and Travion followed closely behind.

"Small wonders," Sereia, a lantern swinging in her hand, muttered. Nothing about this journey had been easy, but at least their quarry did not know how to conceal his trail.

"You'd think someone who has run us on such a merry chase would know not to leave his blood like a path directly to him," Adrik said from behind her.

Sereia snorted. She had to agree with him, though. "It is a fairly amateur thing to do."

"But it tells us a little more about the man we are following," Finn added.

Before she could reply, Sereia tripped over another rock. "Bloody seas and stars!" she growled. "If I trip on one more damn stone, I am going to give this man another scar to remember."

Travion looked over his shoulder at her. "Having troubles?"

"Yes." She glared at him, and he had the nerve to simply smirk before facing forward once more.

The exhaustion that was beginning to set in from this journey did not help with making her way in the darkness. Constant travel, infused with life-threatening danger and battles, did not leave much time for true rest. She knew her temper was getting the best of her right now, but then, keeping it in check had never really been her strong suit.

However, she continued to make her way along the coast, following the steps that Travion took, climbing over small rocky areas, wading through tall beach grasses, and keeping most of her exasperation to herself.

"It looks like he stopped here," Yon announced at last, and the four of them gathered around her. "I can see from the indent in the grasses there"—her hand waved to a portion of flattened grass—"that he sat down. There is a heavy pool of blood, and I would assume weakness from blood loss began to set in at this point."

Together, she and Finn began to walk the circle, their lanterns swaying from their hands as they lifted them into the air, briefly highlighting tall seagrass before returning it to darkness.

"I'm not seeing any more signs of blood," said Finn.

"Neither am I," Yon seconded.

"He has the book," Travion spoke at last. "He likely sat down here to heal himself."

"So we've lost him?" Sereia threaded a hand through her hair angrily, pulling strands free of her braid.

"No," Yon corrected. "He went this way." Her lantern swung through the air to highlight the new trail, and she was on her way once more.

This time Finn joined Yon in the tracking, the two of them holding their lanterns forward to illuminate the path. And they lead the way for several more yards, carrying the group along the coastline, the sound of the rough waves upon the shore nearly drowning out their footsteps over the rocky beach.

But then the man's trail wound farther down to the beach, and his footprints were gone, washed away by the tide currently working its way back out.

"Now we have lost him," Travion growled, angrily throwing his lantern against an outcropping of rocks. Flames flared, oil burning along the stone where it had splashed, before fizzling out.

Sighing, Sereia gazed at the others. "We're all exhausted. Let's build a fire and camp out here for the night. Finn, collect firewood and get a bonfire going. Adrik, Yon, the two of you see what you can catch for us to eat."

The three of them nodded and quickly dispersed. Sereia, taking a deep breath and pushing her own frustrations to the side, stepped up to Travion, pressing a hand to his lower back. He stiffened, and she could feel the way he almost pulled away to hide his current emotions. In response, her fingers tightened in the back of his shirt.

"This isn't a dead end, Travion."

"No?" He spun to face her, anger contorting his features. "It bloody well feels as if it is!"

"Fine!" she snapped back. "By the sea! It's a damn dead end!" He just glared at her. "But it's not the end. Velox and his pod are still out there searching, so are the dolphins, and when we've got a fraction of sunlight and aren't at our wit's end with exhaustion, I'm sure Yon will pick up another trail."

Travion sighed roughly, some of the anger draining from his shoulders as he ran a hand over his face.

"We're going to find this piece of tripe, and we will get our vengeance for everything he has done in the name of some twisted purpose."

Travion slid his arm around her waist and pulled her in against him. "When did you become so optimistic?"

"It's not optimism. It's determination." Travion pressed a kiss to her lips, and Sereia leaned into it, accepting the silent apology for his anger. "Come, your giant has prepared a fire for us."

Together, they moved over to the bonfire, which Finn had diligently built and then discreetly wandered away from, giving them privacy.

The fire crackled, shooting sparks up into the night sky as she and Travion took a seat in the sand before it. A groan left her lips as she settled on her bottom, the true level of her exhaustion setting in as her muscles were able to rest at long last.

Travion sat quietly beside her, the firelight lighting up his features as he stared into the flames. His expression wasn't as stern as his older brother's, but the seriousness was there in the creases around his eyes and the clench of his jaw. While he was not good at saying it, Travion cared deeply. About his people, his family, and his responsibilities. Sereia knew he would not rest until this was all sorted out and his kingdom was safe.

"This may seem foolish to be asking now, but if the book is so dangerous, why didn't you destroy it? Why decide to keep it around?" The question had burnt a hole in her mind as of late. The more she saw of its destruction, the more she couldn't help but wonder why it even still existed.

"We tried to once, my brothers and I. Tore it. Burned it. Struck it with lightning and rain. No matter what we did, once the pieces were brought together, the book would be made whole. If I were to place that page where it had been torn from, it would mend itself. Creation lives within its pages, formed when the very first fae roamed the realms. It was a way to contain the powers of life and death, good and evil. And one family was meant to possess it, with the understanding that it should only be opened for necessity." Travion's eyes never left the fire as he spoke, and he seemed to grow more distant by the minute.

She had not picked a topic to lighten the mood. Sereia watched him, the intensity within his gaze, as he relived some memory of old.

"It was a gift and a curse, one that was never meant to be opened by just anyone. To use it is to take the risk of releasing darkness into the world."

"And yet it has been used, and now we need to contain it once more." Sereia's shoulders felt tight. This was a task for the foolhardy who wished to die. Without thought, her fingers moved to the pendant, coiling the chain around them as she worked out her agitation.

"Yes, we do." Travion looked over at her, his eyes troubled, reflecting her own emotions.

She felt a bitter laugh rising up inside her. "You know, when I left Midniva, I never thought it would be something like this that would draw us back into each other's lives."

"Me either," he muttered.

They both fell silent, the crackle of the fire and the crush of the tide the only sounds around them.

"Why did you leave?" he asked at last, breaking the silence.

Sereia's heart clenched, and she tugged a little at her pendant, the chain biting into the back of her neck. Not at the question that he'd never asked before, but at the unspoken words behind them. The emotion that bubbled just below the surface. It was her turn to stare into the fire, eyes drifting down to the red embers at the bottom. "Because the life my mother had planned out for me felt like shackles pulling me down into the depths of a dark cave I could never escape from."

She sighed and rubbed her face, then leaned back, burying her hands in the cool sand.

"Was I something you needed to escape as well?"

Her eyes slid shut, and she swallowed roughly before shaking her head. "No. It was the life, the expectations. The thought that I would be tied to that place for the rest of my days, and I'd have had done nothing of importance." She sat up and turned to face him, her legs folding crisscrossed beneath her. "From the day each of us was born, my mother drilled into us how important it was to be a lady and to wed well. Every day was lesson upon lesson in music, dance, embroidery, language. Anything and everything to make a well-established lady, but nothing about what truly interested us.

"While my sisters soaked up each lesson, I ached deep within myself. I knew that I didn't belong in that world. That something inside me would die if I were to be trapped on land to live out my days as just someone's wife. The water called to me, *begging* me to go out on it. I wasn't running from you, Travion, I was running toward myself. You've had so many centuries to figure out who you are. To experience life and all that it has to offer. I just needed that time for myself. Needed to discover who I was. To see the world. To actually have a chance to *live*."

"And did you? Find yourself?"

"I did." Her eyes fell to the sand between them. "I've been able to grow and live out from under the shadow of anyone else's expectations or rules. I found who I am as a female and as a fae. For the first time, I was able to live for myself and not for anyone else." Her throat tightened as emotion welled up inside her, and she pondered whether she could be truly vulnerable with him now.

"I'm glad." His words were soft but honest.

"But there wasn't one moment out there that I didn't miss you." She forced her voice not to crack. "That I didn't wonder if someone else had come to claim your heart and be there for you in a way I wasn't able to yet."

Travion seemed shocked at this admission, but then the shock melded into something warmer. "I never wanted to shackle you or cage you like some exotic bird." He sucked in his bottom lip and closed his eyes. "Do you remember our first time together?"

"I do. It was on a beach much like this."

Travion's eyes met hers, and he closed the distance between them, his hands clamping around her waist to pull her easily into his lap. Sereia went willingly, her knees spreading out to either side of him and her hands sliding over his shoulders and up into his hair.

"I knew even then you were a wild creature that should never be tamed," he admitted roughly.

"You almost did," she breathed out on a sigh. Leaning in, Sereia kissed him, her fingers tight in his hair.

"No," he shook his head, breaking the kiss to nip lightly at her lips and jaw.

Her head tipped back, exposing her neck so that his lips and teeth could continue their travels unhindered. Her flesh shivered at the pleasure, toes curling in her boots. "Yes. Spending time with you . . . By the sea, it almost made me stay."

His head lifted from the hollow of her throat, his eyes searching hers. There was a question within his blue depths, one that Sereia wished he would ask but also feared in the same breath.

"Ahem, may I present to you a fish?" a voice cut in, breaking through the intimate moment.

Both of them turned their heads to look at Adrik, who stood on the other side of the fire, holding out a large flounder, his finger hooked in its mouth. Beyond him, Finn and Yon stood together, staring off into the distance.

Grumbling at the reminder that they were not alone, and thus could not continue the intimacy that had been building between them, Sereia slid off Travion's lap. "Did you want me to congratulate you?"

"Maybe?" He shot her a knowing grin.

"Just gut and roast the damn fish, Adrik."

"Aye, aye, Captain." Adrik winked at her and then went about preparing the fish for them to eat.

As the fish was roasted and consumed they fell into silence that was both comfortable and poignant.

While there were moments of distraction to be found on their journey, a dark cloud still remained to shroud them. Tonight, they had felt so close to finding the one behind all of this, and their failure felt like a harsh slap.

Sereia hadn't been lying when she said she wasn't optimistic, just determined. No matter how hopeless this felt at times, she would not give up until they found the man responsible for these horrors and made him pay.

19

Travion

The fire crackled and popped as it died down. Sereia nestled into Travion's side, allowing one of his arms to drape over her back. She breathed softly, deeply, letting him know she was asleep.

Travion peered down at her, only able to see dark lashes fanning her high cheekbones. He should've been sleeping too while they waited. Seas only knew how long they had before the inevitable fight came. Because he was no fool. Travion knew a battle was on the way. But what he wasn't certain of was if he would survive this one. His jaw clenched as he stared up at the night sky, willing the stars to bring forth the man in question, but they only winked at him. He hoped, with a promise. However, it did nothing to soothe his growing tension.

Travion brushed his lips against the top of Sereia's head, letting his eyes shut. Perhaps he could sleep for just a—

A high-pitched clicking squeak rolled along the waves, then the distinct sound of spraying water.

Dolphin.

Travion shifted to ease out from under Sereia, but the

movement was enough to wake her, and she sprang up, glancing around.

"The dolphins have returned." Travion pushed himself to his feet, gathering his clothes, and hurriedly dressed. He padded toward the shoreline, and hermit crabs frantically skittered across the smooth sand.

Sereia wasn't far behind him.

The lead dolphin clicked a greeting to him, slapping his front flipper against the water. Although the dolphin creaked and whistled, images flashed in Travion's mind. Simple words came together too:

Big light in the sky. A winged hippocampus. Dead man in the water. The one you wanted. Blood.

"What?" Travion snapped, taken by surprise. "What do you mean?" But the creature only revisited the same list of information.

Sereia tugged on his wrist. "Travion, what is it?"

He shook himself out of the dolphin's mind. "They say there is a dead man on the shore." Travion shared a look with Sereia, and she sucked in a breath, piecing together what he didn't say. "Can you take us to him?" he asked the creature, and the dolphin bobbed his head in the water and dove away, only to resurface farther away, waiting.

"What good is he to us dead?" Sereia hissed as she jogged forward.

She was right, but . . . "We don't know if he is dead. The dolphins can't reach the shore to inspect." With a newfound burst of energy, Travion ran down the beach as the dolphin led the way. Nearly a quarter mile down the beach, the dolphin paused, slapping the water with its fins.

Travion halted and scanned the shoreline, but Sereia was already rushing toward a gathering of seaweed. Travion focused on it, relying on the moonlight, and he realized it wasn't just plant matter but a lifeless body too.

She hauled the body onto the shore, sucking in a breath as she rolled the man over.

Travion crossed the distance and knelt, swearing a blue streak as he recognized the man to be none other than his steward, Taimon.

Red hair, black eyes. Never in a millennia would he have thought they were describing *Taimon*! His heart raced wildly, and fury rose within him, threatening to consume him. Travion's hands shook, but he shoved the betrayal away.

Crimson trickled into the water, darkening it. Taimon was wounded—Jonathan had mentioned he'd managed to inflict an injury on the redheaded man.

Travion reached down, his brow furrowing as he pulled at the torn linen shirt. "He did heal himself. Look at these wounds, they're scarred over." He rolled the bottom half of the shirt up, exposing Taimon's fresh scar. "This is where Jonathan said he ran him through, but what is this?" Claw marks raked down his side, exposing muscle and bone. Blood seeped from the wound still and spilled into the water.

He wouldn't die. Not before Travion had all the answers he needed. Taimon was the perfect unsuspecting piece in this, wasn't he? While Travion lay in a pool of his blood after being gored by a manticore, Taimon could have swept onto the scene, scarcely noticed, as he was a member of the castle and trusted.

Had been trusted.

"Taimon is behind this?" Sereia whispered, moving her fingers to his throat. "He's alive, but barely."

"Taimon must have grabbed the book while I was being pieced back together," he murmured. "We need to bandage him up as best we can if we have any hopes of saving him." Although he deserved to rot at the bottom of the sea, they needed whatever knowledge the bastard had.

She twisted her lips as if contemplating whether to drive a blade into Taimon's heart. "And carry him back?" Disbelief shone within her gaze.

Travion tilted his head back, summoning more patience that he didn't have. Why couldn't any of this be straightforward or *easy*? "No. Even if we could stabilize him, it would take too long to reach the bloody ship."

Velox surfaced, as if called by Travion's inner turmoil.

"I swear to the seas and shores you are not worth the trouble." He stripped his shirt off. "If I didn't need what's in your head, I'd finish tearing your innards out myself," he hissed, roughly slipping the shirt beneath his steward's body and knotting it so it staunched the flow of blood and kept his innards in place.

"As would I," Sereia agreed.

"Velox, call one of your pod members," Travion said over his shoulder. "Help me carry him into the water," he said to Sereia. "We'll save time and possibly his life if we take to the water."

"Not that he deserves it," she muttered.

"No, but we deserve answers," Travion said as he slid an arm beneath Taimon's upper half and Sereia took care of his lower body. Together, they carried him into the water, keeping Taimon afloat until the hippocampus arrived.

Velox steadied as Taimon was lifted onto his back. He slid forward, slumping against the creature's neck, and Travion climbed behind the limp body. *Live, you wretched bastard. So that I can kill you myself.*

Sereia mounted the other hippocampus, a smaller one

with yellow patches around its muzzle, melding in with the green of its jowls.

From down the beach, Finn, Yon, and Adrik appeared, finally catching up. Sereia waved an arm to capture their attention, and the three quickly ran to join them. Several more members of Velox's pod popped their heads above water.

"Hurry, there's no time to explain, get onto a hippocampus. We have to get back to the ship."

Looking somewhat stunned, the three waded into the water and claimed a willing steed.

In this state or any other, it was difficult for Travion to picture his steward as a villain, especially one who had a hand in his near death. Taimon was reserved, efficient, and dutiful. But how well did Travion know him? How much time and effort had Travion spent learning about him?

Taimon's pallor had grown gray, and Travion worried they were too late.

"His pulse is barely fluttering," Travion muttered as his fingers pressed against the man's throat.

"How unfortunate." Sereia sighed as she twined her fingers around the webbing of her mount's mane. "We'd better ride fast, then."

With a whistle, the hippocampi set off, their fins easily dashing through the water, far faster than Travion or Sereia would have been walking on land.

By the time they reached where *Speedwell* was docked, Taimon's lips were losing their pinkness. Little by little, the life was leeching out of him, and had they carried him, Travion had no doubt he would have died.

Travion slid from Velox and carefully drew Taimon down. Then Sereia was by his side, helping to bring him to shore, where they laid him down. "Go get Lefyr. He's nearly dead!"

Sereia darted away, running up the beach and disappearing from sight.

Finn came to stand over Travion, staring down at the unconscious man on the beach, shock registering on his face.

Taimon's chest barely moved and as Travion checked his pulse again. A faint thrum beat against his fingers.

Lefyr raced down the beach with Sereia leading the way. She sucked in a breath but didn't say a word as Lefyr knelt down beside Taimon and placed a hand against his chest. The soft beating of magic filled the air as the gash running across the half-fae's torso healed, and he sucked in a sputtering breath.

"He's stable for now. Enough so we can move him inside *Speedwell*. I'll do more there." Lefyr looked up at Travion, and a question burned brightly in his gaze, but one he never asked.

There really was no other option, he supposed. Or one that wasn't rash. Taimon had to be brought to the *Speedwell* because, once fully healed, he'd be secured in the brig as a prisoner. Travion wasn't about to chance him escaping.

"Let's carry the bastard to the ship then, because I want answers." He slid an arm beneath Taimon's upper half, and Lefyr tended to the lower portion as they lifted him up. Lefyr matched Travion's stride, and they carried him onto the dock. Finn followed behind, and his expression was now one of absolute fury. Oh, he'd have to get in line, because there was no doubt Sereia would leap at the chance to do Taimon in first.

"So, do you all know this man?" Lefyr asked. "He seems to pull quite the reaction from all of you."

Before Travion could open his mouth, Finn reached forward, plucked the limp body from his arms, and brought him onto the ship, silencing the healer. Taimon looked like no more than a doll in his guard's hold.

Travion clenched his jaw as he stared Lefyr down. "You need to wake him, now. Heal him enough so he can talk."

Lefyr's dark brow furrowed in question. "But you didn't answer—"

Travion lifted a brow. He longed to snap at him, to shake him by the shoulders because he had no idea what *this male* had done. This wasn't the time to question him, and the fae must have seen that written across the tight lines of his face because he stepped back and averted his gaze.

"And he doesn't have to," Sereia said, stepping onto the plank and crossing it. "When Taimon wakes, I want my face to be the first thing that two-faced bastard sees." She tossed her hair over her shoulder, and every muscle of her body tensed, clearly bent on revenge.

Lefyr swallowed roughly but continued, "It is best that he rest—"

"I don't remember asking what is best for him. I ordered you to heal him, and I suggest you do it now," Travion growled as he walked closer to Lefyr.

Lefyr closed his eyes, nodding, but the words he spoke weren't the ones Travion wanted to hear. "I understand, but what *you* must understand is this: I don't have an endless supply of energy, and I've pushed myself to my limits this entire time. That male needs to rest so I can be most useful to you and him."

"By the sea!" Fury rose within Travion, not for the first time, and lightning crackled in the distance. Thunder boomed loudly, rumbling through the town.

Sereia reached out, placing her hand on his back. "Trask," she murmured, pulling him from his well of anger.

His shoulders dropped down a fraction, and he sighed. "Very well, we have no choice. Bring him below."

Finn disappeared from the deck. He wanted his pound of flesh too, but he also wanted Taimon to pay for the crimes against Midniva, Andhera, and Lucem. For the innocents who were slain and those who suffered because of the consequences of Taimon's vile actions. That meant keeping him alive for the time being, as much as he was loath to admit it.

Seahawks circled above, crying in dismay over the loss of a potential meal. Travion crossed the deck and descended the stairs leading toward the captain's quarters. He could hear Sereia speaking but couldn't make out words until he was at the door.

"If we weren't certain about Lefyr knowing before, I think we can safely say now that he *knows* who Travion is," Sereia hissed.

"It wouldn't surprise me. I've seen the way he looks at him," Finn said.

A pause. Then, "Maybe he doesn't need his eyes."

Finn's sigh turned into a groan. "I can't tell if you're serious or not. You cannot just go around plucking eyes out, Captain."

Travion swallowed down a laugh as it bubbled up his throat. He knew for a fact that the lovely Sereia wasn't jesting, and that she wouldn't hesitate to exact her revenge on Taimon for all that he'd done. He'd seen the rage—the hurt—burning in her eyes when she'd first seen his scars.

He slid the door open, and Sereia turned to face him, but his eyes focused on Finn, who looked exasperated. "My dear, loyal Finn Kyros. I promise you that Sereia isn't jesting. Did you know she insulted Draven's wife at the ball? Called her . . . what was it, a childish brat or harlot?" He turned his head to face Sereia, who pressed her lips together and jutted her chin out.

"It was both, actually. And it was a grave misunderstanding. She's a lovely lady," Sereia mumbled, swiping a strand of hair out of her face.

Finn's mouth parted in horror, his brows knitting together as he looked between the two. "And His Grace didn't . . ."

"It turns out, he can be reasonable," Sereia muttered.

Travion lowered into a chair next to the table where his steward lay. A gray wool blanket covered Taimon's body, and his sopping-wet clothes were piled in a heap beside the door. The bastard didn't deserve to lie in his bed. Whatever discomfort he suffered was well deserved. His head lolled to the side, mouth slack, but at least his color was returning to its typical creamy shade. Soon they'd have answers. Soon.

Travion grinned, chuckling. "Oh, I'm sure he was tempted to retaliate," he finally said. But Sereia was his lover, however temporary or infrequent their interactions may be. She was his, and he was hers.

She blew out a breath and leaned forward, poised for an argument, but as she shifted, her eyes squinted and focused on Taimon. "Get Lefyr. He's struggling to breathe."

Finn jumped to his feet and raced out of the quarters before Travion even had the chance to reiterate.

Taimon's chest rose and fell, reminding Travion of a fish gasping for breath on the shore. "He was just fine!" he ground out, but of course this half-wit would try to die before he could face judgment.

"And now he's not." Sereia curled her fingers into her palms as she glared down at the half-fae.

A moment later, Lefyr rushed into the quarters, looking windblown. His white linen shirt hung open at the top, and his silken black hair was in disarray. "Listen, I have to get something out of the way before I continue . . ."

Travion clenched his teeth, seething as the healer took his time. "Do *not* take this moment to—"

Lefyr dipped his head again, then words poured from his mouth so quickly, Travion almost didn't process them. "Apologies, Your Grace, but I know that you're King Travion." Then he darted toward the table, his fingers tugging down the woolen blanket covering Taimon.

"Told you," Sereia and Finn said to each other at the same time.

"I've known since I sat next to you at the tavern. While we've never been introduced, nor have we mingled, I've seen you plenty of times, and I'd be a poor excuse for a Midnivian if I didn't know my king's face," Lefyr supplied, working his fingers down Taimon's torso. A soft, lapping glow crawled along his skin, reminding Travion of a cuttlefish's oscillating fins, then the light disappeared.

Taimon sucked in a breath and sat upright, his eyes wild and feverish. Whatever Lefyr meant to say next was forgotten, because Taimon's eyes locked with Travion's and he bolted from the table. Any doubts Travion may have had about Taimon's guilt disappeared.

Finn darted for the door, blocking it with his body, and Sereia reached for a sword. But Travion rushed for his steward, grabbing him by the neck and forcing him back onto the table. Taimon's nails scraped down his forearm, stinging and bloodying him, but for all the rage that threatened to scald him from the inside, he didn't care.

"I suggest you sit your scrawny self back down, Taimon. You're in quite the predicament." He spoke through gritted teeth and loosened his grip as the male settled.

Sereia rounded the table, blade at the ready. "I will drive this through you and let him heal you only to do it again, understand?" She swung the tip toward Lefyr, then back at Taimon.

Taimon bit down on his lip hard enough to draw blood, and it trickled down his chin. Every inch of the male was tense as his mouth opened and he looked as though he would vomit. But his stomach didn't lurch. Was he trying to speak?

"Are you spelled against speaking about the book?" Travion drawled, dragging his gaze from the table to his steward's eyes. Taimon nodded but didn't utter a word. *By the sea, of course he was spelled!* "If you refuse to speak, you know what will happen, Taimon. You've been in my service for over twenty years, and you know I will cut it out of you if I must."

Taimon's bottom lip quivered, but he said nothing.

"There is a way around the spell. You could avoid suffering at this moment if you comply. Do you agree to try?" It took everything within Travion to offer fairness to a male who deserved to burn to ash, to die alone on the shore of a foreign country.

His steward's ebony eyes slid toward him with such contempt that Travion had a difficult time seeing the frazzled male that sat in on his council meetings and had helped him when Travion needed it most.

"I refuse," Taimon croaked. Contrary to his earlier

attempt at speaking about the spell, the steward wouldn't comply, not even to save himself.

"Very well." Travion glanced at Sereia, and she nodded. "Lefyr, if you don't have the stomach for this, leave now." Fury ebbed from him, and in its wake, calmness reigned. An eerie stillness, like the sea before a storm.

With a careful grace, Travion crossed the room and gathered a spare belt. Taimon flinched but didn't move, not until Travion returned to the table and grabbed his arms. He pulled back, whimpering, but relented as Finn took a step closer.

"Last warning for you, Lefyr, and also for you, Taimon." When neither budged, he coiled the leather belt around Taimon's wrists, and Sereia bound his ankles together with rope. "Finn, hang him from the beam." Travion rolled the sleeves of his shirt to his biceps, watching as his guard hoisted the smaller male up so his wrists held his weight, then yanking his arms up in a painful stretch. "How could I forget?" He turned his back to his steward and walked to a shelf where a blue embroidered handkerchief sat. Travion swiped it and returned to stand before the male, who swung like a pendulum. "To silence your cries and to keep you from biting your tongue off."

"Is he going to . . ." Lefyr stammered.

"I think you should leave, Lefyr," Sereia bit out. "And you'll be called in when you're needed."

Lefyr scrambled for the cabin door and hurriedly exited, slamming the door shut as he left.

"We'll only call for him when it's completely necessary," Travion offered to Taimon as he circled him. He lifted the blade in his hand and let the tip bite into the flesh on

Taimon's shoulder. A muffled cry escaped his steward as blood trickled down his back.

He'd see how long Taimon would hold out.

When his steward's back was reduced to ribbons, and his head hung limply to the side, Finn left to collect Lefyr.

But when they returned, Travion lifted a hand. "Don't fully heal him. I want him to endure this pain, but I need him conscious enough to speak."

Lefyr's pale face appeared quite green around the gills. "As you wish," he murmured, lifting his hands to place around the male's hips.

As Taimon roused, Travion yanked the cloth from his mouth. "Are you ready to talk now?" Sereia came to stand beside him. He hadn't so much as glanced at her during the torture, and part of him was afraid to. What did she see in him then? Did she see he was no better than his father? That Ludari's vile nature ran through his veins too?

Taimon shook violently, no doubt from the pain radiating through his body. "Th-they left me. They took the book. I did everything th-they asked me to." His body convulsed, and then he spewed bile. It splattered on the floor, mingling with his blood.

"Who are they, Taimon?" Travion bit out, but there was no answer. He reached out and grabbed the male's chin, forcing him to look him in the eye. "Why? Why do this to me? After everything?"

Taimon spat in his face. "Because you and your brothers are all the same, and in the end, you'll get what is coming to y—"

Sereia's fist connected with his jaw, and for the second time, Taimon's head lolled to the side. "Speak to him that way again, and I will gut you like the worthless rat you are," she spat. Her eyes were blazing with fury—not fear or hatred toward Travion, but anger directed toward his steward and his involvement in everything. The book, his near death . . .

Travion ran a hand down his face, scrunching his nose as he realized blood caked his fingers. "Oh, he will die, just not now." He motioned for Finn to pull him down from the beam. "Throw him in the brig, and Lefyr, stand by in case he decides to fail on us again."

Because if he did, Lefyr would bring him back, again and again. Until Travion could put him on trial in Midniva.

Sereia crossed the room, closing the door. Then she halted, squinting at the pile of discarded clothes. She knelt down, rummaging through them until she pulled out a wet, crumpled piece of paper.

Even from where Travion stood, from the color of the paper, the length, he knew what it was. A piece of The Creaturae.

20

Sereia

Though not the first page they'd found from the book, it was Sereia's first time holding one. While she had felt the steady thrum of power from the page Travion carried, holding it in her own hands was an entirely different experience. Power tingled through every nerve in her fingers, trailing up her forearms and zinging through her neck to the very top of her head.

The spell written on the page was in a language so old, it was no longer spoken, and Sereia could not read it. "Taimon must have torn it from the book when they left him for dead." She brought it across the room to hand to Travion, who took the page and folded it up with the first. "Will this slow them down? Two pages missing?"

Travion shook his head. "The first page was minor spells, things for regrowing crops or forests." He looked at the newest page. "Taimon managed to tear a page from the destructive side. This spell looks like it is for tearing open the earth."

"Which you can already do . . ." She sighed and dropped down into a chair. "By the sea, I thought when we found

Taimon we would have our answers, yet the book is still missing."

"That has been our issue the entire time. When Naya attacked the realms, my brothers and I believed that we had found the source of our issues. We never dreamed there was another person orchestrating the attacks. Now . . . we find ourselves with the same problem, and whoever they are has left their lackey to die, and we are back to square one!"

Sereia could see the anger and frustration in his eyes. Constantly trailing behind whoever was controlling this had to be leaving him feeling helpless. *Not* an emotion Travion dealt well with. She knew this because she felt the same way.

After all their efforts, there had to be something they could do. Sereia glanced down at the pages in Travion's hands.

"You know," she began, uncertain if she should even bring this up. "There is a tracking spell whispered about amongst pirates. One used for locating lost treasure." Travion's eyes studied her, and she could tell she had his full attention. "Trouble is, it's nigh on impossible to do because it requires having a piece of the treasure itself, and knowing where it was last on land before taking to the sea. The hardest ingredient to get your hands on is the blood of the last known person in possession of the treasure. And if they've already been lost to the sea . . ." She shrugged, eyes locking with Travion's. "But—"

"We've got all that."

Sereia nodded. "I'm not certain it will work, but if we take a little of that chum-bucket's blood, this page, and head to the beach where the battle took place, there should be enough magical residue in the land to give us a heading." It might be a shot in the dark. Sereia had only seen the spell done once and had never performed it herself. She'd be going solely off a memory of a rather drunken and desperate night.

"It would be worth a try. We don't have much to lose at this point." Travion's eyes gleamed with determination and hope.

Sereia prayed she didn't end up dashing it all on the rocks.

The dory bobbed on the choppy water as Adrik rowed them away from the ship and back to the little beach where they had discovered Taimon's body. Finn and Yon sat together in a second dory, neither uttering a word. There was an odd tension between the two of them that Sereia didn't have time to figure out.

When the dory slid through the sand and up onto the beach, Sereia jumped out, her boots splashing in the shallow water. She moved quickly onto the beach itself, clutching a leather satchel. Dropping to her knees in the sand, she wasted no time getting to work.

Sereia brushed extra rocks and seaweed out of her way, creating a flat surface to work on, and dug a large stone bowl out of her bag. Not needing to look up to see if Travion was at her side, she held the bowl out to him. "Please collect some water for me. Only a quarter of the bowl." Once he had taken the bowl, Sereia brought out the remaining items. The page Taimon had torn from the book, a vial of blood, and a map of the entire sea and surrounding nations.

Travion was back at her side shortly, and once the bowl was set on the beach, Sereia pushed the page of The

Creaturae to the bottom. With that in place, she scooped some sand and poured it carefully into the bowl so as not to cloud the seawater. As the sand settled, Sereia took a deep breath and looked up at Travion.

"No promises this will work."

He nodded. "No promises."

Unstopping the vial, Sereia began to murmur the spell, ancient maritime words from some long-gone god of creation. *"Invenire thesauram quaeram."* As she whispered, the words a prickle of heat along the inside of her throat, a cold wind wrapped around her, sliding over her arms and across the back of her neck. A shiver coursed down her spine. Slowly, Sereia poured the droplets of blood into the bowl, her eyes never leaving the sand and water.

She continued to murmur the words, and Travion, kneeling beside her, joined in on the chant. For a moment, nothing happened, just the two of them whispering ancient words and a chilling breeze swirling around them.

She could feel the expectation and held breath of the group, the way they all eagerly watched, and the pressure of that almost made her falter. But Sereia kept uttering the words of the spell, repeating them over and over again, drawing strength from Travion's continued support until, at last, the contents of the bowl began to swirl and mix. A faint light then rose from the water.

Sighing with relief, Sereia sat back on her heels.

"A little lackluster," Travion murmured.

Sereia shot him a glare. "It's not an immediate solution. It has to track, so now we give it the chance to do that. But it's mixing, so I do believe that it's working."

"Do you know how long it'll take?" he pressed.

"I don't know." She shrugged and sighed with irritation. "It's old magic, so it'll take however long it pleases."

At her side Adrik grumbled. "S'all a little anticlimactic, Captain." It was his turn to receive a glare from Sereia. "Well, it is . . ." He smirked at her. "How about the three of us work on fetching us all something to eat?"

Sereia nodded at him, her eyes traveling to Yon, who shifted ever so slightly, but it was enough to show acceptance of this task.

As the sailors all dispersed, Sereia patted the sand beside her. "Sit," she instructed Travion.

He looked like he wanted to protest, but as there wasn't much else to do, he took a seat beside her.

"I don't like all of this waiting."

"Me either. But it's waiting with a purpose. Once this spell works"—and it *would* work, she had decided—"we'll have a proper heading. We'll know where this damn book *is* and can go directly for it instead of this constant searching." It was the searching and never finding that was getting to both of them. She could see it in Travion's weariness. The faint lines of irritation that pinched at the corners of his eyes.

Neither of them were good at not accomplishing what they set out to do, both running into whatever situation was upon them, good or bad, simply because it needed to be done.

"Mmm," he grunted in response.

Her eyes shifted to Travion, who was staring down at the swirling bowl, a frown marring his face.

"How are you doing?"

He blinked, but his expression didn't change. "I'm fine."

"No, Travion." Sereia reached out to take his hand, pulling

it into her lap, forcing him to look at her. "I mean truly, how are you doing? Your kingdom was attacked, your family put in terrible danger . . . You almost died." The word still wanted to lodge in her throat, surrounded by a deep sorrow that threatened to spill out of her in rage and woe so violent, she didn't know if she could contain it. He was safe, so there was no need for it. But how near to death he'd come left her unable to fathom the repercussions. "And now, there is this new, unimaginable threat bearing down on Midniva and all you care about. Forget being king, tell me how *Travion* is doing."

He looked like he wanted to speak about anything other than his actual feelings. And for a moment, she thought he would brush her off. Showing vulnerability was not something Sereia was used to seeing from Travion. But he stilled, falling even more silent, if that were possible, as if thinking on it. Then he finally spoke.

"It's hard to forget the king part," he admitted softly. "It's who I've been for so very long." His fingers coiled around hers. "I don't do well with such violations on my land and people. The threat to my family least of all. I want bloodshed and revenge. I want to ensure that whoever is doing this tastes the cold brunt of steel again and again, until they know such horrors that no one will ever dare attack us again." His fingers tightened on her hand. "And it frustrates me to the deepest, darkest parts of myself that we are still so in the dark as to who is orchestrating all of this."

"We will find them," she assured him. "If we have to scour every last inch of this ocean, dive to the very depths of it, I vow we will find whoever is guilty of this, Travion. And we will make them pay."

She knew then that she would spend the rest of her days

hunting down the culprit if it meant bringing him peace once more.

Travion lifted her hand to his lips and kissed the back of it. "If your spell works, hopefully the depths of the ocean won't be required."

Silence fell between them, and Sereia felt herself being drawn in nearer to him. The desire to lose herself to his touch and his kiss was a strong and heady sensation. That is, until a shout broke her from the spell.

Adrik had built a fire for them but then wandered off down to the water and was currently up to his knees in the shallows. There was a small octopus coiled around his arm that he was chasing Yon around with. It startled Sereia to see Yon looking so out of sorts, trying to evade the one long tentacle not wrapped around Adrik's arm that he was swinging before him in the air like a lasso.

Finn, for all his stoic behavior, seemed to be fighting a grin.

Just as Adrik cornered Yon against an outcropping of rocks, the much smaller woman ducked down and swung her feet, catching the first mate in the ankles and sending him tumbling into the water. When he rose from the waves, it wasn't only his long hair that clung to his face, but also the octopus which had wrapped around his head.

Drawing her calmness back around her, Yon waded out of the water, leaving Adrik to fend for himself. Finn was kinder and moved over to help him extract the creature, plunging a dagger into the center of it.

Sodden with water and boasting several red suction cup marks along his jaw and neck, Adrik hauled himself and the octopus out of the water. "We've caught dinner." He held the dead creature, whose tentacles still writhed even in death, aloft.

"Perhaps you can stop acting like a child and cook it now?" Sereia growled. They had seen such horrors today, and she could understand the need for levity to wash it all away, but now was truly not the time.

Adrik's smile faded, and his face grew grim. Nodding, he looked to Travion and then back at her. "I'll be right on it, Captain."

Silence fell around the fire as Adrik roasted the octopus, and Finn and Yon came to join them, both sitting close to the heat to dry off. With a deep desperation, Sereia sent a prayer up to the spirits of the sea that the spell would truly work. They needed this to end. This exhaustion. This uncertainty. The constant threat to their lives and anyone who lived near or on the water. This kind of devastation could not continue.

"Captain, something's happening," Adrik chimed in suddenly.

Gasping, Sereia rose up onto her knees to loom over the bowl, which was now glowing a faint blue. Travion settled in beside her, his face showing determination.

Inside the bowl, the swirling sand was gradually shifting to the sides, creating what looked like landscape with all the water falling into the middle. The drop of blood, now a faint streak of red like glowing smoke, trailed through what could only be a representation of the sea itself.

"The map!" Sereia shouted, and Adrik moved quickly, tossing the octopus and stick at Finn and coming to kneel beside her. He unfurled the map and flattened it down beside her in the sand, pinning it in place with some rocks.

Together, she and Adrik scoured it over until they found

coves and harbors that matched what they saw before them in the bowl.

Placing her finger on the map to indicate what the bowl was showing them, Sereia looked back down at the working spell. The blood moved subtly, but it moved nonetheless. And it was heading across the sea—toward Midniva.

21

Travion

Travion swore a string of curses as he bolted to his feet and stared down at the map. He jammed his fingers through his hair and growled. "You've got to be jesting. We've traveled this far—for what?"

It was Finn who piped in next. "We've found Taimon, and that alone makes it worth it. If we'd never found him, and his body wasted away on the shores of Sahille, we'd never have our justice. We would have been twiddling our thumbs and waiting."

While that was true, it didn't inspire any warm, cozy feelings inside of Travion. They were so damn far from Midniva, and trouble was hurtling its way closer and closer to home.

Without looking up from the map, Sereia spoke. "Adrik, Yon, we need to get back to *The Saorsa*." She frowned, fingers tightening around the paper.

Adrik sighed, shaking his head. "This was by far the strangest shore leave we've ever had."

Travion chuckled despite the circumstances. It wasn't easy on the weary crew, chasing around an invisible foe who was always one or two steps ahead of them. Yet, he knew it could've been worse, and that *worse* was just on the horizon.

"But have you ever had so much *fun* before?" Travion glanced at Adrik and offered a small grin. Dangerous, exhilarating, and tiresome, but he had to admit that a part of him was enjoying *this*. Out on the sea, with Sereia and free of the crown. But it was a sobering feeling too, knowing how many had died in the process.

"I suppose you've got me there," Adrik admitted.

"Let's head out now, then." Travion kicked sand over the dying fire. Smoke billowed from the hissing embers. "Time is of the essence, and who knows what the sea has prepared for us."

Back on the ship, the rest of *Speedwell*'s crew whispered among themselves, but Travion was no fool. He heard every word and knew they were atwitter about Taimon still. They'd heard his pleas for mercy, but none aboard the king's ship would grant it.

Travion slipped into the captain's quarters, knowing he had to warn Kian of what was barreling his way. He poured water into the basin, pricked his finger, and watched as the blood swirled around until his reflection rippled. When it cleared, Kian's face appeared.

"Kian, I wish I was calling with better news," he said gruffly.

"And break tradition?" Kian sighed. "What is happening?"

Travion loosed a breath. "Where do I begin?" He clenched his teeth, feeling as though they were on the verge of snapping. "Taimon is a traitor and is in league with whoever is racing back to Midniva as we speak."

Kian's eyes narrowed, shock replaced his small smile, and then a fury Travion felt erupted on his features. "The bastard

—he was in on every meeting. He had all of our information regarding strategics—everything!"

"Don't I know it. He is in the brig and will be brought to trial. But you must prepare Midniva for the worst. I fear the destruction out here is only child's play and meant to distract us. With whomever it is fully focused on Midniva . . ." Travion paused and leaned on the table. "I am truly afraid for the kingdom."

"Uncle, I will do everything I can to hold Midniva." Kian waited, then pressed on. "How far out are you?"

Travion tapped his fingers against the table and hung his head. "Nine days. But if we push those with wind and water affinities . . . Five. But we'll be ragged when we arrive."

Kian grimaced. "Do what you must, but do it safely."

"Be well, Kian."

"And you, uncle."

The water rippled once more, and this time, Kian's face was gone. Staring back at Travion was a male who looked bone weary. And this last leg of the journey hadn't even begun yet. They still needed to rejoin *The Saorsa*.

Wind, called on by Travion, blew into the sails, pushing the *Speedwell* into open sea. Aided by the upheaval of the water, courtesy of Sereia, they were able to make exceptional time back to Saventi's port.

In the brig, Travion studied Taimon's sleeping form. Blood caked the side of his head, darkening his red hair. Again, the big question of *why* popped into Travion's mind. Why betray him? What had Taimon been promised that was more than the life Travion had given? He frowned, but his attention was soon drawn toward the stairs.

Sereia descended a moment later and crossed the distance between them. "I'm heading back onto my ship."

"I'll be staying on the *Speedwell* with this bastard." Travion motioned to the half-fae and shook his head.

Sereia pressed her lips together, sighing. "Fine."

He quirked a brow. "Fine?"

"I won't lie, I'm not keen on separating at this point." Her gaze settled on Taimon, and she folded her arms across her chest. "But I understand why." She chewed on the inside of her cheek and turned on her heel. "Just promise me one thing?"

"And what is that?" His curiosity was piqued. A promise between them could mean a thousand things, and few likely anything good. More of an order under the guise of a promise.

"Don't kill him without me. I want to be there when the life fades from his eyes." With that said, she retreated up the stairs and left him with Taimon, who'd roused just in time to hear that last part.

"I can promise you that!" he called to her, and Travion knelt so that he was eye level with the other male. "For your death will be a public display."

Travion leaned on the rail of the *Speedwell*, squinting as the wind whipped his hair into his eyes. Sea spray coated his bare arms, and salt peppered his lips. Being in the open water was like being home to him. The wild and free ocean soothed the deepest, darkest parts of his being.

Two days had passed since setting sail from Saventi's port, and they were still too far out from Midniva to be of any service.

Finn huffed as he leaned over the side, staring down at the churned-up waves. "Have you called to your nephew yet?"

Travion grimaced. "Before we left."

"The prince is more than capable, and with the warning, they're ahead of the book wielder," Finn carefully said, clearing his throat as Travion glowered at him.

He wasn't wrong.

Travion pushed away from the rail, intending to venture into the captain's quarters, but the shrill whistle of Velox stopped him in his tracks. His beast cried out again, racing along the side of the ship until Travion peered down and their eyes met.

"Velox?"

Sharks. Large ones.

"By the sea . . . Velox, hide. Keep you and your pod safe. Go!" Travion shoved away from the rail. "Finn, have them fly the warning flag. We need to pull up beside *The Saorsa*." At that moment, he longed for the ability to teleport or speak to Sereia's mind. Instead, she was a sitting duck on the open water.

Finn's brow furrowed. "We're going too fast."

Travion dragged a hand down his face, sighing. "Then I suppose we'll have to slow down, won't we?"

Without another word, Finn rushed away, barking orders. Soon, the bright yellow flag with a navy dot in the middle was raised. It flapped wildly in the wind, and he was glad for that, because the brightly colored fabric caught someone's eye quickly. Adrik—Sereia? Likely Yon. All that mattered was that they were slowing their speed and circling back.

It took longer than Travion would have liked for *The Saorsa* and *Speedwell* to line up. Every moment that passed by was precious time they couldn't afford. But when the ships were side by side, he and Finn worked to secure the plank in place.

Sereia leaped onto the wooden structure and eased across the way. Her brow furrowed in confusion and in an underlying worry. It was there in the pinched way she held her lips and how her shoulders remained scrunched up.

"What is it?" She glanced around, then homed in on his eyes. Whatever she saw in the depths of his gaze was enough to suck the breath from her. "By the sea! What are we in for?"

"Velox warned of two monstrous sharks." Travion dragged a hand down his face. The land was a dangerous place, with creatures looming in the shadows, waiting to prey on their victims. But the sea? The sea was minacious and unforgiving. Each crevice more unknown than the next.

Sereia whipped her head to the side, glowering at the surface of the water. "Of course there is. We cannot handle a frenzy of them. Our best bet is to go around—"

"No," he bit out, gnashing his teeth together. "As much as I'd prefer that to these abominations . . . if we go around, we'll end up going through the portal to Torskvala." Travion's lips thinned, and he shook his head. "We don't want to involve them."

At the mention of Torskvala, Sereia swore under her breath. Even she wasn't willing to risk involving the barbarians of the north.

"Then we brace ourselves for what lies ahead."

Travion nodded. "That is all we can do." He paused, then closed the distance between them, grabbing her by the elbows. "Don't be foolish. Do you hear me?"

Sereia's features softened, and she grabbed his chin, squeezing. "Me? It's you that shouldn't do anything foolish. If the opportunity arises, don't throw away your life so willingly. Understand me?" Her tone held an edge. One Travion knew came from the unease brewing within her, and from knowing he had a penchant for throwing himself into the fray.

He leaned forward, his forehead pressing against hers. "I will do my best to fight those urges." Travion pressed his lips to hers, tasting their salty warmth. "Prepare yourselves for battle."

She stepped onto the plank, casting him a mischievous glance. "Oh, I'm always ready for battle."

That was a fact Travion knew well. He shook his head, chuckling, and when she crossed the gangway to *The Saorsa*, he and Finn removed the wooden structure.

There was hardly any wind beating against the sails. Normally, Travion would take it to be a calm day out at sea, but it was the quiet before the storm. Not a single cloud marred the blue sky, and the warmth of the sun was welcomed. But as *The Saorsa* pulled away from the *Speedwell*, bigger waves formed, then growing, forcing Finn to slam into Travion. He rooted himself and shook his head. "We're sitting ducks here. Let's move, and ready the harpoons."

The crew shot into action, setting the *Speedwell* into motion once more, and *The Saorsa* led the way. If they could outpace the sharks . . .

Unfortunately, that thought was dashed as soon as one of

the enormous sharks breached. A gray head emerged from the water, two rows of knife-sharp teeth gleaming in the light. It was as Velox said: the sharks were as large as the ships. If it fell on deck . . .

By the sea.

That couldn't happen.

22

Sereia

The horror registered just seconds after the shock, as the monstrous shark broke the surface of the water. It rose into the air, giant snout pointing to the sun. As it crashed back down against the sea, water sprayed twenty feet into the air and sent a tidal wave rushing into the side of *The Saorsa*, rocking her violently.

Sereia grabbed onto the railing. Her heart thudded chaotically, and dread filled her belly. She could not look away from the beast: rows upon rows of razor-sharp teeth the size of boulders, and a jaw large enough to bite their ship in two. "By the sea and all the depths below," Adrik croaked out beside her.

"Harpoons out!" Sereia shouted, pushing herself into action. "Cut off the ropes. We don't need ourselves tied to this thing. Aim for its eyes and gills." All around her, the crew were already moving, following orders before she'd even finished them. "Yon! I want you in that crow's nest with eyes on it at *all* times. Do not let this thing disappear on us and take us by surprise."

Yon leaped onto the rigging and, like a spider, scurried up the mast to the lookout above.

"Adrik!" Sereia shouted at her first mate who, along with Boran, was now bringing armfuls of harpoons from below to the main deck. "Leave Chailai and Boran to harpoons, I want you focused on the cannons. Don't stop firing at it until the thing is a bloody pulp."

Adrik nodded quickly and was off, ordering Donae and Friggid to follow him.

"Captain!" Yon shouted from the crow's nest, pointing to the other side of the ship. "We've got other sharks in the water! Smaller, but many!"

Just as Sereia pulled her eyes away from the massive fin dicing through the water and spun on her heel, the first shark struck, ramming into the bow. *The Saorsa* groaned in protest, shuddering from the impact. Knocked slightly off kilter, Sereia staggered to the rail.

"Not today," Sereia growled and extended her hand to the water.

Around her, the boom of cannons echoed, making her ears ring, while smoke choked her lungs. The iron balls flew through the air, striking one shark in the side and leaving the water bloody. Another did nothing but spray water into the air as it struck the surface.

Calling to the water, Sereia kept her hand outstretched, even as several of the smaller sharks rammed into the side of *The Saorsa*. It sent Sereia staggering backward once more. Several crew members fell over, and one howled in pain as the cannon rolled back on their foot, rocked free of its wheel locks.

Sereia grabbed at railing to keep herself from going overboard and began to form a wall of water around the ship, hoping to push the beasts away. "Tie yourselves down!" she shouted to her crew. The wall of water grew larger and, gritting her teeth, Sereia drew her hand to her chest and then flung it out before her. The wall of water became a tidal wave, rampaging over the sharks and sending them reeling through the water away from the ship.

It worked, but only long enough to give the monstrous shark time to slice through the water toward them. Harpoon guns fired. The sharp spears soared through the air at the massive beast just as another cannon fired. The harpoons struck the shark in the back, just above the fin. They pierced its tough hide, but not deeply enough, bouncing into the air from the powerful motion of the shark's body, then fell away, useless.

The cannon ball had just as little effect, not slowing the beast down in the slightest.

Sereia threw her hand out, trying to create a current to slow its progress.

"*Hold on!*" Adrik shouted just before the shark rammed into their bow and sent *The Saorsa* careening to her side.

Creaking wood snapped through the air around them, and the red sails dipped low toward the water.

The ship would have capsized if Sereia hadn't used all the force of the water below them to push it back into an upright position. *The Saorsa* was saved, but there were several cries for help from those of her crew who had fallen overboard.

"*No!*" Sereia screamed as both Dannae and Hakai were yanked beneath the surface, nothing but a cloud of red left in their wakes.

Frantic, Sereia pushed one shark away with a current of water, while with her free hand, she created a wave beneath Batteo and shot him back onto the deck.

Farther down the ship, Adrik shot a harpoon into the side of a shark, giving Sereia a chance to pluck Yannik from the water, just shy of the beast's jaws. They were not fast enough for Svenik, though, whose cry of agony as two sharks tore at him from below were as an arrow straight through Sereia.

Hollowing in pain and rage, Sereia thrust both hands out in front of her, picturing the water like a forceful wall, and shoved both sharks as far away from them and their ship as possible.

The final crew member was hauled aboard, clutching desperately to a buoy and rope and coughing up mouthfuls of water.

Sereia didn't even have time to be grateful for the ones they had managed to save. The boom of cannons filled the air as both *Speedwell* and *The Saorsa* aimed for the giant shark circling between them. One cannonball hit the creature in the head, while the other struck its gills. The creature seemed to falter for a moment, and then its actions grew more frenzied. It rammed into the stern of *The Saorsa,* causing her to spin violently on the water. Crew screamed, and Sereia tumbled to the deck, rolling head over heels until she finally fetched up against the railing. Her ears rang, and her head throbbed as it collided with the thick wood.

The ship rocked dangerously, rigging creaking as the main boom swung, knocking several crew off their feet. Shaking her head and clinging onto the rail, Sereia fought to slow the spin of the ship, struggling to orient herself with the water enough to know where to put the pressure.

Eventually, they stopped careening out of control long enough that she was able to climb to her feet and look back at the sea.

The giant shark had disappeared. "Yon, where is it?!" She looked up to make sure that Yon was still there.

The woman looked a little green around the collar but had maintained her position in the crow's nest without being thrown from it. "It's nowhere to be seen, Captain," she shouted back down.

Sereia's eyes searched the water rapidly. How could something so huge disappear so easily? It certainly hadn't left. The issue would be where and how it would return.

"There! North-east!" Yon proclaimed.

Sereia caught sight of the tip of its fin, still the size of a dingy, before it disappeared below the surface yet again. The back of her neck prickled as a chill of foreboding washed through her. Everything had gone deadly silent except for the creak of the mast and the flap of the sails above. The very breath in their lungs seemed to have stilled as everyone waited for the next sight of the monstrous shark.

When it breached the water once more, Sereia's heart faltered, leaving her breath to catch in her throat. It crested so high above the water that it made the *Speedwell* seem like a toy, and as it crashed down beside it, the royal ship swayed dangerously on the choppy waves. Sereia did what she could to protect the ship and keep it upright, feeling sweat glisten along her hairline and a strain inside her from the extent to which she was using her magic.

"Fire!" Adrik barked, and soon after, the boom of cannons sounded all around them.

Some missed, others struck, but it did nothing to bring down the monster. The giant only became more furious, its gaping maw widening as it turned on the *Speedwell*. Sereia could do nothing but watch in horror as it bit down on the starboard side, large teeth and powerful jaw tearing through the wood of the hull without issue.

When it came away, an enormous hole had been torn into the side of the ship, which was soon filled with rushing water looking to displace the emptiness. Men and women screamed, bodies torn in half floating along the riotous surface of the ocean. Those that were lucky enough to still be alive fought to get clear of the smaller sharks circling, only to be dragged below.

"We have to get to the survivors!" Sereia waved to her boatswain, who happened to be the closest to the wheel. "Bring us around, now!" Travion was on that ship. Travion could have been right where it had bitten.

Her heart hammered so loudly in her ears, Sereia was dizzy; the world wanted to close in on her. It was becoming difficult to breathe as panic threatened to seize her like a tight fist clenched around her chest. Dread cascaded beneath her skin, traveling her veins and setting her entire body to ice. She couldn't lose him. Not now. Not after everything.

The Saorsa shifted on the water, beginning to turn back toward *Speedwell*, but she wasn't quick enough. Already the ship was tipping forward as the water rushed into it, filling her hull and pulling her down.

To make matters worse, the large shark returned, leaping into the air and crashing through the middle of it, destroying what was left of her hull. The shattered bits of timber scattered over the water, while HMS *Speedwell*, beautiful ship that she had been, steadily sank beneath the waves.

"*Travion!*" Sereia felt the scream tear from her throat rather than hearing it, her senses dulled to everything but the need to get into the water and over to him. She was at the railing and almost over it before she could think.

This wasn't going to happen. She would not let him die. Not before her very eyes.

It was only a firm arm around her waist that kept her from leaping. Frantically, she fought against it, struggling to pull herself that last little bit over the railing.

"Let me go! I have to get to him. He's over there somewhere. *Let me go!*" Desperation made any other thought leave her. There was nothing left but the all-consuming need to be over the side of the ship and into the water, searching for Travion, wherever he may be.

He was still alive. She had to believe it, and she would cut down anyone who got in the way of saving him.

Adrik shook her, trying to jostle the sense back into her perhaps. "And what is it you're going to do against a massive man-eating shark?" Adrik growled in her ear. "You're not going overboard, Rei. I won't let you kill yourself for nothing."

"It's not for nothing! It's for Travion!" Her voice broke, tears of agony threatening to claim her.

"No," was his simple yet firm retort. Adrik kept his firm arms around her, holding tightly enough that she could not break free but not so tight that he would hurt her.

Sereia struggled against him some more before finally letting her body go slack. "Get us over there. Now." Her words were quiet but steely.

"We're going." He hadn't released her yet, as if not trusting that she had her wits about her.

"You can let me go now."

Adrik hesitated, then finally, his arm slipped away from her waist, and she was left free of his sturdy frame that had helped to ground her in the moment. They didn't say anything, just stared at each other, understanding passing between the two of them. "Let's get those survivors! Everyone to the nets, ropes, anything that we can fish 'em out with!" he shouted to the crew.

Sereia took a deep breath. This time when she moved to the railing, she was calmer, at least on the outside. Inside, she was more tumultuous than the water itself, roiling and brewing like a hurricane on the horizon, waiting to descend upon land.

"If we don't find him, Adrik . . ."

"We will."

23

Travion

The moment Travion saw the shark breach and heard the water cascading down over the roar of the waves, he knew the destruction of *Speedwell* was imminent. Relief, though fleeting, filled him, because it wouldn't be *The Saorsa*'s splinters floating in the sea. And at least Sereia was safe—for now.

There was no time to spare, but with a glance in Finn's direction, his guard knew exactly where the king was headed —to the brig. A torn expression filtered across his guard's face, but ultimately, Finn ran toward a panicking Lefyr, grabbed him by the arm, and leaped overboard.

The last individual he saw was the captain, barking orders at his crew in a last-ditch effort to avoid the shark, but even Travion knew it was a lost cause.

Travion descended into the belly of the boat two steps at a time, his hand darting to the skeleton key swinging from his belt. "You'll not die so peacefully, Taimon," he growled, hastily unlocking the small cell.

"What is it? What is happening?" the other male whimpered.

"Several of your little pets have destroyed the ship and are bent on devouring us all."

Travion considered tossing his steward into the turbulent sea, but would the shark's teeth inflict enough pain? He brushed the thought away, knowing any punishment he ordered would be far worse.

An explosion that wasn't cannon fire rocked the entire ship, hurling Taimon into Travion and sending them tumbling to the floor. He knew, without a doubt, that it had been one of the sharks crashing down onto the *Speedwell*. Without thinking, he grabbed his steward by the shirt. In the next moment, the ship rolled. Panic swelled in Travion's chest because he knew what came next: water.

A lot of water.

"Take a deep breath—"

The sea spilled down the stairs, into the brig, and while Travion wondered how he would swim free of the ship, the wall gave way, courtesy of one of the sharks.

A spray of wood shot toward them, but the rushing water worked in their favor, for it collided with the shards, narrowly missing him and Taimon, who he still held in a death grip.

It was disorienting. The ship pulled him downward, but the current threatened to yank him out. Travion kicked hard, swimming toward the hole, only pausing as a gargantuan shadow passed by. The water was too dark, but thank the sea that the sun burned brightly above, showing the surface.

His lungs burned, but he knew he had to relax, that he had more than enough air to get them to the surface. But the added strain of carrying Taimon tired him.

Taimon no longer trod the water, his body an anchor, threatening to sink them.

What had he ever seen in the urchin?

From the corner of his eye, Travion saw a flash of movement and assumed it was only one of the sharks, bent on devouring him. In that moment, he regretted not confessing his love for Sereia on the plank. She'd never know how he felt, how, after all these damn years, he only wanted her.

Travion wouldn't close his eyes on the threat. He wanted to meet it head on. Yet, as it drew nearer, he saw it was no hulking fish but a brightly colored hippocampus. Velox! He didn't click or chirp, only swam close enough so Travion could grip onto his fins, and then his beloved beast sped through the water.

They surfaced violently, and Travion sucked in a precious breath. This time, Velox chattered to *The Saorsa*, his fins fanning to grab their attention.

Travion's eyes burned from the rush of water, but as his vision cleared, he saw Sereia at the rail, hurriedly lowering a dingy.

"To the boat," Travion said hoarsely.

The hippocampus complied, swimming close enough so Travion could hurl Taimon's limp body into the structure then pull himself in.

Shouts rang out above. Orders, but Travion couldn't discern what they were above the wicked waves thrashing around.

"Go now, and this time, I mean it, friend!" His words came out hoarse, which only brought on a coughing fit.

Once the dingy was level with *The Saorsa*'s rail, Travion yanked his steward up and shoved him toward awaiting arms. He blinked, recognizing the thickly muscled arms. "You're alive, Finn."

"It seems I'm as hard to kill as yourself, Your Grace." Finn stepped back, the half-fae draped in his arms. "I'll take him to the brig."

Travion's gaze flicked to the side, catching a glimpse of Lefyr, who vomited a stomach's worth of seawater over the railing. He'd made it too.

"Here's another!" Xiu cried out and threw down a life preserver, then hurriedly yanked on the rope. Adrik joined in, aiding their efforts.

Captain Darragh tumbled over the railing onto the deck, bleeding from his arm and gagging on seawater.

"Lefyr, quit upchucking and attend Captain Darragh!" Adrik's voice cut through the discord around them.

Travion blinked, trying to focus through the sting in his eyes, and as the cloudiness faded a fraction, another rush of movement caught his attention.

Sereia bolted toward him, enfolding him in her arms and holding tight. "You have to stop this nonsense."

His brow arched. "I believe I'm trying to?" But he knew what she meant from the way worry furrowed her brow and anger pinched her lips.

"I mean the almost *dying* part. By the sea, Travion!"

An argument brewed on the tip of his tongue, one of play, but now wasn't the time. He could've easily been swallowed, torn to shreds, or drowned. He wouldn't shame her for worrying, not when he would do the same for her.

He lifted his hand, water dripping from his sleeve to the deck. With care, he tucked a strand of hair behind her pointed ear. "I am not dead yet." Travion's lips twitched into a small smile, which was fleeting, because a moment later, a shark breached, sending a sizable wave toward them.

Sereia dropped her hands to her sides, glowering at the

hulking creature. "We cannot slaughter them all. Our harpoons are no more than sticks, and the cannons may as well be stones!"

She was right, of course. They wouldn't win this by normal force. Not by fire, not by harpoon. Travion's gaze slid toward the turbulent waves, then to the clear sky. What they needed coursed through his veins—and Sereia's too.

He turned on his heel, faced the riotous water, and sighed. "We need to work together. It'll take everything we have, and maybe more." He sucked his bottom lip into his mouth and jammed his fingers through his waterlogged hair. "Do you think you can create a whirlpool strong and large enough they cannot swim outside of its grip?"

Sereia glanced at him, her light eyes sparking with interest. "I believe so. What are you thinking?"

"Creating a harpoon worthy of them."

Understanding washed over Sereia's face, and she nodded. "I will give it everything I have."

Midniva's waters were cold, even in the summer months, but out here, near the islands, it was warmer. These sharks weren't accustomed to frigid temperatures, and to drop so drastic would shock their system. If that wasn't enough to stop their hearts from beating, an ice harpoon surely would be.

Sereia's gaze trained on the rocky waves. The muscles in her jaw leaped, her hand reached out to call to the sea.

Travion squinted. In the distance, a hole formed. It wasn't too far away, but far enough that the ship wouldn't fall victim to the water's rotation.

With each full spin, its force increased, pulling the *Speedwell*'s wreckage into the vortex. The less imposing sharks spiraled, but as Sereia continued to throw her power into the whirlpool, even the more impressive beasts couldn't fight the pull.

Now it was his turn.

Travion looked to the sky, called to the clouds, and for a moment, nothing happened. Then, as if someone had pulled a gray velvet blanket over the blue, the sun faded, and in its place, dark, heavy clouds appeared.

In turn, the water grew inky in appearance. "Sereia, ease back," he ground out, reaching deeper into himself to call on the cold. Snow fell from the sky, dusting the railing. Little by little, the water slowed as it hardened, and Travion fought the natural elements of the sea, the salty water.

He grunted, his chest heaving with the strain. And, as time passed, the smaller sharks rose to the top of the whirlpool. With them at the surface, he summoned the cooler water, and it formed into a spike.

One by one, they impaled themselves on the ice spears.

"Where are the big ones?" Sereia's panicked voice cut through the sound of chunks of frozen water colliding with the side of the ship.

Travion couldn't relinquish his hold yet. "By the sea, I don't know! Can you see them?" He searched for them. Of course it'd be the bigger bastards that went missing. Grinding his teeth together, he dragged in a greedy mouthful of air. "I have an idea. Pull the water toward us."

Sereia whipped her head around to gawk at him. "What? With them in it?"

"Just do it," he said through gritted teeth. "And when I say, propel us backward as far and quickly as you can."

The two sharks breached at the same time, their cavernous mouths opening wide, as if intent on swallowing *The Saorsa* whole. But Travion had other ideas, for as the beasts descended, the water dispersed, and he focused on turning it to ice. Sharp, jagged icebergs jutted from the water, forming the shape of a trident.

"Push now!" he bellowed.

The Saorsa lurched forward but couldn't avoid the tidal wave barreling toward them. Fortunately, everyone was prepared, tied down even. As the water crashed onto the deck, the force of the ship's movement pulled the water back. The moment it splashed over the edge, back into the sea, Travion froze it, creating a free-floating barrier of shards.

Soon, the beasts descended onto the spikes, and they drove through the blubber under their jaws, piercing the tender flesh at the roof of their mouths. Blood rained down from the open wounds, and while they wriggled for a moment, they were soon lifeless.

Part of Travion expected them to stir to life once again, because that would be his luck, but when the beasts made no more movements, he sunk to the deck of the ship and leaned against the side of it. Using his ability in such a way always taxed him, and he knew his limits better than most. But Sereia . . .

She squatted beside him, exhaustion shadowing her eyes. "You can freeze the sea."

He chuckled, head lolling back and forth. "Only a little." Travion reached for her hand, squeezing it. "Besides, you can *control* the sea."

Sereia's legs gave out, and she leaned against him, her hand still in his grasp. "Only a little," she retorted, then grew quiet.

Travion shook his head and closed his eyes. With his hold on the weather loosened, the sun peeked through the clouds and shone down on them. A week of sleep at this point wouldn't be enough. He grimaced, squeezing her hand again. "What shall we face next? Surely it can't get worse than enormous sharks."

Sereia covered his mouth with her free hand, then pulled it away only to tap a finger to his lips. "Never say that. I wouldn't challenge the fates."

Travion kissed the bold finger that was intent on silencing him, then he slanted her a look. "I'm the challenging sort."

"Don't I know it," she murmured.

24

Sereia

Every part of Sereia's body hurt, the exhaustion from overextending her abilities taking its toll. Dropping down to the deck beside Travion, Sereia leaned back against the rail and shut her eyes. The image of Svenik screaming in the water while two sharks tore him apart flashed through her mind. Gasping, her eyes shot open. How long would it take for that sight to fade from vivid memory? How long for the many corpses of Sahille's beach, or the charred corpse of Zaitsev's first mate?

Sereia rubbed at her forehead, then brushed hair back from her face. The knowledge that she was in this for the long haul settled over her. She would not be able to rest until they caught the true monster responsible for this. Whatever happened, she needed to see this through.

Someone had to pay for this hell.

"I'm sorry for your crew, Trav," Sereia said softly. She took his hand, offering a light squeeze.

Travion shifted his hand so their fingers could thread together, hands palm to palm. He didn't say anything, just nodded. There was a turbulent look brewing in his eyes, and

Sereia could only guess how much pain and anger was swirling around inside him over this. "They know we're coming for them," he ground out. "Those sharks were sent deliberately to stop us."

She nodded.

"I can't let them have Midniva as well." His hand tightened on hers.

Sereia leaned in to press a kiss to his damp shoulder. "And we won't." She pulled back a little, only so she could study his face. "We *will* stop them, Travion. Do you know how I know?" His eyes shifted to look at her. "Because neither you nor I are going to cease until we do."

He leaned in then to press a firm kiss to her lips. "No, we will not."

Sereia offered him a tender smile, then stood, dropping his hand. "Rest, you've just survived a nightmare. I am going to see to my crew and the lodging of the remainder of yours."

Sereia stepped away before he could respond, and found Adrik and Chailai looking over the sodden members of their own ship and those from *Speedwell*.

"How many survived?" she asked softly.

Chailai and Adrik shifted around her, so that they could speak quietly amongst themselves. "Only twelve, Captain," Adrik informed her.

Sereia cursed. "Not even half." She looked around them, seeing the harrowed looks on the naval officers' faces. "Shift our crew around, make sure we have space for all of them to bunk down below for the remainder of the trip home."

Adrik nodded. "Will do."

Sereia looked at Chailai. "How bad are the injuries?"

"Not terrible, but hypothermia will be the worst case right now."

"Okay, let's get everyone moved below deck as soon as possible." Sereia turned to the crew, a deep need to console them in some manner surfacing.

She moved to kneel beside Brenid, a younger crewmember who had been close friends with Svenik. He was busy wrapping a bandage around the arm of a *Speedwell* crew member, but there was deep turmoil in his eyes. "Brenid, may I ask a favor of you?"

He looked up, eyes full of held-back tears. "Of course, Captain." His voice broke a little.

"Will you go down and help Cook prepare a nice hot stew for everyone? I'll finish this."

Relief shone in his dark brown eyes, and he nodded quickly. "Thanks," he whispered before he stood and left.

Sereia turned to the officer before her and took up where Brenid had left off. Carefully, she wound the strip of sail fabric around his arm, then tied it off tightly to secure it in place. "Is that the only place you're harmed?"

"Yes, thank you." His fingers rubbed lightly over the bandage. Though he wasn't gravely injured, there was a woundedness to his eyes that spoke of the damage done to his mind and soul.

Would any of them ever be able to sleep again?

Sereia stood and walked over to the next man, but he had already been cared for and was wrapped up in a spare blanket. Yannik approached her then, distracting her from her surveillance of the ship's new inhabitants.

"Captain?"

"Yes?"

"The crew and I . . . we want to know if there's going to be a sendoff for Dannae, Hakai, and Svenik?"

Sereia sighed, fingers working at her forehead once more.

"There isn't time to do it properly." For that, they would need to circle back to where they had lost them. But that shouldn't mean they would be left behind entirely. She reached out and squeezed his shoulder. "Come."

Together, they walked to the bow of the ship. Sereia brought two fingers to her lips and whistled sharply. When all eyes were on her, she began to speak.

"When those who live and work beside us at sea are lost, it is customary to say a true farewell. But we are needed back in Midniva, and there isn't time to stop and do things properly." Even now, Captain Darragh was using his abilities to help push *The Saorsa* more quickly through the water. Once she and Travion had had a chance to rest a little, their abilities would also join his efforts. "But those who have been lost should not be forgotten, and we will say farewell."

Sereia wrapped her fingers around the chain of her pendant, pulling harshly so that it snapped. As she extended her hand over the railing, the pendant slipped down to dangle from her fingertips, the carved selkie spinning in the air before her. Sereia relaxed her fingers and let her offering drop into the water below.

"For Dannae, Hakai, and Svenik."

Following her lead, officers and pirates alike stepped up to the railing and dropped a token into the water below, murmuring the names of those closest to them that had been lost.

Boran, who stood at the helm looking down at all of them, began to sing a sad, mournful Tribonik song of remembrance.

Sereia stepped back, allowing room for everyone to come and pay their respects. She watched Travion step up to the railing, extending his hand and letting a gold coin slip from his palm.

Boran's song continued until the last person had said their goodbyes, and then he let it fade off into the air. As silence fell over them, leaving just the lapping of the waves against the helm, Sereia prayed silently to the gods of before. *Let no one else die.*

Once everyone had been fed and warmed, Adrik and Finn had forced both Sereia and Travion to retire for the night. Darragh assured them he had more than enough energy to keep pushing the ship faster toward Midniva, and promised once he was tired, he would wake them.

However, despite the exhaustion weighing over her body like a heavy blanket, Sereia was unable to sleep. She simply laid there, body aching, soul pained, and stared into the darkness of her quarters.

Travion lay beside her, his arm curled around her, tucking her into his side. His fingers splayed over her hip, pressing lightly into her flesh with just enough tension to tell her that he, too, couldn't get the day's events off his mind.

The sorrow within them was heavy, but Sereia rested comfortably in the crook of his arm with her head on his shoulder. Even in the worst of times, Sereia realized, there was no place she would rather be than in Travion's arms. There was solace here, provided in a way nothing else could. It felt so entirely right and natural.

So natural that it was beginning to make her life on the sea seem hollow. She had been fine for over a century, spending her days exploring the waters and collapsing into her berth at night. It hadn't seemed empty before. Not when she'd visited every country attached to their ocean and the ones beyond.

She'd gone so far as to sail through the veil and drink her way through the vast halls of the ashmanik warriors of Torksvala. They were a fierce people who prided themselves on both exploration and battle skills. To die in battle was an honor and what all of them sought. And their ruling family was the fiercest of all: twin brothers set to burn the world down if so provoked.

It was all she had ever wanted. Experience. Life. Keeping her eye on the ocean before her and letting the wind tangle her hair with the scent of salt water all around her.

But it wasn't enough. Not anymore.

Sereia opened her lips to say as much but found her words stuck in her throat.

Coward.

Travion stirred, his eyes opening and catching her stare. Instead of mocking her, his gaze softened, and his arm pulled her closer. His free hand lifted, and he brushed his fingers tenderly through her wayward tresses. "Sereia . . ." His voice caught, and for a moment, she thought he wasn't going to go on. "I love you."

Her eyes widened as her heart stuttered to a stop in her chest before restarting into a wild gallop. She had to have heard him wrong. He hadn't even said those words when he proposed. "What?" Sereia whispered, needing to know that she had heard him right.

Travion's hand left her hair and drifted down to cup her cheek, his thumb brushing tenderly across her full bottom lip. "I almost died *again* . . . The likelihood I'll come out of this battle is beginning to look pretty grim. I don't want to breathe my last breath without having told you how I feel. How I've always felt." He leaned in to press a soft kiss to the tip of her nose. "You've had my heart since that first moment when you antagonized me on the dance floor at your mother's ball. There has never been another, and I know there never will be."

Her heart tripped along so quickly that Sereia thought perhaps it would burst from her chest and fly around the room. Instead, her own hand traveled up to the side of his neck. Beneath her touch, she felt how his pulse hammered away. Was he nervous?

"Oh, Travion . . . why have you never said so before?"

"The first time I tried to make you mine, you fled from me. In fact, you couldn't get far enough fast enough . . ." He chuckled, but it was a cold, bitter sound, and in it, she could hear how her foolish, younger self had hurt him with her actions. A wound he had carried with him all this time and yet never made her pay for. "I couldn't risk saying it and you fleeing from me again, perhaps never to return."

"Until now."

He nodded. "Until now."

Her heart was stricken. Knowing that he'd held himself back because he didn't want to risk chasing her off. Had, in fact, accepted a partial life with her entirely on her terms.

Sereia felt strangely close to tears. Something she was not used to.

Instead of letting them fall, she leaned in to press a heated kiss to his lips, letting all her feelings spill into it. He growled softly, his fingers burying into the hair at the back of her neck and angling her head back so that he could kiss her more deeply.

Except this wasn't what she had meant to do, not where she wanted to take them. Not yet. So she pulled back to press her forehead against his. Their warm breath mingled, the moment intimate and important. Life altering.

"I love you too, Travion. I loved you even then. It's why I had to flee in such a manner, because if I had resisted for even a second, I would have let you sweep me off my feet and keep me there in Midniva." Her fingers pressed into the back of his neck, needing to reassure herself again, despite it all, that he was here and secure in her arms. "But I carried you with me everywhere I went. It's why I keep coming back. Because I love you too much to stay away."

They were kissing once more, Travion's tongue parting her lips so that it could ravage her mouth, leaving her shaking and pressing into him. He turned onto his side, and her leg moved up over his hip, pulling him in more tightly against her. Rocking her heated core against his hardening member, Sereia felt a thrill run through her at Travion's responding moan of pleasure.

Their kissing became more heated, taking on a frantic quality. She wasn't sure who began taking off who's clothes first, but soon she was out of her top and Travion was out of his slacks, his mouth on her breast ringing cries of pleasure from her while one hand clutched tightly in his hair, and the other wrapped around his length to stroke him.

"Travion," she moaned. She wanted him. Needed him. "Travion—" But there was something sounding in the room, a thumping noise like the call of a drum. Something that was pulling her from the spell Travion had woven around her.

He, too, had stilled, his lips coming off her breast, and his head lifted so he could stare back at her in a mix of frustration and confusion.

"The bowl," they said at the same time.

Grappling for his slacks, Travion stepped into them, tugging them back up as he crossed her quarters and stopped to stoop over the stone bowl attached to her desk.

"I am here."

"Uncle! You're a hard being to track down." Kian sounded strained.

Sereia reached for her top, pulled it back over her head, and thrust her arms through the holes at its sides so that she was covered by the time she reached Travion's side.

"The *Speedwell* has sunk, so my mirror bowl lies at the bottom of the sea."

Kian was silent for a beat before responding. "Sunk? Are you okay?"

"He's alive and injury free, miraculously. But we both lost crew members in the attack," Sereia supplied.

The second prince of Lucem looked harried, his brows pinched, and his vibrant blue eyes stared back through them. "I am so sorry to hear that. I'm afraid I haven't any better news. Mointeach has also suffered an attack."

Travion stiffened. "How bad is it?"

"The spider crabs came out of the ocean in the night. Larger than anything I've ever seen. The watchmen caught them coming and were able to sound the alarm, but there was nothing to be done for those that lived right along the coastline." Kian's eyes were grief-stricken. "The navy besieged them from the water, but they were naught but annoyances against their shells. Uncle Draven and his harpies kept the creatures at bay long enough for your army and his wolves to evacuate the town. But they weren't able to destroy them. I'm sorry, uncle, but Mointeach is gone."

Travion turned and kicked the chair near him, sending it

crashing into the wall. Several items from the shelf above shattered on the floor.

"I've failed you."

"No, you've done what you could under the circumstances. I am only sorry I've left this on your shoulders."

Travion's face was pained, brows pinched and lips pursed tight. Sereia slipped her hand into his, hoping to offer some form of comfort. "What is your status now?" she asked Kian.

"Anyone that wasn't able to travel to landlocked areas of Midniva has been brought into the castle. Between Eden and I, we've woven a barricade of her vines covered in my gold alloy between the castle and the cliffs. It should keep anything from reaching the castle or heading into the capital. For the moment, we're safe. Ruan arrived on the hour, and he and Uncle Draven are convening with the army and the navy. Nothing else has attacked since Mointeach, and we seem to be holding our own now, but I'm not certain how long we'll be able to keep it up if something larger should come from the sea."

Travion's hand tightened on Sereia's, the tension in his body visible. He was nearly vibrating with his need to be there in Midniva, with his family and his people. She knew it didn't sit well with him to be so far away from the battle and danger.

"And what of your father and mother?" Travion asked.

"For the moment, they remain behind, in case this is nothing but a distraction and another attack comes to Lucem. But they are prepared to come here at the first sign of need."

Travion nodded. "You've done well, nephew. Continue to hold firm, rely on your brother and your uncle, and I will push us to be back before there is any more cause for alarm."

"Travel swiftly but safely." Kian then disappeared from the bowl.

Sereia sighed and moved to slip her arms around him. "I am so sorry about Mointeach."

Travion bowed his head to bury his face in her hair. He didn't say anything, but Sereia could feel the pain inside him through the tenseness of his body and the swift beating of his heart against her ear. Instead of saying anything else, she simply held him, trying to give whatever comfort she could offer.

25

Travion

Somehow, in three days, Travion *would* ensure they arrived on Midniva's shores. He'd been pushed harder in his youth, tested until he was certain every fiber in his being would snap, and mayhap this was why. Whether or not Ludari knew it, he had been preparing his son for a moment such as this, when his abilities would be tested to the point of breaking him.

But by the sea! Did his family need to suffer? Did his kingdom need to weather any more than it already had?

Travion clenched his teeth so hard, he thought they'd snap. Gone was the yearning to sink his fingers into the curve of Sereia's bottom. He'd prefer *that* to the grating sensation in his mind, pushing and pressing him to be home. *Faster, faster, faster.* Even the wind seemed to groan the very thought.

There was nothing Sereia could do to soothe him, either.

She pressed a kiss to his temple and stroked the hair back from his eyes. "I'll prepare the crew. We will be home soon, I swear it, Travion."

Home.

A place she'd run from for so long, and now it was suddenly home. His heart soared, but before he could pick apart what she meant by it, Sereia was gone. A moment later, her voice rang out as she busied herself relaying the plan to the crew.

If it was home to her, did that mean she was willing to compromise? That she'd be willing to stay when all was said and done?

A small knock on the door pulled him from his thoughts.

Finn entered the captain's quarters, his brow furrowing as it often did when he was trying to read Travion's mood. "Your Grace." He bowed his head. "Everyone is waiting for you topside." When he didn't answer, Finn trudged forward and placed his hand on his shoulder. "We will get to them in time. And when we do, whoever is responsible for this madness will pay for their crimes." His tone was firm—as if he were vowing it.

Travion nodded. "And they will suffer greatly." The promise of bringing the culprit to justice was enough to drive him out of the cabin and up to the deck.

The journey to Midniva wasn't an easy one. Even the most experienced seafarers were green around the gills, including Travion. With the high wind in the sails and the sea hurtling them along faster, the ship didn't glide through the water effortlessly. Instead, it was rough, and the ship slammed against the rising waves, jarring and bouncing the crew.

Travion sank onto a barrel, brow furrowing with

exhaustion. His reserves were nearly depleted, and he desperately needed to rest.

"Your Grace, allow me to take over," Darragh said as he strode up. His hazel eyes filled with understanding as Travion said nothing. "Beg your pardon, but you're no good to us if you pass out."

Travion grumbled. "Very well." He wanted to argue, especially when they were so close, but as soon as they touched land, Travion would be leaping into battle. He relinquished his hold on the wind, and the ship jerked as it slowed, but Darragh soon took over, and the sails were filled once more.

Lefyr retched again. Since the *Speedwell* had sunk to its watery grave, the fae hadn't recovered. He groaned, then wiped the corner of his mouth before glancing at the sky. Travion followed his line of sight and saw what appeared to be birds diving toward the cliffside.

His gaze dipped, and there, on the horizon, were Midniva's shores.

Those weren't birds plummeting from the sky. They were griffins.

A kraken, the size of *The Saorsa*, if not larger, climbed up the side of the cliff, dangerously close to his castle. Inky tentacles whipped through the air, lashing at the swooping griffins, and to Travion's horror, the beast snatched one of the castle's defenders and hurled it down the cliffside.

"By the sea!" Lefyr cried, fixated on the tentacled beast, even as it ensnared a new writhing victim and brought it to its gleaming beak. "We cannot hope to fight this abomination."

Travion clenched his fists, and any exhaustion he may have felt before vanished as a fresh wave of adrenaline coursed through him. This was his home, his people, and these wretched creations wouldn't destroy what belonged to them. Not while breath remained in his lungs.

"You won't be." Travion turned away from the scene, grinding his teeth together. "You'll be aiding the wounded."

Lefyr opened his mouth to argue but quickly snapped it shut. He must have sensed Travion's alternate suggestion —fighting.

Sereia pushed her way through her crew and stopped in front of him. She cupped his face and shook her head. In part, he knew what was tumbling around in her mind. She didn't want to leave his side, and certainly didn't want to face the possibility that this could be their last moment together.

Travion slid his fingers through her windswept hair, committing the way her eyes blazed with anger for Midniva and concern for *him*. Why was it now, after all these years, they'd finally grown comfortable enough to share their vulnerabilities?

He leaned his forehead against hers. And by the sea, his chest ached with the threat of losing her. "My heart, if there is a way to come out of this alive, I will find it, and I *will* find you on the other side of it."

She nodded and bit her bottom lip. "I need to stay down here, where I am suited best. But you . . ." Her gaze drifted toward the castle, and her hands slid to the back of his neck, pulling him in for a lingering kiss. "Go to your people."

Travion reluctantly withdrew from her, then looked toward the hull. "First, I need to ensure Taimon is thrown in the dungeon where he belongs."

Before Sereia turned away, she smiled and uttered the words, "I love you, Travion of Midniva." And they sounded as much like a threat as they were a promise.

He couldn't help but grin. "And I love you, Sereia Ferox." Before he could prolong the moment, she dashed away into the throng of her crew.

Finn approached his side with Taimon in tow. Iron manacles bound his wrists and ankles. "I thought you'd want to take him with you. Otherwise, the crew here might take matters into their own hands."

Not that they'd have time. But should anything happen to *The Saorsa* or its crew members, Travion didn't want his steward escaping or dying without his say-so.

The half-fae tilted his head back to watch as a team of griffins flew overhead. A peculiar expression washed over his face, torn between horror and amazement. The latter only caused Travion's palms to itch with the need to bash his skull in.

Nevertheless, Travion hopped onto the rail. Grabbing ahold of one of the riggings, he brought his fingers to his mouth and produced a shrill whistle.

Above, the riders glanced down, and much to Travion's delight, he saw that one was his nephew, Ruan.

The winged creature descended, landing as lightly as it could on the deck. Clawed front feet tapped the wooden planks, and its beaked mouth opened as it released a clicking purr.

"By the sun, uncle!" Ruan bellowed as he hopped down from his mount. His dark eyes assessed Travion, then the two males at his side. The prince of war didn't seem distressed but delighted as battle cries rang out around them. He wore a tan leather vest with thicker straps expanding over his shoulders, and on the front, a gilded chest piece with the emblem of Lucem shining on it.

He strode forward, his sandal-clad feet looking more than

a touch out of place. A sneer formed on his face as he glanced at Taimon. "So, you're the one who nearly got my uncle killed." The surrounding air crackled with not only tension but electricity.

Travion stepped between his nephew and the captive. "It's good to see you too, Ruan." He moved in, embracing him, for lightning raining down on them all would do no good for anyone.

Ruan pounded Travion on the back, then withdrew. "What do you need?" He turned his hawk-like gaze on him once more.

"I need to get Taimon to the dungeon and my healer on the shore. Do you think you or another can fly us to the courtyard?"

His nephew lifted a dark brow, and he grinned. "To the dungeons, you say? I think I can help with that. And I know someone down there who will be most pleased to have your company while the sun is still up, traitor." Ruan scowled at Taimon, who, in return, shrank all the more. He glanced over at Lefyr and nodded. "We could use another healer."

Draven. Travion's chest constricted. There hadn't been a doubt in his mind that his brother would come, but there was the complication of his *condition* that would deter him. The sun was an obstacle even Draven couldn't overcome.

"How long has Midniva been under attack?"

"This morning, the kraken arrived, and with it, the smaller crustaceans." Ruan lifted his hand, signaling for a comrade to join him. A golden-maned griffin lighted onto the deck, ruffling its feathers as it squawked to Ruan's black-maned mount. "Take the king to the courtyard. I'll join you after I deliver this bastard to Andhera's king."

The armor-clad warrior bowed his head. "When you're ready, Your Majesty."

Finn shoved Taimon forward, and the half-fae stumbled. Ruan only watched as he fell hard against the deck.

"Be sure to tell Draven he's allowed a little fun but to keep him alive." With that said, Travion crossed the distance and climbed onto the back of the griffin. A moment later, it took flight.

The wind ruffled the feathers of the great beast as it rose higher and higher. Travion narrowed his eyes on the wall Kian and Eden had erected. At first glance, it just looked like a gilded structure, but when Travion took a moment, he saw the jagged thorns, rooted trees, and even blooms that had been hardened with the metal.

It was impressive, but how much longer could it hold? And who knew when the next round of creatures would emerge from the sea?

The griffin swooped over the castle, and from this vantage point, Travion saw the depths of the kraken's mouth, the obsidian beak, oozing with venom that longed to liquefy its prey. Light gray suckers dotted along the tentacles, and as they slapped down on the ground, they adhered to whoever was unlucky enough to be within reach.

Travion gnashed his teeth together. Once more, his castle was under attack and his people were threatened.

Below, soldiers combated spider crabs and attempted to sever the kraken's appendages. They were faring better with the crabs, as several carcasses scattered the hillside. If they all survived this, the griffins would have a grand feast after.

The rider brought the griffin down to the courtyard, and Travion quickly slid from its back.

"May you fight well and survive the day," he murmured, and the other male lowered his head.

"And you as well, Your Majesty." The winged beast leaped into the sky once more, joining the others.

Travion scanned the courtyard, grimacing as his gaze landed on a fallen soldier. He quickly closed the distance between them, kneeling beside the fallen male. His head was turned at an unnatural angle, and blood oozed from the corner of his mouth. His legs were snapped, twisted around, and all Travion could think was that he was one of the kraken's victims.

"Rest well," Travion murmured, dragging his hands down the fae's open eyes. Frowning, his hand went to the sword still in the soldier's scabbard. He withdrew it, and as he did, the earth rumbled beneath him in response to his growing ire.

The beast was an oversized octopus. If they could rapidly fire the cannons on its head, there was a good chance they could slay the kraken. Just like slamming the hilt of a blade down on the head to end its life . . .

But in the meantime, they'd have to keep the creature from gaining ground.

Ruan ran up beside him, spear in hand. "Draven sends his regards," he said breathlessly.

Travion arched a brow, then peered over at his nephew. "Ruan," he murmured, rapping his fingers along the hilt of the sword. "Do you think you could push—"

"I'll push it back as much as I can. It's mostly water, isn't it?" Ruan turned his free hand over, and electricity skated across his palm, bouncing along his fingertips. "I don't think lightning will play well with it." Then he ran forward, leaping upward, and when he inevitably crashed down, he drove the spear into one of the tentacles reaching over the cliffside.

Before the other appendages could crash down on him, Ruan darted away, and lightning flashed and homed in on the metal rod.

His nephew could hold the ground for a little while. For now, the others battling the crustaceans needed help.

26

Sereia

Separating from Travion wasn't easy. Who was going to make sure he didn't run headlong into death if she wasn't there to pull him back? But this was war, and while Travion needed to be on land with his people, Sereia belonged on the water with hers.

She stood at the helm, surveying the battle laid out before them. Spider crabs littered the shoreline, soldiers holding them off as best they could, but too many bodies lay strewn about to say they were making any true headway in killing them. Other still unseen creatures were likely converging on the shore by way of the seafloor. What was left of Travion's naval fleet was mainly focused on firing at two giant crabs, similar to the one that had decimated Sahille. Cannon fire sounded as they fought off the monsters. Yet, the biggest and most imminent threat was the kraken scaling the cliff and heading straight for the castle. The shining vine wall that Queen Eden and Prince Kian had constructed was a fabulous piece, but it would only hold so long against a creature with no bones and suction cups.

"What's the plan, Captain?" Adrik asked from her right.

His back was straight, and there was a defiant smirk curling his lips.

Sereia's eyes narrowed on the creature. It possessed only seven tentacles, with a small slender one growing in replacement of the missing limb. She had faced it down once before, as had Zaitsev's crew. And by the sea, this time, she was going to kill it.

Sereia looked at Adrik and then at the rest of her crew, who all gazed up at her from the main deck. There was some fear in the depths of their gazes—they had faced this beast before and barely escaped—but mostly there was a bright fighting spirit shining back at her.

"I know that a lot of you don't call Midniva home, but *The Saorsa* has become renowned for coming to the aid of those in need. Today is no different. Let this be the day that Midniva and her king learn to sing praises of the prowess of *The Saorsa* and her crew." A loud cheer went up from the ship's deck, and Sereia met Adrik's eyes. "Prepare the cannons for battle and have every pirate at their station. I'm going to bring us up alongside the lone naval ship focusing on the kraken and see if we can't sway them to our way of thinking."

"Aye, aye, Captain. And don't worry, your man is more than aware of your prowess." He winked at her, then headed down the stairs, just out of reach of her swinging hand.

"Adrik!" she called after him, and he paused to look back at her.

"Aye?"

"I noticed no one seemed surprised at Travion being called uncle by Prince Ruan. When did they figure out who he was?"

Adrik's grin was full of delight. "Captain, they've known

all along." He shook his head at her and laughed as he walked away.

Sereia supposed she shouldn't be surprised to learn that she hadn't done a very good job hiding Travion's true identity. They were a family, after all, and no secret remained a secret for very long.

Hands tightening on the wheel, Sereia swung her ship hard to the left and cut through the water toward the naval ship. From the mainmast above, Yon switched out their flags to proclaim that they were looking to parlay, not attack.

The naval ship and its officers were at the ready nonetheless—the sailors prepared for attack as Sereia drew *The Saorsa* close. "Drop anchor!" she shouted.

She felt the tug against the keel as the anchor dragged along the seafloor before fetching up and bringing her ship to a halt alongside HMS *Hastings*. The wind was fierce along the coast, so Sereia signaled for her crew to drop a plank. There would be no shouting from one ship to the next. Once it was in place, she jumped down the stairs and walked over the board to stand at the railing of *Hastings*, letting her knees naturally shift with the slightly off-sync bobbing of the two ships.

A cannon boomed, making Sereia's ears ring. The iron ball flew across the water to collide with the meaty portion of the kraken's body. The beast didn't even react.

"Pirate," the captain of HMS *Hastings* spat out. "We haven't the time to parlay, we're in the midst of a battle, if you hadn't taken note."

Sereia's eyes narrowed, and she fought the urge to slap him where he stood. Instead, her hand gripped the sword at her hip, the fabric of the grip squeaking from the pressure.

"Bootlicker." She dipped her head in greeting. "I've come to offer our assistance in the battle currently facing you. I have faced off with crabs as large as those ones." She motioned to the giant beasts the ships were trying to destroy. "Going through the mouth is the only way to kill them. Your ships would be best off dredging the bottom of the seafloor and stopping whatever creatures they can from reaching land. Tell them to prepare for sharks." Sereia gazed over the water. It wouldn't be long before those monsters joined in on this too, she was sure of it.

The naval captain was frowning up at her, and at the bow, another cannon fired.

"If your force, along with the infantry, can handle land and sea, then I will focus *The Saorsa* and all her power on the kraken currently scaling the cliff. I have a score to settle with the beast, and I won't stop until it's dead. All I need is for your ship to continue as is but aim more for the tentacles." As far as plans went, it was not perfect. But it was what she had to work with at the moment. If any of them came out of this alive, it would be a miracle.

The captain's brows shot up. "Might I ask why we should be taking battle instruction from a pirate?" His eyes drifted over her with disdain.

Sereia's lip curled, and she only stood straighter beneath his disdain. "I *am* a pirate. I am also Lady Ferox of Midniva, and you will take instruction from me because I am the only one to have faced off with a kraken that size and come out the other side alive. And furthermore"—at these words, she stepped closer so that she was properly looming over him—"your lord and king trusts me, you egotistical flea. So you can either get behind me and this plan, or you can keep floundering out here on the water, wasting cannonballs.

Either way, *The Saorsa* is heading for that cliffside, and we are going to stop that monster from reaching the castle."

Sereia spun on her booted heel and walked the plank back to her ship. Once on deck, she scowled at Adrik. "We may be on our own. Be that as it may . . . we're taking down that kraken." She surveyed her crew, nodding before she shouted, *"Anchor up and man your stations!"* Fueled by *The Saorsa*'s new purpose, she raced back up to the quarterdeck, reclaiming the helm.

Adrik followed behind her, waiting for instructions.

Sereia took just a moment to eye the kraken, preparing herself for what was to come. "Mount the largest harpoon you have to the front of the ship. Tie it off at all the masts to secure it, and then I'm going to use every ounce of my strength to pull that sodding beast off the cliff." Their eyes met, matching determination within their depths.

"These are the days I signed up for." Adrik grinned over at her, excitement taking over his face so much so that it made her laugh.

"So pleased to hear one of us is happy about what is about to happen," she grumbled, but there was a matching grin on her lips.

Sereia steered *The Saorsa* away from HMS *Hastings*, bringing them closer to the cliff. Any other day, she'd have made sure the captain paid for his disdain toward her. Today, however, she was focused on more important things.

Adrik sprinted down the stairs to the main deck, dropping down into the hatch to fetch their largest harpoon. Upon his return, he loaded the gun and shouted for Yannik and another to join him in tying off the ropes. They trailed three thick lines from the back of the harpoon and wrapped around the masts of the ship, tying them off tightly.

Hopefully, it would be enough to secure the weapon once it was lodged inside the kraken and not bring her bright scarlet sails down.

The sight of the beast up close was daunting. It was equally the size of her ship at its head and body, its long tentacles putting her masts to shame. The creature could easily crush *The Saorsa* and everyone on it. Sereia took a deep breath. She would need to give it her all if she was going to pull this off.

The Lucemite soldiers on their flying griffins dove around the tentacles, throwing spears and swiping with swords in an attempt to sever the limbs. But the monster was quick, and its tentacles agile. Crackles of electricity lit up the sky and crashed against the rocks. It was enough to wring howls from the beast, but it wasn't forcing it to recede into the water.

Overhead, a griffin flew by, and sudden inspiration sprang to mind. Releasing the ship's wheel, Sereia waved her arms wildly in the air until a soldier turned and looked at her. The large paws of the griffin touched down on the deck, and the soldier surveyed her quickly.

"You beckoned, Captain?" It pleased her, more than a little, to be recognized as a captain rather than a pirate.

"We are about to harpoon the kraken. I'll attempt to pull it from the cliff with my affinity for water and lure it after us instead." The soldier's brows shot up in surprise, but he was listening. "It would be helpful if, while we are doing this, you and some of your fellow soldiers would pester the beast even more so than you are now. Give it every reason to remove its tentacles from the cliff. The less it has to cling on with, the more likely we will be able to pull it down."

He seemed a little shocked, but then a fierce look replaced his initial bewilderment. "I believe my men and I are up for the challenge. I'll let Prince Ruan know what you are planning."

"Let Prince Ruan know that once the beast is in the water, I plan to trap it at the bottom of the seafloor with a whirlpool. That would be the perfect time for him to focus all his power on it." The soldier nodded in understanding and launched into the air.

Sereia watched him corral his comrades. "Adrik!" she shouted. "We've got some help! Give the griffin infantry time to distract the creature, and only then will we fire. We've only got one shot at this, so don't miss."

"Wouldn't dream of it, Captain!"

Standing at the helm, Sereia reached out to the water around her, her mind and ability wrapping around the currents and the force of the moving tide. As she watched the efforts of the griffins and Prince Ruan double, she wrapped the currents around the hull of *The Saorsa*.

The Lucemites attacked from all sides, thrusting spears at the tentacles, tearing through flesh with claws, striking it with everything they had. Lightning struck the hide, tearing screeches from the Kraken. Not all were fortunate enough to make it out, and she watched more than one griffin and soldier plummet to the land below or be grabbed and crushed by a tentacle itself.

It only made her more determined to succeed.

When the kraken was holding on by only two of its tentacles, Adrik lined up the harpoon and shot it into the air. Sereia's breath caught as she watched the giant spear launch toward the creature. It only released when the head of the harpoon sunk deep into the body of the kraken. A loud roar of anger and pain echoed through the air, ricocheting off the cliffside and back out over the water.

"Boran, take the helm!" she shouted and ran to the railing. Calling to the currents she'd already created around them, Sereia pulled at the hull of her ship, and the line of the harpoon grew taught. Nothing happened at first, and *The Saorsa* lurched forward as the kraken pulled at the rope.

Sereia eyed the taut line, and above them, the wooden masts creaked from the strain. She refused to lose her ship to this beast. "Not on my watch, dammit!" Gritting her teeth, Sereia increased the strength of the current running beneath the keel and began pushing *The Saorsa* back.

Wood groaned harshly, but her masts held.

As *The Saorsa* pulled more forcibly on the kraken, Prince Ruan and his soldiers increased their assault on the beast. Several bolts of lightning crackled, zipping across the sky. They struck one large tentacle, finally severing it. The appendage crashed into the surf below, spraying water high into the air. The kraken wailed a piercing cry that reverberated within Sereia's chest.

She increased the strength of her pull, groaning at the agony inside her own body from the strain. Above, the masts creaked in protest, and she prayed to whatever water spirits were listening that they would hold.

A deafening crack sounded, echoing over the water. The last of the kraken's hold on the cliff gave way. Large gray tentacles writhed helplessly in the air as the monster fell to the shoreline below.

The land shuddered, and aboard her ship, a short-lived cheer went up. "Not yet!" she screamed through the strain, propelling them farther into the water before the creature could regain its wits and take them down.

Once the kraken was deep enough in the water to be fully submerged, Sereia wove her arms in the air, the chill of the sea washing over her form and the scent of salt coiling around her. Her muscles strained, and her legs grew weak as all her energy was channeled into changing the direction of the current so that it was no longer beneath *The Saorsa* but circling around the kraken.

The ship rocked beneath them as the sea itself shifted, and a giant whirlpool opened up.

The creature, finally regaining its equilibrium, rushed the wall of water, trying to swim free. It fell back into the center of the whirlpool. One tentacle shot out to wrap around the front of *The Saorsa,* seeking an anchor point. Adrik, along with several others, fell upon it with swords, hacking at the tip of the tentacle. With each swing, blood sprayed over the deck and crew. From above, Prince Ruan and his soldiers attacked once more, diving toward the kraken threateningly while avoiding tentacles. It helped to distract the kraken long enough for Sereia to increase the strength of the whirlpool to such an extent that it bared the seafloor and dragged the creature down.

Screaming through her own pain and exhaustion, her body giving all it had left to give, Sereia finally trapped the monster in a cage of roaring water, nothing but the sand of the seafloor for it to cling to.

"Any day now, Your Highness!" Adrik shouted over the roar of water, and Sereia couldn't help but laugh at his audacity. Not many would get pushy with the Prince of War.

Though she could only agree. Her knees were shaking beneath her. The strain on her body to keep up this influence over the sea was draining her of all energy. If they didn't kill the beast soon, she was going to pass out, and all their efforts would be for naught.

It was then that the remaining naval ships came to their

aid, circling around the whirlpool, cannons aiming for the kraken at the bottom.

Prince Ruan released a war cry, a storm cloud brewing so dark it, sent shivers down Sereia's spine. Thunder rumbled, and sparks crackled in the air. When the blast of electricity finally erupted, every cannon upon the naval ships unleashed as well.

The noise was deafening, and it brought Sereia to her knees. Still, she would not release her hold on the ocean water. Not until she had proof that the creature was dead.

When the smoke cleared from the cannons, all that remained was a charred carcass riddled with holes.

A proper cheer went up from all the ships, and Sereia let her hands fall at last, the sea rushing in to fill the hole. The force of it rocked all the ships dangerously and sent the remains of the kraken—torn free from the ropes—forward to wash up on the beach.

"By the sea! We did it!" Adrik hurried to her side, stooping to wrap his arm around her waist and help her back up to her feet. "That was a bloody brilliant display of prowess, Captain. Something they're all bound to be talking about for many years to come." He winked at her.

"Well, don't count our scallops yet, this thing isn't over."

As if her words had called forth hell, screams could suddenly be heard all over the harbor as large sharks crested the waves, ripping men nearly out of the air and smashing through hulls.

On a small island in the middle of the harbor, a volcano erupted. From the molten lava, creatures straight from the pits of hell emerged. They were like crabs, with long spindly legs, and yet where their claws should have been were long, pointed tusks instead. Their faces, or what could only be assumed to be a face, were nothing but row upon row of teeth leading to a giant cavern of a throat. From the tops of their heads, long spindles protruded like those of an angler fish, topped with the abominations' eyes.

The seawater began to froth and bubble, so many of them streamed into it, and with horror, Sereia could see them fast approaching all the ships in the harbor.

A lone figure stood on the island. Sereia pulled her spyglass from her hip and saw that it was a woman, beautiful, with a touch of madness about her. She was watching the avalanche of horror head into the water, a look of delight on her face and a glowing, golden book in her hands. Sereia lowered the spyglass and shoved it back into its holster. "Boran, take us to that island!"

"What?" Adrik squawked, grabbing at the railing to keep them up as *The Saorsa* tilted at the sudden change in direction. "What is going through your head?"

"She's got The Creaturae, Adrik. She's the one behind all this. If we can kill her and take it, all of this can end." She pushed off of him, finding the strength to stand on her own two feet again.

There would be time to wilt later. Now was the time for battle.

"Well, then let's go end this war." He flashed her a grin, only for his lips to quiver and cringe. A frown puckered his brow, and then he coughed, red spattering his lips and dripping down the sides of his chin.

Sereia stared at him, seeing her own confusion mirrored back at her from the depths of his pained blue eyes.

Together, they looked down to his chest, where a sharp tusk pierced through. Behind him, one of the monstrous creatures finished climbing up over the railing and onto the deck of the ship.

Sereia's mind went blank, her ears ringing and blocking out all sound as she pulled her sword free of its scabbard and launched herself at the beast. Several other crewmen joined her. One lost their arm to the blade-like teeth, another just missed being speared by its other tusk. With a rage that was all-consuming, Sereia clambered over razor-sharp legs that sliced at her limbs and climbed onto the creature's back. With one fell swoop, she severed its antenna eyes, blinding it.

The creature reared up and sent her flying through the air. Her back hit the mast, breath rushing out of her, and she crumpled to the deck. Black spots swam in front of her eyes, but she clung onto consciousness and watched Yon take her place on top of the beast. She lifted her sword into the air and drove it into the fleshy top of the creature's head. It shuddered, then collapsed to the deck.

Pushing up onto her hands and knees, Sereia hurried to Adrik's side, shouting at her crew to blind the beasts as more crawled up over the sides.

Adrik's bronze skin was pale, his long hair matted to the side of his face and the deck red with his blood. Sereia pulled him onto her lap, pressing a futile hand to one side of the gaping hole in his chest.

"Gods, Adrik . . . why?" Her face was wet, and something like rain dripped onto Adrik's shirt, dampening it.

He chuckled, then winced, coughing up more blood. "I always knew you'd be the death of me, Rei." There was no anger in his eyes as he said it, only something akin to fondness and love. "But by the sea, I wouldn't change a thing about my life. You've given me the best years."

Sereia shook her head. "Stop speaking like this. This isn't how you go down. Not like this. Not by surprise."

"Only way—" He winced. "To get me." He lifted his hand to cover hers. The slickness of the warm red coating them both filled her with more horror than it ever had before.

"Adrik—"

"Listen to me, Rei."

"No, Adrik—"

"Captain!" She finally shut up at his shout. "I need you to do something for me."

"Of course, anything."

"Promise me you won't run this time."

"What?" She wanted to say she didn't know what he was talking about. But she did. Brushing the back of her hand across her face, smearing tears and blood alike, Sereia nodded.

"Doesn't . . . mean anything . . . if you don't say . . . it." His words were interrupted by fits of coughing, a wet sound gurgling in his lungs.

"I promise I won't run this time," she rasped.

"That'a girl." He squeezed her hand, smiled gently, and then the light faded from his eyes.

"Don't die on me! Adrik! I forbid you to go out like this!" She shook him, but there was a stillness to his form that could not be reinvigorated. Pain caught at her throat, ripping through her flesh, and her fingers tightened on him. Pulling Adrik against her, she bowed over him for a moment, rocking back and forth as grief swelled like a tidal wave, all-consuming and powerful.

A roar of fury exploded from her lips at last, and Sereia climbed to her feet, blood soaked and sword in hand.

There were no thoughts in her mind as she raced across

her ship's deck and mounted the next beast. Her sword swung and her knife was pulled from her boot to aid in her climb, stabbing into any area where flesh could be found.

The creatures would pay for this senseless slaughter. The woman behind it all would pay.

The world would pay.

27

Travion

Low grinding hisses filled the air as the crabs converged beneath the castle's cliffside in hopes of finding purchase or a way to the land. It wouldn't take long for them to figure it out—the other crustaceans already had.

"Can you hold the castle?" Travion called out to Ruan.

"We have, and we will continue to. If they need you on the shore, go!"

Travion ran down the hill, toward the beach beneath the cliff. He barreled forward, sword in hand, as he lunged beneath a rearing crustacean and jabbed the length of the blade into the exposed underbelly. Before it crashed onto the sand, he rolled out of the way.

Dozens upon dozens of slain crabs littered the sand with their legs cut off, underbellies torn out. They were the same creations he and Sereia had battled in Saventi, each roughly the size of a cow, but their numbers were harder to determine. Four dozen? More? He didn't want to take the time to count. Two rushed forward, and Travion called upon the earth. It shook in response.

As three more crabs raced toward him, the ground gave way in front of them, emptying into a deep, watery grave. Before they could hope to dig out or climb, a soldier ran up beside him, lifted his hand, summoned the sand, and covered the hole once again.

"Good work," he yelled before running toward a small horde overtaking a group of soldiers. Lightning crackled across this sky, and this time, it had nothing to do with Ruan and everything to do with Travion, who sent the bolts directly into the crustaceans.

Booms rang out, echoing off the water, rolling onto the land. The ground shook with the shock of it, and Travion turned his gaze toward the cliff. More lightning sizzled, caging the beast between electrical currents. Movement from the water caught Travion's attention, and he saw the harpoon connect with the kraken, sending it tumbling into the water below.

His heart hammered in his chest. Was Sereia all right? The beast was gone. But was *she* alive? Travion shook his head. Sereia was more than capable, that much he'd learned on this journey.

Travion searched for Kian amid the melee. Swords clashed with hard shells, and as he walked down the sandbank, a soldier crashed to her knees, preparing for a lethal blow from a crab.

He hurried forward, sword lashing out, deflecting the lowering claw. At the same time, another sword cut through one of its joints. Travion craned his neck only to see a grim-faced Kian.

"You're safe now," Kian murmured to the soldier, aiding the female to her feet. "Head up the bank. They seem to have slowed, but you can be of help with the wounded."

"Where is your brother?" Travion slid the blade's edge along his trousers, wiping off the collection of fluids and meat.

Kian wiped the sweat from his brow and jerked his head toward the sky. "There."

Before the griffin could land, another shockwave shook the ground, and Travion fought to keep his balance. "By the sea! What is it now?" He searched the waters, hoping that it wasn't the ships splintering into the sea. However, his worst fears came to fruition. Part of the fleet erupted with rounds of cannon blasts as what he could only assume were enormous sharks surfaced. Again.

Travion muttered a curse as the head of one breached, but it was *small* compared to the monstrous sharks they had battled.

He opened his mouth to speak but was promptly cut off.

Smoke billowed high from the island close to the shoreline, and large chunks of debris rained down, striking friend and foe alike. Travion sucked in a breath. "By the sea," he whispered. He felt as though the wind had been knocked out of him. "The book is near," he ground out. "Whoever is holding it is orchestrating this madness. This is too much for someone to play out from afar."

Ruan growled in frustration. "Send Kian's metal griffins in as a distraction, then we can assault from all sides. The sea, air, and ground."

"Sounds solid enough to me. But someone needs to get to that blasted island *now!* So send the griffins to the sky, and meet me there." Travion turned away, jogging toward the dock.

"Uncle!" Kian sputtered.

"He's been out at sea for too long," Ruan dryly offered.

Is that what they thought of him? After all these years, that he'd lose his cognitive abilities after less than a month at sea? He shot a glare at them over his shoulder. "My mind is sound, you fools! We can't let this continue until dark! If we lose that book, this will seem like child's play!" Because he'd seen what it could do to a living being: it could twist and contort them until they were an abomination. It could stop a beating heart with one word. Travion swallowed roughly. "To rush in would be certain death. If the pages can create those monsters, what else do you think it's capable of?"

His nephews hadn't the slightest clue, because they'd never held the book in their hands or uttered spells from it. They didn't know the horror that book could create. This was only a fraction of it.

Travion's feet touched the wooden planks of the dock, and he bolted down the row to the very end. The island was far enough that swimming wasn't a possibility, but did he really want to call on Velox amid this madness?

Sea water bubbled like a stew in a cauldron, swirling and rising, and from the foam, nightmares, far worse than any creature he'd seen in Andhera, flowed. Twisted versions of crabs spilled from the water, floated on the waves, and drew dangerously close to the beach. Instead of claws at the end of their arms, they boasted long, gnarled tusks.

Still, the naval fleet waged war on more damn sharks, and Sereia, by the sea, from what he could discern was alive and well.

Travion turned around, his eyes widening as his nephews halted before him. "Get your griffins! Ready them for another att—" He plunged into the water as the dock gave out, and before he was shoved beneath the surface, he heard his nephews shout something.

The cold current tore at his body, tossing him downward, then back up. His eyes adjusted to the murky blue water, and he spotted a mass racing toward him. Not wanting to waste more time, he kicked hard. The creature was meant for the sea, and he couldn't cut through the water or crawl on the seafloor as it could.

Travion surfaced, gasping for breath.

"Grab ahold!" It was Ruan who called to him, swooping down along the surface. His griffin lowered until its claws skimmed the waves, and when it drew closer, it wasn't Travion who held on, it was the winged beast.

Talons gripped onto Travion's shoulders, lifting him out of harm's way, and quickly deposited him onto the sandy beach. He coughed a mouthful of water up, gathering his wits quickly, for a moment later, the same abomination launched from the sea and at him.

A roar erupted from Travion as one of the crab's tusks grazed his bicep, tearing it open. He rolled out of the way, searching for a weapon he no longer had. A winged shadow moved across the sand, and Travion pushed himself up, running.

"By the sea, when will they stop!" Travion growled, his anger mounting as the sound of legs scuttling across the sand intensified. He was going to be impaled, but he wouldn't do it with his back to his foe.

Travion turned around and dropped to his knees, half hoping his attacker would rush past him, but as he reached deep within himself, calling on the electric currents in the sky, a metallic screech filled the air. He chanced a glance just in time to see one of the metal griffins collide with the creature. Claws scraped along the hardened hide of Kian's creation but didn't harm it. The crab protested angrily as it uselessly clawed at the metal griffin, but it died off as the beak tore into the hard shell and yanked the meat out.

When it was dead, Travion approached the metal griffin, smoothing his hand down its back. Kian's craft never ceased to amaze him, what he could bring to life with fire and iron. For a moment, he thought the creature would deny him as a rider, but when he drew nearer, the gilded creation let loose a soft clicking purr.

"Easy," he murmured softly. "I hope to the depths you have enough sense to know I'm not a foe . . ."

The griffin's ears swiveled, but it kept an eye on Travion, watching and waiting. When Travion was certain the beast wouldn't tear into him, he hopped onto its back, and it leaped into the sky. "By the sea!" His hands slid up the griffin's neck, hoping to find a piece of jutting metal somewhere. Travion's heart hammered so loudly in his ears that he wasn't certain if he was hearing Ruan or not.

"Not how I would've done it, but well done," Ruan's gravelly voice rose over the sound of crashing waves and the battle below. "Do you want us to scout or stay behind?"

"Follow closely, but first I need to speak with Sereia." Selfishly, he needed to see if she was truly well.

Ruan nodded. "Of course."

Once Travion gained balance on his mount, he urged it downward, and it swooped toward *The Saorsa*.

Sereia lifted her blood-soaked sword toward the sails, then pointed it down at the fallen beast on the deck.

The griffin lighted on the ship's deck, then took off toward another abomination, plowing through its skeletal structure.

She was halfway to him when Travion realized something was wrong. Tears streaked her sun-kissed face, but hatred hardened her expression. "It killed him," she ground out. "It killed Adrik, and there was nothing I could do but watch."

His shoulders sagged, and he closed the distance between them, embracing her for a moment too short, in his opinion. "You will have your revenge tenfold. I swear it to you." He cupped her face, kissing her forehead before withdrawing. Guilt gnawed at him. Travion didn't want to ask her for anything else, but they needed to get to the island . . .

"Don't start handling me with kid gloves now, Travion," she spat, the words less aimed at him and more at the circumstance. "I will kill as many as I need to. Including that female!"

A female? His brow furrowed, but he nodded and turned to assess the threat before them. From here, he couldn't make out many details, only that a sleek figure held the book. "Hold as many beasts back as you can . . . I'm taking Velox to the island's shore." Sereia opened her mouth to argue, but he continued. "I need you here because I trust your abilities. You'll know when to join us."

Sereia pulled away, scowling at the island. "Come back to me," was all she said before walking away.

He'd do his damnedest to do just that.

Travion motioned for Ruan to come down, and when he did, he called to him. "How do you feel about using your lightning for a diversion? Kian's griffins can assault the book wielder, as we decided before."

"Sounds like another day of play to me." Ruan grinned darkly. His pearly whites flashed against his tan skin.

"Stick to the skies!" Travion closed his eyes, allowing the hum of the sea to fill him. He reached out, searching for the tie between him and Velox. The warmth of the bond wound around him, and a moment later, the whistling call of the hippocampus echoed off the ship.

Travion leaped from the side of the ship into the turbulent water, and his faithful sea steed was there to greet him. He twined his fingers in the seaweed-like mane, and off they went.

Velox dipped below the surface, streamlining himself as much as he could. When Travion's lungs burned, he surfaced again, but by that time, they'd already made it far enough around the backside of the island that the female couldn't see him. Just as he caught his breath, Velox dipped beneath the water again, taking Travion by surprise.

He pulled on the hippocampus' frills to no response. Travion glanced over his shoulder, and all he saw were white jagged teeth and the throat of the shark.

Bubbles of air left him as he pressed himself closer to Velox's neck, who swam through the water at breakneck speed.

As close to the shore as you can get.

But the shark bobbed in the water, cutting Velox off. It moved fast, too fast for a beast that size, and Velox couldn't surface without losing momentum.

The hippocampus dove deep, then dodged to the side, nearly tossing Travion off in the process. As Travion's eyes focused, another shark swam toward them—they were being hunted.

By the sea!

He leaned against his mount's neck, searching for the strands of the nearby orcas. When he found them, he mentally plucked them. If he were fortunate enough, they'd find him in time. But as it was, Travion's chest burned with the need for air.

A familiar *click-squeal* echoed in the water, then a flash of black and white as the orcas rammed into the sharks.

Travion urged Velox forward as the whales distracted the beasts, and the hippocampus gladly obeyed. He surfaced, gasping greedily for breath. His mount swam so close to the shore that his fins brushed the sand, but the massive sharks couldn't draw closer without beaching themselves. Still, their jaws snapped in fury.

Travion slid from his mount and rubbed the creature's slippery cheek. *Be safe, Velox.* Travion dipped his head forward, pressing his forehead against Velox's. *Swim fast and far from here.* Then, the hippocampus dipped below the turbulent water, and all Travion could do was hope he'd survive.

He trudged his way through the water and onto the wet beach, collapsing. He had to keep going, had to push himself on. The book wielder—a female—was on the island. He drew in another breath.

Ruan and Kian flew above, waiting for the signal.

Travion crept along the beach and swallowed the tickling at the back of his throat. Volcanic ash fell from the sky, blanketing the ground and covering his form. The air was stifling, but he pushed through, ignoring the ache in his lungs.

He wove through the scrub pines and trees. The branches sliced across his skin. Blood welled to the surface, coating his arms in the crimson liquid. He angrily swiped it away, flinging his blood to the ground.

A deer rushed out, and he stumbled, righting himself at the last minute. "By the sea!" he bit out. Sweat coated his skin, mixing in with the soot. His heart hammered in his chest, and every muscle threatened to give out, but anger helped him push on.

Travion ventured farther through the woods and eventually came upon the female. She stood with her back to him, facing Midniva's shoreline. She held the book in her grasp and moved her hand about, as if conducting an orchestra. He stopped in his tracks, assessing the female's figure. Long, light brown hair tumbled freely down her back, and she wore a navy dress befitting that of a Lucemite. Gauzy fabric cascaded down her curves, and he realized this was no Midnivian citizen.

He crept down into the open, still shielded from the wielder of the book by the line of trees, but in view of the sky, so his nephews could spot him. He waved his hands, and Ruan and Kian caught the signal.

They rode forward as the sky blackened, and an electric current filled the surrounding area.

Once they began, Travion darted into the trees again, moving in closer behind the female. A squadron of griffins flew down, disappearing beneath the tree line. With the chaos ensuing, all he had to do was wait for her to loosen her grip on the book . . .

Lightning struck in a purple flash, hitting not far from where she stood. The female spun around, seemingly losing her confidence as she closed the book and headed directly toward him.

Her face, which had been concealed before, was now visible, and Travion's galloping heart deafened him.

His eyes widened in shock.

He wanted to scream.

Phaedora? The book wielder was Phaedora?

Long ago, Zryan had been betrothed to her. An

arrangement their father had forced on him, so he'd heard, but Travion had seen her snake her way into the palace. Attempting to stake her claim on his brother even though he'd called it off the moment Ludari was dead. By then, Zryan had set his eyes on Alessia, and there was no chance for Phaedora.

Travion stepped out from behind the cover of trees and growled. "Phaedora!"

Phaedora smirked, seemingly unsurprised that he'd arrived, and she pinned him with her hazel eyes. "It's been a long time, Travion."

Before she could dart away, he launched forward and grabbed the book. However, he'd underestimated her strength, and she pulled back. Despite the magic that wove the book together, the binding was still ancient, and as Travion yanked it harder, the book tore in half.

A shockwave threw him back, and he groaned as he landed on the rocky soil. The island itself seemed to groan, and a wall of water rose up, then fell, coating the shore in its salty liquid.

She scowled at him from the ground, clutching the book like a lifeline. "This was a meeting that was never meant to happen. Naya, Taimon . . . They were rather easy to convince that this was the best way for *everyone*. When I heard you were alive, their failure disappointed me."

She was mad. Truly mad. The centuries hadn't been kind to her.

"I'm not so easy to kill, Phaedora."

"So it seems, but we'll change that." She glanced down at the torn half of the book and frowned, prompting him to do the same.

On the faded painted pages, scripted in gold, the title winked at him in the fading light.

Interitus.

Destruction.

Travion possessed the destructive portion of the book, and he knew exactly how he wanted to use it.

He grinned wickedly at her.

28

Sereia

The ache was bone deep, her muscles almost beyond movement, but Sereia's fury fueled her, silencing all protests. Energized further by the knowledge that, for the moment at least, Travion was still alive.

As he dove into the ocean, Sereia made her way to Batteo. "Take Adrik below and make sure he is secure in his bed." His remains would be safer there, until she was ready for a proper goodbye.

"Aye, aye, Captain." He nodded and motioned to another sailor. Together, they tenderly gathered up their comrade's body.

She hated herself for the weakness, but Sereia had to look away and focus on something other than the lifeless form of her first mate. She turned to Chailai instead. "You're first mate now. Begin reloading all of our cannons, and fire at anything and everything in the water. We're heading toward that island."

"The one with the volcano, Captain?" She looked like she wanted to protest.

"The king is on his way there now, and we need to

provide a distraction for the beasts in the water and clear his way." There was no time for idle chatter, so she turned to call up to Boran, still at the helm. "You need to get me as close to that island as you can without running us aground. Understood?"

He saluted her, then spun the helm, turning *The Saorsa* in the direction of the island, her cannons firing as a large shark crested the water before them. The cannon stopped it from falling down onto their bow, pushing it back into the water. Several more of the monstrous, crab-like creatures climbed onto the deck; her crew was on them in haste.

Xiu staggered as a tusk went through his leg but captured the second in his hand to stop it from impaling him. Batteo, coming to his aid, thrust his sword into the monster's mouth, ceasing its motions quickly.

Brenid was fighting a second but lost his balance and fell onto his back. He cried out in pain as the crab-beast pinned him to the deck with a tusk through his shoulder. Sereia ran forward, blocking the free tusk with her own sword.

"Don't give them time to attack!" she screamed. They had to strike preemptively if they wished to survive. "Yon, keep your eyes peeled for anything climbing the sides!" Sereia shouted up to the crow's nest as her sword slid down the length of the tusk. She ducked beneath the arm and drove her dagger into the side of the monster's face. The bulbous antenna eyes swiveled to pin her with a look. She didn't allow it to attack again. Pulling her sword back to her chest, Sereia then drove it up into the roof of its mouth, piercing the beast's primitive brain.

As it collapsed, Sereia struck out at the joint above the tusk, chopping it free. Together, she and Brenid yanked the severed tusk out of his shoulder.

The young lad got to his feet, a hand pressed to his wound. "Thank you, Captain."

Sereia pressed a quick hand to his good shoulder, nodded, and then moved down the side of her ship, slicing through the joint of another crab, enabling Yannik to deliver the killing blow.

Above, Yon called out the location of a new monster mounting the starboard side. Several crewmembers rushed to stop it before it could get on deck. Four more hurried to the bow at her guidance.

Sereia's eyes shifted to the shoreline, searching for a form climbing the beaches. She wasn't sure where Travion was going to come up, but she needed to make certain that he made it. Her insides were too raw, every nerve overexposed. The world couldn't handle her losing him. Not today.

While watching the shoreline, a large fin slicing through the water caught her eye and hauled her attention that way. Familiar apprehension shivered down her spine. It wasn't the size of the monster that had attacked them at sea, but it was still abnormally big and heading directly for them.

Sereia rushed over to Yannik, who was manning the closest cannon. Yannik, who was also missing the lower half of his right arm. "What are you doing?" she sputtered. "Get below deck and bandage that!"

Yannik looked at her in surprise, then shrugged. "No time, Captain. We're down men—"

"Yannik, *now*! Preferably before you bleed out on my deck." She glared at him until he stepped away from the cannon and nodded. She watched him until she was certain he had gone below—she would not be losing any more crewmembers if she could avoid it—and then turned her attention back to the shark.

Sereia sheathed her sword and took Yannik's place at the cannon, the slightly rough iron surprisingly cool in her hands. As she pushed down on the heavy cannon, her biceps shook with weakness. But Sereia ignored her sore body and the weariness running through her. Angling the cannon, she lined it up with the approaching shark. Grabbing the flint dangling from the end, she held it ready in her hand. When the shark was close enough, she sparked the flint and lit the slow match, inserting it quickly into the vent hole. The cannon erupted, spewing the solid ball of iron forward and rocking back on its base. Sereia withstood the shock, her ears ringing.

The ball struck the shark dead-on, driving it below the water. Sereia watched and waited. However, it wasn't long before the shark breached the surface again, angrier than before. "By the sun, moon, and sea!"

"I think they're armor-plated, Captain."

Sereia looked over her shoulder at Xiu. "What makes you think that?"

"I saw a glint from the sunlight."

Frowning, Sereia pulled her spyglass off the holster on her thigh and extended it to take a look. Sure enough, there appeared to be an almost metal-like sheen to the shark's hide. Their enemy had increased their defenses.

Sereia cursed as she lowered the spyglass. "If that's the case, then the only soft spot is likely to be inside its mouth."

The shark, deciding it had had enough of circling, dove beneath the water only to come back up beneath them, slamming into their hull and making *The Saorsa* sway, dangerously close to tipping over.

Sereia and Xiu both went down, as did the rest of the crew, tumbling and sliding across the deck.

Grabbing on to the mast as she slid by it, Sereia kept herself aboard, but there was a terrifying sound of several splashes that could only mean one thing.

She pulled on her reserves and righted the ship with her powers, pushing *The Saorsa* up with a wall of water. "Get them out of the water!" she screamed, climbing to her feet, and turned to Xiu. "I'm going in and I'm going to distract that thing. Once its mouth is open, do not waste any time firing. Do you hear me?" Xiu nodded. "And Xiu? Don't miss."

Sereia ran for the railing and launched herself into the water. From its depths, she was able to see the shark just below *The Saorsa,* dark gray form cutting swiftly through the water and headed for someone floundering at the surface. Propelling herself toward it with a burst of water behind her, Sereia managed to grab on to its tail fin.

As she leeched on, the shark shook its body, rolling in the water to try to dislodge her. Sereia clutched more tightly, digging her nails into the un-plated flesh of its tail. She allowed her body to move with the coiling motion, keeping her place. When it was unable to remove her, the shark swam for the surface, leaping into the air, only to slam back down on its back.

The impact left her breathless and forced her to let go. She had barely enough time to gather herself as the shark came for her, its jaw wide.

Sereia threw her hands out in front of her, forcing a jet of water directly into the shark's mouth. The creature stopped, shaking its head to try to right itself. Taking this as her chance, Sereia created a swirling vortex of water around herself that lifted her up into the air.

As she came above the surface, Sereia glanced over her

shoulder at the ship. Xiu was there, prepared to fire when she had lined the shot up for him.

They didn't have long to wait; the shark, both hungry and agitated, leaped from the water, its maw open wide as it sought to grab her out of the air. Just as the sound of the cannon echoed through the air, Sereia released the water below her and let herself fall back into the sea.

It was the exploding of flesh and raining of blood around her that let Sereia know they had succeeded in taking out the beast.

As she resurfaced, Sereia looked at the island once more. She didn't require her spyglass to recognize Travion sneaking across the shore. Not trusting him to face off with the female responsible for all of this alone, she took this as her sign to join him. Her crew would be fine. She would just have to have faith that they would do what they had always done and come out on top.

Creating another current around herself, Sereia pushed herself toward land. A smaller shark shot through the sea toward her. Sereia kicked at its snout with her feet, shoving herself away and also deterring it a little. Shooting a blast of water at it, she drove it farther away. Fortunately, the vast majority of the creatures seemed to be deterred by Lucem's princes, or her very own ship, and she was able to swim past the last of the crabs.

She released her pull on the water just as she reached the shallows, her body catching on the sand beneath and tumbling through the waves until she finally stopped.

Sereia climbed to her feet and waded through the last of the water, up onto the beach. She could no longer see Travion, but she knew the direction he had gone. Just as she stepped out of the water, a shockwave rushed over the entire island, knocking her to her hands and knees.

Her ears were ringing, and Sereia felt like she was underwater. Her head swam, and her eyes were unable to concentrate on anything, leaving her body wobbling and falling over into the sand. Groaning, Sereia shut her eyes, taking deep, slow breaths and counting to ten before she opened her eyes once more.

Now able to focus, Sereia pushed herself up onto her knees and carefully climbed to her feet. Her ears were still ringing, so she carefully made her way over the rocky beach and in the direction that she had seen Travion disappear.

When at last she broke through a cluster of trees, her hearing finally returned, and she found Travion and the brown-headed female. Both were holding half of The Creaturae in their hands.

Unsure of the situation, Sereia leaned against the trunk of the nearest tree and hoped they wouldn't notice her as she got the lay of the land and figured out how she could best help Travion.

"So, it seems we remain at odds," the woman spoke, waving her portion of the book.

"And I have the destructive side," Travion responded.

The woman only smirked. "Mm, so you do. But that isn't enough to stop me."

"You don't think so?" Travion began flipping through the pages, until he stopped suddenly, his mouth beginning to form words.

The woman reacted, shouting something that caused a large stone wall to burst from the ground, separating the two of them. But as Travion's words finished, and he pointed his finger toward her, the wall exploded, sending rocks hurtling through the air.

Sereia ducked down quickly, narrowly dodging a rock that came whizzing past. The brunette was not so lucky, and a rock struck her in the head, causing her to drop down to one knee. Long, pale fingers pressed against the wound, and she glared across the way at Travion.

"Lucky strike, that one."

"It'll be a larger rock next time." His hand angled toward the volcano, and a sharp crack was followed by a rumble as the side of the volcano broke open.

"You're going to kill us both, you fool!" Her hand lifted toward the volcano, and as she murmured soft words, more rocks formed along the side of it to catch and block the lava beginning to rush from the divide.

"Better we both die than any more perish for your nonsense."

"Nonsense? *Nonsense?!* I've come only for what I am owed after my family gave your father my most precious gift! The Creaturae was formed for my family, for *me,* and we gave it to Ludari with the understanding that I would become a part of the royal family. And your *brother*—"

"Oh, I'm aware. He broke the pact, and then we refused to give The Creaturae back once it was understood the power that resided within. It was three thousand years ago, Phaedora. You must get—"

"Do not tell me to get past it," Phaedora spat out.

The book—in the end this was all about a stupid book more powerful than anything had the right to be. Greed was a heady thing, and it could drive even the sanest people to madness. If Travion and his brothers had managed to destroy it, they'd all be better for it.

Sereia began to stealthily make her way along the tree line while they spoke. They were both distracted, and if Travion could keep the madwoman speaking, perhaps she could get behind her and tackle the other half of the book out of her hands.

It was a good plan—until one of the crab monsters appeared from behind a boulder and hissed at her, swinging one of its tusked claws at her head. She ducked out of the way, throwing herself to the side and rolling away from it in time to avoid being struck, but it drew the attention of both Travion and Phaedora.

Rising onto her knees, Sereia brought her sword up. But the crab was faster, and its tusk collided with her wrist, sending her sword flying. A gasp left her as one of its shelled legs hit her in the chest and pinned her to the ground. Sereia groaned and grabbed at the leg, but lifting it was useless and only sliced up her hands on its sharpness.

"Sereia," Travion growled in concern.

"I'm okay!" she grunted back, her breathing hampered by the press of the foot against her chest.

"Oh," Phaedora spoke with understanding. "Does this one belong to you?" She looked from Sereia to Travion.

Travion didn't answer that, but the flex of his jaw said all that was needed. "Don't, Phaedora . . ."

The brunette smirked. "You have something I want, Travion. I'm sure we can come to some sort of agreement." She tapped her finger against her lips, eyeing Sereia and the crab with delight.

Sereia, not wishing to be held against Travion, struggled to reach her sword, but it lay just too far out of reach. Above her, the crab hissed once more, its giant cavernous mouth opening and closing with a snap as drool streamed from the sides.

"Do you know, Travion, that while your half may be the destructive portion, it is my half that possesses the resurrection spell?" She cackled, and with a snap of her fingers, the crab reacted.

Its pointed foot increased its pressure and drove through Sereia's middle, crushing and tearing everything beneath it. Sereia screamed, pain beyond anything she had ever felt before lancing through her, racing through every nerve and firing every synapse. Her ribs fractured, her heart lurched and spasmed, and for the first time in her life, she felt what it was to drown.

A roar of fury and agony sounded out, and then the crab above her shattered into a million pieces. Travion was at her side shortly after, pulling her into his lap.

Sereia now understood what Adrik had felt in those final moments. The coldness. The pain. The surprising acceptance.

Her skin ached, and her lips pulled at the smile she struggled to put on them. "I'm so glad I came back, and that I've had this time with you." Weakly, her hand curled into a fist in the front of Travion's shirt. "I was going to stay this time," she rasped and forced the smile on.

"Sereia, don't you dare—"

Everything became foggy. She was beneath the water again; it was filling her lungs, pulling everything inside her apart. Sereia coughed, trying to clear the blockage inside her. But her lungs burned. Her heart faltered. She gasped, unable to get oxygen. She was falling, pulled into the cold. Into the emptiness.

And then it all stopped.

29

Travion

"No!" Travion howled, his fingers gripping Sereia's lifeless body. In all his years, he'd only ever loved her so deeply. And now she was gone. Travion didn't want to believe the other half of his soul had been taken from him. That she was irreversibly *gone*.

No. No. No. No.

Tears spilled down his cheeks, and as fury bled with sorrow, the ground quaked violently. "Phaedora," he whispered, and in reply, the wind roared and skated across the sand. Two cyclones spun on the edges of the island, darkening and growing with his rage. Hatred clouded his senses, and he knew at once that Phaedora could hide behind a book, but he didn't need such a thing to rip her to pieces.

"My heart, in another lifetime." Travion brushed a kiss to Sereia's cool lips and gently laid her down. Every muscle in his body quaked with rage. Every inch of him yearned to obliterate Phaedora.

He scooped up the discarded half of the book and stood.

Phaedora lifted her half of the book, and fear glimmered in her eyes. "No!" She turned away, as if to run, but Travion was going to ensure she would not escape this island—not alive.

The sky blackened, and lightning zig-zagged across the sky, sizzling as the bolts rained down on the sand, blocking the female in.

His knuckles turned white from the pressure of his grip. Slowly, he walked toward Phaedora, his chest rising and falling with each determined step. "Tell me," he growled lowly, "why I shouldn't just end you now, because I see no reason to stop." His fingers flicked through the dusty pages, but his eyes were trained on the female.

Phaedora's posture stiffened. "You wouldn't dare kill me." Her expression shifted from arrogant to pensive, with a hint of doubt.

Travion laughed bitterly, his eyes narrowing on her. "Is that what you think, Phaedora? It *has* been too long if you believe for one moment I won't tear you asunder. And, in case you forgot. I don't need a spell of destruction to end you!" he bellowed, and at the same instant, the ground shook, splitting and giving way around her.

Phaedora meant nothing to him, and considering she'd tried killing him several times, and now *his* Sereia . . . she deserved something *worse* than death.

Above them, the winds grew in strength, kicking sand and volcanic ash up around them. The larger cyclone danced over the beach, sucking plant matter and stones up as it careened closer to Phaedora.

Travion's finger landed in the middle of a page. He glanced down, curious as to what instinct or the pull of magic had brought him to. It wasn't as if the book was *alive,* but it wasn't entirely lifeless either. A somewhat sentient being that could influence a holder and direct them to the most suitable spell.

And this page suited his needs: an insatiable inferno that wouldn't extinguish until Travion deemed it finished.

"Stop!" Phaedora gathered her skirt and took one bold step toward him. "I have the resurrection spell!"

Travion narrowed his eyes on her. What was her play, instilling false hope within him? "I don't believe you." He cast his gaze on the page before him, then murmured the opening lines of the spell. The ground rumbled in discontent, then cracks formed, spider-webbing toward Phaedora. Steam burst from the seams, and even he felt the heat against his face.

"Travion!" Phaedora screamed. "Who knows the book better than me? I swear it on my own life."

The words gave him pause, only because that was all Phaedora valued—her life, her ways. She was as shallow as they came, but she was not dimwitted. However, to relinquish his hold on the Interitus portion would not bode well for anyone. He'd need to trust Phaedora, and he didn't trust her to serve anyone but herself. She could easily run away as soon as he handed his half over.

When he didn't answer, she stepped closer, halting as the sand cyclones threatened to consume her. "She is your lover, this one?" Her gaze flicked to where Sereia's body lay. "Let me help you."

"Don't speak!" he growled, then recited more from the book. From the gaps in the ground, flames leaped at Phaedora, chasing her back from the crevices.

"I didn't take you for a fool, Travion. I could easily reunite you with her." She raised her voice over the roar of the wind and growing flames.

She didn't know him. Shared space nearly three thousand years ago didn't make them any more than acquaintances now. Then again, if the roles were reversed, it was probably easy to see how much he cared for Sereia, and that made him weak. A weak individual could be controlled. He loathed the feeling and despised the situation he was in. Save the realms from destruction or the one he loved more than anyone from death?

Travion spat in her direction.

"If what you say is true, you will do it before I give you this half." He sounded desperate even to his own ears, but if there was a chance, he wasn't going to cast it aside. Together, he and his family could take down Phaedora.

The flames between them died down, and the winds calmed, but the sky still raged on, and the sea lashed waves against the shore in all its fury.

Phaedora pursed her lips and openly contemplated the dilemma. "It seems we're at an impasse. For I don't trust you to deliver on your promise." She tapped her fingers against the front of the cover. "Unless we make a blood pact and we are bound to our word. I also demand the two missing pages."

Travion wasn't keen on being bound to anything as far as Phaedora was concerned. He scowled. But was there any other way?

In the blackened sky, griffins screeched, and the beating of their wings drew closer. He heard his nephews shouting back and forth to one another, but their words jumbled in his mind as he considered his options.

"I don't have them. Your abominations are to blame for that when they sank my ship," he hissed. The pages were at the bottom of the sea, but he wasn't foolish enough to believe that was where they'd stay for long. The spelled pages would call to one another, and Phaedora would have her bloody book in one piece again.

She wasn't to be trusted. And yet, he had no other option. If she chose to confront him so closely, he would be certain to end her life on the spot, even if it cost him his own.

Travion nodded solemnly. "A blood pact it is." He crossed the distance between them and shoved his half of the wretched book beneath his arm, then crouched to lift a piece of volcanic glass from the ground. As he drew the sharp tip against his palm, crimson bubbled forth and dripped onto the sand.

He offered the glass to Phaedora, unable to keep himself from glaring at her.

"Uncle!" Ruan bellowed from behind Phaedora, his griffin barreling through the air toward them.

She didn't flinch as she sliced her own hand open, Travion had to give her that. Phaedora gripped his hand, pressing their palms together. She chanted, and Travion hissed as a sharp sting circled his wrist. When she was through, he repeated the words, and she whimpered from the binding too.

"It is done," she said.

"Get down!" Travion grabbed Phaedora, shoving her to the ground. He derived a speck of pleasure from that but directed a glower in Ruan's direction. "Cease your assault at once."

Kian flew in from the other direction, his gaze lingering on Sereia's body. "Ruan, fall back."

"No! I won't let the book get away again." But as Ruan glanced over at Kian, he finally noticed what his brother had —Sereia. He shifted uncomfortably, frowning.

Travion understood the frustration, and part of him was riddled with guilt, but his overriding pain screamed at him to continue, to follow through with the pact and resurrect Sereia.

Phaedora rose, dusting her skirt off with one hand, then motioned toward Sereia. "Shall we, Your Majesty?" she purred.

This was wrong, bargaining with the wretched female. Yet, that selfish piece of him yearned to have vibrant life shining within Sereia's eyes once again. And that dismissed his sensibilities.

Travion nodded and led the way. He knelt by Sereia's side and eyed Phaedora as she lowered herself too. She flicked through the pages of her half of the book and stopped on a page filled with bright words and a smear of aged blood.

Who had this spell been used on before?

"Ah, yes . . ." She placed the book on the ground by her knee, then let her hands hover over Sereia's still body. The chanting was soft at first, then grew louder. Streams of teal light poured from her fingertips, like a jellyfish's tentacles, and they dove into Sereia's flesh, skating beneath the surface.

Tension coiled so tightly in his body that his muscles ached. Time seemed to stretch on endlessly, and nothing was happening. Sereia didn't twitch, nor did she suck in a breath. Anger replaced hope, and when Travion's eyes met Phaedora's, she flinched.

"It takes a moment, Your Majesty." She hissed his title, but her fingers knotted in the gauzy fabric of her gown.

She was nervous it wouldn't work? The notion didn't inspire confidence in him.

"It wasn't *me* who made a blood vow," Ruan growled from behind. "Can't I end her now?"

As much as Travion may have wanted to, the binding wouldn't allow for it unless this was a farce. Yet, if it were, it wouldn't bode well for Phaedora, magically or physically. If it wasn't by his hand, Ruan would run her through with his blade all too gladly.

"No," he snapped, squeezing Sereia's hand. "You will do no such thing, Ruan." Travion closed his eyes, willing the life back into her. "You cannot leave me," he whispered softly to Sereia's still form, then he lowered his mouth to her ear. "Not like this. Do you hear me? Come back to me." He pressed his forehead against her shoulder, wanting more than anything to scream his rage at the sky, to throw Phaedora to the ground and exact his revenge, but none of it would bring *her* back.

But then Sereia drew in a soft breath. A movement and sound so subtle that he nearly missed it over the roaring sea.

Travion drew back immediately and stared down at her as if he'd only imagined it. However, her chest moved again. "Sereia!" He cupped her face gently and lowered his ear to her mouth. Whispers of breath washed over his flesh. "By the Sea! Take another breath."

This time, she drew in a ragged breath that resulted in a hacking cough. Sereia groaned, but her eyes remained shut, and she was unresponsive still.

Phaedora's eyes glittered with contempt as she stared at him. "My end of the bargain is done, Travion."

He wished Ruan would cut her down then and there, yet . . . She had saved Sereia.

"A deal is a deal," Travion grunted, then reached for his portion of The Creaturae. The moment his fingers touched the leather backing, the ground began to rumble. He turned to look at where the volcano had erupted and idly wondered if it was about to blast again.

Phaedora snatched the half of the volume away from him and stumbled backward. The ground split behind her, sending her scrambling off to the side.

"She's going to get away!" Ruan roared in fury.

"Get to the sky!" Travion demanded, and neither one of his nephews argued further. He slid his arms beneath Sereia's prone body and started running toward the shoreline, where the cracks hadn't yet spread.

They hadn't made it this far to die.

30

Sereia

Sereia opened her eyes. She was sitting on a hillside, looking down at a vast, black lake. She remembered it being close to sunset, but somehow it was now dark, and a bright yellow moon glowed overhead. It lit the landside enough that she could see what was around her, though not clearly.

The lake was beautiful, flanked by tall mountains on either side. The moon's glow reflected off the surface, and a half-circle of a rainbow wrapped around it in the sky. Eerie but lovely.

Sereia lifted her hand, shifting it back and forth in front of her. Something was off. Her hand seemed to flicker as she squinted more closely at it. When she tried to grab it with her other hand, the two passed right through each other.

Dead.

There should have been a heart pounding wildly in her chest, filling her with adrenaline and anxiety. Instead, there was nothing. Just an empty lightness. Nothing to ground her to this world except for an inexplicable pull drawing her somewhere over the hill.

Was this all there was to the afterlife?

As suddenly as she realized she was dead, Sereia was drawn from the landscape around her and into darkness again.

Pain filled her entire body, racing along every nerve ending, coursing through her bloodstream, all centering on her abdomen. Her ribs snapped back into place with agonizing swiftness, her muscles began to knit back together, and all of it was with razor-sharp pain coursing through each of her cells.

As her final rib pulled from her lung, Sereia gasped deeply, and her eyes opened to the fading sun and Travion's face above her. His arms were wrapped tightly around her, and the entire world seemed unsteady.

"Trav?" she rasped, a hand lifting to clutch on to his chest.

When he looked down at her, there was a depth of relief in his eyes that struck her down to her core.

"Sereia!" He halted, his arms tightening around her, and he kissed her fiercely, until the world shuddered once more and he staggered. "We need to get off this island," he growled, then clutched her firmly to him as he ran.

When they reached the shore, he shouted to those on *The Saorsa.*

"Travion, put me down," Sereia argued. "They'll never see or hear you if you're unable to signal them."

"No." His response was short and clipped. "You aren't steady enough yet. Your body is barely knit together." He glanced down at her, glaring as her lips opened to respond. "Don't. Not right now."

Finding herself too weary to argue further, Sereia laid her head against his chest and shut her eyes. Somehow, Travion managed to signal her crew, and a dory was rowed ashore to retrieve them.

"She suffered a grievous injury and won't be able to climb the ladder," Travion muttered to Xiu, who'd come to fetch them.

Sereia squinted in annoyance as Xiu looked at her with concern. "I'm fine. I'm alive." She could feel Travion stiffen where she leaned against him. Turning slightly and feeling her entire body revolt in protest, Sereia had to silently agree that Travion was correct. She *was* barely knit back together. "But I wasn't . . . was I?" Sereia searched his face. "What did you do?"

Travion's face was dark, and he shook his head. "Only what I had to."

"Travion . . ."

"No. Listen to me." His hand slid up to cup her cheek, tilting her head back so that she was forced to meet his gaze fully. "I did what I had to do to bring you back. That is all that matters."

He kissed her then, firmly and thoroughly. It was full of loss and anger, desperation and love. It shook Sereia to her core, leaving her feeling seared to her very soul. She was Travion's as wholly as she was her own.

The trip back to the ship was blessedly uneventful. Xiu held onto the rope ladder and called for a net to be dropped down. Carefully, he and Travion settled her into the net, and she was hoisted up onto her ship, into the waiting arms of her crew, who pulled her aboard and settled her onto a barrel with more care and grace than she had ever seen from them before. If she were one to give in to her emotions, she would have shed a tear.

There was no time for peace or explanations, though, for

no sooner had they climbed on deck than Ruan landed his griffin on the deck and slid off. "Uncle! She's gone! I chased after her, but in the chaos of the volcano and the earth splitting, Phaedora disappeared. I have failed!" With a growl of anger, Ruan lashed out and drove a fist into the mast.

"Dammit to the seas," Travion growled. "You did your best, Ruan."

"It shouldn't have even been a possibility," he snapped, glaring at his uncle. "Had you not—"

"Enough!" Travion snarled at his nephew, warring with the hot-headed male.

"What did you do, Travion?" Sereia demanded once more, as angry silence settled between the two of them.

"He traded his portion of the book for you," Ruan responded angrily.

His words were a fresh blow as Sereia realized the book was gone once more, and this time, it was because of her. Her jaw clenched, and she pressed a hand to her agonized middle. "Then I guess I will just have to help you get it back."

Sereia lay back on a chaise in Travion's office, with her torn and bloodied blouse fully open at her sides, while Queen Eden knelt beside her. Her soft, pale hands rested on Sereia's darker torso, a warmth spreading from them as she poured magic into her wounds, helping to strengthen what was still weak inside her. While the spell had brought her back from the dead and repaired her, there was still healing to be done from the death wound.

With each wave of warmth, Sereia could feel the pain within her lessening. "Thank you," she said at last, when the pain was manageable. Resting a hand on her wrist, she pulled Eden's hand away. "I feel much better."

Eden frowned at her. "You're not finished. I can still feel the damage inside of you."

"I'm done enough for now." She shook her head when Eden made to protest. "I know that there are plenty of others who need your help. The castle healers must be pushed beyond their limits. Don't waste your abilities on making certain that I am painless. I've felt far worse than I currently do."

Eden sighed. "I would argue, but I can already tell it will be pointless."

Sereia offered a pitying smile. "I am sorry that we are all such troublesome individuals."

"I have grown quite used to the stubborn nature of the royal family." Eden's smile was softer and more lovely.

As Eden stood, Sereia carefully forced herself up onto legs still weak from blood loss and actual *death*. Travion was at her side quickly, a hand coming to support her at her back. "I'm okay," she assured him, and drew the pieces of her blouse back together, tying the ends over her abdomen to offer a semblance of decorum.

"She is," Eden confirmed. "Don't allow her to perform any rigorous activities, and certainly no fighting, but she will be okay."

Travion pulled Eden into his arms, giving her a firm hug and pressing a kiss to her cheek. "Thank you."

"It is my pleasure." She pulled away, offering both of them a caring smile. "I'll excuse myself to go and aid the other injured soldiers." At the door, she was greeted by her husband, who pulled her into his own arms after giving her a quick once-over. They murmured something to each other, then Eden left the room, and Draven continued into the office, searching out his brother.

"What happened out there?"

"He threw it all away is what happened!" Prince Ruan came storming into the office behind him, throwing his golden helmet across the room to crash against the bookcase. Behind him, Prince Kian entered in a far calmer manner.

"The sharks in the harbor have retreated, and the crabs on the beach have been subdued. For the moment, we seem to have overcome the worst of it. I have soldiers down on the beach killing anything else that moves," Kian supplied to the room at large.

"Yes, we've subdued them for *now*, but that bitch is still out there with The Creaturae, and so our battle and our losses have achieved nothing." Ruan paced the room.

"What *happened?*" Draven demanded once more, frustration glimmering in his blue eyes.

"I managed to tear The Creaturae in two and possessed the destruction side. But Phaedora used one of her monsters to kill Sereia." His voice didn't crack at the words, but there was a strain in his features that told Sereia the mere thought of it still tore at him. Remembering her own desperation when she thought he had been killed, she couldn't imagine having to watch it.

Sereia reached out to take Travion's hand, stepping up more fully beside him so that they could present a united front.

"And you did what?" Draven asked carefully.

"I traded my half in return for the resurrection spell in the creation portion she possessed." Travion did not balk.

Did not try to excuse himself, nor did he seem apologetic. He stood by his decision.

"For her. We've lost it once again because of *her*." Ruan pointed an accusing finger at Sereia.

She could feel her back bristling. She and that callous bastard were going to have words. But before she could respond at all, Travion was speaking.

"Careful with your words, boy."

"Ruan, go and tell Father and Mother what has occurred, and reassure them that for the moment, all has been secured in Midniva," Kian said, his voice steady, bringing a sense of calm to the room.

Ruan growled but nodded. He took a moment to shoot another glare at both her and his uncle before storming out the door.

"Charming as ever, Ruan," Sereia drawled.

Draven eyed her dryly, his own ire just below the surface. "While I cannot condone what has taken place, I also cannot say I would have done anything differently had I been in the same situation."

Travion sighed, his fingers scratching at his jaw. "What have you learned from Taimon?"

Draven's eyes darkened further, and true anger filtered across his face. "I fed from him, there's nothing I don't know of what he has been up to. He was fully involved with all of Naya's plans. He helped to orchestrate the chaos here in Midniva and was responsible for dropping the drained bodies along the shoreline."

Travion cursed and pulled away from Sereia to kick a nearby chair, sending it scraping across the floor. "Phaedora said as much. She admitted they were her puppets but never said how many others belonged to her."

Draven's jaw muscles leaped. "He and Phaedora began their attack here on Midniva as a distraction, but unfortunately, Taimon wasn't told all of her plans. I don't know what she was distracting us *from.*"

Travion nodded. "Whatever it is, it can't be good."

"No, it won't be." Draven sighed. "We always get so close, but it's never enough." He shook his head. "I'm going down to the beaches to see where I can be of help with the cleanup." He nodded to them both and then left. Sereia had the distinct feeling that the king of nightmares was giving them some time alone.

It felt oddly like acceptance.

Sereia sighed and turned to Travion. "You should have just let me remain dead . . . It wasn't worth losing what grasp you had regained on the book."

Travion stormed back to her side, his hands grasping her face and holding her tightly. "Not worth it?" His eyes were stormy, and Sereia could swear she heard thunder rumble in the distance. "What would you have had me do? I watched you fade away before my eyes, your blood staining my clothes. Your very last words promising me the one thing I have always wanted from you."

I was going to stay this time.

Sereia's heart stuttered in her chest, reminding her that she was, indeed, alive once again. "Yes, I did," she whispered.

"Did you mean it?" His face suddenly softened, the anger leaving him as quickly as it had taken him over. "Or was that just death-speak?"

Sereia reached out to grip his waist, pulling him closer. Her chest ached, more than just from the injuries still healing. "I meant it, Travion. I'm here to stay. I am yours, now and forevermore." His eyes were brightening. "I'm tired of being where you aren't and fighting the knowledge that this is my home. *You* are my home."

Their lips met in a deep kiss that tingled down to her toes. Warmth and comfort wrapped around her.

"Home," he whispered.

"Home." Sereia pressed another soft kiss to his lips. "And even though you shouldn't have given up the book for me, thank you for loving me so much."

Travion shook his head as if denying that there was ever a choice. "I'm not losing you again, not ever. I will fight to keep you at my side—no matter what it takes."

"Well, then I suppose we will simply have to face the consequences of this together and somehow make it right."

31

Travion

Travion gritted his teeth as he strode back inside the castle. He'd just returned from surveying the true damage Phaedora's creations had caused. Mointeach was in ruins. The death toll was high, but no number had been officially counted. *Too many.* Bodies littered the shoreline, monster and Midnivian alike. But the discord she brought didn't stop at Midniva's shores; it stemmed to Andhera and Lucem, to Tribonik, Sahille, and Saventi.

His heart ached for his people, for the devastation, the losses. And when the smoke finally settled, he'd see to the monument in Mointeach, as he'd planned, before he left Midniva's shores again.

Phaedora had woven a complex web of deceit, and she plucked the strings at will.

And she would pay for it.

Fury didn't begin to describe what Travion had experienced. He'd nearly lost Sereia, and although it cost them the book, he would do it again if he had to. Ruan had been rightfully incensed, but Draven, despite his initial look of contempt, had shown understanding.

Travion entered his study and glanced outside the floor-to-ceiling window. Even the sky reflected the state of the kingdom, deep crimson hues melding with orange and almost black clouds. In minutes, Midniva would be in darkness, and the trial could begin.

Taimon was to be put on trial and inevitably executed. There was no way the royal family would decide otherwise. The kingdom had been invited to witness it, to let them see what happened to traitors.

Taimon would pay for his crimes. *All* of them.

A moment later, a knock sounded on the door.

Travion turned his head to see who it was, and his toga-clad brother strolled in wearing a smile that didn't quite reach his eyes. Ruan, no doubt, had relayed every single detail to his father, including how furious he was with the outcome and the distinct lack of Phaedora's head on a pike.

However, no such irritation was written on his brother's face, nor was there a hint of disappointment. But there was tension.

"You have returned in one piece," Zryan said, assessing him to ensure what he said was true. "I have to say that I'm surprised." He crossed the room and half-embraced Travion, pounding him on the back lightly. Zryan withdrew and sat in a blue velvet chair in front of the massive window, drumming his thumbs along the clawed armrest.

Travion would have laughed, but the weight of the situation still threatened to pull him down to his knees. His younger brother must have picked up on that because he only inhaled deeply instead of prodding.

"Sereia is . . . ?"

"Resting, I suspect. I just returned from surveying the

damages and I didn't want to give her more reason to leap out of bed with a report. The trial will rile her up again."

"As any good trial should," Zryan murmured. "It seems the two of you are a match, given your penchant for near-death experiences." He didn't say it teasingly but rather matter-of-factly, yet it still made Travion bristle.

He crossed the distance between them, narrowing his eyes on his brother. "There was nothing *near* about her experience. She died in my arms. By the sea, every time I close my eyes, I see it over and over." Travion's voice broke, and he rammed his fingers through his hair.

Zryan lifted his hands in surrender. "I wasn't making light of the situation, brother. But I am glad for you both that she is alive."

Travion clenched his jaw as he closed his eyes. "Yes, and the book is gone."

"For now," Zryan offered in a reassuring tone. "But about that . . . was it truly Phaedora?" He leaned forward, clasping his hands together as he glanced up at Travion.

Travion pinched the bridge of his nose and began pacing as flashes of Phaedora's smirking face surfaced in his mind. The wicked gleam, the triumph . . .

"It was without a doubt Phaedora, but why she has waited this long to make herself known is beyond me."

Zryan shrugged a shoulder, and his green gaze flicked to the window. "She's always been mildly obsessed." His hand brushed down over his torso. "But none of it bodes well for us. However, we're on alert now, and our family has only grown stronger."

"Stronger than The Creaturae?" This time, Travion *did* laugh, and it was a cold, hollow sound. "We need to begin planning how to counteract any of her inevitable attacks. And since she has assembled a following that we have no way of knowing how large it is nor who is in it, we're behind in this game."

Travion turned to the window, which had darkened as the sun made its final descent, but across the starless sky, purple streaks of lightning danced.

Zryan stood from the chair and joined him at the window, his eyes searching for something, perhaps an answer. "Midniva doesn't need torrential rains for the execution, Travion. We want them to see what happens to those who trifle with us, don't we?"

A storm would chase a crowd away, but the mounting frustration of *not knowing* made it difficult to restrain his anger.

"It's almost time for the trial," Zryan drawled as he reached his hand out and squeezed Travion's shoulder. "Take a breath, retrieve Sereia, and we can all talk after."

Although quite the rarity when it came to most things, his younger brother was correct.

They had time to assess the situation deeper and hash out strategies. However, at this very moment, his kingdom needed him, and he needed Sereia.

"Until later." He inclined his head toward Zryan, then left his brother to the still, dark room.

Upstairs, Travion nudged open the door to his bedroom only to find all the candles unlit and the room quite empty. He frowned, but the soft padding of slippered feet caught his attention, and he peered down the hall as one of his servants came into view.

"Evening, Your Majesty." She bobbed a curtsy, glanced up at him, and her brow furrowed. "If you're looking for Lady Sereia, she is in her rooms."

Her rooms? Then, Sereia's laugh carried toward him, and accompanying it was a voice he knew all too well—Evun.

By the sea, what was that rapscallion of a fae up to now?

"Thank you," Travion murmured and promptly headed into Sereia's room. Not long ago, Eden had stayed in this very room, resting as Midniva ended the first battle. But it belonged to only one, and as he rounded the corner, his breath caught.

Sereia faced the floor-length mirror dressed in a powder-blue gown with silver embroidery on the edges. A layered skirt wrapped around her curvy figure, looking much like waves crashing onto the shore. The bodice boasted more of the embroidery, as did the sheer fabric covering her arms.

His valet fiddled with restraining her silken strands, pinning them into a tidy updo.

She looked every bit a queen.

Evun caught him staring in the mirror and grinned. "Come to see my work, have you?"

His lips twitched into a small smile. "I didn't take you for a handmaiden, Evun." His valet only tutted in response. Travion moved deeper into the room, pausing a few feet from Sereia. "Leave us."

"Don't muss her hair up before the trial." Evun sighed, shaking his head. "I will have your clothes situated momentarily." The valet left the room, closing the door behind him.

Sereia smoothed her hands down her sides and tilted her chin up. "It seems I've rendered you speechless, Your Majesty."

Indeed, she had. For she was his and his alone. She was as beautiful as she was fierce and intelligent.

Travion stepped behind her, his head lowering so his chin

rested on her shoulder ever so lightly. "A rare thing, indeed." Her scent invaded his senses, but instead of sweat and sea air, he caught a whiff of something sweeter, almost floral. He closed his eyes, arms encircling her from behind, and simply embraced her, absorbing her presence. "I love you," he murmured against her neck, feeling the need to express the truth now every chance he got. He'd come so close to losing her . . .

Sereia's fingers squeezed his hand. "And I love you. Now go clean up. I can appreciate the windswept appearance, and even the smell of horse and leather, but I don't think your courtiers will."

He chuckled and pressed a kiss to the spot between her neck and shoulder, letting his lips linger on the tender flesh.

"Trav, if you don't leave now . . ." she whispered.

They'd be late to the trial, and her hair, much to Evun's dismay, would be ruined. Sighing, he withdrew from her, but not before he placed a kiss on the tip of her ear.

"Very well. I'll meet you in the foyer." He departed from the room, smiling to himself.

After Evun had fussed over how *unkempt* he'd arrived, Travion dressed in the clothes that had been laid out for him.

Form-fitting black trousers, a crisp linen shirt, navy vest, and finally, the last cumbersome layer, a tailcoat in the same hue as his vest. Much like Sereia's gown, his coat had silver embroidery on the edges.

Good enough.

He left the privacy of his room and ventured to the foyer. Sereia was waiting for him, the candlelight bathing her in a warm glow. Much to his surprise, she didn't seem bored or like she was readying to leap from the nearest window.

"Lady Sereia, can I escort you to the platform?" He

grinned down at her, and in this lighting, her eyes sparkled like the sea under the sun.

"I thought you'd never ask."

Travion pursed his lips. "You'll need to stand with the family—"

"I'll make sure Queen Eden and Prince Kian are between me and everyone else."

Movement at the door caught his attention. Finn nodded his head, and it was time to begin.

Outside of the castle, Finn led the way down the torch-lit path, taking them farther away from the seaside and to the rolling hills of Midniva. Eventually, it gave way to a wide-open space. Despite the dark of night, the area was illuminated by rows and rows of torches.

A crowd, far more numerous than Travion could count, drew around them, facing the platform. Nearest to him and Sereia, the royal family was lined up in high-backed chairs. Draven sat grim-faced, while Eden held his hand, and between her and Kian was an empty seat.

"It's almost as if they know me," Sereia teased.

"Almost, my heart." He dipped his head and brushed a kiss to her brow. "I will find you after." Travion led her to the seat, then ascended the platform.

For as many citizens of Midniva that were present, he was certain if a pin dropped, he'd hear it loud and clear.

"My beloved subjects, tonight we make an example of those who threaten us and who dare to betray us." Travion turned to his right, and Finn stood with another guard who held Taimon by his manacles. With a small nod, the guard brought the traitor up and secured him to a wooden post. His hands behind his back and ankles secured in place.

"Taimon Mustela, we are here to try you for your

involvement with Naya Damaris' plots, conspiring against the crown, and attempted regicide. What have you to say for yourself?"

The half-fae spat in his direction, laughing maniacally. "May the Old Ways rise. And if any of you value your life, you'll see the light. You'll see that *this* is the only way. I refuse to repent for what I've done."

The Old Ways? His eyes darted toward his brothers. Draven's jaw muscles feathered, and even Zryan's brows knit together in a mixture of surprise and disgust. The Old Ways were in place when Ludari ruled. When he was absolute and freedom was naught more than a dream.

"Very well. Since this involvement is beyond Midniva and encompasses the three realms, let us cast our votes. What say the royal family?"

Draven stood. "Guilty," he grunted.

Eden pressed her lips together and joined her husband. "Guilty."

Sereia was next, and when she stood, the crowd murmured. Likely because they weren't certain *who* she was and why she was sitting among the royal family. "Guilty."

Kian's metal arm glinted in the firelight, and he nodded. "Guilty."

Zryan, for all his foolishness, looked as though he longed to peel the flesh from Taimon himself. "Guilty."

Travion turned to look down at Taimon, who trembled but wore a smile of pure madness. "You are guilty, Taimon, and as such, you will be executed by beheading." He stalked forward, leaning in so he could growl into his ear. "I trusted you with everything, and you betrayed me."

Taimon lifted his eyes and stared hard at him, then he

spoke in a tongue few knew. *"May the Old Ways rise and the new ways crumble."*

How did he know that language? It'd all but been forgotten, save for the families that had managed to survive Ludari's reign and the fallout.

"Who else is involved with Phaedora's web, Taimon?" Travion asked lowly.

Taimon smiled up at him, his eyes void of remorse. *"You'll know soon enough."*

Travion walked to the side of the platform, grabbing the sword Finn handed to him. The other guard unchained the half-fae and shoved him to his knees. Foolishly, Taimon kept muttering the same phrase over and over, which only served to infuriate Travion all the more.

"Let your death be an example," he growled and lifted the sword upward, only to bring it crashing down onto the male's neck. His head tumbled away, blood spraying onto the wooden planks, and his body collapsed.

It was done.

For now.

Long after the execution, Travion couldn't find sleep, and it seemed Sereia couldn't either. For she huffed and stared up at the ceiling in his chambers. Neither one was in the mood for a *distraction*, too ramped up from the earlier events.

"Since we're not sleeping, can we talk? The silence could deafen me," Travion grumbled and rolled over to face her.

She lifted onto her elbow and peered down at him. "Talk about what? How you're *not* trailing your lips along my neck?" she teased but made no move to tempt him any further.

"By the sea, Sereia. Is that all you think about?"

"When I'm nestled up next to you, it most certainly is." She scooted closer, pushing him onto his back, and climbed on top of him. She didn't grind against him, only traced the raised scar on his chest.

He lifted his hand, brushing his fingers against a fresh scar, where a gaping hole had been. "Aren't we the pair?"

Sereia scooped his hand into hers and brought it to her lips, kissing his knuckles. "Something like that."

"Sereia," he whispered, "you said you'd stay this time." Travion carefully selected his words, not wanting to ruin the moment, not wanting to ask for too much. But he dared to speak, dared to love her with everything that he was. "Will you be my queen?"

She stilled, scarcely breathing.

"Yes," she finally said.

He loosed a breath, sitting up so quickly, his forehead nearly collided with hers. Travion's lips captured hers in a quick kiss. "Truly?"

Sereia nudged his nose with hers. "In case you haven't noticed, I am not a liar." She wound her arms around his neck, playing with the longer strands at the back. "But I will need something for myself. Something that will allow me to remain true to who I am."

She was a lady of the sea and belonged to the water as much as the ocean belonged to her. To rob her of that would only tear her in half. And Travion didn't want that.

After a time, he sighed. "Well, tragically, there is an opening for admiral in my navy. I think it would suit you, but that is entirely up to you."

The words were barely out of his mouth when Sereia's lips covered his once again.

"Do you mean it?"

He leaned back until he hit the mattress once more, and Sereia was sprawled out on top of him. "In case you haven't noticed, I am not a liar." Travion mimicked her tone, tossing her words back at her. Then he chuckled, threading his fingers in her hair. "What will bring you happiness, my heart?"

"You and the sea."

"Then you shall have us both."

32

Sereia

The sun glistened on the harbor, and Sereia squinted at the brightness. The waves crashing on the shoreline rocks and gulls crying in the air filled her with a sense of peace that warred with the whirlpool of grief inside her.

Pirates died. Every day. The sea life was not a safe life, which had been made even more apparent in the past few months. The knowledge, however, did not make the loss of her first mate, her friend, her *brother*, any easier.

Since the day she bailed him from that prison in Tribonik, Adrik had been loyal to her and dedicated to his life aboard *The Saorsa*. He'd also learned to deal with her and her temper, learned how to help her through her muddled thoughts and get herself out of her own way. A first mate could be replaced, but family could not. There would never be another Adrik.

Sereia lifted her hand to press against the leather corset surrounding her midsection. Beneath it rested the fresh scar that told the tale of her death. She thought of Andhera's bright yellow moon and beautiful dark lake. If she had gone there, perhaps—

"Sereia," a soft voice called from behind her, and Sereia turned on the wharf to see Queen Eden making her way toward her. She was dressed in a lovely gown that spoke of two worlds, not clashing but blending beautifully.

The bottom layer was the stark red of *The Saorsa*'s sails, a kind and intentional dedication Sereia was sure. The top layer of the gown was made of black gauze that wove lovingly around Eden's form in soft curls, much like a whirlpool, before the full skirt finally ended in several layers of waves at her feet. All through the black gauze ran lines of sparkling pink and purple, hints of light and hope within the darkness.

In her coiled red hair nestled a purple and black flower that reminded Sereia of a bat. Eden was without a doubt the queen of Andhera, and it amused her that she had been so wrong at the beginning.

"Your Highness," she greeted.

"I think that we're at the point where you can call me Eden." She stopped before her, a soft smile on her lips. "We are to be sisters, after all."

Sereia grinned a touch. "We are, and will spend a fair share of time together, if I am not mistaken?"

"You are correct. Every six months or so, I must leave Andhera before its atmosphere can change me into a vampire like Draven." A distant look passed in her gaze, but when she refocused on Sereia, she nodded. "Travion has kindly offered me a home here during the months I must stay away. I have a family home in Lucem, but here the sun sets, so Draven is able to visit me."

"Well, I look forward to getting to know you better." And she meant it. Eden was soft and tender, in a way that Sereia was not. Oftentimes, it was a personality trait Sereia would keep clear of, as she didn't often share much in common with people like that. Eden, though, was married to Draven, king of nightmares. There had to be more to her than softness and smiles.

"As do I."

Sereia sighed and moved her hands onto her hips, feeling the need to brace herself for the next admission. "I, however, feel that I owe you an apology. The night we first met, I said some things about you out of jealousy and loss. I misunderstood when a courtier referred to you as the new queen and thought that you had stepped in and married Travion. I—"

Eden held up her hand. "You do not have to explain yourself. I fully understand. When I first moved to Andhera, there was a vampiress who thought she could come between Draven and me. In the end, I killed her."

Sereia's face split into a wide grin at this, and she laughed heartily. "Oh, I knew I was going to like you." There was a quiet fierceness about Eden that was clear once Sereia looked close enough. Her position in Andhera and at Draven's side made more sense now.

They shared a smile, and then Eden grew more solemn. "I did come down here for a purpose. Everything is ready for Adrik's sendoff."

The weight of grief shrouded Sereia once more, digging into her bones and reawakening an ache that could not be defined. She nodded. "Thank you."

In the days that had passed after the battle, there were too many injured to see to, a trial to be held, and defenses to be reinforced. Sereia herself had been recouping from the injury inflicted upon her. There had not been time to bury the dead. After they had all been gathered from the ships and the beaches, each had been returned to their families for burial. Adrik, however, had remained in the castle infirmary, waiting for her and their crew. They were his family.

"Let us go, then," Sereia said, straightening herself up.

Eden looked like she wished to hug her. But, seeming to understand that Sereia didn't need that form of comfort in the moment, Eden nodded and turned.

Sereia drew her hands down over her hips. While she was now Midniva's future queen, and newly appointed admiral of the naval fleet, she had chosen to dress for neither role. Today, she was Sereia Ferox, Captain of *The Saorsa*, and she was laying to rest a member of her crew, her family.

She was dressed in a linen blouse with long, billowy sleeves. A dark leather corset wrapped around her waist, supporting her back and her still healing body, and boosted her breasts from beneath. The curve of them peaked out from the scooped, ruffled neckline of her linen shirt. Instead of leather slacks, Sereia had chosen a deep red skirt that fell to the ground in the back but was gathered by leather laces in the front and tied to the belt around her waist.

A layer of linen petticoat showed below, adding a ruffle of white along the gathered portion of the skirt. It fell to about her knees, leaving her more than capable of climbing the gangway, and showed off her knee-high leather boots and the brass buckles up the front of them. To her hip was strapped her sword, and right beside it, her spyglass.

Sereia had argued with Evun—and won—over her hair, which had been simply plaited on both sides and pulled into a single braid that hung over her shoulder.

As they walked, the heavy sound of their footsteps reverberated up from the wood and bounced off the ocean water below. It was hollow and yet steadying. So familiar while also being a first. Today it brought no comfort like it usually did.

Her head and shoulders were hot from the noonday sun, and the wind whipped briskly against her cheeks, but all her senses dulled as she and Eden reached the end of the wharf where her crew stood silent and ready.

Boran, Xiu, Yon, and Yannik each held onto the wooden handle of a stretcher, his body, wrapped in first a layer of linen and then a bright red scrap of sail from their ship, nestled carefully on top. They had come to Sereia, asking for this honor, wanting to pay tribute to their friend and brother.

Eden squeezed her elbow lightly, then disappeared into the crowd.

Sereia looked over her crew, registered the grief and pain on their faces, and did her best to meet the eyes of each one. "Let us take our brother home."

A chorus of "aye, aye" rang out.

Chailai moved to stand beside her, and together, they walked the length of the wharf to where *The Saorsa* sat ready to carry them. Behind her, the crew moved quietly yet steadily.

Once the procession was all aboard the ship, Sereia shouted for them to haul anchor and cut the ropes.

The wind, clearly on their side today, filled the sails as soon as they were unfurled, and they were bright swathes of red against the blue sky, pulling them out to the middle of the harbor already speckled with floating wreaths of farewell. She brought the ship to the center of the Midnivian naval fleet, which bobbed respectfully in wait.

Travion was aboard one of the ships, watching with his

sailors, paying respect to a comrade who had fallen in aid of his home.

As the anchor was dropped once more, Sereia left the helm to stand at the railing of the quarterdeck. Her hand slid into the pocket of her skirt, fingers curling around the carved stone handle of the knife she had gifted Adrik before this all began. The knife had been in his boot when they'd started preparing him for burial.

"Adrik Drozdov was a member of this crew for nearly three decades. He joined as a lad and dedicated his life to the service of this ship, this crew, and myself. Adrik lived for the adventure a seafaring life brings and died just where he wanted to be. Today, we return him to the depths of the waters he loved and pray to the gods of the sea for a peaceful journey to the lands of darkness, or beyond, wherever his soul should take him."

"Aye, aye!"

As Sereia descended the steps to the main deck, Adrik's body was lowered to rest on its surface. Chailai appeared at his feet with two small cannon balls, each lovingly etched with the names of his crewmembers. Carefully, she rested them on top of his ankles, and with Yon's help, wound red cloth around them and his shrouded form, binding them together. Sereia knelt by his head and picked up the needle that still rested on top.

It was her duty as captain to stitch up the last of the red fabric over his face, the final goodbye and preparation for his burial. Sereia took a deep breath and leaned down, wetness gathering in her eyes but not falling. Not now. Not when everyone looking on needed strength.

"Goodbye, my brother. Thank you for your loyalty and your laughter. Thank you for the years of your unwavering support. You will live on in memory, forever." She pressed a kiss to his linen-clad forehead and then began the tedious work of stitching the red cloth.

When she was done, she knotted the end and ripped the needle off the thread.

Sereia stood and stepped back. Nodding to Chailai and his carriers, she signaled that they were ready. From somewhere in the crowd, a mournful song began, which each member took up, and as Adrik's body slid into the waves of the ocean, the naval ships shot off their cannons. Smoke filled the air around them, creating a ring of seclusion as the crew gathered at the railing and watched his scarlet form sink into the depths.

A single tear slipped from the corner of Sereia's eye, and she let it trail down to her chin. Adrik deserved it.

The tavern was filled with the crew of *The Saorsa*. Some sat together, others held a serving wench on their knee, and all held a tankard of ale in their hands.

"To Adrik of Tribonik!" Sereia lifted her tankard as she shouted, and a cheer rang out before all drank.

They were heavy with sorrow, the lot of them, but they had laid their brother to sleep, and now it was time to celebrate his life.

"Captain," Chailai called out, signaling with her hand for all to quiet. "While I appreciate the solemnity of this occasion, I feel I must also ask for myself, and for the crew. What is our direction from here? Many a rumor has been circling, and we worry."

Sereia had known that this discussion would come, but she had not been anticipating it tonight. She supposed, though, they had a right to know what was becoming of them and their ship.

"Some of you will have heard, others not, that I have accepted His Majesty's offer of becoming his wife."

There was silence, and then Boran shouted from the back, "Midniva's going to have a bloody pirate for a queen!"

There was a round of chuckles and cheers, tankards were lifted and another gulp taken.

Sereia laughed and, shaking her head, she lifted her hand to silence them once more. "You are correct, as terrible an idea as it is." From across the room, Sereia met Travion's eyes for a brief moment, seeing only love and support in their depths. "Midniva will have a pirate sitting on the queen's throne. But not only that, she will have a pirate as admiral of her naval fleet."

An uproar of voices and questions broke out as everyone fought to be heard over each other.

Sereia brought her fingers to her lips and released a sharp whistle. "Enough! Let me finish. I have accepted the role as admiral, and *The Saorsa*'s hull will be repainted in the naval colors." Though she'd be keeping her red sails. Sereia couldn't bear to part with those. "Anyone who wishes to give up the life of piracy and keep their position aboard *The Saorsa* is welcome to." Sereia met Chailai's eyes, and then Yon's beyond her, silently letting them both know how much she wished for them to stay. "Any who do not wish to fight in the name of Midniva and her king, I will allow to walk away, no questions asked, no repercussions."

There was silence for a moment as everyone soaked up this information.

"Personally, I think we could teach the fleet a thing or two," Boran shouted out.

"My place is by your side, Captain." Yon bowed slightly, which brought a grin to Sereia's lips.

And then Chailai stepped forward. She took a moment to assess the crew and then met Sereia's eyes. "Captain, I think I speak for most of us when I say it would be the greatest honor of our lives to serve on *The Saorsa* for the queen of Midniva."

Sereia's throat felt tight, and she nodded. Clearing her throat, she lifted her tankard. "To *The Saorsa*, the best damn ship on the seas!"

Cheers went up and tankards clanked together. Soon there was a fiddle being played in the corner, and the celebration truly began.

In the end, a handful of the young crew members approached her and took their leave, wishing to remain free on the seas, and her cook, old and grizzled, announced his decision to take this as his chance to retire to a small seaside cottage and live out the rest of his days. But the rest had decided to remain.

Sereia made her way through the crowd. Moving up to Travion, she allowed him to pull her by the waist to his side.

"I didn't expect so many to pledge allegiance to your crown," she admitted.

"They didn't," Travion replied. "Their allegiance is to you and whatever cause you decide is worth the fight." He kissed her brow. "How are you? Today was . . ."

"Today was rough." Sereia nodded. "But I spoke true when I said he died exactly where he wanted to be, and that is all any of us can hope for."

"And you?" he asked. "Are you exactly where you wish to be?"

Sereia studied his face. The sun-kissed cheeks, the windswept hair, the bright blue eyes that still spoke of devilment after all these centuries, and the depth of his fierceness and loyalty. While she would always require a part of her life to be on the sea, Travion was where Sereia now needed to be.

Marriage and the throne no longer felt like a chain weighing her down to the bottom of a deep trap. Instead, it felt like a new adventure. To stand at his side as queen, to help protect these shores from any threat, to claim a space each night in his bed.

Sereia lifted her hand and cupped his cheek, the pad of her thumb brushing lightly over his lips. "I have never wished to be any place more than I now wish to be here, at your side. I am yours, and you are mine, and I pity anyone who dares try and part us."

They locked eyes, and matching smirks claimed a place on their lips.

"I second that, my heart."

Ignoring the inhabitants of the room, Sereia slid into his arms, and Travion claimed her lips. Heat and love swept through her on a tide of desire, pulling her so naturally into the storm that was King Travion.

Finally, she was home.

Epilogue

Travion

"Just think, Your Majesty, it has only taken a century to woo your bride," Evun tittered as he tucked in the excess fabric of Travion's white ascot.

It was beyond him as to why he needed such a ridiculous accessory. He scowled at the bulk of it. However, his irritation grew at his valet's boldness. "I think you forget to whom you're speaking."

Evun pressed his lips together, tilting his head. "Have I?" He stepped back, assessing his handiwork. "One day, that is all, just one day of frills and perfection. Then you can run through the mud and look as you wish. Just give me *one day*."

"Very well. One day."

Evun winked and turned on his heel to leave, but before he did, he cast a glance over his slender shoulder. "Know that this makes me happy. That, a century ago, I was dressing you for an event that you were loath to attend. And here we are."

Travion smiled, chuckling to himself. "And here we are," he echoed.

Evun whistled as he left the small quarters of Cathair Cathedral.

Moments from now, Travion would be bound to Sereia until the end of their days. And despite the tumultuous events leading up to this day, the last two weeks had been quiet, allowing the kingdom to heal, and Sereia to mourn the loss of Adrik. Blood or not, he had been her kin, and his death had left its mark on her.

But this evening was a moment of joy and a new beginning for them—for Midniva.

Nerves were not something Travion was familiar with. Unease, certainly, but anxiousness? He flexed his fingers as he stepped from the room and walked down the hall toward the door leading to the altar.

The soft whine of a violin filled the air, and before he could allow himself to overthink the moment, he strode down the carpeted aisle. Row upon row of pews were full of courtiers, Sereia's family and his own.

For all the pomp and circumstance, they'd both agreed no high priest would wed them, but a captain of the sea instead. Darragh, one of the finest captains in Midniva's navy, inclined his head as Travion approached the dais.

The captain wore no robes, only tall boots, fitted breeches, and a hip-length overcoat. His clever brown eyes danced with laughter, but he remained quiet as Travion reached the dais.

A war raged on inside of him as he stood to the side. His fingers flexed and toyed with the hem of his overcoat, the polished buttons . . . How many times had Travion addressed the kingdom? Spoken to a room full of lords and ladies? Yet here he was, picking at the embroidery lining the bottom of his overcoat.

Soft murmurs filled the cathedral, but they all blended together.

Then, the bow of the violin dragged along the strings, indicating a change in the song to garner everyone's attention. A deep, slow melody played, and the creaking of wood echoed around them as the inhabitants of the building turned to watch as the bride entered.

Sereia was an absolute *vision* swathed in midnight blue. The skirt split high enough to show the tanned skin of her thigh, which he longed to cover in lingering kisses. At her waist, an intricate silver belt tapered the fabric, and his eyes dragged upward to the deep V-cut that enhanced her full breasts.

The same silver workmanship rested on her shoulders, lending her a domineering appearance befitting of a queen and admiral. And in her tidy updo, dozens of pearls winked in the candlelight.

His heart roared in his ears because seeing Sereia like *this* . . . would never grow old.

Travion swallowed and grasped her hand as she came to stand before him, squeezing it as they held one another's gaze.

"What a beautiful evening to celebrate His Majesty King Travion and his lovely bride Lady Sereia Ferox's union. Now, I'm not in the business of marriage, but rather of tending to the sea, so without further ado, let us begin." Darragh reached inside his coat pocket and produced a braided rope. He draped it over their joined hands.

They'd recited the words prior to today, they'd memorized them . . .

Sereia glanced down at their hands, and if he wasn't mistaken, Travion thought he saw her pulse leaping wildly in her throat, matching his racing heart.

Together, they spoke, and as they did, Darragh wound the

silken strand around their hands. "You are the blood of my blood and bone of my bone. I give you my body, that we two might be one. I give you my spirit until our life shall be done."

"Let none come between them." Darragh smiled, nodding. "Your Majesty, you may kiss your bride."

Elation filled Travion, and at that moment, no one else existed. Only them. He moved forward, and with his free hand, cupped Sereia's face. He grinned and captured her lips in a deep, sensual kiss.

They had barely pulled apart when the cathedral's door burst open, and wispy shadows snaked along the red rug.

A shrouded figure strode farther into their space, and guards immediately rushed into action. But as the unknown individual lifted a hand, they were halted, frozen in place.

Draven rushed to his feet, poised to run at the threat, but as the shadows eased away from the intruder, Phaedora's light brown hair and growing smirk came into view.

"Congratulations. I hope you enjoyed this gift of time, because you won't be this fortunate again." Her gaze slid toward Zryan as he rounded the pews, and she eyed him like a long-lost possession. "I'll see you *very* soon."

The room seemed to shrink, then expand as a piercing light filled the cathedral, blinding Travion. He winced, blinking rapidly to gain his sight back.

Guests screamed or shouted. But the royal family stood, bristling and ready for battle.

"Zryan," Alessia said lowly, fury blazing in her eyes.

"By the sea!" Sereia hissed.

"Guards, search the surrounding area in case she might be found!" Draven's voice boomed.

"This isn't my fault!" Zryan looked from Travion to

Alessia, his eyes wide in surprise and muscles tense with anger.

Travion reached for the rope dangling from his and Sereia's joined hands and tugged on it, freeing them both. "We had our moment," he whispered softly, and when his gaze met hers, she nodded in understanding.

"It is time for war."

And at least they were all together. A family united.

Travel back to the Immortal Realms…

The trilogy isn't complete yet!
Wages of War is the conclusion to the epic trilogy, featuring Zryan and Alessia.

Pre-order Now
books2read.com/wagesofwar
(Available February 14, 2024)

ACKNOWLEDGMENTS

Thank you so much for reading our take on Poseidon and Amphitrite! Travion and Sereia haven't had it easy, but hopefully their happily ever after brought a smile to your face.

We are grateful for everyone who excitedly asked about Tides. Who loved Seeds of Sorrows enough that they couldn't wait to get their hands on the next. You're the ones who've helped fuel our muse to write this story.

Our novel wouldn't have made it to greatness without Lou, who always takes the time to beta-read our crazy stories. Carla, for providing in-depth help to make this the best book ever! And Melana, whose favorite thing is a great pirate tale.

A big shout out to our proofreader, Amber H., for taking the time to comb through our adventurous tale!

We also want to send out a massive thank you to our comma goblin, Meg Dailey! We love you more than you know!

To our loyal Patron supporters, Donna and Kristen! You inspire us to continue writing more stories.

THE OFFICIAL PLAYLIST

Want to listen along while you read and immerse yourself into the world of Tides of Torment? Listen to the playlist below!

SCAN FOR SPOTIFY PLAYLIST

1. Head Above Water by Avril Lavigne
2. What the Whiskey Won't Do by Alan Doyle ft Jess Moskaluke
3. All I Want by Shavi ft. Emie
4. If You're Still In I'm In by The East Pointers
5. Dancing Without Music by BRDGS
6. She's a Rare One by Ashley MacIsaac
7. Bridge Over Troubled Waters by Stephen Stanley
8. Hold Her by for KING & COUNTRY
9. Ocean Eyes by Billie Eilish
10. Sailors Eyes by Joel Plaskett

ABOUT ELLE BEAUMONT

 Elle Beaumont loves creating vivid and fantastical worlds. She lives in southeastern Massachusetts with her husband and two children. When not writing or chasing around her children, she enjoys making candles. More than once she has proclaimed that coffee is the lifeblood and it is how she refrains from becoming a zombie.

Stay up to date and receive some free books by signing up for her newsletter! ellebeaumontbooks.com/newsletter

Join Elle's Facebook group and hang out with her facebook.com/groups/ElleBeaumontStreetTeam

For more information visit
www.ellebeaumontbooks.com
Follow Elle on social media!

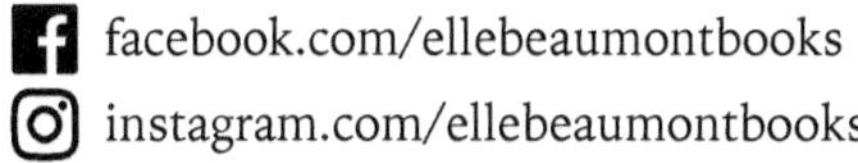 facebook.com/ellebeaumontbooks

instagram.com/ellebeaumontbooks

MORE FROM ELLE

Demons of Frosteria

Frost Mate

Frost Claim

Immortal Realms Trilogy

Seeds of Sorrow

Tides of Torment

Wages of War (Feb '24)

The Hunter Series

Hunter's Truce

Royal's Vow

Assassin's Gambit

Queen's Edge

Secrets of Galathea

Brotherhood of the Sea

Bindings of the Sea

Voice of the Sea

King of the Sea

Standalones

The Dragon's Bride

The Castle of Thorns

Slaying the Frost King

ABOUT CHRISTIS CHRISTIE

Christis Christie lives on the east coast of Canada, in Nova Scotia. She gets most excited about diving into a new fantasy world while writing, but also loves a good supernatural plot. Tiss, as she is affectionately called by her friends, enjoys being creative in any way she can, so if she's not writing then she's crocheting or she's embroidering. Her favorite animal is the sloth, and her favorite retellings are anything Beauty and the Beast related.

Follow Christis on social media!

facebook.com/ChristisChristieWrites

instagram.com/tiss.writes

MORE FROM CHRISTIS

Standalones

Spun Gold

The Dragon's Bride

Sanctuary of the Lost

Of Loyalties & Wreckage

Of Love & Ruin (Oct '23)

Immortal Realms Trilogy

Seeds of Sorrow

Tides of Torment

Wages of War (Feb '24)

Reaping Series

Ephesus

Anthologies

Emporium of Superstition

Granted by Brindi Quinn

Some villains have reasons for sticking to the shadows.

Recent college graduate Dolly Jones has spent the last week shacked up with her genie boyfriend in a pompous fantasyland manor avoiding the three vengeful brothers determined to sully her relationship with the new Laird. The rest of the world may be against Velis Reilhander taking a human for a mate, but Dolly is committed to being the person on his side, at his side—her own anxieties be damned. But when a trip to the nymph realm doesn't go as planned, Dolly's newfound strength will be tested as she quickly learns there are more secrets surrounding the Reilhander legacy than even Velis knows.

Veteran genie Arrik Reilhander will do anything to make himself feel better, anything. Even if it means jumping into someone else's story. *Especially* if it means jumping into someone else's story. And as for Dolly f*cking Jones . . .

Available Now

Fires of the Forsaken by Stephanie E. Donahue

Addie did not have "getting plucked from the 21st century and thrown into a rudimentary fantasy world" on her "fun things to do at 30" checklist. Yet here she is, struggling to survive in the hellscape known as Sakar, a place where Wraiths flame-broil humans and Celestial armies wage war with each other over a centuries-old spat. Thankfully, Cheriour, the hunky commander of the human army, takes her under his wing—although he's allergic to giving straight answers. And talking.

As Addie reluctantly starts to care for him, and the rest of the Sakarians, she also learns why she was sent to this world. And it's a doozy…

The violent society of Sakar is the only home Lass has ever known, and it's been a wretched one. She has spent her life being tormented and twisted into an inhuman hybrid by the Celestials and hunted by the humans who fear her. But she finds solace with a cocky, blue-eyed boy who comforts her, even after she accidentally slaughters innocents.

As Lass struggles to control her volatile powers, she slowly transforms into the monster the humans believe her to be. And even the boy she loves is in peril…

At the end of time, there is only fire. And neither Addie nor Lass will escape unscathed.

Available Now